THE HIDDEN STORYTELLER

Mandy Robotham saw herself as an aspiring author since the age of nine, but was waylaid by journalism and later enticed by birth. She's now a former midwife, who writes about birth, death, love and anything else in between. She graduated with an MA in Creative Writing from Oxford Brookes University. This is her seventh novel – her first six have been *Globe and Mail*, *USA Today* and Kindle Top 100 bestsellers.

By the same author:

A Woman of War (published as *The German Midwife* in North America, Australia and New Zealand)
The Secret Messenger
The Berlin Girl
The Girl Behind the Wall
The Resistance Girl
The War Pianist

THE
HIDDEN
STORYTELLER

MANDY ROBOTHAM

avon.

HarperCollins*Publishers*
1 London Bridge Street
London SE1 9GF

www.harpercollins.co.uk

HarperCollins*Publishers*
Macken House
39/40 Mayor Street Upper
Dublin 1
D01 C9W8

A Paperback Original 2024

1

First published in Great Britain by HarperCollins*Publishers* 2024

Copyright © Mandy Robotham 2024

Mandy Robotham asserts the moral right
to be identified as the author of this work.

A catalogue copy of this book is available from the British Library.

ISBN: 978-0-00-859922-5

Typeset in Bembo Std by Palimpsest Book Production Ltd, Falkirk, Stirlingshire

Printed and bound in the UK using
100% renewable electricity at CPI Group (UK) Ltd

This book contains FSC™ certified paper and other controlled sources
to ensure responsible forest management.

For more information visit: www.harpercollins.co.uk/green

To Molly Walker-Sharp, my first editor, and an enduring third eye — many, many thanks.

AUTHOR'S NOTE

We know from modern day conflict zones, and those painful images from Syria and Afghanistan, that suffering does not automatically cease when the weapons of war are laid down. Vast swathes of land are scarred, and so too the people. The same is true of WWII, though from the iconic pictures of Victory Day parades and the sheer joy and relief, you might not think so. Still, as the ticker-tape dispersed, London and Britain as a whole took time to rebuild. In Europe, fierce ground battles and aerial raids caused untold devastation, with entire nations broken. Sadly, death lingered all too frequently.

When I started to read about the hard facts of recovery from five long years of war, I was shocked – at the continuing loss of life, and the remaining fissures between peoples. The war's end did not signal an end to suffering, and it's this reality that I wanted to view through Georgie's eyes. Many of her observations are guided by commentators who travelled to Europe and reported back on the war's fallout, including the renowned publisher Victor Gollancz with *In Darkest Germany*, plus German journalists Margaret Boveri and Ursula Von Kardoff, who documented everyday struggles of the displaced – the 'shoe absenteeism', a widespread currency of cigarettes, and the value of a simple suitcase.

But this remains a story: Georgie and Harri are fictional, as are the crimes they investigate, though readers of Philip Kerr's Bernie Gunther books might recognise a few grumpy traits in Kripo man Harri. It's my little tribute to the work of the late, wonderful Mr Kerr. Georgie was a joy to re-visit after *The Berlin Girl*, and to discover that she's still kicking against the expectations for women in the 1940s.

As ever, I have weaved in shades of real people within my own characters: British-born Walter Purdy was an acolyte of the traitor and radio broadcaster Lord Haw-Haw. Enticed by the Nazi regime, the young Purdy went on to broadcast propaganda in Germany, subsequently labelled 'the man with the golden voice' by the Nazis, as documented in Ben McIntyre's excellent history of *Colditz*. His treason exposed; Purdy narrowly escaped the noose. And, of course, there's tiny waif-like Meta – a walking metaphor for the enduring tenacity of people everywhere, with that ability to pick themselves up, dust themselves off and simple carry on, in the face of adversity. Without such determined souls, there's every chance that you and I wouldn't be here now.

PROLOGUE

Early February 1946, Hamburg, northern Germany

I see her, the vitality in her face, and what looks to me like a hunger for life, as she laughs with her friends, swaying with the music and tapping her feet on the edge of the dancefloor. Under the lights, the shine in her chestnut hair draws my eye, as she flirts openly with a man smiling at her. She pushes away a stray wisp and takes up the offer of his outstretched hand, stepping onto the floor gingerly, as if testing the thickness of a vast frozen pond. So much like Liselle. And just like Liselle, this woman's face is all innocence, a benevolent smile and white teeth on show as she gains confidence, spinning and looking intently into the man's features, as if she is interested. But as with Liselle – all of them, in fact – she is not artless. How can this man courting her not see beyond the cleverly painted mask? To me, it's obvious. I know that behind her smile, she is assessing her dance partner, weighing up how much the British squaddie is worth, in units of cigarettes, or jars of coffee, or loaves of bread to take home to her family. Maybe even a wedding ring, if she maintains her disguise for long enough. They all want something, this new race utterly devoid of loyalty and allegiance to Germany. The men are bad enough, but these women are worse, nothing but bloody scavengers under the make-up and their pinned, preened hair. There are lessons to be learnt. Things that I must teach them.

Liselle was the same. She pretended to be interested, wanted to talk and engage. She beguiled me, and I fell for it – at first. But her veneer melted away when it became obvious I wanted something too. Of her. Oh yes! Then she wasn't so attentive, avoiding me at all costs. How dare she play me, lie to me. In the end, though, I gained the upper hand. Before long, it was me who called the shots, steering the way. Leading her into . . . let's just say she was very attentive when her future became clear.

Still, I have plenty of work left to do; there are hundreds out there, dotted in and around this dancefloor, on the streets, throughout Hamburg, and Germany beyond. It's down to me to track them down, seek out where they congregate and live, and offer them the choice. Someone should test the loyalties of those left, and cleanse a country that has become so filthy, wipe away these harlots who will betray a nation without a second's hesitation. Turncoats and liars, all of them. Traitors.

Look at her now, with her white teeth and brown, shiny hair, smiling her lies as she trips and twirls under the lights, grasping at that innocent dupe in a uniform.

I see through her. And for that, she should pay. In full.

CHAPTER ONE:
THE RETURN

11 February 1946, Hamburg, northern Germany

Georgie

She's aware of her own shoes echoing on the rough concrete, soles slapping noisily as she looks left and right for the man who's set to meet her. As with any arrival in a strange place – and there have been many over the last six or seven years – Georgie pitches her nose into the air, to gain the scent. To place herself, not so much in the geography of a town or country, but in the atlas of humanity. Good or bad, safety or danger. Too often it has been cordite and destruction, and death. Now, above her own scent of magnolia, the smell under her nose is unexpectedly worse: peacetime despair and decay has replaced dynamite. Death, too, remains firmly in the mix, bubbling under. Is that right now the war is over?

'Miss Young?' A man steps forward, marked out less by his khaki uniform than his frame, not weighty as such, but well-covered, his webbing belt snug against his waist. In comparison, the clusters of people gathered outside Hamburg's military airport waver like blades of grass – even those whose clothes are not rags, but still hang loosely over shoulders that have little more substance than a wire coat-hanger.

The man's rounded face broadens as his bristled moustache branches upwards with a smile. 'Can I take that from you?' he adds, gesturing towards her suitcase.

'No. Thank you.' Instinctively, Georgie pulls the brown leather valise tighter towards her knees, a reflex from past years. Through experience, she's learnt to travel light, and so anything packed into her battered old suitcase is necessary, always guarded closely as she and husband Max moved over Europe's battlefields – notebook, pens, toothbrush and at least one pair of clean underwear, a legacy from her mother that she hasn't been able to shed, despite a world war. Max teased endlessly about her 'extra pair', until he ran out of his own supply one day and was forced to borrow hers. And for years afterwards wished he hadn't, unable to escape her gentle mocking; the mere mention of the 'battle knickers' still has them laughing at their own, very private joke. The suitcase she carries now is the old and battered warhorse that's been her constant through the entire conflict, Max having bought it for her in Paris as a wedding gift. Not romantic to some, but better than any sparkling bauble in the circumstances, just days after Hitler declared war on Europe. In truth, it belongs to a different era, and she really should retire it to the top of the wardrobe. Start afresh, along with several other elements of life. Somehow, that's easier said than done.

'I'm fine to carry it myself,' Georgie says, remembering her manners. 'Sergeant . . .?'

'Dawson, miss. Or is it mrs? They didn't say.'

'Miss,' she says swiftly, biting back on her sharpness. How many times has she had to say it over past years? Except Sergeant Dawson is probably more used to greeting the wives who have come to join their British officer husbands in the peace and enjoy the spoils of victory. She wonders when, if ever, she'll get used to being addressed as 'Mrs Max Spender'. She is his wife – willingly, and without regret – but so far it has never meant forsaking herself. Here in Hamburg, she is Miss Georgina Young. A journalist in her own right.

'Sorry, miss.' Dawson purses his lips and smiles nervously, bringing her back to the bustle of the airport. 'I'm to take you to your hotel, and then the headquarters. Is that correct?'

'Yes, thank you. Apologies, Sergeant – I'm just tired.' He nods as if he understands, as if fatigue is a given after years of warring, seeping into your pores in the same way fire smoke invades and clings to every fibre. It sits alongside the same question common to all battle-weary survivors: will this so-called peace be any less exhausting?

This isn't the way that Georgie Young, freelance correspondent, would have chosen to arrive in any European town, city or hamlet. The military transport she is well used to – jostling in the back of a jeep, or thrown around the innards of a troop carrier – but any arrangements over the course of a long war have tended to be ad hoc; her and Max cadging a ride on a requisitioned train, a notebook tucked in the inside of her jacket, his camera swinging from the strap around his neck. As with most of the press, they piggy-backed on the action wherever they could, always with the prospect of danger, but of excitement, too. Looking death in the face was not something she and Max had pledged in their wedding vows – an impromptu ceremony back in Paris in the opening days of the war – but it was never destined to be a conventional marriage. And they'd both come out alive, hadn't they?

Now, there's no Max alongside, courtesy of a broken leg sustained while skiing in Scotland over Christmas, and she has to contend with the organisation in the British army. Or what passes as organisation. Back in England, she'd been warned that reliance on rail travel through Germany was a risk in terms of timing, comfort and the very existence of a train. Some apparently took weeks to reach their destination, packed like sardines with throngs of Displaced Persons. So, the occupying army of the British Zone has arranged air travel, and the very presence of Sergeant Dawson at the airport seems to suggest the military's aim is to chaperone her, in favourably promoting their corner in the new dawn of occupied Germany.

They might need to reconsider, Georgie thinks, since she's never been in need of a minder. The first time she set foot in the country as a news reporter, way back in 1938, she was a twenty-six-year-old novice, raw and naïve, but her innocence was short-lived. The black crow of Nazism hovered across Berlin, mistrust multiplying daily as Europe hurtled towards bloody conflict, forcing her and Max to learn swiftly. Then, the true battle, with tanks and guns and cruelty beyond measure. They both worked the war principally as a words-and-pictures press duo, but not exclusively. And always in partnership rather than as

6

a married couple. In love, but never reliant. Dependence is not in Georgie Young's nature.

But that life is over. Hitler is dead, the Third Reich conquered. Georgie is better travelled, and wiser – hopefully. Peace for almost a year now, though the world is far from back on its axis. The London that she and Max now call home is slowly hauling itself back on its feet with a building frenzy, but rationing remains harsher than ever, and the food queues as lengthy as those days of the Blitz. With Churchill no longer at the helm, Britain's new Labour government talks of renewal and fresh ideas.

And what of Germany, the losers in that bloody game? Do they share the same hope? Can they? Are they even allowed?

It's what she's here to find out.

CHAPTER TWO:
THE WAIF

11th February 1946

Meta

Her head lifts at the sound of the door opening, and the first in a new parade of travellers exiting the terminal building, their shoes smacking on the crystallised concrete and patches of hard, packed ice. It's a sign – the first flight has landed, and with it a fresh influx of spoils.

She and her fellow loiterers shuffle with expectation. Some prepare to beg with a fixed vacant gaze, others to pickpocket with light fingers, and the rest simply mill about, because being displaced is the only thing they know how to be these days. Meta narrows her eyes to focus but doesn't look directly at this fresh batch streaming from the airport building. Instead, she keeps her gaze low, at knee-height, scanning and surveying, picking over her would-be treasure. Briefly, her attention flicks upwards to scrutinise several faces, but it's fleeting; the people interest her only in so much as they have something she wants. Covets. Men and women who are lucky enough – rich enough in some cases – to fly in out and of this post-war chaos that is Hamburg inevitably have need of clean clothes, of fresh underwear and toothbrushes, and perhaps a book to read at bedtime. And for that they require luggage.

Meta, in turn, has great need of that. Centuries ago, Hamburg was founded on dockside haggling, but in this new dawn of post-Hitler Germany, trade is *everything*. The contents of these suitcases she can barter for cigarettes; ironically, for something that goes up in smoke, a packet of Player's or Lucky Strikes represents a far more solid currency than the inflationary Reichsmark, which wavers up and down like a strong tide on the River Elbe. But for Meta, the container is her trophy. In the dawn of 1946, a good, sturdy suitcase has value. With it, you can store the meagre collection of things that have become your entire life, ensuring movement across the city at less of a shuffle as you keep your precious belongings close and confined, not likely to spill with abandon onto the slush-ridden streets. Once in a safe spot, between the slough of winter street grime, you're able to plant the case on any pavement or surface, and sit on it. Instantly, it becomes a home. Barely a metre square, maybe, but it's yours, for as long as you squat on the leather joins and the old metal clasps. Despite the swarms of nomads seeking new homes, people oddly respect your claim on it, taking pains to sidestep around you, as if you'd taken bricks and mortar and constructed a solid boundary with a castle moat. And that, nowadays, is a lucky place to be, in a shifting world where countries have borders that stretch like elastic, bending to the will of the Allied troops, or refugees trudging across the lines, smudging any claim on land. For Meta, her own invisible wall is the best that she and her fellow survivors can hope for.

She wrinkles her nose and sniffs. Above the thermal waves of aviation fuel and general fug of pollution, a scent tweaks inside her nostrils. Not an odour that's rancid or foul, but something pleasant. Of lavender water, perhaps, or magnolia. Perfume. Not cloying or expensive, but fresh, and that almost brings tears to her eyes.

Mother.

Meta pushes herself to focus again, her gaze set just above the knees of a khaki-green swathe, the hordes of military personnel toing and froing from the terminal to the landing strip. Her eyes are drawn towards a pair of grey-fleck trousers, two slender legs in a thinner tweed that can only be female. The clip of low heels tells her the rest. Bobbing and nudging against this woman's knees is the prize. Meta's pupils widen, and her dry mouth runs with a little spit: this target is sturdy brown leather, well-used by the looks of it, though the clasps may have been shined recently. Just the right size, too. Perfect.

Her desire burns inside. She shivers beneath her layers to inject some energy and feels her bones rattle with complaint, stamps to push life into her frozen toes. Her legs are weary today, flaccid and wiry in unison, and increasingly devoid of energy. Women, however, are generally easy prey for her, even though Meta hates to admit it. They will rarely give chase, particularly on the ice and snow, afraid of snagging their stockings or falling on the filthy winter fallout. And she's so thin nowadays that her body can weave through the tiniest of gaps, disappearing like a whisper on a breeze. She just has to time it right.

Meta sniffs the air again. Let the hunt begin.

CHAPTER THREE:
A SURPRISE WELCOME

11th February 1946

Georgie

'HEY!' Georgie is wrenched from her thoughts by a blur of limbs by her left side, a sudden yank as the hand clutching the leather strap of her case is left swinging in the air. She feels the chilled breeze weaving around her empty fingers. 'STOP! Come back!' she yells.

Instinctively, Georgie takes off after the culprit, sensing Sergeant Dawson hesitate for a half-second before he pursues, though at a much slower pace. 'Stop that thief!' she hears him bellow from behind, the volume of his voice thrown further than his body.

The blur ahead is fast, weaving in and out of people who startle at the human missile coming towards them, too sudden for them to snatch and stop. Georgie is panting, her shoes slipping on the icy surface, and yet she can't give up. She won't. There are the precious knickers, but also more. Her notes and notebook are inside – tiny props to some, but which make up her being as a reporter. And the picture, dog-eared and blood-smeared, of Max on their wedding day tucked inside the case that made it all the way through the war. She will not allow a common thief to snatch her life away.

As Georgie's legs struggle to keep up, it seems the blur is slowing, the heavy case impeding the progress of its human slalom. She watches the moving vision stumble and falter, then fall again, a small crowd closing in around it. By the time she reaches it, bodies have enveloped the robber in a human cage, cat-calling and baying for blood. 'Let me through, let me through!' she cries, pulling out her rusty German. 'It's my suitcase.'

The circle of people opens out to reveal their catch, and it takes Georgie half a second to spy the 'blur' on the ground, little more than a waifish head cloaked in a strange concoction of clothing, a mobile jumble sale of layers. Skinny fingers clasp the case in front of it, an expression of outrage between the wide eyes and pinched nose, as if they're the one who's been wronged.

'Someone call the police,' says a man, jabbing his walking stick at the waif and receiving a loud hiss in response.

'What can they do?' a woman asks the crowd. 'Stealing is like breathing these days. Someone needs to teach her a lesson.'

Her? Georgie realises for the first time that yes, the blur is female. Woman or girl it's hard to say, even when she reaches down and grabs at what looks like a pyjama jacket, the thin weave beginning to split under her nails and releasing a stale, unwashed odour.

'Hoi!' the waif says indignantly, squirming away from

12

Georgie's grasp, a possessive grip still on the case. Despite the smell, Georgie moves closer, aware the thief might be planning to dart sideways in a second attempt to escape. A breathless Sergeant Dawson catches up, causing the group to quickly disperse at the sight of his army uniform, slinking back into the human fabric milling about.

'I can call the local police,' Dawson says officiously. 'Have her taken away.'

Georgie watches fear bloom in the waif's eyes, then a determination close behind it. After five years of conflict reporting, it's an emotion she recognises all too easily. 'To where?' she asks.

'I'm sure a night in the cells will teach this wretch a lesson.' He prods at a thin shoulder through the layers, but without any real malice or intent. The waif doesn't shrink, remaining as firm as her gaunt form will allow.

Judging by her appearance, Georgie feels that a lesson is not a priority. 'No, Sergeant,' she says in English. 'I just want the case back.' She beckons for the girl to get up.

The waif cocks her head, wisps of dark hair poking out through the holes in a loosely knitted hat. She stands, using the case as leverage but not taking her eyes off Dawson, visibly pulling back her bony shoulders. There's a clear message in this gesture that Georgie recognises – defiance. At times, it might signal aggression, but in this instance, it's like staring at her own reflection, back in the day.

'Give it back and you can go,' Georgie says in abrupt German.

The girl's eyes, protruding from her gaunt cheeks, dim several shades. She looks more defeated than if she were facing the certainty of a night in jail. Reluctantly, her grimy digits peel away from the leather, and she seems to sniff the hide on letting go, as if to bank the smell.

'Sorry Fräulein,' she says quietly, in broken English. 'I don't want what's in it.'

Georgie cocks her own head in confusion. 'Then what is it you do want?'

'The suitcase,' Dawson interjects with a huff. 'That's what they all crave. It's good for bartering.'

'Not this one!' the girl protests. Her hand strokes at it again. 'I would have this one. For myself.'

The exchange is attracting attention, and Georgie is keen to defuse the situation. She wants to get to her hotel, have a hot bath and get to work. It's what she's here for. And this former blur, this waif, is holding her up. But more than that, this encounter has tweaked something within her stomach, rippling up towards her heart; the filth of this girl, and her ragged, inadequate clothes. The look on her face is worse. Tenacious, and yet so needy. As if her life depended on a bloody suitcase. And perhaps, in some way, it does?

'Just the suitcase?' Georgie queries. The pull on her heartstrings she's used to, having witnessed so much human suffering, but this girl . . .

The waif nods.

'All right, you can meet me at the entrance to the Baseler Hof Hotel at six p.m.'

'Is that wise, Miss Young?' Dawson starts. 'I mean you don't want to encourage . . .'

'Wise or not, it's my choice, Sergeant,' she says in English, intentionally clipped this time.

Waif's eyes switch from left to right briskly, Georgie to Dawson, woman to man, between hope and penalty.

'Do you know where that is?' Georgie says.

The girl nods mutely and pushes the case towards Georgie, confirming her limbs are spent of the will to pick it up.

'What's your name?' Georgie asks.

'Meta.'

'Well, Meta, I'll see you at six.' Georgie offers a smile, to signal there's no threat. Of Dawson, or those like him. It's an odd thing to be offering after minutes on foreign soil, but years of war have taught Miss Georgina Young that you take your chances when present. On many occasions, her and Max's survival has been down to providence; lingering for an extra coffee on a roadside, only to watch a mine or a grenade explode in the near distance just minutes later; accepting a ride offered in the opposite direction, and then hearing their intended destination had been flattened by an aerial raid. Today, chance has offered up Meta, and Georgie reasons it might be a fleeting acquaintance. Equally, it could be fated, perhaps for them both. For now, the hope is that her intended good deed will be helpful. She reaches into the pocket of her coat and finds a crumpled paper bag, still half full with lemon bonbons, her favourites. Despite his heavily plastered leg, Max had clearly limped out to their local corner shop on crutches, leaving the bag for her to find as she left in the early hours for the airport. Sweets for my sweet, his note had said. It was his way of apology, of trying to mend the singed bridges between them. Of saying, 'I love you' and 'Come back' with rationed sugar baubles, of patching up those fractured few days before she left. Now, she holds out the same gift to Meta, whose already bulbous eyes protrude at the

15

yellow jewels poking through the paper. Georgie knows a square meal is what she and half the population really crave, but sugar will do for now. 'Here.'

Meta's thin digits reach out hesitantly, almost in disbelief. She wipes her mouth with the other hand, perhaps salivating. 'For me?'

Georgie nods, and the grimy hand snatches at the bag. Suddenly, she's a blur again – has turned, ducked and disappeared in the blink of an eye.

Dawson huffs. 'I wouldn't worry, you won't see her again.'

'Really? What makes you so sure?'

'She's *trümmerkinder*, more than likely – groups of kids living in some rat-infested hole in the ground. Those sweets will be swapped within the hour, for cigarettes probably.'

Georgie looks beyond the clusters of people, into the space where the waif has ghosted away. 'Hmm, perhaps. Let's see. In the meantime, Sergeant, I need to get to work. By way of a bath.'

CHAPTER FOUR:
A STARTLING REFLECTION

11th February 1946

Harri

At this time of year, the grey of daylight is never quite strong enough to split his sleep. Today, though, the thin shaft of brightness before his eyes is a sword, a huge, glinting shard that hovers just inches above his body, ready to strike at the space below the window, where Harri Schroder lies inert, seemingly pinned to the mattress. Helpless. Upright and deadly, the steely blade is preparing to stab at him with brute force – once, twice, three times! Fighting his groggy sleep with panic, his eyelids prise open and he hurls himself bolt upright, chest pulsing like a set of bellows, the thin membrane of his lungs rammed against his ribcage; one more breath and surely they will burst. He holds it for a second in abject fear, and when the sword miraculously doesn't plunge downwards, Harri gently frees up the air inside his chest, watching his breath curl white in the dim light.

'Oh Jesus,' he pants, his gaze swiping left and right. Blinking rapidly, the sword melts away as Harri's bleary vision clears, his vivid dreams receding alongside. Gradually, he sees that it's no weapon splicing the gloom of the room, but a new dawn outside, drab but bright enough to plough through a lengthy split in the dark, patched fabric that doesn't quite span the window space. Still, he's grateful to have curtains. Or curtain – singular. And glass in the window, something else to be thankful for, even if it is crusted on the inside with a white, thick frost.

Fully conscious, Harri flops back into the pillow and reviews his sudden jolt into this new day, now that his heart has limped back into its rightful space. It's not his usual nightmare, at least – not the one where he stumbles blindly through the inferno of a building, scrabbling and searching, molten hands grabbing at his ankles from a floor in flames, scuppering any attempt to move forward. Always searching. Never getting anywhere. It's terrifying each and every time, and yet he's also become quite jaded by it, the same vision having invaded his sleep countless times over the space of three years. And not once has he managed to escape that burning building, or those pawing, clawing hands. Last night's visitation represents a change, and was mercifully shorter – had it played out, it might have meant sudden death from that blade. On certain days, he might even welcome it.

The heat from his body drains rapidly, and Harri pulls the meagre blankets up and around his chin, shivering to incite some warmth, knowing that soon he will have to leave his sanctuary and brave the freezing apartment, for hot water, weak ersatz coffee and a shave. He puts a hand to the bristles on his chin; on any other day, he would forgo the razor and no one at work would be any the wiser. But he's been told that today he needs to 'smarten up', to greet some dignitary or other, no doubt come to view the rewards of victory, albeit in ruins. As if he hasn't got enough to do. Harri eyes the few clothes hanging limply from the picture rail (the wardrobe sacrificed long ago for firewood) and sighs at the challenge of looking presentable when every item is either torn, threadbare or patched, a consequence of five long years of war. The result, too, of being in a country of occupation. The nation that lost.

When he finally makes his move, the sprint to the kitchen sink is necessarily quick, like plunging into an ice-cold lake in autumn, though in his clutch of happy memories Harri recalls that sensation as refreshing and pleasurable once. Now, it's merely shocking. The water that emerges coughing and spluttering from the tap is freezing, and he puts a pan onto the small stove to boil, jiggling up and down on the spot to keep his blood flowing. The tiny cracked mirror propped above the sink confirms what he already knows.

'Christ, Harri Schroder,' he murmurs to his own reflection. 'The only certain thing about today is that you look like shit.'

CHAPTER FIVE:
MAP MAKING

11th February 1946

Meta

Six o'clock can't come soon enough. Meta spends the remainder of the morning on her 'rounds', surveying the line of bodies at several soup kitchens and judging if the lengthy queue is worth the wait. Her stomach says so, the lining tugging painfully at her insides rather than grumbling with hunger; for it to growl she thinks there must be some substance to the tissue, and hers shrivelled to nothing long ago. And yet, in the time it takes to wait her turn for a cup of thin broth, she could barter the acquired trinkets in her bag for a few cigarettes, exchanged for a bread roll and perhaps some stale sausage, if it's near to growing mould and those without a strong stomach won't chance it.

She walks to a pawnbrokers near the Alster basin and trades several watches stowed under her layers – a recent hoard from an abandoned house – though only one is ticking, and she's forced to check the time against the clock on the imposing Rathaus, the age-old town hall centrepiece of Hamburg that miraculously escaped annihilation under the bombings. If the Rathaus clock is wrong, then time really has stopped still in Hamburg. Isn't that what the Allies dubbed it anyway, the day of German surrender, in May 1945 – 'Germany's Zero Hour'?

By midday, Meta is exhausted from hauling her body and bag around. She pays calls on two *trümmerkinder* squats to make minor swaps, grateful for the meagre fires the rubble kids manage to keep burning with their constant foraging of house furniture. She needs light and warmth for her fingers, because there's something she has to do. At her third port of call, the fire is sufficient, and the ruin deserted, except for one of the gang keeping vigil.

'Hey, Meta, where have you been lately?' A boy with one damaged, unseeing eye turns his head as she crouches beside him, holding out her fingers to the shallow flames.

'Here and there,' she says.

'Any good pickings?'

'Some.'

It's like a polite exchange from before the horror, similar to how their parents might have passed the time of day at a tram stop perhaps. Except neither Meta or one-eyed boy have any family left alive, or the twenty pfennigs for a luxury ride across town, in places where the meagre tram service lurches and weaves between the piles of rubble. Besides, each of them knows a single ticket price equals as many as three decent cigarettes, duly exchanged for a meal or a hot drink. Which means survival, for another day at least.

Neither will they reveal their prized 'picking' spots, usually among the grand houses of Hamburg's pre-war rich facing onto the wide, watery expanse of the Elbe, now requisitioned by the British for their higher-ranking officers. The mansions are often unoccupied, waiting for Mrs Smith or Jones to arrive and take up residence, and, in the meantime, the elaborate contents are a prime target for any thief brave enough to risk a British patrol and their snarling dogs. While these huge houses stand empty, thousands of Germans, Russians, Poles and Jews crowd into the city's bunkers, living in squalor and filth, wandering aimlessly to nowhere, to scavenge almost nothing. So what are Meta and her fellow rubble kids to do, but help themselves to the treasure of the once wealthy Hamburgers? It's not stealing, they reason, merely the laws of survival. Even one of the highest churchmen in Germany has sanctioned it as necessity. It's every man, woman and child for himself. In Zero Hour, time has been reset and the rules redrafted. Nothing and no one is the same any more.

'What you doing?' The boy – who's known as Popo – shuffles closer, in his equally ragged outfit, squinting with his remaining good eye. Meta can smell his rank breath, and realises with sadness that it's probably no better than her own. He's around her age – sixteen – and was on the way to being handsome, before the burn across one side of his face and the milky maiming of his eye. Now, he's just a filthy *trümmerkinder*, smelly and unwanted. Like her.

'It's a map, stupid,' she grunts, at which Popo throws himself backwards with a loud belly-laugh, rolling on the wooden pallets roughly fashioned as a hard sofa.

'Who on earth would want a map in this shit-show of a city?' he cries. 'You'll be doing guided tours next.'

She doesn't baulk at his obviously un-German way of speaking, since all the boys talk like Tommies nowadays, purporting to hate them and yet adopting anything of the 'free' world – accents, mannerisms, and sucking in the strains of jazz music – when they can. Instead, Meta stares at the marks scratched into a single sheet of paper that she's traded one of her good watches for, along with a stubby but precious pencil.

'I just need to draw,' she says. 'Someone needs it.'

'They paying you for it? How much? One of those idiot *Englisch*?' He sniggers again to himself and pokes at the dying fire. 'Come on, Meta, why don't you join us here? The gang? We could clean up, fleece those bastards for every cigarette and coffee ration they have. Make maps and pilfer their pockets at the same time.'

She only shrugs. Having posed the question many times before, Popo knows the answer. Meta works alone. In a city where the homeless often roam in shoals, searching for fertile feeding grounds, she guards her privacy closely. It's true that she can't gather enough fuel by herself for a fire most nights, but her rudimentary home is just that – hers. A refuge. A place where she can shed her bravado, drop the steely gaze she's forced to adopt in fighting for every morsel on the streets. Where she can weep in solitude for her mother and sisters, for her father who marched to the Eastern Front and never came back. And never will. It's where she can shiver and sob herself into sleep, and – at the moment of drifting – often wish not to wake up.

Having finished her pencil scratchings, Meta looks at Popo, his good eye trained on the glowing embers of the fire, deep in thought. He looks like he needs a good cry, she thinks. Or a hug. She inches closer and nudges her shoulder against his. Clad in so many layers, their bodies have no hope of contact, and so she reaches for his hand, blackened from the fire, foraging and months of city grime. Popo doesn't startle or pull away as she thought he might, but wraps his fingers around hers and squeezes. Tight. When he turns to reveal the unburnt, mobile side of his face, there is a river of tears streaming towards his mouth that ripples with the reality of defeat.

She pulls out a torn bag from inside her coat and offers him the sweet succour of a lemon jewel.

CHAPTER SIX:
GOOD MORNING HARRI

11th February 1946

Harri

'There's been another one.'

Harri is barely through the door of the staunch, upright (and still standing) police station on David Strasse when he's met with the news. He doesn't need to ask what, only where.

'In the ruins of Weiland Strasse,' Paula reports, blinking through her round, wiry glasses. 'Found this morning.'

'Do we know how old she is?' he asks, moving towards the burner in the corner of the office, though it's already starved of fuel. With this news and the chill, he doesn't bother removing his coat.

'Difficult to say,' Paula reports, 'but we think between fifteen and twenty.'

Harri's chest deflates. Another life lost is nothing new, even after the bombs have stopped – starvation, disease and the freezing weather are the new agents of death. But this . . . needlessly, at the hands of another: one culprit, they suspect, who's waging his own, private war against Hamburg's women. So far, everything smacks of one perpetrator, a single maniac wreaking havoc. A true madman. And that's an all too familiar scenario the German nation would like to condemn to a bloody, besmirched portion of their history.

'Are there similarities with the others?' Harri asks, fingering his chin and realising he missed a patch with his blunt razor.

Paula swallows and nods. 'Strangled and cut, I'm told, so probably. Though no chance to check over the whole body yet. Do you want to head to the scene now?'

'I'm afraid it − she − will have to wait for an hour or so,' Harri says. 'We're expecting a visitor, someone important, apparently, from the British side. I can't get out of it.' He's been told, very firmly, by his senior officer at the Kriminalpolizei *not* to duck out of it. To shake hands and nod in all the right places, to reassure the British authorities that Hamburg's home-grown detective division − the 'Kripo' − is no longer staffed by former Nazis and is capable of solving crime, despite losing half their number to war and the subsequent peace, plus an upward trend in suicides of low-ranking officials. Some would rather face the cyanide capsule than the probing de-Nazification process.

'Send a message to ensure the scene is preserved,' Harri tells Paula. 'If those bomb site kids get anywhere near, we'll have no evidence at all.' With luck, the freezing temperatures will do the rest of conserving the scene until he gets there.

The dignitary, some visiting busybody, keeps them waiting for half an hour, which does nothing for Harri's mood, the meagre fire having burnt down to nothing by the time he arrives. As a British Member of Parliament, the Right Honourable Henry Portman is not in uniform under his thick overcoat, though he looks unimpressed that the entire Kripo department have shed theirs. Even smartened in honour of his visit, the office apparel is 'relaxed' and downright shabby alongside his pin-striped suit and British worsted wool.

'Sir, uniforms from the old regime tend to make the German public nervous nowadays,' the man standing behind Portman whispers in his ear, clearly sensing the MP's disquiet. In turn, the guide is in the navy blue of the Control Commission Germany – known widely as the CCG – those administrators now charged with bringing calm to the post-war chaos in the British zone. And for today, his unenviable job is to pilot this parliamentary do-gooder towards the vital work of the Commission, in feeding and housing the thousands of officially Displaced Persons that have poured into Hamburg in the nine months since German surrender: refugees, former prisoners from both sides, and the generally dispossessed.

'Does he speak English?' Portman enquires, in a tone that the British upper class imagine is discreet, but plainly isn't.

Harri deflates. It's bad enough having the British military oversee almost everything they do, without the pomposity of others poking their noses in. 'He does,' he bats back, with a smile that's obviously forced. 'I mean, I do.'

'Good man.' Portman coughs, momentarily off balance. 'Well, I hear theft is rising dramatically,' he adds officiously. 'And I'm told the black market is rife. How are you proposing to put a cap on the numbers, Inspector?'

Harri can't help it when his smile drops in surprise, at the sheer naivety of this man. Has he not just lived through a war himself? Albeit in London, cushioned by the privilege of the British Government. Yet surely, he can see from a single journey across Hamburg that it's pure chaos out there. There's little order, and scant law to go with it. Robberies up not by one hundred per cent, but eight times that, Harri's desk piled high with case reports, everything from a loaf of bread to a diamond tiara and, in one instance, a bicycle actually robbed from under someone's backside. Each report is scratched in pencil because they have one typewriter in the entire building, no pens and a single telephone line for one of the busiest stations in Hamburg. Tackling a tenth of the unsolved crimes feels more impossible than resurrecting Adolf Hitler from his grave – not that Harri would ever relish that prospect.

'We do what we can, sir,' he says in his accomplished English, gathering every ounce of calm from within. 'I can assure you my officers are working very hard, in very challenging circumstances. Inevitably, we have to prioritise.'

'Yes, well. I can see it's tricky for you.' Portman trawls his gaze over the pocked walls, peeling plaster and desks patchworked from every shade and shape of wood. 'Perhaps we can talk to the Commission about some more resources for you. Eh?' The MP looks hopefully at the CCG man, who nods in deference.

Harri's smile of gratitude is a reflex. Along with the CCG man, he knows full well that while there may be a small surplus of resources available, the German Kripo are low on the list of priorities. Nearing the bottom of a large pile, in fact. So, for the time being, the Right Honourable's visit means precisely nothing, aside from a good hour's delay getting to a prime murder scene.

'Sir, perhaps we should move on?' CCG man urges into the uncomfortable pause. 'We've quite a day in store, and I think you will definitely want to see one of our resettlement centres . . .'

Harri is stood down as Portman is led out, enduring yet again the half-second hesitation so common between Allies and Germans these days: the MP deciding if it's the 'done thing' to shake hands with the enemy, then determining that it's perfectly acceptable, not because the war is over, but because they – the British – are on the winning side.

Paula re-emerges from the office shadows when Portman has finally gone. 'What did he want?'

'To show who's boss. As if we don't already know.' Harri sighs and rubs warmth and life into his face. 'Right, let's get going to the scene. How many bikes have we got?'

'Two.'

'Ah!' Some good news at last to beat against the gloom of the day so far – one bicycle apiece. Almost a luxury. The joy dims a second later. 'How many have flat tyres?'

'One,' Paula says matter-of-factly. 'But it's my turn on the best one. Remember?'

He does. He knows, too, that a bone-shaking ride across the pocked concrete of Hamburg is not the worst of today's prospects for Harri Schroder. Not by a long stretch.

The dead girl in a ruin will trump anything on his daily shit-list.

CHAPTER SEVEN:
CREAM CAKES AND CHAOS

11th February 1946

Georgie

The desolation she is prepared for, having seen towns and countries across Europe reduced to a shadow of their prime, some almost completely flattened. But jostling alongside Sergeant Dawson in the passenger seat of his jeep, wind whistling through the broken window, Georgie is shocked. Utterly. What's more, she's lost for words.

As the aircraft made its approach into Hamburg, she'd had to blink twice at the ground below and reset her perspective; skeletons of buildings standing like ghosts, mere bones of whole apartment blocks and offices backing onto a swathe of forest trees, which in winter are mere carcasses themselves. Where the concrete ended and nature began you simply couldn't tell. From the air, they were all just spindles clinging to existence. The trees at least have nature on their side and a chance of replenishment come the spring.

Down at street level, the devastation feels more acute – not just the obvious destruction of a city, but total annihilation of a way of life. It's just gone ten, and there are people everywhere, on the roads that necessarily merge into pavements, moving in throngs, with handcarts, some pulled by emaciated donkeys, children riding on top with withered faces and sunken cheeks wrapped in threadbare blankets. The parents leading the way look hopeless, trudging on a road to nowhere. Georgie, naïve or not, had never imagined the ending of a war looking like this.

The vehicles weaving around the trains of people are largely military, with a few black Mercedes in the mix. Requisitioned, no doubt, because in the back sit starchy officers in the khaki green of the BAOR, the British Army of the Rhine. Po-faced and important.

'Didn't you fancy staying at the Atlantic, Miss Young?' Dawson says brightly. He's trying hard at his charm offensive, and she's beginning to warm to his effort, given her rather prickly ripostes at the airport. 'I'd have thought the CCG would be more than happy to put you up there. It's the sort of hotel my wife can only dream of, even now.'

'I have heard it's very nice, but I prefer something smaller, a bit quieter,' she says. In truth, she dreads the thought of having to sit daily in the Atlantic's plush interior, hemmed in by high-ranking officers and service wives, in a place notorious for its wartime menu of kangaroo tail soup. She's here to do a job, not to drink tea and pick at cucumber sandwiches.

'And how long do you plan on staying? Oh Christ!' He swerves suddenly to avoid a motorcycle that's been upended in a large pothole, the rider tossed several feet

31

across the road. 'Sorry, miss, occupational hazard. Are the roads just as bad back in London?'

'No, not any more,' Georgie mumbles. 'The road crews have been busy for months.'

The jolt tosses her mind back to a London ravaged in the war's later stages by Hitler's V2 rockets, even though it's a city on the rise again, a grand old dame that's fought off war, pestilence and fire for centuries. A daily percussion of hammers and nails is the soundtrack to life in Britain's capital now. True, there are returning soldiers being demobbed, a portion of whom are disabled and depressed, or both, but nothing like the nomadic swathes she's seeing right now. She knows from her research that the British face an uphill struggle in dealing with untold numbers of *Voelkerwanderung* pouring into Hamburg from the industrial wastelands – a drifting shoal of forced labourers, refugees, abductees, those poor wretches from the camps, German POWs being released in stages, and bombed-out families; Germans, Czechs, Hungarians, Slavs and Poles. A shared compendium of sorrow and death. And that's only what she gleans from the expressions on their faces. Lord knows what stories simmer underneath. For the first time in years, she doubts her ability to distil such loss into words.

She checks into the Baseler Hof and asks – politely – if Dawson might call back in an hour. The bath water is warm, her room small but clean, and Georgie is refreshed and back in the downstairs lobby with ten minutes to spare, a steady stream of middle-rank officers coming and going who don't give her a second glance. And that pleases her. With her short blonde hair, dark knits and tweeds, Georgie has become adept at blending into the smudgy tones of war, of not sticking out like a sore thumb as a Woman Among the Boys. The cosy shabbiness of the Baseler Hof is a perfect base for her, with a private lounge area for work and a small bar for those long, dark evenings. It's also in direct contrast to the grandiose entrance of the Hotel Atlantic, an age-old monolith overlooking the water basin of the Alster river, where Dawson deposits her twenty minutes later, in time for her first official meeting.

'Can you wait half an hour, please?' she asks.

'Not a problem, miss,' Dawson says. 'I've been allocated to you for the entire day.'

Stepping into the Atlantic's once-ornate and lofty foyer feels like entering so many requisitioned grand hotels across Europe, the ones where the British military had a knack for making themselves at home in any given place, as they pushed back Nazi forces in the closing days of the war. There's a muffled clatter of typewriters, though none in sight, and a general shroud of khaki green masking the faded glamour of this establishment that, she's been told, was once the haunt of the wealthy cruising classes in the 1920s and 30s. Alongside the placard signalling the 'Adjutant's Office', a painted sign points towards the 'Palm Court', and Georgie follows the strains of a lone piano player doing his best against the excited chatter of ladies taking tea. In among the crowd, uniformed men huddle around several tables, a mix of military green and the navy blue of the CCG, busy planning Germany's future, no doubt, or at least a portion of it. Hamburg's destiny, certainly.

'A table, Fräulein?' A waiter guides her towards a discreet

corner, past a collection of service wives distinguished by their penchant for talking too loudly in affected English and layers of bright lipstick.

'The tea here is dreadful,' one woman complains loudly. 'Why is it the Germans can't brew a better pot?

For the same reason that the British don't 'do' anything other than weak, insipid coffee, Georgie thinks with irritation, cringing with embarrassment for her own countrywomen. It's not merely their attitude which makes her feel so out of place; the ladies who lunch are well-turned-out, chauffeured in their expensive, purloined Mercedes-Benz, to save their high heels from making contact with the filthy pavement slush. Hair is carefully styled and pinned, in contrast to Georgie's gamine style, kept purposely short throughout the war, a practical and timely disguise in several tricky moments. Now, she's too lazy and distracted to grow it out and tend to a new style. Besides, Max professes to love it. Here, she is glad to be different.

Georgie sits only a minute or two before her contact approaches, his look distinguished by the CCG uniform, and a lean, pallid face that says he spent his war cocooned not in a foxhole, but the corridors of Whitehall, battle-weary in an altogether different way.

'Lieutenant Howarth?' Georgie rises and offers a hand to shake.

'Pleased to meet you, Miss Young.'

She doubts it, wondering how Howarth drew the short straw of eliciting favourable publicity from a freelance reporter with her reputation. It's not that she's intent on digging the dirt, merely telling the truth to readers back in England and across the world.

He is, however, enthusiastic in reeling off a list of 'sights' she should see in her tour of Hamburg – the soup kitchens, resettlement centres and factories kept functioning with British funds. 'I'm afraid I won't be able to accompany you on all of your visits, but I have a contact lined up at each point to show you around,' he concludes.

Georgie coughs, and takes a sip of tea. 'That's very kind, Lieutenant Howarth, but it's not how I'm used to working. Of course, I am grateful for the CCG's help, for the flight and the billet especially. Perhaps in the first few days, it would be useful to have a driver, and accreditation to allow me access. Beyond that, I usually go where my nose takes me.' She rounds off her speech with a fixed, determined smile.

Howarth's face falls, with disappointment she thinks, but perhaps a glimmer of relief mixed in? 'But, er . . . The work we're doing here . . .' he tries.

'Will be written about in the way it deserves, and in the context,' Georgie steps in firmly, the only pledge she'll commit to for now. She draws in a breath. 'I promise you, Lieutenant, I'm not here to demean the effort you and your colleagues are making. Far from it. But from what I've heard, there is a long way to go yet, in winning the peace.'

She shoots him the line so often quoted in the press, in politics and on the street: the infamous General 'Monty' Montgomery's warning as he took over the unenviable task of co-ordinating the British zone in north-west Germany, when the nation was carved into four separate areas after the surrender. The American- and French-occupied areas to the south, Russians to the east, while Britain got the battle-scarred industrial zone of the Ruhr and more than twenty million souls. 'We have won the German war, now we need to win the peace,' Monty pronounced with optimism, though – to Georgie – his words will have been spoken with reservation. Of all people, the celebrated general must have recognised the colossal challenge before him, perhaps even trickier than defeating Rommel in the deserts of North Africa.

Howarth sips his own tea and considers. His shoulders droop and something seems to fall away within him. After several seconds, he sits upright and nods to himself. 'Can I speak off the record, Miss Young?'

'Of course.' She splays her hands, proving she has no notebook hidden under her jacket, and fixes him with her practised look, the one that says: *I'm listening*.

'It's chaos out there,' Howarth says definitively. 'It's estimated there are nine million displaced people across Europe, though that's likely to be conservative. There's nowhere to house them, and very little food, since the railway lines moving supplies into Hamburg alone are shot to pieces, and the weather this past winter caused so many roads to close.'

Georgie remains silent in his pause. The surroundings of the Palm Court tell her that some do indeed have plenty – plates of sumptuous cakes are being waved away by women lamenting their expanding waistlines. She also knows that such inequality is not confined to Hamburg or Germany, merely the way of the world.

'That's before you've even got to the politics,' Howarth pushes on with his confessional. 'We need to move tons of grain in from the east to make the bread, but the Russians are playing hard to get, and they'll only open the transport corridors if we pledge to dismantle German factories and ship out the hardware. But if we do that, the Germans have nowhere to work, and no way of earning even a pathetic amount of Reichsmarks. A good proportion of Germans hate us being here, and more than a few British feel all Germans should pay dearly for Hitler's crimes – in blood, sweat and tears.' He sips again, eyes skittering left and right, as if his words will somehow send up a toxic cloud above his head, marking him out as a traitor to the British cause. 'This *is* all off the record, isn't it?'

'Yes, it is,' Georgie reassures. 'But I am curious. Why tell me this? Why not just pilot me around the sites that will make a good story, and hope I don't dig any deeper?'

'Because, Miss Young, I've read your pieces throughout the war.' A faint smile creeps across his lips. 'I know for a fact you will see through it. Personally, I would like you to tell it like it is – not that we British are having a hard time dealing with the chaos, but the real existence of German people, day to day.' He swallows, and scans the sumptuous surroundings with disdain. 'Quite literally, it's hand to mouth. Of course, it is necessary to weed out the complicit Nazis who've gone to ground, and I agree that the whole thing must never be allowed to happen again. But most people out there can barely function' – he pushes out a hand to beyond the palm frills and sanctity of the Atlantic – 'let alone raise another army, if that's what people back in Britain are really frightened of. Whether or not the Germans bear the guilt of a nation is irrelevant right this minute. Mostly, they are simply hungry.'

Howarth flops back, looking relieved, unburdened. Still weary, but lighter.

'Thank you for your honesty,' Georgie says. 'And I promise you one thing – that whatever I see here, I will tell it like it is.'

'Then, Miss Young, that's all I can ask.'

Georgie appreciates Howarth's candour, but it's not news to her. Details of the chaos are what's brought her here, stirrings in the press from visitors to post-war Europe – a trickle of academics and writers appalled by what they saw – and confirmed by a letter from an old school friend. Posted first as an army nurse to France, Eleanor had trailed the British army on the final advance into Germany, staying on to help with the huge task of repatriation in Hamburg's largest public hospital.

Naïvely, I thought the dying would stop with the surrender, she'd written to Georgie. But there are hundreds succumbing every day – from starvation, TB, and typhus. People have fought for years to survive Hitler's madness, and they're dying because we can't feed the peace.

She was exhausted, Eleanor added, and planning to head home for respite.

But Georgie, people in England need to know what's happening. We can't tar everyone with the same brush and exact revenge on a whole nation, just because we won. Of all people, you can shed light on the truth.

Since that eye-opening first year in Berlin with Max, back in 1938, it's been Georgie's task to report with both accuracy and empathy. There, she witnessed first-hand how Jews were treated, how the German nation was systematically hoodwinked by Hitler and his finely tuned propaganda machine. She saw then it wasn't right, but equally how some were powerless to fight the mighty Third Reich and its insidious tyranny, the underlying threat of violence around every corner, in every loaded smile from a Gestapo officer. The following years have only clarified those first impressions; in her eyes, it doesn't matter where you come from, your religion, or which way you lean, it's about being certain of your actions, having a morality to push against evil. Being human.

But after almost six years of war, millions lost – husbands and sons, wives and daughters – are Britons ready to hear that truth? That peace, too, is ugly? In her last assignment before leaving London, Georgie had toured the suburbs, talking to women queuing outside butcher shops and greengrocers, for butter and meat rations that had been cut yet again only the week before, with bread supplies restricted for the first time. The women knew their sacrifice was needed to ship food to the British zone in Germany, and they were livid. 'What on earth did we fight a war for?' some spat in anger. 'Our children are going hungry to feed the people who supported Hitler.'

She heard them, understood their resentment and reported their wrath faithfully. So, how does Georgie garner their sympathy against the swell of hatred for the German people, reported time and again in the British press? How does she ask the average housewife to see her German counterpart as a victim of the tyranny too? As human. It might prove her toughest assignment yet.

And yet, if she's demanding understanding and honesty from her readers, she must look to herself, to her own life that's hardly been rosy of late. Candour from within. Isn't there another reason why she's here, and not in London, tending to Max and his fractured leg?

Don't kid yourself, George.

CHAPTER EIGHT:
THE PUPPET MASTER

11th February 1946

Harri

Against the dimness of the day and charring of the ruins, it looks as if the woman has tied an ornate choker around her throat as a fashion statement, in a deep shade of velvet red, perhaps in readiness for a night's energetic dancing at the Alster Pavilion, in the days before it became a ruin. Harri has to peer closer to ensure that it's part of her own fabric, and not just decoration. It is: her crusted, crimson self. The wound isn't neat, but the freezing temperatures have played their part in reducing the flow of blood snaking into the crevice of her bare breast.

Harri's heart shrinks. 'How long?' he asks Paula.

The police doctor has left, overworked with so many deaths to attend to in and out of the hospital, and so Paula consults her notes. 'At least six hours, possibly ten.'

'Early hours of the morning, then, and still dark?' He's thinking aloud, as he always does on first inspection, ordering his thoughts as he mumbles. He peers outside the ground-floor ruin. There's no sign of life, the surrounding buildings little more than brick ghosts.

'Who found her?' Harri scans for the blackened seat of an old fire among the rubble, the evidence of *trümmerkinder*, and valuable witnesses.

Paula consults her notes again. 'A local man scouting for old furniture and firewood.'

'Is he a suspect?'

'I very much doubt it.'

'Why not?' Harri recalls several other cases from the past where the perpetrator tried to cover their tracks by posing as a Good Samaritan.

'He's a returning POW with one arm and a pronounced limp. And he nearly lost the insides of his stomach just looking at her.'

'Strike him off the list then.' It's obvious that this poor woman – a girl at first glance – met her death at the hands of someone both able and robust, since she's been hauled into a sitting position and fixed, strung under her arms with what looks like shipping rope from the docks, head tapered by a scarf around it, fastened to the rope. Despite the stiff rigor of her limbs, she appears to Harri as a larger-than-life marionette left slumped, her features frozen, eyes closed, lips just ajar. If this were a stage, her eyelids could snap open any second and her limbs come alive, dancing to a jaunty tune. But strings or no strings, there's no life in her now, no spring in any future step. Harri's entire being sags; it's the saddest sight he knows, for her to have endured the war and survived attack from all angles – the Allied bombings and the Nazi scourge – only to succumb to a different monster. Because this killer is just that: bloodthirsty and determined. He's done this before. Too many times now.

'The Puppet Master again?' Paula sidles up beside Harri and peers at the familiar positioning, the third woman in as many months to be maimed and posed in this way, a clear signal that the killer is pulling all the strings.

'It's not helpful to give him a name,' the inspektor bites back. 'There's enough paranoia in this city, and affording him credence – if he finds out – might only fuel his ego.'

'Sorry,' the detective constable mumbles. 'Only some back at the station . . .'

'I know what they say.' His voice is tinged with irritation and defeat, already well aware of the feelings inside Davidwache, of whisperings that say this has gone on long enough. The simple truth is that if Harri Schroder does his job and hunts down this so-called 'Puppet Master', it will safeguard women *and* deprive this madman of a nametag. And yet, he shouldn't be too hard on Paula, since less than four months ago she was a widowed housewife, whose only other job had been in police administration. The enthusiastic cull of the Kripo meant recruitment became both fast and necessary – anyone with their faculties and proof of not being a Nazi was considered suitable for officer employment, signed up and trained on the job. And yet those prior years of tracking down food for her children and places to live have made Paula an excellent officer; intuitive and insightful. She's damned good at the paperwork, too. Maybe he should tell her so, instead of showering censure and his foul mood?

The Kripo forensics team is a thing of the past, having been either arrested or killed, and the two detectives spend almost an hour meticulously combing the rubble for any trails of blood, footprints or traces of their killer. Harri breaks for a second as two orderlies from the morgue untie the victim and lift her to reveal a small pool of blood beneath. He surveys their movements almost paternally, his heavy frown reminding them to support her limp, skinny limbs as they carry her away. She *is* another body, one of many, but like all the others, she shouldn't be treated with anything less than respect. Through the entire catastrophe of war and beyond, Harri Schroder has pledged never to lose sight of it.

'Damn it! He's been careful again,' Paula huffs, levering up and stretching her back with a wince. She stops halfway, and Harri watches her nose dip towards the ground again, twitching like a hound dog seeking out a bone.

'What is it?' he asks.

'A scent,' she says, face close to the floor. 'Fleeting, but I swear I smelt the same at the last murder scene.' She closes her eyes and sniffs, as if rifling through her own memory bank. He waits, statue-like, careful not to disrupt her concentration. There's no point approaching; Harri's own sense of smell has been reduced to almost nothing, bar a constant, acrid odour of blood and ash lodged in his nostrils for almost three years now. Ever since that day. His own zero hour. A doctor friend has said his loss of smell is likely to be psychological, and may well return one day, out of blue. When he begins to heal, perhaps. It stands as an irritating hindrance to his role as an investigator, if a handy asset in among the stink and filth of Hamburg.

Paula is still analysing. 'Earthy,' she mutters. 'A little sweet, a bit like soil.'

Harri begins to move away. Clearly, she's latched onto the miasma of Hamburg – unpleasant, but hardly significant either.

'Wait!' Paula pushes out her palm and closes her eyes, retrieving a fine strand of memory from deep inside her brain. 'I've got it! Patchouli.'

'Patchouli?' Harri can't help but be sceptical. 'Are you sure?'

'Yes, my father-in-law used to wear it – too much.' She's wide-eyed now, with a faint smile. 'I always hated it.'

'Well, it's something to consider.'

'But vapour is hardly evidence, is it?' Paula adds with disappointment.

'True. But it might well be a small piece of the puzzle, especially when we have nothing else.' Harri squints beyond the spaces that were once window frames. 'I think that's enough for now. There's little point us going house to house with so few people about.' Instead, he orders a uniformed officer to remain outside, watching for those bodies scurrying from the 'rabbit holes', the cellars and basements that have become makeshift homes for the bombed-out and displaced. As darkness descends, the underground dwellers tend to break cover like small creatures bent on foraging in the dark. Maybe they saw something. Anything.

Harri draws both hands across his face, nails catching on his stubble and pulling purposely at his jowls made loose by the war. His fingers smell of death and he wants to find a street standpipe and wash them, however freezing it might be.

'You head back to the station and go through recent missing persons,' he instructs. 'There's a chance she might have a family, someone to miss her. I'll head over to the morgue. Get the team on identification and any background, and assemble in the office for a briefing at nine tomorrow?'

Paula nods, obviously relieved to be spared morgue duties, and perhaps Harri's company too, given this mood he can't seem to shake off. He picks his way over the street rubble outside and talks to a few street traders who set up shop each day on the kerbside to raise a pfennig or two, the odd cigarette if they're lucky. They've seen nothing since the daylight hours.

'We'll keep our eyes open, though,' says Emil, who was once a chief engineer, and now scrapes a living selling ephemera from a worn sailor's kitbag. Harri struggles to select anything remotely useful from his paltry collection laid out, but he picks up a small lighter, and hands over coins way beyond its worth, plus two cigarettes from his pack. He draws a policeman's wage, while Emil's mind is too ravaged to pick up his job at the old Volkswagen plant, warped by the loss of his entire family in the firestorm of '43. And even though Emil is hungry and gaunt, he's too proud a man to be in receipt of charity. For a city that's thrived on trade for centuries, nothing less than a sale is acceptable.

'We'll keep our eyes open,' Emil pledges, handling the cigarettes with kid gloves and placing them in a hard case alongside his other tobacco treasure.

'Send me word with any detail,' Harri says with a parting wave. 'You know where to find me.'

★   ★   ★

Corridors of any morgue are depressing by nature, echoey and necessarily cold at the best of times. Worse is when the echo is dulled and padded by too much custom, orderlies walking back and forth, scratching their chins about where to store the latest influx. Harri draws in a last, semi-fetid lungful of air as he enters the autopsy room and spies the pathologist, who drags hard on a thin cigarette, a swift interlude as one body is wheeled away and he pulls back the sheet on the next.

'This your girl?' He gestures, dousing the cigarette and carefully setting it aside.

Harri nods reluctantly to Dr Edelman, a pre-war dermatologist forced to rapidly expand his medical expertise during the conflict, but who has since become a shrewd pathologist, largely through practice. He's pretty good on skin, too. Which is just as well, since they are both compelled to peer closely at the girl's pale flesh, their eyes focused on her shallow navel smeared with dried blood.

'Can you read the letters?' Harri queries.

Edelman reaches for a magnifying glass and pulls the overhead light closer. 'L . . . U . . . G . . . N . . . E . . . R . . . I . . . N.' He spells it out like a child reciting their homework, handing the glass to Harri, who can only just make out the letters carved into her skin by what seems the finest of knife points. 'Lugnerin,' he repeats. *Liar.*

'The same, then?' Harri stands erect and hears his spine creak, like an old ship. That's what he feels these days. At thirty-two, he's an aged, washed-up vessel.

'Hmm, I would say so,' Edelman agrees. It's a moot question really, since this is the only killer in Harri's career who seeks to score messages on his victim's flesh.

On the previous two, he'd etched 'fraud', and 'cheat'. Evidently, this is a man who feels slighted by war or women. Or both.

'Cause of death?' Harri asks.

'Strangled, like the others, and the throat cut almost immediately afterwards, given what you say about the pool of blood beneath her at the scene.' Edelman peers through his tortoiseshell glasses, a tiny fleck of blood sitting on the lens.

'Any other bruising to indicate she put up a fight?'

'A little on the wrists, but less than I would expect, given the violence of the crime.'

'Sexual interference?' Harri feels his chest constrict in readiness, even though the other two victims were spared that brutality. *Please, not that sufferance as well.*

'No evidence of it,' Edelman reports with obvious relief.

'So, she was killed where we found her . . .' Harri is thinking aloud again. 'Why on earth would she follow her killer into an abandoned ruin in the dark?' He looks intently at her face, so innocent under her pale mask of death. Everything above the fatal gash to her neck is untouched, and Harri – as much as it pains him – forces himself to imagine her animated face just twenty-four hours before, talking and laughing, turning to a grimace at the end. Her skin is untarnished by make-up and she looks eighteen at most. Dark welts pepper her legs, a sign of vitamin deficiency that so many in Hamburg sport nowadays, which tells him she's not rich or privileged. Neither, though, does she look like a working girl, giving good service to the British service boys and breaking the rules on 'fraternisation' between the occupiers and the conquered. So, who is she, and why was she there?

'Thanks, I'll await your full report,' Harri says to Edelman as he makes for the door. Even without a sense of smell, the dense ether claws at his skin and he's eager to escape.

Edelman looks up from his scrutiny of the body. 'Schroder – catch this one, will you?' His tiny pupils shine through thick lenses. 'It's bad enough people dying from war, starvation and disease. But this . . . we've had enough inhumanity. Enough.'

Inspektor Harri Schroder nods. He couldn't agree more.

CHAPTER NINE:
SAVIOUR ON THE STREET

11th February 1946

Georgie

Sergeant Dawson is waiting patiently outside the Atlantic when Georgie emerges, seeming genuinely upbeat that his role as her driver had been extended for a few days, after the meeting with Howarth. 'Makes a change from ferrying stuffy old generals about,' he chirps, then stops himself and looks at her with alarm. 'Sorry, miss. I don't mean any disrespect.'

Georgie looks sideways with a smile. 'Believe me, I've spent many an evening with stuffy old majors and colonels, and I agree entirely. Give me a military mess or the local café culture any day.'

'Well, if you're keen to witness service life in Hamburg, then the Victory Club is the place to go,' Dawson suggests. 'There's a decent NAAFI canteen, and plenty of good music on some nights. I like a bit of Benny Goodman, don't you?'

'I do, Sergeant. Very much.' The mention of Benny the band leader draws Georgie back to London again, and one of the last evenings out with Max, before he left for the mountains of Scotland and put a hold on his dancing days by breaking his leg spectacularly in two places. They'd gone to a club in Piccadilly, drunk on the music and spinning on the floor until the early hours, as if making up for the honeymoon Hitler robbed them of back in 1939. She smiles to herself and pockets the memory for later, a hand moving unconsciously over the waistband of her trousers. Contemplation and nostalgia will have to wait.

Dawson drives north-east, navigating the uneven thoroughfares, a few with recognisable streets, and others where the rubble simply melds to a continuous moonscape, forcing the caravans of wanderers to constantly dodge the handcarts, horse-drawn wagons and military vehicles. Some on foot are too lethargic to even bother, and simply leave it up the driver to swerve and save them. Or destiny perhaps.

'Where are they all *going*?' Georgie says in a true expression of wonder, her breath steamy against the jeep's grubby window.

'Hmm, often nowhere,' Dawson says. 'Some will collect around the soup kitchens, others to the makeshift camps on the outskirts of the city. Mostly, they just move around, picking up food or work where they can. It's all they've known for so long, and I'm not sure they know how to stop. How to have a home any more. Not that there's anywhere to put them.'

For a brief second, Georgie recognises that nomadic element within herself, the difficulty she and Max had in

51

grounding themselves each time they landed back in London after an assignment, and the way in which they both dawdled over putting a deposit on their flat in Islington at the war's end, somewhere to call home. The way in which it felt so strange to be cosied up in the warmth of their own parlour, not in some trench or run-down billet, and the months it took for their feet to stop itching.

But then she realises it's not the same. Not at all. London is damaged rather than obliterated, and Britain's homeless aren't forced to trudge the streets endlessly. It's not the same because she and Max have a choice to roam, freely if they want to. And choice is freedom.

'Here we are,' says Dawson, as he pulls up with a screech of brakes, with the air of a man enjoying his new role as tour guide. 'Hamburg's old zoo, turned resettlement camp.'

At first glance, there's little evidence of the low-level crumpled landscape once having been a zoo, and the earthy scent she recognises isn't visceral, but human in origin. Lines of people snake around the makeshift buildings, though these are ordered queues, of women and children mostly, who seem to be waiting for something tangible in exchange for their patience.

Clutching her hastily typed letter of accreditation from Lieutenant Howarth, Georgie strides to the front of the line, forging towards a woman whose voice is the loudest, directing bodies in a staccato mix of German and English. She appears to be someone who knows the score, one of that type Max dubs 'the movers and the shakers of this world'.

Georgie thrusts out a hand and a firm introduction. 'Accredited journalist,' she adds. Tall and austere, with her

52

relatively healthy complexion, hair pinned into submission and clothes that are practical and well-worn, rather than rags, the woman stands out from the surrounding sea of gaunt cheeks and sallow skin. She palms away dust and dirt from her fingers before taking Georgie's hand gingerly.

'Margaret Gilbey,' she replies. 'British Red Cross. Are you . . . with someone?' Her eyes search into the distance for an official chaperone, and settle on Dawson lurking in the background, puffing on a cigarette. 'I wasn't aware we were expecting visitors, the press especially.'

'Apologies,' Georgie says. 'I only arrived in Hamburg today, and I'm anxious to begin work straightaway.' She fixes a determined look on Margaret, still clutching at her hand, another trick that always seems to work particularly well with high-ranking army officials who baulk at female reporters anywhere near the front line.

But Margaret — who looks nothing like a 'Maggie' — may prove a tougher nut to crack than any brigadier-general. 'Perhaps you can come back tomorrow?' she responds briskly. 'We're busy with de-lousing and registering today. I really haven't the time to guide you around.' Her voice is as firm as the hand that steers a small child into the queue.

'Oh, I won't need a guide,' Georgie says cheerfully. Equally, she won't be rebuffed; more than once Max has decreed that 'pushy' is his wife's middle name. 'In fact, I'd like to see it exactly as it is. The British people need to hear about this. Without a shine on it.' She fixes Margaret Gilbey with an expression that reads like an international language between all women.

Margaret's pale pursed lips seem to reflect an understanding: *I hear you*. She expels a large sigh. 'All right. I may well get it in the neck for this, but if you want to witness the reality, it's about time someone shouted about it. Welcome to Number Seventeen Displaced Persons Assembly Centre, otherwise known as "Zoo Camp".'

Notebook in hand, Georgie trails Margaret on her checks of the de-lousing process – children's faces turned ghost-like as DDT powder is sprayed liberally over their clothes and hair. They flinch but don't complain.

'All very necessary, I'm afraid,' Margaret explains, as she switches between her pidgin German and orders in English to the other Red Cross staff. She is abrupt and sometimes curt, but with the enormous numbers needing attention, Georgie sees why. It's a huge undertaking to furnish the endless queues with clean clothes, a purpose and a glimmer of hope.

'The families here are supposed to be on their way to other more permanent camps,' Margaret explains, forging at a pace through corridors of the hastily built wooden huts, 'but in fact we have a hard time convincing some to head back east, the Poles especially. They're not keen on being sent to the Russian sector.'

Together, they visit the soup kitchen, with children hungrily eyeing the watery broth on offer, and the lines of families needing registration; Georgie's attention is drawn to the anxiety etched in every mother's face as they pull their young into the folds of shabby coats, a constant grip in place. *Is this what it's like? To harbour a heavy swell of worry, all day, every day?* For the second time in less than an hour, a hand hovers above her own abdomen. *Could I do that?*

It's not long before Georgie's German is struggling to keep up with the stories pouring forth from parents as they pitch for food coupons, clothing and a place to stay. Constantly, she looks to Margaret for explanation, but Miss Gilbey's attention is taken elsewhere. Hovering alongside the registration desk, Georgie is lured by the timid murmurings of a lone woman wrapped in sour-smelling cloth, her thin face sprouting from two heavy blankets, which appear as if they are both weighing her down and propping her upright at the same time. Barely audible, she unfolds a tale in her native German, one that's undoubtedly tragic. If only Georgie could understand every word.

'She's from south of Berlin originally,' another voice cuts in from behind, English with a heavy German accent. 'But she's come from the camp at Ravensbrück.'

'Thank you.' Georgie turns towards the voice, and a young, pale-faced woman just feet away in the queue. 'Could you ask her how she came to be here, and where she's going?'

The story that is patiently interpreted, line by line, is all too common, though still shocking in its intensity; a family of four sisters, all German-Jews, transported to the infamous female camp outside of Berlin. The gaunt woman relays impassively how two of her sisters were worked to death, one later beaten into her grave. She is the last standing, she says, her stalk-like legs barely supporting her meagre form.

'She's searching for a cousin – her only relative she thinks might be alive, last heard of in Hamburg,' the translator relays.

The desperate woman is keen to tell her story, to push her relative's name forward, though it's evident she has no expectations of a swift resolution. When there's no recognition, she smiles meekly and shuffles away to join another line of hopefuls.

Georgie turns to her impromptu interpreter again. 'What are the chances of finding her family alive?'

She shakes her head. 'Not good. But you keep going. We're all searching for something.'

'And you . . .?'

'Zofia,' the woman offers. 'Zofia Dreyfus.'

'Are you looking for someone, Zofia?' Georgie is curious now, not only as a journalist seeking the human elements of a story, but as a woman, a wife and a daughter. The face in front of her has a look of youth, with maturity etched into her dry skin and the cracks around her eyes. Her sunken cheeks and dull head of hair pay testament to a difficult war.

'My sister,' she says. 'She was in Ravensbrück, too. I was . . .' – her tired eyes mist over – '. . . elsewhere.'

'And where are you going now?'

'Another camp, probably. Hopefully nearby, so I can keep searching.'

Georgie hesitates, but only momentarily. 'Well, Zofia, would you like a job, for a week or so, maybe more? As my translator?'

It's spontaneous, and very possibly rash to anyone else. To Georgie, however, the path is immediately clear; while she's heard battlefield philosophers and war-weary generals tell her time and again that you can 'only look at the bigger picture', that helping one soul at a time is no better than spitting on an inferno, her own morality doesn't hold with that. Whether it's one person or a hundred, it's still better than nothing. And no, she doesn't possess the selflessness of Margaret Gilbey and her staff to dedicate her life to a cause, and she is definitely no martyr, but Georgie Young has always strived to help where she can – spare rations, cigarettes, or a little money has often made a difference to someone in dire need. Here and now, her rusty German needs oiling. Zofia's English is patently good, fluent in Polish, too, and some Russian. It's a perfect match made in this hell.

'Sergeant Dawson?' Georgie marches towards the jeep, catching him staring with wonder at two elephants – former zoo residents, she presumes – overturning the wreck of a car with their trunks. She, too, pauses for a second at the extraordinary image, nature amid the broken shards of concrete and humanity.

'Isn't that a sight for sore eyes?' he murmurs wistfully. 'A miracle they survived. And more efficient than any forklift, I'll bet.'

'I'm sure they are.' Georgie makes a mental note to capture the image for her final article, but there are more pressing issues at hand. 'Can we make some room for another passenger, Sergeant?'

'Of course, Miss Young.'

If he has an opinion about Georgie collecting a stray on their travels, Dawson hides it well, lifting up Zofia's small knapsack and helping her into the back seat with true decorum. They drive south towards Hamburg's centre, weaving between tramlines and horse-drawn carts, but as they reach the fallen, compacted landscape of the Reeperbahn, Georgie is struck with a sudden urge to roam. Max calls it her 'itchy self', and when he senses it, he'll often be first to suggest they go out scavenging for a story. Some of their best news features during the war were captured by simply following their noses. Now, she feels a strong need to read Hamburg from beyond the safe confines of a vehicle. The broken glass of the jeep feels more of a barrier than a safety net.

'Sergeant, can you let me off here, please? I'll make my way back to the hotel.'

He rolls the jeep into what was once a kerbside. 'Are you sure, Miss Young? This area isn't always that safe. I could take the young lady back to the hotel and come with y—'

'Thank you but no. I'll be fine.' She's trying to be patient with Dawson's paternalism, reminding herself that it comes of genuine concern. 'Can you take Fräulein Dreyfus to the Baseler Hof and secure a room for her, please? I'll sort out the details with reception later.'

Zofia's face from the back of the jeep seems to glow not with fear but fresh uncertainty.

'I won't be long, I promise,' Georgie assures her. 'Take a nice bath and order a hot meal, whatever you like. It will go on my bill. I'll join you before six.'

As Dawson drives away, Georgie pulls the strap of her worn leather satchel across her body and scans the scene. *Hamburg, here I come.* She's glad to have changed from flat travelling brogues to her sturdy boots, as she begins to clamber over the wasteland of bricks and rocks between the building façades that stand like paper cutouts against a grey, brooding sky. The remaining walls act as divides in the mounds of rubble, some stacked into small piles, and others waiting to be sorted and processed by the 'brick *omas*' she's heard of, the staunch women in headscarves who look at her now as she walks past, at her good clothes and clean hair. Yet they stare with what seems like wonder rather than bitterness, their thick overalls and jackets as pocked as the walls on which they lean, one or two drawing on a tiny stub of a cigarette. She smiles and says, *Hallo*, but the faces reflect only bewilderment and a vacancy she hasn't seen since her visit to the newly liberated Nazi camp at Sachsenhausen almost a year before.

She wanders on, reluctant to pull out her notebook and attract undue attention, blinking instead like the shutter of Max's camera to set the image in her mind. Up close, the stone frontages possess an endurance Georgie hasn't appreciated so far; from the air, the concrete left standing looked so fragile, but the fascia of so many apartment blocks here have refused to lie down, their ornate art deco porticos fixed and unyielding, the fabric of the flats and homes behind crushed into dust. It prompts images of Christmas at home and her mother's attempts to build a gingerbread house each year, fusing her thinly baked walls of biscuit with sugar icing, and the shrieks of dismay from the kitchen as her structure cracked or toppled. Mercifully, Hamburg's doorways are made of sturdier stuff.

That memory, plus a rumble in her stomach, reminds Georgie she's had nothing to eat since a very early breakfast, and it's already gone two. It's untimely and irritating, but without something inside, her reserves will begin to flag. She scouts around for anything resembling a shop, and spies a makeshift sign, rough paint daubed on a ragged piece of wood propped up next to an alleyway: *Backerei*. Even a bread roll will boost her energy.

The alleyway is dark and uninviting, but Georgie's insides protest again and she ducks into the freezing space leading to a small courtyard enclosed on three sides, one having simply fallen away to reveal more desolation beyond.

Several children, thin, pale and underdressed, hover opposite an ad-hoc shop doorway with weary expectation. Georgie smiles as she walks past, but they only stare wantonly. Inside the shop, there's little choice – one loaf of black bread and several unappealing rolls sit on an upturned box, but the woman squatting next to it jumps up like a jack-in-a-box. Georgie's clothes may be classed as dowdy amid the glitz of the Atlantic, but here they shine like finely spun gold, her very being screaming wealth. The woman gabbles in rapid German, perhaps attempting her best sales pitch, offering up all her wares with grubby fingers. Georgie nods, pulling out several dollar notes and Reichsmarks from her leather satchel.

'*Danke, danke*,' the woman repeats over and over, grabbing at the dollars and pushing the bread into Georgie's arms. With nothing left to sell, it's clear the shop is now shut and she retreats to a room in the back. Outside, the gaggle of small hopefuls twitch with a renewed zeal, milling closely around her, not pawing, but staring, pulling at the produce with their gaze, unable to tear their eyes away. They murmur under their breath: '*Bitte, bitte.*' Please, please. Suddenly, Georgie's hunger has vanished. She breaks the rough, leaden bread into pieces, as evenly as she can, and distributes it among the children, who grab, smile, spin and scurry away in little more than a heartbeat.

Beyond the alleyway and back out into the street, she scans left and right. Which direction did she come from? It's daylight, though a heavy snow cloud overhead has cast a gloomy shadow. Suddenly, the mounds look all the same, with fewer people about, leaving Georgie disorientated. In conflict, she and Max became experts at using their ears and eyes for navigation – towards or away from the dull thud of artillery, depending on whether they were chasing a story, or craving a semblance of peace to write up copy. Here and now, there's just a scrape of bricks and a hum of disquiet. She's not panicked, but there is a tingling of unease in her still empty stomach. In war, the same stir was as common as breathing, and yet it's much less comfortable in peacetime.

Damn it! Perhaps Dawson was right to warn me?

They come out of nowhere, just like at the airport. Fingers tugging feverishly at the satchel slung across her body, so fast she can't even count the bodies or hands pushing into her coat pockets, like the tentacles of a sea creature. Her own hands go immediately to the thick leather strap, as the thieves yank hard on where her money and precious notebooks are, and her mouth lets out a shriek of alarm and shock. Being fired on in a theatre of war is one thing, but targeted by thieves for the second time in one day is another. How lawless *is* this place?

There are two hands jerking at her bag, another two – she thinks – tugging at her coat from behind. The bodies are shorter than her, thin and reedy, but with the strength of barbed wire. She smells sour breath close and unwashed clothes, but also determination. In her experience, desperation has a knack of fuelling commitment to the task.

Despite her flagging energy, Georgie is equally committed to not being a victim. The satchel represents a smaller version of her beloved suitcase, worn with overuse and re-stitched through necessity, a constant through so many assignments. It's her second skin.

The tussle lasts only seconds, even though such an intense struggle seems like an eternity. She locks eyes with the gangly boy pulling with all his might, almost sent off balance by the startling milkiness of his eye and the candle-wax flesh below. He is defaced and determined, unable to let go. It's a battle of wills as much as strength, neither prepared to relinquish the prize.

Within seconds, Georgie feels the heavy twine on the bag strap begin to give, one stitch at a time, almost cracking away from her – several more tugs and it will split completely and the bag will be lost. *NO!* she screams inside herself, watching the boy's head suddenly swivel as tension on the strap falls away to almost nothing, while her own ears register a sound, a yell maybe, somewhere in the distance.

'*Achtung! Achtung!*' the thief behind her shouts, and the one with the maimed face has to turn fully to see the cause of alarm, a man running towards them, hollering, 'Halt! Halt!' a baton of some sort held aloft in one hand. Georgie sees the two boys exchange a swift look, turn on a penny and run full pelt into the ruins, their bodies soon swallowed by the gloom and grime. Crucially, they flee empty-handed, her satchel still hanging by a thread from the strap.

The man must see them go because he begins to slow up as he reaches Georgie. Breathless, he bends, hands on his knees, scooping in air. '*Geht's ihnen gut, Fräulein?*' he pants.

'I . . . I . . . I'm fine, thank you,' she stutters in German.

His attention is piqued and he stands upright. 'You're English?' he says, switching instantly to her native language.

'Is my German that bad?'

The man half-smiles diplomatically. 'Well, you're shaken, understandably.' His command of English, by comparison, is very accomplished. 'Did those boys get away with anything?'

Georgie checks her pockets hastily. 'Just a few Reichsmarks, perhaps, but not this thankfully.' She pats the satchel. 'All down to you. My thanks.'

'It's my . . . pleasure.' He stops, his face suddenly quizzical. 'What are you doing out here, anyway? So far from the British HQ?'

'Oh, I'm not with the British,' she bats back. Georgie wonders if she can claim such a thing, but she's still loath to align herself with the occupiers, so accustomed to being a neutral observer. 'I'm a reporter.'

He sniffs and shrugs. 'In that case, we'd better get off to the station, to report this incident properly.' He begins turning, in the direction he came from, as if expecting her to follow.

'No, really,' she protests. 'There's no harm done. A scuffle, at the most. I think it's very unlikely the police will ever catch those boys.'

'So do I,' he says with a note of defeatism. 'But we should report it anyway.'

'Herr . . . I'm sorry, I don't know your name.'

'Schroder. Harri Schroder.'

'Well, Herr Schroder . . .'

'Detective Schroder. Kripo division.'

'Ah.'

'Yes, Fräulein. And as much as I'm reluctant to add to the teetering pile of paperwork on my desk, it's more than my job's worth to ignore a crime perpetrated on a British visitor.'

'But I won't say anything, I promise,' she entreats. Georgie is feeling a burden now, as well as foolish, heat rising up through her neck. Oddly, being shot at has afforded less stress in the past.

He turns back and faces her, hands planted in the pockets of his overcoat, which she sees now is not ragged, but worn and patched in places. 'I'm sure you won't, but in my experience, someone might, Miss . . .'

'Young.'

'Well, Miss Young, I sometimes like my job. I certainly need it. So, please, if you'll come with me?'

She hoists up her satchel and pulls it close into her body, reminded of the debt of gratitude she owes. 'All right.'

CHAPTER TEN:
PRYING EYES

11th February 1946

Harri

He forces purpose into his stride, in backtracking towards the four-storey red-brick citadel of Davidwache station, one of the more distinct buildings facing onto the Reeperbahn, given its escape from too much bomb damage. With as much as goodwill as he can muster, Harri opens the imposing doors and climbs the stone stairs to the first floor. By this hour, he had hoped to be in a basement café on Erich Strasse, where the company is discreet and for ten pfennigs and two cigarettes, you can get a decent cup of Maxwell House and a portion of solace and quiet in the late lunchtime hour. They don't volunteer where the coffee comes from and he doesn't ask. But that opportunity – and a chance for a personal slice of peace – is rapidly disappearing.

Eyebrows are raised around the office as Inspektor

Schroder leads this newest victim towards his desk and hastily swaps his own, fairly solid chair for the one where visitors usually perch, but which now wobbles significantly on a spare leg. 'Please, have a seat.'

Watching Miss Young's eyes comb over the ramshackle surroundings, he wonders if any part of London's infamous Scotland Yard has ever looked this shabby. Her focus falls on Paula, scribbling at her desk in the corner, and on Erwin who – at approaching seventy – has been pulled out of retirement to make up the numbers.

'It might not look like much, but it does have the advantage of being solid, and still standing,' Harri remarks, fishing out keys from his desk drawer and unlocking a battered cupboard, from which he pulls an ancient typewriter and a single piece of paper. She looks oddly dumbfounded and knits her brows together under her short boyish fringe. 'It's our only functioning machine,' he explains. 'And being British, you are therefore entitled to a typed report.'

'Well then, I am honoured,' she concedes. 'But I'd make it brief if I were you, to save your precious ink.'

He likes her more then, for a distinct lack of sarcasm, a playful edge to her voice and a wry twist to her full lips. Perhaps he won't lament the loss of his Maxwell House too much. They run through the details quickly; she talks almost in shorthand and he is economical with the facts, using up only five lines of print and half a page. Glancing up from the keyboard, he watches as her attention wanders to the blackboard Erwin is currently updating, pinning the drawings of the murder scene that Jonni – a promising art student – has made in place of photographs they can no longer afford or process.

Her eyes flick back and forth, and he deflates at the thought of her mind being equally nimble. Will he regret blithely bringing her here, into their think tank, exposing the news of a killer of women? So far, the small detective department has managed to keep it under wraps, in not introducing panic into a city already steeped in turmoil. It'll be Harri's fault if she 'breaks' the story and sends their killer further into Hamburg's underbelly, either to kill again or disappear without trace.

'It's in the early stages,' he ventures, hoping to quash her curiosity before it multiplies.

'What is?' Her voice is innocent, but she palpably isn't.

'The investigation.'

'Into?'

'A murder.'

She cocks her head, eyes still fixed on the board.

'I know. It's quite incredible that some people haven't had their fill of it,' Harri says without humour. She's gazing at drawings of his latest cadaver, and he's staring at her, wondering what machinations are going on behind her very wide eyes.

'How many?' she murmurs.

'How many what?'

'Bodies. All women, I presume?'

He stands, the scrape of his chair signalling a reluctance to reveal any more, and of course, she'll sense that. She's a bloody reporter, after all. 'Well, Miss Young. I will contact you at your hotel if we happen to apprehend these young bandits.'

'But I promise not to hold my breath, Inspector.' She smiles weakly and rises, patting her satchel. 'I'm merely grateful to keep hold of this. My thanks again.'

He shuffles. 'I would like to be able to offer you a lift back to the Baseler Hof, but I'm afraid we have no appropriate transport. I can, however, provide an officer to walk you to the nearest U-Bahn. Once you're there, it's relatively safe these days.'

She hesitates, but only briefly. 'Thank you, that's kind. In the circumstances . . .' she looks to the window and the darkness descending outside '. . . I think I'd be wise to accept your offer.'

Through the office window, he watches her easily keep pace with the uniformed Schupo officer as they stride down the Reeperbahn, her confidence apparent. Something pulses at his temple. A suspicion, perhaps, that Harri Schroder has not seen the last of Miss Georgina Young.

CHAPTER ELEVEN:
THE SWELL OF REGRET

11th February 1946

Georgie

It's five by the time she puts her key in the door of the hotel room, and only then does a combination of exhaustion and hunger hit Georgie with a tidal force. She thinks of knocking on Zofia's door and renewing their acquaintance, but she hasn't forgotten the six o'clock arrangement with the waif, and she wants space to dwell beforehand. It is silly, but she needs to prepare, prompted in part by the telegram waiting for her at reception.

Hope you arrived safely. Stop. Missing you already. Stop. Mr Young.

Their little joke, Max pretending to work in her shadow, although he never has. Through the day, he's inevitably popped into her consciousness, but 'it' – the issue, part of the reason she's actually here – has been duly suppressed. With his telegram, will it stay buried for much longer?

Chewing on a sandwich in her room, Georgie unpacks the remainder of her suitcase, feeling deep into the corners and under the straps where she secures small notes, and where Max often slips in tiny missives whenever she leaves for a solo assignment. *Get that story, Georgie girl!* Or *You are the best of the best*, he'll scribble. But nothing today, manifesting another tug to her stomach. The last item she pulls out is the photograph with frayed edges – their wedding snap in front of the Paris Ritz, flanked by reporter reprobates Rod Faber and Bill Porter, fellow survivors from that daunting but precious time in Berlin when Hitler was busy honing his menace and stockpiling for war. Georgie stares at their fixed grins, hiding a mixture of pure joy, anticipation and abject terror at the prospect of what lay ahead, Prime Minister Neville Chamberlain having declared war just the day before. How is she the same person now? She's isn't – that's the truth. Neither is Max. They are more resilient, though their sacrifice has been innocence, both left with a distinct cynical edge at the war's close. Having survived, she'd imagined herself almost untouchable. How wrong can you be?

Holding the wedding picture to her nose, Georgie draws in a scent that's so familiar – the paper infused with a bitter char of smoke, alongside the sweetness of cologne; war and love, washed and unwashed. The scent of life. Their past life.

Is it really over? All of it?

That last evening, the night before she'd left, they'd each tried so hard to make it nice. Despite rationing, they managed a good meal in a restaurant, with windows now stripped of their taped crosses and peals of laughter rising up from the surrounding tables. Their own conversation skirted around the real issue, with Max sensing it too. He wondered aloud if she might bump into any of the old press crew in Hamburg, while she talked about leads to focus on and new contacts to make. Anything to avoid the crucial subject of them. Max rubbed at his leg under the plaster as his regret arose. And yet, if they'd been brutally honest, both were relishing the space to come. From each other.

That need became most apparent on reaching home. Climbing into bed, Max wanted to be close, to cement the evening and make love. Inevitably, it became awkward, and not just the uninvited extra guest of his leg plaster. Then, the heavy question: should they take precautions?

She'd wriggled away, claiming tiredness, needing to sleep. 'I've such an early start,' she had muttered. She knows Max, knows his person inside and out – he would never, ever force her. Never has. If anything, she's been the leader. But that night – only last night – it sparked sadness, and the hurt inside him forced its way to the surface.

'So when?' He'd sat up in bed, his voice entreating, yet with an edge.

'I don't know, Max. I'm not ready yet. Not after . . .'

'The baby,' he said solidly, irritation flooding in. 'You can say it, you know. Pregnancy. Baby. The baby we lost.'

'It was very early . . .' she'd tried. 'A miscarriage.'

'It was still there, Georgie. Part of us. A future as a family – or is that what you can't bear to think about?'

The acrimony had turned to silence, backs to each other under the eiderdown, and halfway through the night,

Max had hobbled out of bed and she surfaced to hear him muttering about the ache in his leg, and he would sleep on the sofa. He's always been such a bad liar.

Now, alone in her room hundreds of miles away, the guilt descends. A burning shame that she doesn't feel their loss with the same intensity, or an equal level of regret. At the time, when it happened, she had been genuinely distraught, a falling away of the physical joy at having created something together, after years of witnessing so much loss and destruction. Relief too, that their bodies – hers especially – had not failed them. She'd convinced herself the time was right for a family. At thirty-two, she was old compared to some of her friends, and yes, they should stop wandering and create a stable, loving home. It's what couples do. Her reputation would surely secure a job on one of the Fleet Street newspapers after a year of playing house, perhaps as a features writer. She'd always seen herself as a working mother – they'd never discussed it outright, but Max would understand, wouldn't he? She was too headstrong to be tethered completely.

And that had been the problem. Max saw their baby, in the three months it was inside her, as growth, conceived in that joyful aftermath of victory parades and liberation. She, by contrast, couldn't help sensing that fresh barricades were going up, on her life at least.

And when it slipped away – just one of those things, the doctor said at the time – Georgie felt acute pain and a physical stab to her heart. Let down by her body. But with it, a sense of release too, nicely infused with guilt. She'd kept those feelings to herself in softening Max's overarching grief. In time, though, he suspected. Of course he did. He's an astute journalist, a keen observer since swapping his notebook for a camera. He saw right through her.

So much so that, after several months of recovery time, when she made the decision to renew the intimacy between them, the subject could no longer be avoided. He raised it gently. 'When do you think we should try again, George?'

The row that ensued was bitter, acrimony fed by sorrow and a new cuckoo in the nest of their marriage that each recognised as mistrust. 'Perhaps you might have told me that you didn't want a baby in the first place!' he blazed.

'It's not like that, Max. I did, or I thought I did,' she protested, weakly at first and then with more vigour. 'It's different for you. For men. You're not expected to give it all up. To stay at home and deal with nappies and washing, your brain slowly dying.'

'So, will it happen, ever?' he spat back, a question that only just masked the real dilemma: *Do we even have a future?* He never said it, but they both sensed a tightrope being yanked firmly at either end. Would it tip them off the thinning wire of their marriage?

Come the morning, he was contrite, sorry and understanding. Genuinely. But the hurt and the desire linger, even now. Georgie sees that Max wants to be a father so badly because of his own parents, the early loss of his beloved mother and an absent, demanding father who cares only about the stock market and social standing. Max wants to do better for his own children. And in this new world, who can blame him?

So that's where they are, why Max is sneaking small bags of bonbons into her luggage, in trying to express his love, yet still bound in sorrow and need. Why Georgie felt almost relieved to receive Eleanor's letter from Hamburg and a sudden excuse to flee, that once again someone else's distress becomes her saviour. And the extra slice of guilt that goes with it.

So, is that why she's forcing herself to hand over her precious suitcase – a portion of the old Georgie – to a total stranger? Assuaging several layers of self-reproach, and convincing herself that she is ready to move forward?

She moves a hand from stroking her empty belly to the tough, worn leather, feeling with her fingertips the clasp that still has a grain or two of North African desert sand in its working, the patched-up gash on the leather that saved her own leg from a potentially deadly piece of shrapnel. But with such vivid recollections still fresh in her mind, and the rest set in print, it's no longer a lifeline, or a necessity.

She loves this case. She will miss it, but she doesn't need its presence to move forwards. Perhaps, though, someone else does.

CHAPTER TWELVE:
THE HANDOVER

11th February 1946

Meta

The Rathaus clock says 5.35 p.m. as she passes it, and so it must be quarter to by the time Meta reaches the Baseler Hof, the entrance facing directly on the street, in the midst of a terrace largely untouched by the war. It's not a hotel with a grand visage, not like the Atlantic or the Four Seasons, which she avoids, since the well-dressed women who swan in and out are mean and the pickings equally lean. She hovers by the side of the door, hunkering down inside her coat fashioned for a man three times her size. Squatting, her feet disappear and it becomes an instant tent and she's almost comforted by the acrid smell rising from the insides, pulling her arms inwards and fingering the extra pockets that she's painstakingly stitched into the lining, courtesy of an old sewing box discovered by chance in a bombed-out house, unscathed and full of treasure. She tried hard not to think of her grandmother as she sewed in the extra pouches, and yet strived to make her stitches neat, in the way that *Oma* Giselle would have approved of. The resulting pockets are robust and can carry a good weight. At times, Meta pictures herself as an aged tortoise, carrying an entire existence on her back.

'Hey, you, move on!' A bellboy emerges from the hotel door, trailed by a British officer, and makes a point of shooing her away. But when the soldier disappears from view, the boy walks on and lights up a cigarette further along the street, as if to signal he doesn't really care whether she's there or not. She'd stand her ground anyway – the Allies might control the country overall, the British with their grip on the city, but they don't own the damned pavement. Not yet, anyway.

The one functioning timepiece in her possession gave up hours ago, the second hand now in permanent limbo, and now Meta has to judge the wait by how cold her feet and fingers are, how many times she has to cup her palms and blow on them to transform cold breath into a degree of warmth. It must be six o'clock soon, she estimates. Or that woman has forgotten, or never intended to be here anyway. That's the most likely possibility, isn't it? Why on earth would anyone give a second thought – or their time – to a thief who attempted robbery the minute they set foot in the country? She reaches into a pocket and fingers the carefully folded paper; it's obvious now that she's been deluding herself all day, imagining the woman would be true to her promise. Huh, ironic really, Meta thinks, since most of her day is spent duping others. 'Tit-for-tat', she's heard some of the rubble boys say in their Tommy soldier-speak. Except Meta is certain of being a benefit to anyone newly arrived in this ghost of a city – she's keen-eyed and knows things, and if she doesn't, those nuggets of information are easily detected. Something tells Meta this woman could be the perfect client for her services. If only she would damn well turn up.

The bellboy gives her a wan smile as he heads back up the steps and into the hotel, the inner light shining weakly onto the pavement that's now sparkling with a fresh night-time frost.

Deflated, Meta would leave, if it weren't for the fact that her feet have gone to sleep, and until they become painful, it's oddly comfortable in her self-styled bivouac. If she stays out of the light, the uniforms going in and out won't notice her for a while and she's safe from their testy comments. They've come here to sort and order the city and the nomads within, but it's another thing to tolerate one hovering outside their hotel, a place of safety away from 'those bloody Krauts'.

The inevitable, creeping burn to her feet causes Meta to shift and contemplate leaving. She's given up looking towards the door any more and the flow of people going in and out. Instead, her mind is on the cube of bouillon that she'll use for supper, and the few crumbs of bread she'll pinch together with her fingers to make it solid enough for dipping into the hot liquid. She'll use only a quarter of the precious bouillon cube to give some taste, and enough wood to heat a small can of water. And then to her shivering, and eventual dreams . . .

'Meta?' The voice comes from the dark. Not 'Oi', or 'You!' and so she doesn't shrink into her coat shell, but stands and wavers with an odd, tingly feeling in her toes and ankles.

'You came?' she says in English, the language she learnt from a nice Tommy last year, one who didn't try to touch her or take advantage, but gave her food and cigarettes, simply out of kindness. Then he got posted elsewhere, leaving her to improve her fledgling English from the Red Cross *omas* in the soup kitchens.

'Of course I came,' the woman says with surprise. 'It's freezing out here. Do you want to come inside?'

Meta is horrified – no, she doesn't. The people in there will look at her and wonder what such an excuse for a human is doing in their midst, wrinkle their noses, and not discreetly either. She shakes her head. 'No.'

Even in the gloom, she notes what the woman has in her hand – the golden goose of a suitcase, that one she tried to steal less than twelve hours before. The battered but sturdy and coveted one. Does she really mean to give it up? Meta imagined the woman would placate her with food coupons and a few cigarettes, or a loaf of bread. And yet, why else would she have hold of the suitcase now?

'Here,' the woman proffers. Incredibly, the case is held aloft, clearly lighter than before.

Unusually, Meta's hand extends tentatively, when her normal reaction would be to snatch and run. She stares at the woman's face for signs of a smirk, that it's all a big joke and several soldiers behind her are waiting to laugh out loud at Meta's audacity to even think she can have something for nothing; their sweet revenge on a scrawny German wretch trying to rob the benevolent British.

But there's only the woman's hand and a sturdy strap

78

in her eyeline. Meta takes it, feels the leather warm against her freezing flesh. '*Danke*,' she says.

Plainly, the woman really means it. The case is now hers. More space for things to trade, but also for her precious hoard, the tiny trinkets of her old life she will no longer have to bury in the stinking ground, in fear of thieves invading her home camp.

'I've put a few items in there,' the woman says, gesturing at the case. 'Cigarettes, some food from the hotel kitchen. I hope you don't mind.'

Mind? The British say that a lot. Why would she mind? She's a beggar and a thief living on scraps. There's no dignity in starvation or dying. No, she doesn't mind at all.

'Thank you,' she says, mimicking the refined replies of the Allied women she hears outside the Victory Club when they accept a light from a man in uniform. 'Thank you very much.'

Car headlights briefly light up the woman's face, enough for Meta to glimpse a forlorn gaze, as if she is saying goodbye to a true friend. And then the flicker of light is gone and the woman coughs, placing a palm to her chest. 'I'm Georgie,' she says.

Meta nods. 'Georgie,' she repeats aloud.

In the brief pause that follows, she remembers her own gift, some small repayment, if it has any value at all. From an inside pocket of her tent-coat, Meta retrieves the folded piece of paper and opens it out. It looks grubby, but she alone knows there's a purpose to where the ashes from Popo's fire were applied and smudged, in distinguishing the roadways from the rubble sites. She holds it out to Georgie, who takes it and angles the paper towards a sliver of window light, this time a look of bewilderment moving across her face.

'*Karte*,' Meta says, not knowing the English. 'Hamburg. For you. To search.'

'Oh, a map!' Georgie says, with what seems like real appreciation, peering closely at the drawing, a faithful imprint from Meta's mind of the city streets that are recognisable only by what buildings still stand, where the rubble is piled highest, and the lines of British Nissen huts peppering the landscape like giant caterpillars on a slow march. With her pencil, she's marked out the mesh of streets with icons that any visiting British woman will soon come to know well and be able to navigate by: the Victory Club, the Rathaus, Café Paris, Hotel Atlantic and – because it is custom-made – the Baseler Hof.

'For me? This is wonderful,' Georgie says. It prompts Meta's face to glow; she has mixed feelings over the Allies who have seized their city. It's true they bring in vital food, but a good portion of bad feeling too. She has known one or two decent Tommies over the months, some with genuine sympathy for the plight of the homeless like her. In her eyes, though, plenty more are contemptuous of the defeated Germans they are forced to oversee, convinced of their guilt as a nation – of a secret, slavish devotion to Hitler – and disdainful of the moving cloud of odours the nomads create. 'Piss off! You stink!' is a common response when she approaches for a cigarette or spare pfennig, of which they seem to have plenty.

Of course she stinks. She has no real home, no water to wash in that doesn't have a sheet of ice as a skin, and no clothes to change into. Life stinks.

Georgie is standing closer to her now, still holding the map. 'Meta, if you need anything . . .' She repeats something similar in German. 'Come to me, here. At the hotel. Georgie Young.'

Meta nods, pleased at not being dismissed the instant that this woman's conscience has been quieted by giving something to a poor German soul.

'And I'll pay for information, anything good,' Georgie adds. '*Zigaretten.*'

Already, Meta likes Georgie, this woman who has kept her word. But business is business. 'How many?' she demands.

'Two or three.'

Meta's face falls. Out of two or three loose cigarettes, one may be usable, the others stuffed with sawdust or ground leaves that are definitely not tobacco. One sniff and her astute nose detects those duds instantly.

'Packets,' Georgie follows up. '*Sealed* packets.'

Now she's talking. Meta can't calculate what one sealed carton of Lucky Strikes or Chesterfields will buy any more, let alone several. Something towards a train ticket to Berlin, perhaps, where she thinks an old aunt might still be, plus some clothes to make her look presentable on the journey.

'What information? What is good?' she asks of Georgie, already sensing the soft give of the packet under her fingers and the unspoilt paper tab to signal its purity.

'Missing women. Anything you hear. Anything at all.'

Meta nods eagerly. 'Yes. Yes, I will.' She was right all along – this woman does need her services.

Even her bones are cold now, and she's keen to unclasp the suitcase in private and see what treasures hide inside.

Meta holds it up and smooths her hand across the leather, as further proof that she will look after the gift, safeguarding this woman's faith in her.

'*Danke. Danke sehr.*'

CHAPTER THIRTEEN:
THE INTERLOPER

11th February 1946

Harri

The need for coffee has passed, and he opts for a beer instead, though the basement café is busier and his window of calm has all but disappeared. With each sip of the precious Holsten brew, Harri tastes guilt amid the golden hops, in knowing that it's black market, and he really ought to be arresting the purveyors and dragging them down to the station, rather than sampling their wares.

The truth is that, much like every post-war city in Germany, Hamburg runs on a flourishing trade in contraband, despite the best efforts of the British hierarchy and the German police to shut it down. Somehow, it's only the fat cats that Harri despises, the already wealthy businessmen who endeavour to get richer, using desperation to drive the prices higher, insensible to the poverty on the streets and the families who simply cannot survive without illicit trade. Those he would happily lock up and toss away the key. But Fritz, the barman who serves up Maxwell House and other sundries from under the counter, always with a smile, is no fat feline. He's a returning POW with a gouged-out leg and three children to support.

So, each sip becomes a moral judgement for Harri, served with a side order of reproach – adding to his overstuffed daily quota. Even the simple task of scaling his mountain of crime reports pulls on his moral fibres; only one case in every four warrants investigation, the rest filed away in a corner of the office dubbed 'the black hole'. He's become a veteran at shouldering the shame: *Just pass it all my way, boys*, he smiles into his glass as the alcohol takes slow effect. The guilt of an entire nation? Yes, pile it on. Why not? He might as well have it all, because no amount of blame will ever outweigh what he already holds inside himself, the self-loathing burning inside for almost three years now. Because of what he couldn't prevent. What's left are the crackling embers that have eaten his insides, leaving behind the brittle shell that people still recognise as Harri Schroder.

Outside, the freezing night air doesn't have the desired effect of sobering him up. Harri sways towards home, stumbling in the dark over rubble and hoping that no thief comes running across his path tonight, as with that woman earlier, because he's in no fit state to give chase.

That woman. In the hours since she left Davidwache, he hasn't been able to delete Georgie Young from his consciousness. It's not so much her solid good looks and striking cut of hair that have forced this lasting impression, he decides, but the air about her, her confidence and a subtle note of humour which, if teased out, he imagines might be quite wicked. He misses that, having an adversary in wit, someone to laugh at life with. And God knows they all need that nowadays.

He glimpsed a wisp of it in Georgie Young. So that now, he cannot shift her imprint, her aura sliding into his vision and bobbing behind his eyelids weighing heavy with too much beer. And that's irritating, when Harri Schroder has so many other things to think about, starting with the urgent matter of life and death on his caseload.

Climbing the stairs to his apartment block, he senses a layer of dust and grit on the stone stairs, lighting a match and holding it upwards. He knows Frau Kessler from the first floor will have swept the stairway earlier today, and so the debris that's drifted down is fresh, a fine coating for now, but worrisome when the five-storey building is already semi-condemned and yet fully occupied. A decent gust of wind might do for them all. Still, he climbs higher, and until or unless the collapse happens, he won't go searching for a new apartment. Principally because there's nothing available with a full complement of walls, let alone the added luxury of a ceiling.

In truth, he's comforted by the familiarity; the temperature as he opens the door to his rooms is only a degree or two warmer than the air outside, but the chill is expected. There's the rhythmic flap of the tarpaulin hanging from one corner of the kitchen parlour and which he prods at with a broom handle on entering, an action more about the ritual of homecoming than dislodging a fresh fall of snow through the gaping hole in his skylight. But it's his place, his space. High into the remaining rooftops of Hamburg and so out of sight. And where sometimes, if the mood takes him, and Fritz has come good with supplies of home-brewed *Korn* liquor from under his counter, Harri can get slowly and completely out of his mind.

Except that woman, she's still there, a flickering reel moving in and out, stopping and starting, sticking on the frame where her sardonic smile tickled at the corners of her mouth and her eyes became impish. She's an interloper, trespassing on him without permission. Maybe though – just maybe – her presence will oust his dreams of fire and destruction tonight, of flames and swords, and the trappings of death and hell that cloud his half-sleep.

And Harri muses, as he sinks into his mattress: *Wouldn't that be nice?*

CHAPTER FOURTEEN:
A GIFT

12th February 1946

Georgie

Georgie sleeps surprisingly well, with no shadows of robbers and thieves, or the shoals of homeless souls. No Max either. By eight a.m., she and Zofia are having breakfast in the Baseler Hof dining room, surrounded by lower-rank officers and CCG in uniform. Zofia's eyes are wide and wary, still marked by dark circles beneath, but her skin is, Georgie thinks, a little brighter and less like paper, hair with a light sheen. She's just twenty-five, though clearly aged by imprisonment, her thin shoulders swamped by the spare sweater and trousers from Georgie's case, until they can drop by the NAAFI later in the day and pick out a new set of clothes from the second-hand shop.

'Did you sleep well?' Georgie asks her.

'Yes, thank you. Too well perhaps.' Zofia looks apologetic.

'I'm so sorry I didn't wake when you knocked on my door last night. I had something to eat, and I lay down on the bed, and then . . .'

'Not to worry,' Georgie reassures. 'I was beyond tired myself, and I must have been asleep by nine. We'll make up for it today.'

The waiter places toast and eggs in front of them, causing Zofia's face to take on more surprise. 'Is that all for me?'

'Yes.'

'But . . .'

'You need it,' Georgie insists. 'You're a working woman, and we have a busy day ahead.' She watches Zofia closing her eyes as she forks scrambled egg into her mouth, chewing diligently, and Georgie wonders what memories are reignited by the long-lost taste of food once shared with her family. Good or bad? Welcome or not? Zofia offers little but polite conversation, and Georgie doesn't press her, sensing that patience is definitely a virtue in this case. She'll talk when she's ready. Or not.

By 8.30, both are seated in the back of Sergeant Dawson's jeep and bumping their way through the streets towards the Atlantic. Georgie disappears inside and emerges ten minutes later, staggering a little under the weight of a large office typewriter.

Dawson rushes to unburden her. 'How on earth did you get that, Miss Young?'

'A very nice man inside, a few promises and a large smile,' Georgie puffs. 'Can you take us to Davidwache police station, please? After that, we'll arrange our own transport for the day.'

'Yes, Miss Young, of course.' His tone suggests a slight wounding at being relieved of his duties so soon.

Parking up on David Strasse, Zofia's face is suddenly awash with anxiety at the imposing building, as she and Georgie shoulder the weight of the typewriter between them. Although Zofia hasn't said, it's a fair guess that any authority is a threat to this girl who has suffered and lost, all at the hands of her own countrymen. A police station is the last place she'll want to be.

'Zofia, it's fine,' Georgie is at pains to assure her. 'You're safe. I've been inside myself, and there are good people who work here.' On the first floor, they knock on the door signposted 'Kripo', but with the heft of the machine, Georgie doesn't wait too long before forging into the office.

Inspektor Schroder swivels in his chair at the sudden invasion. His face sports a look of alarm and embarrassment, not least because there's a cloth around his shoulders and a woman is standing behind with a pair of scissors, snipping away at his hair. He swipes the cloth away, wisps scattering across the floor.

'Ah, you've caught us red-handed, Miss Young.' He's half-smiling as he says it, gesturing to the woman behind, the comb held aloft in her hand. 'Anna here was a hairdresser in a former life, and we don't waste such skills nowadays.' His eyes fall on their heavy cargo, and he moves quickly to relieve the two women of its weight.

'I thought you might be able to make use of it,' Georgie explains. 'It's British–issue, with an English alphabet, of course. But I dare say you can work around that. Oh, and these.' She dives into her satchel and pulls out several spare typewriter ribbons wrapped in paper, plus a handful of army-issue pens and pencils.

It's only when she looks up again that her offering registers as a possible mistake. A big one. The inspektor's eyes switch from the typewriter in his grasp to Georgie, still holding out her wares. Is he affronted? Worse, insulted?

'Thank you,' he says, eyeing the pens with suspicion.

'I didn't mean to offend,' she rambles. 'I just thought . . . only yesterday, you said . . .'

He coughs, spilling wisps of greying hair from his jacket. 'No, it's just . . . well. I've never been given a typewriter before. It's quite the gift.' Now, his expression is teasing, his ample lips working their way into a smile, causing the sudden tension within her to fall away. 'Here, let's make room,' he says, and sweeps aside a stack of files with his elbow to land the machine with a clump onto a small table. 'You can be sure of it getting good use. And being much appreciated.'

Anna of the scissors retreats into the background, and the hum of the office moves into a lengthy pause, Zofia's feet shuffling on the scuffed wooden floor. Georgie has never been backwards about coming forwards, with work especially – there's no such thing as a shy war reporter – and yet, she finds herself suddenly hesitant, wrong-footed by this man, and it takes several seconds for her nerve to push through.

'I'd like to follow the case,' she blurts.

Again, his eyes snap to the typewriter. 'In exchange?' His brow knits. 'I'm not quite sure how things work in England, Miss Young, but as poorly resourced as the Kripo is, we don't accept . . .'

'The machine isn't a bribe,' she counters quickly. 'I simply thought you could use it. There are scores at British HQ sitting idle and you have far more need of one.'

'And the investigation?' A rippled forehead says he's not convinced of her motives.

She takes in a breath as fuel for the pitch she's made countless times before, in persuading a string of editors to accept, commission and print her stories. Any proposal has to be convincing in twenty words or less. Much more than that and you risk losing their interest.

'I want to highlight everything in Hamburg – the good and the bad, British and German. People back home should see what you're fighting against.' It is more than twenty, but her petition spills out rapidly.

It's Harri Schroder's turn to take a breath, and Georgie gauges that he's walking the fine line that all Germans are forced to nowadays, especially those 'allowed' to retain their positions: keep the British sweet. Comply and smile. And yet, he is still a policeman, charged with keeping order rather than inciting panic of a murderer on the loose.

'I trust that I'm able to speak frankly, and off the record?' he says.

'Yes, of course.'

'I' – he swivels his head around the office – '*we* appreciate what you are saying, Miss Young, but any progress on this case depends on us *not* alerting the killer to what we know, that we have linked each of his crimes.'

Georgie shakes her head fervently. 'But my article would be written in hindsight, for a readership outside Hamburg, and so nothing your killer might read. I only want to see the process unfold, and once you've caught this man, your' – she stops herself using the word 'overseers' – 'those in charge can see what you're achieving. Against the odds.' She pauses for effect. 'Surely that's a good thing, for all of you?'

'I'm pleased that you possess so much confidence in us,' he starts. 'But as much as we want to stop this man instantly, murders rarely come to a quick conclusion. It might be months.'

'Or not,' she bats back. 'There's nothing lost, surely? And Zofia and I will be out there anyway, across the city, with our ears to the ground.'

'Miss Young, there's no question of you helpi—' Inspektor Schroder's protest is cut short by the sudden arrival of a man and woman into the office.

The woman stops mid-stride, her eyes tacking back and forth with interest. 'Sorry, Harri. I thought we had a briefing at nine?'

'Yes, we do,' he says, reverting to German. 'Paula, Erwin, these are Fräuleins Young and Dreyfus, from . . .'

'Independent Press,' Georgie cuts in, extending a hand to Paula, and making brief introductions in German. 'We're going to be following the case, for a possible . . .'

'. . . article,' Zofia pitches in seamlessly. 'A newspaper article.'

Paula shoots a look at Harri, who shrugs an acceptance, though it's very much resigned. Despite his silence, Georgie has the feeling that Inspektor Schroder may take some persuading yet.

It takes all her powers of concentration to make sense of the briefing that follows; her German, once near fluent, is in need of fine tuning. Once again, Zofia is already adept at predicting the words she might know and fills in with the trickier vocabulary.

'This latest body makes three that we know about, and so far, it looks to be a thread,' Harri starts. He stands to the side of a blackboard, chalked with a crude map of the city and marked with the three discovery sites. It's easy to see they are clustered around the north-west of Hamburg, where the bombing has left little more than a wasteland in some areas. Pinned alongside are the detailed, coloured drawings made by their young artist, a collection both harrowing and beautifully sketched.

'We know all the women were killed and mutilated in the place they were found,' Harri goes on. 'It poses the question: why were they there, and what would have made them follow a man into such an area, with so few people about?'

'Are we certain that none of the women were prostitutes?' Paula asks.

'Nothing points to it so far.' Anna looks up from her notebook. 'One was a nurse, another an administrator and the third we're still waiting to identify. The first two had a decent income, so it seems unlikely they would be working for extra money in that way.'

'And I think it's fair to say none of them had an obvious appearance of working girls,' Harri adds.

Briefly, the office falls silent and Georgie's eyes read the room. With life on permanent hold, nothing is beyond imagination. Saddest still is the realisation, among the women especially, that no one of their sex is exempt from need; all have families, children, mouths to feed and a desire to survive. A girl down on her luck can so quickly translate to a girl on the game.

'Let's keep an open mind about that,' Harri cuts into the pause. 'In the meantime, anything at all to link them

– families, places they frequented, or friends?'

'I'm still looking, but nothing so far,' Anna reports, resignation in her voice. 'It takes time, getting across the city.'

Harri nods his understanding, and Georgie thinks back to her short stint on the London crime desk of the daily *News Chronicle* just before the war. Detectives had cars and telephones to speed up their investigations, and still it was all about legwork. From what she's gauged so far, the legwork within the Kripo is all too literal.

'Without forensics, we can't be a hundred per cent sure that it's the same sick bastard carrying out the killings. But I think it doesn't take a genius to conclude that we are looking for a single offender, given the messages he is leaving on the victims.' Harri Schroder points to the list of three words scored on each of the bodies – translated as 'fraud', 'cheat' and the latest, 'liar' – and the team nod in agreement. 'There's a clear theme of betrayal, I'd say. However, if we go looking for one man among the millions out there who feel slighted by the war, we're going to fail. So, let's try and narrow it down. He's giving us clues, maybe because he can't help it, but they are clues all the same.'

Harri lays a finger on the close-up drawings made of the flesh, on the belly, breasts and navel: 'What does this tell us?'

'The lettering is clumsy, but he had time to do it,' Anna says.

Harri chalks 'time' on the blackboard. 'And?'

'He came prepared,' says Erwin. 'It's pitch black out there. He would have needed light to pose and' – he swallows uncomfortably – 'do that to them.'

Harri adds 'preparation/intent' to the list.

'And if he's not targeting the women specifically, he does seem to be working through a motive that's personal to him,' Paula suggests.

'Yes, good!' Harri jabs at the air. 'If we isolate the reason he's doing it, we might get a better idea of who he is and where to find him.'

'Are we assuming he's German?' Erwin asks. 'Given the writing?'

'Not necessarily,' Anna comes in. 'I've spoken to plenty who've picked up a good amount of language through the war – refugees, those from the camps, aid workers . . .'

'British soldiers,' Georgie punts from the sidelines, as several heads snap towards her in surprise. She shrugs. 'It's possible, isn't it, and shouldn't be ruled out?'

Inspektor Schroder nods in her direction. 'Fräulein Young is right. For now, nothing is excluded. Everything – and I mean *everything* – is to be written up on this board, no matter how trivial you think it is. And each day, we meet to go over it again, and again, until we wheedle out our needle in the haystack' – again he glances at Georgie – 'right here in this office.'

They break into groups to allot their tasks, and Georgie watches Paula head to the board and chalk a word to the side.

'I think that means "patchouli",' Zofia whispers to Georgie, who is busy noting it down when Schroder approaches, on his way to opening the office door, no doubt his own subtle way of shooing her and Zofia off the premises, albeit diplomatically.

'I've no need to emphasise the delicacy of this case?' he says, eyebrows raised.

'No, you haven't,' she replies emphatically. 'You can count on us to keep a confidence. But we will keep our ears open, for what it's worth.'

He nods, though he's still not fully convinced. Georgie makes one more attempt at her pitch, which – in the course of the past day – has transformed itself into more of a pledge. 'I promise you I'm not doing this for glory, Inspector Schroder, either my own, or for the British Establishment. I want to tell the story of these women because, to me, they are victims of war as much as anyone else. And like all those who suffer, they deserve to be remembered.'

Now she has him. His hand drops away from the doorknob, and when his eyes move up to look at her directly, there's a light behind them, a spark that she can identify. Now Georgie Young has the measure and motivation of the seemingly dour Harri Schroder, and with it, something to work with. Like almost everyone she's come across in her life, he possesses an Achilles heel.

Under that brusque exterior, he cares.

CHAPTER FIFTEEN: FORAGING

12th February 1946

Meta

Up and on the streets as dawn breaks, Meta harbours more energy than she has in weeks. More than likely, it's down to the treasures discovered in the suitcase as she prised it open last night; the hunk of bread that didn't fall apart like sawdust in her hands, a piece of slightly stale but sweet cake and, best of all, a hardboiled egg and a tin of ham. Real meat, encased in its tin, untampered and unsullied! She'd stared at it for some minutes, pondering over saving it and making do with only the egg for supper, or throwing caution to the wind and combining the two, bathing in the pleasure of a favourite breakfast her mother used to cook at weekends – ham and eggs together.

The recollection and the snarl of her stomach had been too much. She'd banked up her tiny fire and set to work on opening the tin with a knife, and though it caused her to sweat in releasing it, the resulting smell and sizzle as it cooked was worth every effort. Oh, the taste on her tongue, melting in her mouth. There she was, back in the family kitchen, Mama on one side, sisters Rosa and Monika on the other, and Papa at the end of the table, his head buried in his paper, as always. The strong coffee aroma she'd needed to conjure, but it came easily as she closed her eyes and hummed a tune on the radio from before the war, a clear image of Rosa teasing Meta that she was tone-deaf and couldn't hope to hold a note. The recall of that engaging laugh melded with the music of old and Meta gorged on slices of meat and memory.

With the remaining half of the ham tin snuck into her best hiding place, she had slept, her feet clamped around the suitcase, and a single pack of sealed Player's cigarettes tucked against her slightly distended stomach for safekeeping. And for the first time in an age, Meta drifted off with the clear intent of waking again; in the daytime, the innate human spirit to endure serves to keep her moving, begging and trading for food, feeding off the survival instinct of her fellow *trümmerkinder* when the temperature and her resolve dips. In the night hours, however, she's often too tired to battle the will of the earth's elements which might take her. Last night, she lay down with a full belly and a determination to see in a new dawn.

Come daylight, the spring in Meta's step is down to that sated feeling – the stale cake that she chewed slowly for breakfast – and from today's purpose. It's the fact that she has one at all, aside from the usual grind of stealing and bartering. In the Hamburg of today, some might say her task is near impossible, but she's unfazed. If anyone can coax out details from strangers, it's Meta Hertzig. Didn't her Tommy friend used to say she could 'charm the birds out of the trees', as well as the cigarettes from his pockets? So, if it's information the British woman wants, then she shall have it. The more packets of Player's vying for space in Meta's suitcase, the better.

Despite her determination, she's prepared for an uphill task. In post-war Germany, millions are still absent, either transported to work camps, Nazi-run factories or across borders, husbands and brothers unreturned. Many are dead; shot, starved, worked to death, or gone mad and wandering in a pitiful state, not even knowing their own names. 'Missing' encapsulates them all. But from what she's heard on the street, several women have disappeared quite recently – from proper homes, with jobs and a reason to stay. Meta knows there are scores of young fräuleins planning their transport out of Germany, with a wedding ring on their finger and a Tommy in tow. But that's not happening officially, not yet, and there are strict rules over 'non-fraternisation' with the troops. So, why would these women suddenly disappear, and where to?

She avoids the obvious points like Dammtor railway station, the central Hauptbahnhof, and the hundreds of women who hover outside each day, holding up torn, faded pictures of their loved ones, hoping that, by some incredible stroke of luck, a traveller or passer-by will miraculously recognise their husband, sister or daughter. It's never worked for Meta. 'They're dead,' she wants to say to their pained faces. Cruel, but kind in the long run. 'Stop wasting your time. Go home and grieve.'

Instead, she heads for the docks, to the once bustling

heart of Hamburg, with its soaring giraffe-like cranes and heavy machinery, all of which now slump with inertia, mangled and warped and bombed out of shape. The few boats that putter in and out of the harbour are mostly military, or fishing vessels small enough to weave their way around the graveyard of scuttled boats and the broken bows poking out through the oily waterline. Once the life force of the city, the mighty Elbe still flows, but these days it's with a polluted, turgid rhythm. Bustling it is not, and Meta doesn't often come here, saddened by the sight and the stench of defeat.

A few old sailors loiter on the wharfside, probably out of habit, and it's those she works on first. It doesn't help that she has neither name nor picture to prompt their memories, just a 'young woman gone missing'. For an hour or more, she tours the water's edge, with a stream of shaking heads. 'Have you seen . . .?' or 'Have you heard . . .?' tends to have people turning away towards their own problems, and for a second Meta is almost glad she knows with certainty that her family is gone, because the endless search is surely worse. Almost.

Deflated but undeterred, she works the streets inwards towards the city centre, and then back out again to a part of town that was once a thriving suburb, now commonly known as the 'underbelly', where the landscape is a wasteland, the horizon bumpy, and below ground is a city warren teeming with life. Reluctantly, she reaches into the suitcase for her precious packet of Player's, slips a grubby nail under the tab and releases the distinct scent of good tobacco, running a hand gingerly over her wares. Unlike a lot of *trümmerkinder*, Meta doesn't smoke herself, and so there's no temptation. The value of a sealed packet is markedly higher, but she'll need the lure of a single cigarette to loosen mouths.

Within the hour, she is several cigarettes down and has two possible leads on women who have disappeared suddenly and without reason. One is patently a false alarm, where the woman turns up during Meta's interrogation of her mother, hungover and contrite after a night at the Victory Club. The other tip, however, leads her towards an address in St Pauli.

The stout landlady looks at Meta as if she's something off the bottom of a dirty shoe, but doesn't hesitate in pocketing a couple of Player's, revealing that the young woman who rents her top room hasn't been home for two nights. 'I know because her shoes make a god-awful clatter on the stairs,' the landlady says with derision. 'She's bound to be in a soldier's bed, or in the gutter. I'm not sure which is worse. Frankly, I did think she was better than that. She's got a good job over at the pharmacy on Dammtor Strasse. But it's right opposite that British club.' Her lips make as if sucking on a lemon. 'These days, it seems to be a magnet for young girls.'

Further information costs Meta two more cigarettes, though she can't very well go waltzing into the pharmacy to look for an employee, not in her dishevelled state. Surely the name alone is worth something to Fräulein Young?

With the suitcase bumping against her calf in a reassuring fashion, she heads back into the centre of town, traversing the large square in front of the Rathaus and eyeing the queue of young men and women being forced – press-ganged, she thinks – into signing up for labour work that the British insist is vital for the city's survival.

Meta prefers to forgo the bribe of a ration card and rely on her own hunting skills, rather than be bound by the lies of politicians again. Her mother and father had once believed in someone, in those early years, when she'd been little more than a toddler. Adolf Hitler and his National Socialists had promised so much to working people: stability and pride, putting a ravaged and defeated Germany back on its feet after the debacle of the Great War. That was before their glorious Führer showed his true colours, the methods finally revealing his promises to be a fatal façade, and his ego steering an entire country into a war that burnt so many. The personal vendetta of one man that took everything she had. Every precious particle.

So why would she have faith in anyone else promising to improve her life? Better to be alone, Meta reasons. Trust only in yourself.

So, she gives a wide berth to the snaking lines of people in winding her way towards the Baseler Hof, the whine of her stomach mollified by a sense of expectation and more than a little satisfaction at today's rather different type of foraging.

CHAPTER SIXTEEN:
THE HARSH PEACE

12th February 1946

Georgie

Georgie and Zofia set out on foot after leaving Davidwache, slipping down into the U-Bahn for speed. The platforms are crowded, and in the carriage, bodies stand and sway like bottles in a crate, feet planted on a floor made wet and greasy by the slush. Few people utter a word, and Georgie's eyes flick from one flat expression to another, as if speech and soul have been automatically sucked out the further they go below ground. In the airless space of the rickety train, a sour odour of sweat hovers above the homburg hats and shoulders wrapped against the cold. Georgie searches for the tiniest glimmer of lightness or joy, but finds none.

She and Zofia alight near the skeleton of Dammtor station, its ribbed rack of iron girders the only elements giving structure to a domed lofty shape, the glass shattered long ago in the inferno of '43. Underneath the flakes of snow drifting through the gables, trains shunt to and fro in chaotic fashion, people leaping onto carriages as they pull out of the station to a shrill whistle, squatting on the heavy metal couplings when the coaches are sardine-packed. Georgie notes that – much like any travelling point across Europe – it's a microcosm of hope and expectation, but also of despair and loss, concentrated under a once-spectacular roof that's only present in people's memories.

'If the city is chaos, then this is multiplied ten times,' Zofia murmurs under her breath, causing Georgie to wonder how many hours she's spent here, searching the throngs of bodies for her sister's face.

In each waiting room they visit, every inch of floor space is taken up with suitcases, piles of belongings or rags that slowly reveal themselves to be bodies, shifting and whimpering, parents spooning their limbs around sleeping children in a bid to instil some warmth. 'Some come to wait for a train that never arrives, and yet they never manage to leave,' Zofia sighs with her personal insight.

With Zofia at her side, Georgie hears the stories of women who make a life out of waiting – for husbands, and relatives, or a direction to make itself plain. 'Why here?' she asks.

One mother tells her the solid confines of the waiting room outweigh its overbearing stench and filth. 'Everything is a trade nowadays, isn't it?' she says mournfully, as her baby sucks listlessly on a deflated, sagging breast.

* * *

Outside the station entrance, the longing is more acute and visual. Boards span the length of the brickwork, carpeted in photographs and messages, of men, women and children, the fabric of the missing, rain-soaked, blistered and smudged, fluttering wildly with the gusts that send up a snow spray at intervals. The crowds along the wall are principally women, whose only occupation is to loiter each day in hope, through rain, snow and bitter winds, pushing the image of their loved ones in the faces of anyone who will look, desperate for recognition. Georgie scribbles in her notebook: *Hope has replaced trade as Hamburg's bedrock.* Within half an hour, she has scored a firm line through *Hope* and replaced it with *Misery.* The stories are heartbreaking, with not one or two family members lost, but great swathes of personal history torn apart. *This war will take generations of repair,* she writes.

Zofia is at her shoulder constantly, on hand with translations, though in the moments when Georgie is catching up with her notes, out of the corner of her eye she sees the focus drift, Zofia's gaze picking over the crowds and scrutinising the sea of faces, never at rest, constantly scouring for any morsel of light and a timely sighting of her sister.

Their next visit, to the hospital, offers little relief. School friend Eleanor has given Georgie a list of nurses' names, her former colleagues at Hamburg's public infirmary, and in the turmoil of the overcrowded corridors and wards, it's easy for them to show Georgie the stark reality of life on less than a thousand calories a day, the bloating that makes adult and infant bellies look replete, but serves as a severe sign of malnutrition, the TB rifling its way through already depleted bodies, and the open sores of vitamin deficiency. Some patients are nursing injuries caused by storming the coal trains; when city supplies ran out last winter, the desperate risked a maiming rather than certain death from hypothermia. 'Sometimes, there's very little we can do, except watch them fade away,' one British nurse sobs in a quiet corner. 'People talk about enemies and the Germans paying reparation, but you wouldn't wish this on anyone. This isn't winning.'

'I think that's enough research for now, don't you?' Georgie blows out her frustration to Zofia on the hospital steps, a new fall of snow drifting down, each flake cold and refreshing on her face. Editors back home will be demanding a 'colour' piece, perhaps illustrating to Britons that life in post-war England is really not so bad in comparison, and yet Georgie has yet to find any brightness. And while she is all too aware that those around them cannot take a convenient break from constant drudgery, the war years have taught her that suffering another's pain is of no benefit to anyone.

'If you broke your leg and fell in a ditch, would it help me to sympathise if I broke mine too and got down in the ditch with you?' Max once challenged, on a day somewhere in the battlefields of France, when the endless tableaux of death finally broke through her resolve. 'It wouldn't, would it?' he'd pressed her, though not unkindly. 'We can still empathise, George, and show concern from above that ditch. We can also help a good deal more with our legs intact.' His sensible, impassioned voice rings clearly in her head now, and the logic holds firm as she shivers in the cold. Mostly, it's the supreme irony of Max's own analogy that prompts her to smile right then.

'How about we swing by the NAAFI shop for clothes, and then head to the Café Paris for something to eat,' Georgie suggests. 'Both are places on my list to visit, and so we kill two birds with one stone. What do you say?'

Zofia smiles weakly and nods silently, causing Georgie to wonder what horrors have gone before those eyes and what's running through her mind now, confronted with today's sorrowful panorama. In the zoo's resettlement centre, she at least had a small window of stability, surrounded by people in a similar dilemma. Has Zofia been robbed of what little sanity she could cling to?

'Are you all right?' Georgie asks. 'Is this too much?'

'No! No,' Zofia protests with alarm, her voice determined. 'I'm glad to be here. Honestly, Fräulein Young. I want to help, and this is so much better than being stuck at the camp.'

Rummaging through the racks at the NAAFI is something of a pleasure, the slightly muddled stacks of clothes reminding Georgie of sales day at Selfridges in Oxford Street before the war, plucking out bargains with great satisfaction. Zofia has to be reminded she can choose whatever is needed, but once Georgie insists, she does seem to enjoy herself a little. Almost everything she selects fits easily on her withered frame, and so they come away with several bags of good-quality second-hand items. By the time they finish, both are flagging and in need of sustenance.

Zofia seems a little less assured on entering the renowned Café Paris, whose doors have lain open to Hamburg's great and good since 1882, followed by the not-so-good of the Reich during the war years. As with so much of the world, war has faded the once-shiny opulence, and Georgie has to imagine the well-to-do-ladies of pre-war Hamburg lunching under the beautifully painted ceiling, smoke curling around their expensive furs. Now, beneath the bleached frescos extolling the virtues of shipping, trade and industry, men in British uniforms are free with their laughter and disdain of the local population. The German waiters are too busy to notice, or they do a good job of hiding their bitterness.

With her everlasting fondness of café culture ignited by Kranzler's in Berlin, Georgie basks in the strong aroma and the echo of conversation bouncing off the pillars of white tiles. She orders real coffee and sandwiches, and two slices of whatever cake is freshest. 'Large slices, *bitte*.'

Zofia shuffles in her seat, eyes grazing over clutches of men engaging German women, her mouth in a thin line.

'Have you been here before?' Georgie asks.

'With my mother and sisters, before the war. It was always my birthday treat.'

'And in the war?'

Zofia shakes her head defiantly. 'Full of Gestapo and SS,' she says. 'My family was . . . let's say they were out of favour after my father took a quiet stand against the Reich.' She swallows and her eyes grow dim. 'Though it wasn't quiet enough.'

Georgie considers Zofia's words carefully, analysing her lips that are tightly pursed. *Is that why you were imprisoned, and perhaps your father, too? And why your sister is still missing?* Deliberately, she curbs her curiosity. Zofia's trust is more important, her translations essential, and if that faith is gently nurtured, the story may well emerge in time. If not, there is no shortage of tragic tales to tell; after just one day, Georgie's notebook is groaning under the weight of distress.

Good coffee and sweet cake hit both women instantly, the real caffeine working its way through, and the sugar prompting a much-needed buzz. Around them, the tables are filled with a mixture of military and CCG, with what looks like a handful of well-to-do Germans. In time, however, Georgie is regretting her decision to bring Zofia here, surrounded as they are on all sides by indiscreet conversation.

'Bloody Krauts, I hear they're complaining about the daily ration again,' the plummy voice of an officer punts between puffs of his cigar. 'Should be grateful they get anything at all, since we're bankrolling it.'

'They could always move to the Russian sector and let Stalin look after them,' his colleague sniggers. 'See how they like that.'

Seething and ashamed, Georgie wonders how many calories these two faceless men have consumed in their short time at Café Paris. Far more than the average daily quota, she fathoms. Then looks at her own plate of half-eaten torte and feels penitent for enjoying it so much. It's all such a moral maze.

'Aren't you hungry?' Zofia asks. She's already finished her torte, and is eyeing Georgie's leftovers with an interest she can't hide.

'Suddenly, I'm not any more. Would you like it?'

Zofia has manners enough not to grab at the plate, but Georgie sees that time as a refugee means there are no moral conundrums. Food is food. You eat it when you can. And when Zofia picks up the last crumb with her finger, her cheeks almost seem plumper, certainly with a look of satisfaction. 'It tastes so good,' she breathes. 'So, where are we going next?'

'We've had a full morning and I need to take stock of my notes,' Georgie says. 'Why don't you head back to the hotel? I might drop into the NAAFI canteen on my way back briefly and talk to a few of the servicemen there. I won't need an interpreter for that.'

'But . . .'

'Take the time,' Georgie encourages. 'We still have a lot to cover over the next week or so, but I'm sure there are things you need to do in the meantime?'

They are crossing the Rathaus square together and preparing to part when a voice closes in from behind, urgent and unrelenting. 'Fräulein! Fräulein! Fräulein Young!'

Both turn to see a small figure swamped by cloth half-running towards them, slowed by a leather suitcase almost dragging along the ground. Zofia's face grows instantly dark.

'It's all right, I know her,' Georgie assures.

The moving column of material catches up, breathless, her face alight under the grime. 'Fräulein, I was just making to find you.'

'What is it, Meta? Are you all right?'

'Yes,' she replies. 'But I have some news. About a woman. The missing one.'

Georgie pulls two full packs of Player's from her satchel and watches Meta's eyes glow again. 'There's more if you come across any other news,' Georgie says. 'So, keep it in mind, yes?'

'Ja.' Meta's twitching fingers close over the cigarettes. She goes to turn and scarper, as if it's a natural reflex once the goods are secured.

'Wait!' Georgie calls her back and dips a hand deep into her bag again. When she pulls out a small chocolate bar bought from the NAAFI shop, perfectly wrapped, there's an audible gasp from Meta's tiny mouth, rising above the noise of the square. 'I'm sure you could use this. And come and see me at the hotel tomorrow evening. Six o'clock?'

The girl nods, pulling the chocolate close to her chest. '*Danke, Fräulein.*' And then she is gone, swallowed instantly by the weave of bodies.

'How do you know her?' Zofia asks as they walk on.

'Meta? Oh, she tried to steal my suitcase when I arrived.'

'That suitcase? The one she was carrying?'

'Yes.' Georgie shrugs. 'What could I do? She's got far more need of it.'

Zofia looks suddenly scornful. '*Trümmerkinder* – they're all thieves,' she mutters with a deep contempt.

In her surprise – and shock – Georgie can think of nothing to say, in response to Zofia of all people, a refugee in a queue until yesterday. How can she be so ungenerous? Or is it that there's already a new post-war class system operating, with refugees sitting above *trümmerkinder*, viewed as the lowest of all?

Stark reality cuts through Georgie's naivety . . . no, she's beyond naivety now. It's her need to believe that the war was fought to bring some good and understanding from so much suffering. The good hasn't triumphed – not yet. She realises that, much like the war, it's not a simple case of one nation against each other, democracy against fascism, Allies against Nazis. There are Germans on both sides of the fence, those who hate Poles and Russians and resent the returning refugees getting increased rations, the

111

lawless of Hamburg who steal from each other like rats. Like Meta. As General Montgomery hinted, the peace is far from won. So Zofia's scorn may simply be the natural reaction of someone who has nothing, after a war that stole everything. And who is Georgie to question it?

As Zofia peels away, Georgie takes two steps towards the Victory Club and then spins on her heels, remembering at the last minute that she needs to check some facts and figures with Lieutenant Howarth before the next day's research. Grudgingly, she guides herself towards the Atlantic, not relishing the atmosphere or the clientele, a world away from the bonhomie of a services canteen. She pulls Meta's map from one pocket, and − avoiding the closed-off streets − arrives in time to see Sergeant Dawson emerge from the hotel, face grim and shoulders hunched.

'Sergeant, you look like you've lost a pound and found a penny,' she says, as he sparks up a cigarette.

'Oh, hello, Miss Young.' He blows out smoke with a heavy sigh. 'You could say that. Seems I drew the short straw. Remember what I said about stuffy generals? Well, I bagged Major Stephens this afternoon. And he's in a foul mood, which is about as bad as it gets.'

Dawson takes another long drag. 'Absolutely sure you don't need me to drive you somewhere this afternoon?' he entreats. 'Anywhere? Timbuktu perhaps? I hear it's very nice this time of year.'

'Sorry, Sergeant, I'm almost done for the day. But I very much hope you stay out of the line of fire.'

Howarth is stuck in a meeting, and Georgie is forced to wait in the Palm Court, sidling into a corner table behind a convenient fern and ordering tea. The room is only half full, with its high ceiling absorbing the low-level

112

chatter – a great relief as she can feel a headache descending. She buries her head in a copy of the *Daily Telegraph* that's several days old, hoping to look busy.

No such luck.

'Anything of interest in there?'

Georgie's gaze swipes to her left, at a man at the next table, sitting alone. He's a civilian in a smart suit, fair and mid-thirties, she guesses, with an eager, friendly face, and a crisp English accent. What's more, his expression says he's keen for conversation.

'Nothing much,' she sighs. 'Just the usual political strife of the British trying to sort themselves out.' She's trying not to be rude in capping off the exchange, fiddling with the empty space on her left hand and wishing she hadn't left her wedding ring at home, having convinced herself it had become loose in recent months and she was wary of losing it.

'Victors in war, and yet we still can't seem to get it right, can we?' the man goes on, undeterred. His chair and body shift an inch or so towards her, readying for a debate. 'Makes you wonder who are the real winners, doesn't it?'

'Hmm.' Georgie lowers her head again, her temples aching properly now. *Where the hell is Howarth?*

'So, are you new to Hamburg?' he tries again. 'I haven't seen you here before.'

Giving up on any peace, she goes for a different tack. 'Georgie Young,' she says with a forced smile. 'I'm a journalist. Freelance.' It's worked in the past, in scaring away men afraid of either strong or curious women, or a combination of both.

Once again, no such luck with this individual. 'Oh, and

what are you reporting on?' he presses, angling his chair purposefully towards her.

'Um, all sorts really,' she says vaguely. 'Post-war life, how people are coping, the crime rate, that sort of thing.'

'Crime?' His interest seems further piqued. 'What aspect of—'

'Miss Young, *so* sorry to keep you waiting.' A figure in navy blue strides up and offers his hand to shake; Georgie is loath to admit being saved by a man, but right now she could kiss Lieutenant Howarth for his judicious arrival. As he sits alongside, the chatty man sags into his chair, drains his teacup and leaves.

'Sorry, was I interrupting?' Howarth asks.

'Absolutely not,' Georgie says. 'Your timing is perfect.'

Georgie stands on the steps of the Atlantic, suddenly awash with fatigue. In her mind she's already in a warm bath, with perhaps a decent glass of whisky beside her, followed by a good book and bed. Against the chill of the wind, she plunges both hands into her coat pockets, her fingers touching on the scrap of paper Meta has given her, containing the dirty scrawl of name. It might well be a dead end – simply a woman who's had enough of Hamburg and has squeezed herself on a train to escape the city. It could wait until tomorrow, in telling the doleful Inspektor Schroder, who may not thank her anyway. But what if it *is* more than that? Someone else's need could well be greater. Shouldering her bag, Georgie pushes the comforts of the Baseler Hof to the back of her mind and hitches herself a ride with a willing private heading west towards the Reeperbahn.

CHAPTER SEVENTEEN:
ONE STEP FORWARD

12th February 1946

Harri

A hand on his chin, he stands looking at the board, only for the fifth or sixth time that day, as if inspiration will come floating off the chalk marks. Or leaping towards him. Except it hasn't so far. Damn! Who is this latest victim, and why was she targeted? And why hasn't anyone missed her?

Murder is murder, Harri reasons – someone has lost their life – but before the war it was far easier to engage others in such a tragedy. Now, people are shocked momentarily, at the manner of death and the unnecessary loss of someone's future. But the violence? When you've witnessed your nearest and dearest swept away in a man-made inferno, or people opting to drown themselves rather than face a fatal burning, sympathy is in short supply. There's a numbness to the grotesque nature of death that wasn't present in people before the war. Perhaps understandable, but it doesn't help the likes of Harri Schroder and his team.

It means Paula and Anna have been out trawling the streets for witnesses most of the day, Erwin is touring the bars and haunts of prostitutes, while Jonni the artist is at the morgue again. Dr Edelman sent word that he's worked his magic on the latest corpse and they need a faithful but palatable image of her face to reproduce and take to the streets. Harri feels sure that identifying this latest victim will provide a crucial piece of the jigsaw. But his own concentration is flagging.

It's not been helped by an unscheduled flying visit from Major Gordon Stephens, who blew into Davidwache just an hour ago, expecting a full briefing. 'Flying' seemed to be apt, given the major's combustible rage at the news of yet another body and no tangible leads to report. As Harri's overseer, the military man berated him over the lack of progress, plus the obvious drawbacks of news reaching the general public.

The word 'incendiary' had been breathed like fire into Harri's face more than once.

'Sort it, Schroder! Or we will move someone in who can,' he'd barked as a parting ultimatum.

In truth, Harri had been seconds away from snapping: 'Fine! Have your thankless job.' If he'd possessed any handcuffs, he might have thrown them in a childish fit of pique at the major's feet. Somehow, a broken pencil wouldn't have carried quite the same weight. The problem remains that he can't give up or let go, or have it taken away. Harri needs to see this through to the end – for the women, and the team. For his own pride, too, even though he hates to admit it.

'Yes, sir,' he'd said pathetically, to Stephens' glowering face. And hated himself all over again.

It's little wonder that, by late afternoon, Fritz and his cup of Maxwell House is calling again, with something stronger as a chaser.

A resounding knock snaps his attention from the board, and the sight of Georgina Young lifts his energy and mood. Much to his own surprise, he finds himself quite pleased to see her. Or is it that she's simply a welcome distraction from the writing on the wall?

'Fräulein Young. What can I do for you?'

She's proffering a scrap of paper as she approaches, eyes skating over the empty office as she walks forward. 'I'm not sure if this will help,' she says.

'What is it?'

'A name. Of a missing girl. As in recently missing.'

'Ursula Reinhart,' he reads slowly off the note. 'Where did you get this?'

'Someone off the street,' she admits, though her look appears sheepish. Uncharacteristically so. 'A girl, who went searching on my behalf.'

'*Trümmerkinder*, you mean?' he quizzes.

'Yes, I suppose that's what you'd call her.'

'Is she reliable?' He's not being deliberately difficult, though his fatigue is producing a hostile tone.

'I . . . I don't know,' she says. 'Only that she seemed keen.'

'For cigarettes in return?'

'*Yes*, for cigarettes.' Now there's definite irritation in her voice. 'Look, I might be new to Hamburg, Inspector Schroder,' she goes on. 'But I am not naïve when it comes to contacts, spies and snitches.'

'Snitches?'

117

'Informants,' she explains huffily, turning to go.

'No, wait,' Harri says. 'I'm sorry. I've been very rude, when you've taken the time to come here, and made the effort. My apologies, Fräulein Young.'

'Georgie,' she comes back briskly. 'Everyone calls me Georgie.'

'Even rude Kripo officers?'

That does bring a smile creeping across her face. 'Yes, even those.'

'In that case, you should call me Harri, rather than Inspektor Schroder.'

'Listen, *Harri*, I agree this name might be nothing, but from what I can see' – she nods towards the chalkboard – 'you're still scratching for leads.'

Despite the lingering wrath of Major Stephens, a resigned laugh escapes him. 'That is one way of putting it. Tell me, are you this direct in print?'

'I tell it like it is,' she says. 'But I suppose I can dress it with words a little more on the page. Even so, there's never any veneer in what I write.'

'I'm very glad to hear it.' He reaches for his coat. 'No time like the present, I believe the British say. We'd better see if this name leads us anywhere.'

Over in St Pauli, Ursula Reinhart's landlady seems annoyed instead of concerned, though she's more attentive when Harri flashes his Kripo ID on the doorstep. She merely eyes Georgie with suspicion, reluctantly leading them into her parlour, dark and dusty and unlived-in.

'You're a step up from that urchin who came earlier,' she says. 'Though I hope the police aren't so desperate as to employ the rubble rats nowadays?'

Harri smiles weakly. 'So, Frau Heske, precisely how long is it since you've seen Ursula?'

'I told that girl before, I didn't see her, as much as hear her clumping on the stairs, probably around eight o'clock Sunday evening. Then the front door slamming shut.'

'Do you know where she would have been going?'

Frau Heske rolls her eyes, heavy with disdain.

'And where does she work?' Harri asks.

'Schwan's pharmacy, opposite that big place, where the British hang about.'

'The Victory Club?'

'Yes, I think they call it that – Victory. Rubbing our noses in it, as if we haven't got enough—'

'Can we see her room, please?' Harri cuts her off.

'I suppose so. Though, if she doesn't come back within the week, I'll be advertising it.'

'Did you follow any of that?' Harri asks Georgie as they are led up the dark stairway and left alone in Ursula's room. 'What our gem of a landlady said?'

'Most of it, I think,' she says. 'Strange how women like that of all nationalities are able to complain in the same tone. Maybe, if Hitler had known how similar his own citizens were to those in the rest of the world, he might not have started a war.'

'I'm not sure similarity was his main aim,' Harri mutters, sorting through the few trinkets on the small dressing table. The wardrobe is empty and possessions sparse, so it's difficult to tell if Fräulein Reinhart has packed for a trip or not.

'She's definitely not left of her own accord,' Georgie says, her nose in the drawer of an old, dilapidated tallboy.

Harri's head springs up. 'What makes you so sure?'

119

'She's left her best underwear behind.' Georgie pulls out a pair of silk knickers and a single silk stocking. 'She'd never leave these, just in case that old crone downstairs comes poking around and helps herself. They'd be sold within a day.'

'I really need to get you and Paula working together,' Harri says. 'The criminal fraternity in Hamburg wouldn't stand a chance.'

'Then you'd be out of a job.'

'Would that be such a bad thing?'

Down below, Frau Heske has moved on from complaints about loss of rent to general grousing over the state of Hamburg, Germany, the world and the universe. 'Young people, they really have no priorities — spending money on dancing and cosmetics and the like, when they should—'

A thought bulldozes its way into Harri's head and he cuts her off. 'Tell me, had Ursula always been blonde?'

It silences the landlady for all of half a second. 'Now you come to mention it, no. She's always been dark. Then one day last week, I saw her on the stairs and she was bright blonde. I barely recognised her.'

'Thank you, Frau Heske.'

'What was that about the colour of her hair?' Out on the doorstep, Georgie turns to Harri as they button coats against the whip of a fierce gust, and she pulls a beret over her hair.

'Nothing that we can check out today,' he says, eyeing his watch. 'And unless the team have come up with something fresh, then we'll have to wait until tomorrow for Frau Heske to view the body in the morgue. The pharmacy will be closed by now, but we'll visit first thing.'

120

'But what's the feeling, in your gut?' She angles her head, wrinkling her nose in a way he finds interesting.

Harri pulls down the brim of his homburg and looks out into the descending gloom. These days, darkness suits Hamburg. 'Sadly, my guts tell me it is her. You could well have put a name to our victim.' He scoops in a breath. 'Otherwise, my insides tell me I'm very hungry. Are you?'

She considers for a second. 'Now you mention it, yes.'

'In that case, can I buy you dinner, to show my gratitude? I can't promise anything as good as your hotel food, but some genuine German atmosphere might make up for it. To help with your article.'

'In the interests of Anglo-German relations, and excellent research, I can't possibly refuse.'

As he leads her back into the populated streets, Harri's fatigue has all but been wiped away, in part by a possible move on the case, but driven also by this exchange with Georgie Young. It's that repartee he misses, the affectionate mockery, and – though he has no designs on affection in this case – it does lift him. More than anything, it's a timely reminder he is a man again, rather than a police officer going through the motions, or a solitary drudge destined to be alone forever.

The old creaking ship of Harri Schroder feels a little bit seaworthy again.

CHAPTER EIGHTEEN: PROBING

12th February 1946

Georgie

'So, where did you learn to speak English so well?' Georgie nods her thanks as Harri places a beer in front of her, a creamy foam top inviting her to take a first swig and leaving a white deposit on her top lip. While Hamburg itself does not lack low temperatures, the cold amber liquid is very welcome. 'Oh, that's so good. The best I've tasted for a while.'

'Good local Holsten, a rarity these days,' he says, wiping away his own foamy moustache with the back of his hand. 'Er, the language? I had a pen pal in England when I was a teenager, back in the late twenties. His family was very generous, and they had me to stay for weeks over several summer holidays. Aside from my friend, no one in the house spoke any German, so I learnt through necessity. Very much the King's English too. His mother insisted on it.'

'And since then?' Georgie imagines it would have been easy to let his skill lapse over the war years.

'I was careful to practise, making myself indispensable to the Gestapo.' He flashes a wry look. 'In my experience, it's good to provide that lot with a reason not to kill you.'

'*The Gestapo?*' Georgie's surprise sends a spray of beer over the sides of her glass, though she's wary of keeping her voice low. Even with Hitler in his grave and the scourge being weeded out, Germans don't welcome reminders of the Führer's legacy.

But Harri only raises his eyebrows, and she suspects he might be enjoying the joke, playing it out. 'I thought you of all people would have known, Fräulein Young, that everyone in the Kripo was on the SS payroll. Himmler was very clever in making sure we were implicated in his little band of brotherly endeavour. Our dubious morality afforded him some sort of loyalty.'

'But does that mean . . .?' Her eyes are wide, aghast like a rookie reporter of old.

Sipping at his beer, Harri leans over the table. 'There are ways and means of retreating into the background,' he says, voice at barely a whisper, 'to preserve what little personal integrity is left.'

'What do you mean? How?'

He shrugs and sits back into the old wooden chair, looks around the small basement club they are in, noisy enough to absorb their conversation. 'You absent yourself when you know there's a raid on Jews being planned, make yourself available at all times to do real police work instead of bully-boy duty, you keep your ears open and your mouth shut. More than anything, you try hard not to be noticed by anyone of rank. You become a nobody except when it suits you.'

'And that worked for you?' Georgie is too curious to be mindful of her manners or any sensitivity.

'Mostly.'

'What does that mean?'

Now he does laugh, perhaps at her childlike inability to hold back from interrogation. 'Are you asking if I did anything unsavoury or shameful on behalf of the Reich?'

Georgie only looks, certain that a prolonged pause can be the best method of teasing out a confession. Though this grilling is purely for her benefit, rather than her notebook.

He hugs his beer glass to his chest and pushes out a breath. 'I'm bound to say no, aren't I? But if you really are that curious, the answer truly is no. Not to my knowledge, anyway.'

Georgie feels her shoulders relax back into her body. Despite his lugubrious nature, and the initial standoffishness, she wants permission to like Harri Schroder as a friend. And maybe an ally too.

'You don't look convinced,' he says. 'But I promise you, I have been vetted by the British forces and duly filled out my *Fragebogen*, answering all their spurious questions – all a hundred and thirty-three of them – in reassuring the victors that I am in no way damaged by seeing more than half my city burnt to a crisp by Allied firepower, that I am totally intact, and ready to pledge my allegiance to a new command.' He's wide-eyed and thin-lipped, waiting for her reaction, as if daring her to be incensed. Shocked by his audacity as a German.

And now it's Georgie's turn to laugh heartily. Far from being wounded by his overt sarcasm, she's amused by it, not least that Harri can find humour in the Allies' de-Nazification process, and the frankly farcical, long-winded questionnaire designed to weed out collaborators and Nazis hiding in plain sight.

'Tell me then, which one of those *Fragebogen* questions was your particular favourite?' she punts lightly.

'I like the one asking if I'd ever played with toy soldiers.'

'Which would surely make you a natural warmonger?' Her brow is crimped in disbelief. 'Any more perceptive enquiries?'

'Yes, the one which asked if any of my family had been affected by the Allied bombings and, presumably, the resulting inferno.'

'And how did you answer that one?' Georgie is too amused, too carried away by the exchange, beer drunk too quickly on an empty stomach. Too late she hears his tone darken and sees his face fall.

'I wrote in one sentence that I lost my wife and only child,' he says flatly, swallowing the last of his beer. 'Which, ironically, they took as provocation, earning me a further interrogation from a senior officer before I was fully cleared.'

Georgie stares into her beer. The bubbles have disappeared. Her heart physically aches for him. Can she not stop being a reporter for just one bloody second? At times, she's seen even Max wincing at how deeply she dares to prod at her interviewees. 'I'm so sorry,' she mumbles.

'No, it's me who should apologise,' he says, looking into his lap. 'Sometimes it escapes in ways that surprise even me. I shouldn't have said . . . I hardly know you.'

'It's my fault, Harri. I've no right to be so nosy.'

'But it is your job,' he says plainly. 'Mine too. We just can't help ourselves. I am sorry, though, if I've made you feel awkward.'

'I think I've seen too much to feel awkward any more,' she says. 'Which is an awful admission. It does make me feel sad. For you, and everyone who lost.'

'We all lost.' He says it without emotion, reaching for her glass. 'Another beer? I'll order some food, too.'

'Right, Miss Young – my turn to pry now.' Minutes later, they are leaning over plates of stew and fresh beer: the meat is a mystery but Georgie detects with relief that it is not horse, having eaten enough to know. Mercifully, not dog either. The club has begun to fill up with couples, those with jobs and some spare income, and there's a trio in the corner playing gentle jazz.

'Fire away,' she says. 'I think I'm ready.'

'So, where are your family, and your husband?'

Georgie's eyes snap upwards, away from her plate. Disappointed, if she's honest. 'Oh Lord, do I look married?'

'And is that a problem?'

Fork aloft, she considers. 'No, not really. I like being married, and I love my husband, but . . .'

'But what?'

'I don't actually want to look like a "wife". A *frau*.'

'So, what does a *frau* look like? Tell me.' He's playing with her again, she can tell. Just like Rod and Bill back in Berlin, her beloved mentors as she cut her teeth in the newspaper world, teasing her mercilessly and maintaining a poker face as they took turns prodding at her innocence. Harri's face is similarly deadpan.

'I don't know,' she admits. 'A bit staid, I suppose. Unexciting.'

'I never thought of my wife as unexciting,' he says, wincing as he plucks a large piece of gristle from his fork. 'Are you sure that's not just your own prejudice coming through?'

She stops and looks at him, aghast. Is he right? Is that what she's afraid of, with Max, and then the baby? Becoming dull, only able to talk about domestic affairs and newborn feed times. Because that's not what the mothers she knows are like, not at all. So why should it be her? And does reading her so acutely make him a good detective?

'Don't look so serious,' he says, his face breaking open. 'I am joking. You don't look like a wife at all, if there is such a thing. I just happened to ring the hotel and they told me you were registered under two names.'

She remembers then leaving 'Spender' as a contact, in the event of telegrams from Max.

'And why would you ring the hotel?'

'I was checking you out.' He smiles wryly, suppressing the humour he's so clearly enjoying. 'You didn't think I could let just anyone into the investigation, did you? That wouldn't make me a very good policeman. Don't forget, I was technically SS, only the most suspicious organisation known to man. So yes, Fräulein Young, I went digging.'

'And what did you find, Herr Schroder?'

'That you're good at your job. Thorough. Undeterred. The CCG are scared stiff of you and the articles you will write for the world at large, and so they are determined to keep you sweet at all costs.'

She chews thoughtfully. 'What does that tell *you*?'

'I only wish I had the funds to offer you a job. Like I say – you, Paula and Anna could probably clean up this town, like avenging angels. Erwin and I would sit back and drink coffee and schnapps to our hearts' content.'

'Now you're dreaming,' she bats back.

'At this point, Georgie, dreaming is all we have.'

Harri walks her back to the hotel via the U-Bahn, and while it does make her feel a little like a defenceless female, she is grateful. In the dark and away from the main thoroughfares, Hamburg feels edgy. In post-war London, Georgie has finally become accustomed to *not* seeing bodies leap from battlefield bunkers, emerging instead from doorways at ground level, or stepping off the platform of a big red bus. Here, the city's underbelly is not so much thriving as relying on the sanctity of the subterranean world to survive. People materialise from their underground homes in the pitch darkness, ghosting out of thin air on Hamburg's streets. With the embedded, unwashed grime, it's often not until they come close that you register their faces alongside. Sometimes it startles, throwing her back into a world of conflict, artillery and gunshots ringing in her ears. Georgie Young has to remind herself time and again: *We are at peace.*

Seconds later, she is apt to ponder: *Are we really?*

She and Harri part at the hotel entrance, he choosing sleep over a nightcap in the bar, though Georgie suspects – understandably – that he might not want to be surrounded by British uniforms. He's surely had enough of those. Wearily, she climbs the stairs, hears a gentle snoring as she presses an ear to the door of Zofia's room, and heads to her own. There's no putting off her task any longer, no pleading exhaustion to herself or erecting spurious barriers to delay the inevitable. And really, the prospect should not feel like facing the gallows or walking the plank. She undresses, slips into bed and pulls some fresh paper onto her lap.

Dear Max (AKA hopalong husband),

I hope you and the leg are well, and that you're not going too mad without work to distract you. Perhaps you ought to get going on that book you've been threatening to write — or have you forgotten you were once a writer too? (Ha ha, I can see your eyes rolling and hear your teeth grinding from here.)

Oh Max, how to describe Hamburg? You might have to wait for my article to get the full picture, because my notes, my mind and my own opinion are so far scrambled. Enough to say that once the joy of VE Day and the parades has dissipated, what remains is confusion, regret, sorrow, death, and perhaps even harder than death to see: hatred. But then, how would we feel if the Nazis were strutting down the Strand, or hoisting the swastika over the Houses of Parliament? I haven't yet found the word to express the mood in Hamburg. I do know it's harder to describe than battle or conflict, because we were certain then which side held the moral high ground. Here, I'm not sure there even is one. There's no black and white, not even grey. It's just muddy.

Hell, I'm becoming very literal and far too flowery for a letter — I will save it for my written piece.

On the plus side, I have a comfortable hotel room, away from the dreaded wives' gatherings, and I've found a fabulous translator, a young woman from the resettlement camp who is already a godsend. The CCG and army boys are being helpful too, though I suspect they are treating me with kid gloves for a reason.

Max, I'm not sure yet how long I'll stay – from what I've seen so far, this might turn into a syndicated piece, from several different angles. And while the leg is putting you out of action, the money will be more than welcome. Don't you agree?

Missing you, of course. I won't tell you what great images of daily life there are to capture on camera, because you'll be very jealous, but I yearn for more than your skill through the lens.

We'll talk when I come home. We'll work it out, Max – we always have, and always will.

Look after the leg.

Your darling scribe, Georgie XX

From under the warmth of her eiderdown, she reads it over twice. Is it enough to slip in that brief, conciliatory sentence at the tail end? Will he be expecting more – of her sadness, and her readiness to try again? More emotion? It's odd that she finds it hard to write sentiment to someone she knows so well, and yet her articles have attracted praise (and sometimes censure) for the ability to 'wring out tears from the page', to quote one reviewer. Max says she has a finite 'pot of angst' and often uses up her quota on the keyboard, so there's little left for loved ones, something Georgie's mother has hinted at more than once. Of course, Max has never really needed comfort before, given they've generally been together, and when they haven't, there's been little time to write. Or a reason. Now, there is a purpose, and he might be craving something of her, reassurance that they have a future. In those brief words, has she succeeded? Is she even capable? Brevity on the page has never been Georgie's forte, always better at the more verbose lengthier articles, where she paints a vivid picture with the typewriter. So there's little consolation woven into this all too brief missive.

What's missing, of course, is any mention of the murder investigation, or Meta and her precious suitcase. Or Harri Schroder. But what's to tell, she reasons. Very little so far.

Georgie flips back the blanket, feeling a sharp chill to her legs as she steps towards the small writing desk, pulling out an envelope from the drawer. In moving around, she notices that her palm rests automatically on her stomach in thinking of home, propelling her towards the full-length mirror fixed to the wardrobe door. Pulling up her nightdress, she takes in a breath and pushes out the flesh of her belly, not so taut as it once was after months of peacetime inactivity. She would have been what . . .? Seven months pregnant by now, rounded and expectant. And not here in Hamburg, for sure, but safely back in London. She and Max might be readying the spare room as a nursery, her mother inevitably fretting over where she would give birth, encouraging her to head back to the Cotswolds, instead of a busy London suburb and exposing the baby to the post-war dust and grime. What sort of work would she be doing, feeling heavy and cumbersome? Perhaps ingratiating herself with women's magazines, priming the way for those freelance projects she might be able to complete when the baby slept, if they ever do. She might even be feeling happy at such prospects.

Georgie smooths her hand over the silhouette of her distended skin and, for the first time, allows herself to imagine the sensation of the baby moving inside, a leg or a hand pushing out to say, 'Hello, I'm here. Are you ready for me?' It's then that her breath runs out and the bump retracts, returning to its slim, unrounded state. To being a void. And her hand moves upwards to her face, wiping away a stream of tears that she doesn't welcome, but won't be denied all the same.

She swipes at the loose letter and places it firmly in the desk drawer, slamming it shut. She's not ready. Not yet.

CHAPTER NINETEEN:
ANYONE FOR A DANCE?

13th February 1946

Harri

For the first time in weeks, there are no dreams splintering his sleep, and Harri wakes with a curious sensation of feeling refreshed. He scratches his memory for his usual hellish recollections, but finds nothing under the surface. Not even a tremor of distress or a lick of a flame. To his further amazement, the face reflected between the cracks of his kitchen mirror seems less crumpled, lifted maybe. With the murder case still very much pending, he wonders why. And while he shaves, he finds himself whistling a tune. Is it one from *The Blue Angel*, recalling the time he took Hella to see it at the picture house in the city centre? Yes, it's the same song, a sudden memory of their first date together. And yet, rather than a painful pinch within his chest, there's a lopsided smile in the mirror. What *is* going on? Has his devilish night goblin been replaced with a deity spreading fairy dust?

'Don't kid yourself, it won't last,' he mutters into the reflection that purports to be Harri Schroder.

There's good and bad news on reaching the office. Bad for a portion of the women in Hamburg, but potentially good for Harri and the investigation team, who are huddled around the fire on a day that's especially bitter. Someone has secured real coffee and the precious pot sits on the stove, chairs pulled in close and fingers wrapped around mugs of the hot brew.

'There's enough for one more cup.' Anna gestures to Harri.

'Wonderful.' He pours coffee and presses the fingers of his free hand directly to the hot metal. Even when it singes his skin, it's somehow a relief. 'Anything new?'

'Possibly,' Paula comes in. 'Doctor Edelman sent word – Frau Heske, the landlady, identified the body this morning as Ursula Reinhart, so we have a firm identification. He's also completed the post-mortem. Nothing to add on the cause of death, but in answer to your query last night – yes, she had dyed her hair very recently. Underneath the blonde, she's naturally dark.'

Given the first two victims had dark hair, Harri's suspicions prove right. And yet, he's visibly confused. 'But I saw her on the slab – naked,' he says, brow skewed. He struggles to temper his words. 'She was blonde. I mean, I saw *everything*.'

Anna and Paula exchange knowing looks. 'It does happen, Harri,' Anna says. 'Uncomfortable. Painful even, but women are sometimes very thorough with the dye – eyebrows, and yes, everything. Men like it, apparently.'

He takes a second to appreciate the oddity, though his mind is already working on the consequences. 'If all three victims are naturally dark, have we got a common thread?' he throws into the group. 'Considering half the women in Hamburg have the same colouring, I wonder if it's significant. Because if he is targeting those women, would our killer have known about Ursula, given that we didn't detect it immediately?'

Paula jolts upright. 'She might have dyed her hair as a way of avoiding him, if he was pursuing her over several days or weeks.'

'Possibly,' Harri muses. 'It's certainly worth thinking about.'

Erwin blows out his sagging cheeks and drains his coffee. 'Then that's another piece of the bloody puzzle.'

'Damn it!' Harri sets his cup down noisily on the stove and paces in a small circle, though his frustration is directed entirely at the board and not poor Erwin. 'Why are there only fragments? Do we really have to wait for another victim before we start to fit them together?'

'All we can do is keep on adding those pieces until we find the answer,' Paula assures. Her rational, even temper is always the team's best asset when their mood is low.

'Well, if that's the case, let's get out there,' Harri says with a sudden urgency, looking beyond the office window. He swallows the last dregs of coffee. 'Paula and Anna, you try to track down any of Ursula's relatives, and I'll visit her place of work, see what I can discover there. Erwin, can you find Jonni? We need to update his likeness of Ursula to include her blonde and dark looks, and then get both pictures out there on the streets.'

Using her name spurs on the team to shift from the

135

relative warmth. Along with Liselle Mauser and Rita Essig, Ursula is no longer a number among the millions of dead, but a person with a name, and family, even if they are lost. She mattered to someone, perhaps even to peevish Frau Heske a little.

The pharmacy is directly opposite the Allied Victory Club, and Harri runs the gamut of the female lines outside Dammtor station, thinned out because of today's perishing weather. He slows and looks dutifully at each picture thrust towards him – given his job, there's a small chance he might have come across one lost husband or brother, albeit in the cells. A second of his attention might mean the world to someone. Not today, however. His head shakes with regret at each woman, noses blue in the cold. '*Danke*,' they chorus, even when there's nothing to be thankful for.

Behind the counter of Schwan's pharmacy, and clad in his spotless white coat, Ursula's boss is clearly devastated. 'But how? Why?' he mutters, choked with emotion. 'She was such a sweet girl. Always reliable and diligent.'

Harri skates over the grisly details and, in the privacy of a cluttered back room, notes down that she'd been employed since the surrender. According to the chemist, Ursula was twenty-one, older than her looks. 'Were you not concerned when she didn't turn up for work?' he asks.

Herr Schwan shakes his head. 'No. She'd asked for three days' holiday, starting on Monday . . . the day you found her.'

'Was she planning a trip somewhere on her days off, out of the city perhaps?'

'I wouldn't know. She was pleasant, but very quiet. She didn't talk much.'

'Did she have any family?' Harri asks.

Again, Herr Schwan shakes his head. 'She never spoke of anyone, and so we assumed they were lost. It tends to make you wary about asking, just in case. Though she never seemed sad, always pleasant and charming.'

'Is there anyone else who works here, someone who might know her a little better?'

The pharmacist calls up the stairs for his wife to join them.

'Did Ursula have a particular friend, either man or woman?' Harri asks a shocked Frau Schwan.

She dabs at her tears with a handkerchief. 'Not really. I don't remember anyone calling for her during lunchtime or after work. But I do know she used to go somewhere to dance regularly. Once, she asked me for some eyeliner to draw on her stockings, when she'd forgotten hers.'

'Do you mean opposite, at the Victory Club?'

Frau Schwan shakes her head. 'I would be very surprised. She didn't like the British soldiers, hinted that they were only after one thing, when she was there to dance.'

'Thank you, that's helpful,' Harri says, though he's not entirely sure what he's learnt has much value. For now, it's just another sliver of that damned whole. 'We'll keep you informed about funeral details when we know.'

Outside, he ties his scarf tight into his neck, cursing the bleak sky above for offloading more snow on a city already under siege from everything else. He trudges not towards the U-Bahn and the office, but walks the short route towards the Baseler Hof. At this time of the morning, he guesses Georgie is likely to be out touring the city with her translator, but he wants to leave a note. She should know her information has been valuable and, in

137

turn, he's reminded not to be so disparaging in future about *trümmerkinder* and their worth.

Your hunch – and your 'snitch' – was right, he scribbles. *We've identified the woman from the name you supplied. Can I repay you with a dinner, in a good restaurant this time (or what passes for good in Hamburg!)? If tomorrow night suits, then leave a message for me at the station.* He scrawls the number of the one remaining telephone line, and deposits the note at the hotel reception.

The truth being, Harri is grateful, and it's the least he can do for the most promising lead they've had so far. But journeying back to Davidwache, hands deep in his pockets and head buried in his coat collar, he is forced to admit his offer is also personal, that he's glad to have a reason to spend more time in Georgie's company. She's married, and happily so, but there's no crime in enjoying the company of an intelligent woman. Inspektor Schroder is widowed, wounded, scarred and scraped out inside, and yet underneath the weight of sorrow and remorse, he recognises himself as a man still, one who enjoys female friendship and always has. Is that really so wrong?

Back at the station, Anna is busy at the ancient mimeograph machine, rolling off copies of the updated image Jonni has provided.

'Where did you get the paper?' Harri asks, marvelling at the small pile beside her. For months, they've been reduced to reusing scraps. 'On second thoughts, I don't want to know.' He busies himself updating the board, deep in thought as to where Ursula would have gone dancing. The ornate Alster Pavilion on the edge of the river basin is – or was – an obvious magnet for dancers, but lies crumpled after the Allied wartime attacks. The lively Café Heinz and the Trocadero are similarly closed. So where?

By late afternoon, the team is assembled in the office, cold and weary, and so more than grateful for the decent loaf and small portion of butter Harri has acquired en route and laid out for all to share. It cost him a quarter of a week's wages, but the reaction is worth every pfennig.

'Ooh, that butter is so good,' Paula groans with delight as she chews. 'Right now, that's better than any pastry laden with jam.'

'Pastries!' cries Anna. 'With jam! I can't even remember what they taste like. For now, we'll just have to imagine the sugar crust on top.'

Harri brings them to attention, relaying what he's discovered from the pharmacy. 'Now your bellies are a little bit full, spill what information you have.'

'I have a sighting of a blonde woman just west of the bridge by the Central Market, on the evening before Ursula Reinhart disappeared,' Erwin says. 'The description of her clothes roughly matches what she was wearing.'

'Isn't that area fairly damaged?' Paula says.

'Yes, but I talked to a few locals, and they say people gather under the bridge for impromptu dances. You've seen them dotted about, haven't you? Someone brings a gramophone, there's often a put-up bar, and they dance. That night, there was a meet that apparently lasted several hours.'

'Given what Ursula's employers reported, I think we'll have to look at the area more carefully,' Harri says. 'I've heard these street dances are getting more popular, so it's entirely feasible that the other two women could have gone there. So, who fancies moving to a bit of swing?'

Erwin shrinks back into his chair, and Anna fidgets noticeably, pulling at the scarf she wears each day like a turban. Underneath it, mere wisps of her own hair remain, a by-product of the war and all its stresses. Harri knows she is deeply self-conscious when it comes to strangers and social events.

Paula takes a breath. 'I'm game, if my mother can sit with my children. I think I remember how to dance, as long as you don't expect any cartwheels.'

Harri nods. 'We'll need two of us, minimum – I'll hover on the outskirts and watch for potential predators, while Paula mingles among the dancers.'

'Aw, Harri, does that mean you won't dance with me?' Paula simpers like a schoolgirl, her expression pure mockery.

'You wouldn't ask if you value your feet being in one piece,' he shoots back. 'My wife had me tagged as the worst dancer in Germany. Anything else?'

Anna fidgets again. 'I've been thinking about our man, and who he would be,' she says. 'We're guessing the girls weren't forced or dragged to follow him into those buildings, so it's a good bet that he's quite charming, and maybe even fairly good looking? Youngish?'

'A valid point,' says Harri. 'Perhaps someone who seems trustworthy.'

'Does that mean we're back to a military man?' Erwin suggests.

They all shift uncomfortably. It's the biggest fear for the Kripo, because if they do track down a culprit who is part of the British occupying force, there's almost no chance of a conviction. Unofficially, the military are largely protected from criminal charges, and the best they can hope for is that this monster will be ghosted out. What the British do with him after that is largely their own affair.

'Let's pray he isn't,' Harri says decisively. 'What we can do is check out any common threads the women had – doctors, dentists, shops they went to for rations. Anyone who, on the face of it, seems reliable, and watch if any of the names overlap. Given Anna's theory, I don't think we're looking at a DP, or returning POW with rage in their belly. This man is smart inside and out – and he offers them something these women have found irresistible. Our job is to find what that is.'

CHAPTER TWENTY: INVITATIONS

13th February 1946

Georgie

Georgie's been in Hamburg a little over forty-eight hours, but on walking into the Baseler Hof at the end of the day it already feels like a bunker, an oasis and a home-from-home rolled into one, with its gentle murmur of footfall, the tinkle of the reception telephone, and a very welcome clink of glasses as officers partake of an early evening drink. Zofia heads straight up to her room for a bath, where the novelty of sinking into a tub of warm water hasn't yet worn off.

'Fräulein Young, there are messages for you.' The man at reception holds out a chit with a written note and a separate envelope. The dinner invite from Harri lifts her tired self, surprised at how much it makes her smile. It's the second invitation that pulls her mood in the opposite direction, producing a deep sigh as she slumps into a battered leather chair and reads the formally printed card.

Miss Georgina Young - Major and Mrs Stephens request the pleasure of your company at dinner, 15th February, 6.30 for 7 p.m. RSVP.

The name is immediately familiar as Sergeant Dawson's fearsome passenger, since it's unlikely there are two Major Stephens. Underneath is an address that can only be one of those grand houses just outside of the city, on the banks of the Elbe. Below that are handwritten words from Lieutenant Howarth.

Sorry, he's penned. The major caught a whiff of your visit and I couldn't steer him away from issuing the invite. He's extremely keen to meet you. I will be there (as an ally) if it's any consolation.

It is – good old Howarth – but the mere prospect still drags on Georgie's scant energy. Hobnobbing with senior military from any nation is easily her least favourite part of the job, especially those who have a high opinion as to how connected they are with 'the people'. They aren't – that's the truth of it, not when they are routinely served good wine in large, well-heated houses. It's only 5.30 p.m., but the message creates a sudden need for a stiff whisky, before she climbs the stairs to her own bath, followed by a quiet dinner with Zofia and an early night.

It's while she's staring into the amber liquid that Georgie is hit with a thought. Energised by her brainwave, she checks her watch and heads towards the reception desk. If he's working late, she might just catch him. 'May I use your telephone, please?'

Harri takes several minutes to come to the phone, and

143

she pictures him having to leave the relative warmth of the Kripo office to descend the cold, stony stairs towards the station's own front desk.

'Yes?' he says into the receiver, with a slight irritation. Perhaps he's shivering in the draughty hallway.

'Harri, it's Georgie.'

'Oh, hello. I wasn't expecting you to leave a message until tomorrow.' At the end of the line, his tone goes up a notch. 'I'm assuming you've got my note?'

'Yes, thank you,' she says. 'I would love dinner. But, instead of a restaurant, could we eat at your place? Is that an awful imposition?'

The seconds of ensuing silence tick slowly away.

'Harri?' she quizzes. 'Are you still there?'

'Yes, yes, I am.'

Clearly, she's done it again, in overstepping the mark. A huge part of being a reporter is intuition and sensitivity, especially now. And she has both, mostly. Sometimes, though, her enthusiasm overrides all. Sitting there with her whisky in the hotel lounge, she pictured the contrast, could hear how she would phrase it on the page – dinner with the major, against dining in the midst of Hamburg's ruins. The perfect juxtaposition. Any editor worth their salt would recognise the power in print.

And now, in Harri's silence, she kicks herself for it, for seeing him as a story opportunity. For being a journalist first, above all else.

'I mean, if you really want to,' he says finally. 'I can't promise restaurant cuisine and it will be a bit like eating al fresco. In winter.'

'I really shouldn't do that,' she says with sudden and genuine remorse.

144

'Do what, Georgie?'

'Invite myself to dinner, when you've been kind enough to suggest going out. It's very improper.'

'Because you're a married woman and I'm a single man?'

'No, because it's just downright rude.'

'It is direct,' he agrees, though he's not remonstrating. In fact, he sounds slightly amused. 'And from anyone else . . .? But yes, why not? And here's me thinking that my entertaining days were over. If nothing else, it will force me to tidy up.'

'I'll bring the wine and dessert,' she says, her attempt at a sweetener.

'There's just one more thing,' he adds.

'Yes?'

'Wear plenty of layers. You'll need them.'

It's a few minutes to six when Georgie lays down the receiver, and something nags at her memory, only just recalling her pledge to meet Meta outside the hotel. Pulling on her coat, she makes a rapid visit to the kitchen, rifles in her satchel and trips down the hotel steps. To one side and tucked against the wall, she finds the young girl squatting sentry-like in her portable bivouac. Meta's eyes light up on seeing someone approach, and Georgie feels that punch to her chest again. If her own presence is a high point in Meta's day, what sort of life is that?

As ever, the waif looks hungry. But beyond the bony cheeks, papery skin and sunken eyes, another appetite is apparent; Georgie reads in her a will to please, to progress, to never stay still and succumb to an existence that isn't yet a life proper. If only this state, this country – the world at large – would allow it.

Georgie holds out a paper bag of goods, not offended when Meta's nose is instantly within, sniffing and surveying like a voracious rodent. The smile as she lifts her head from the bag says it all, plucking out a sealed pack of American Chesterfield cigarettes – the gold standard for the *zigaretten* populace. '*Danke, Fräulein.*'

'Well, the name you gave me – it was good information,' Georgie tells her.

'Yes?' Meta stands to full height. 'I can get more. What do you need, Fräulein?'

Georgie holds up both palms. 'Just to keep your ears open, that's all. Nothing more.'

Now, Meta looks slighted, as if she hasn't quite come up to scratch, as if she's being 'let go' gently. 'I can get more. Go anywhere, Fräulein,' she beseeches. 'Meta goes anywhere.'

It's then that Georgie takes her by the shoulders, searching for a bony skeleton under the layers of cloth. 'It's dangerous, Meta,' she says firmly. 'This man who we're looking for, he could hurt you. You need to understand that.'

Georgie has pledged a certain confidentiality to Harri over the case, but this is not like advertising the details. It's survival. While Meta is not a woman in employment, with nice clothes and a touch of lipstick, there's no saying what any monster could turn towards in desperation. To Georgie, the killer is an enemy of every woman out there, and will be until he's caught.

'Promise me,' she says, her eyes meeting Meta's. 'Promise me you won't go hunting?'

'Hunt . . . ing?'

'*Jagd,*' Georgie dredges from her memory. '*Jagen verboten.*' No hunting.

Again, that injured look from Meta, though she does nod her head in agreement.

'I'll still bring you cigarettes, I promise. But, you know, I can help you to get into a place with a bed, with the Red Cross, somewhere to help you settle.' Georgie deliberately avoids the word 'camp', and yet the alarm floods Meta's face.

'*Nein!* No, Fräulein. Thank you. Meta is fine. Good. Alone.'

It's nothing less than Georgie expected. Dawson, Howarth and Zofia, plus her own eyes, have demonstrated that living without a home is now so entrenched within some DPs that they simply can't tolerate four walls. Add a solid roof and it feels like a prison, which is tantamount to hell. They crave stability and yet shun the confines of it. The war has turned concrete and confidence into dust. How on earth do you even begin to build that back up?

Georgie pulls out a small notepad and two pencils from her pocket and hands them to Meta. 'I'll see you in three days,' she asserts in German. 'But if you need me before then, mark the paper with an "M"' – she scrawls a large letter on the paper – 'and ask the bellboy to leave it at reception for me. Then I'll meet you out here. Same time.'

Meta nods, fervent this time. 'Three days. A note if I need you. I have it. *Danke, Fräulein.*'

Georgie pulls her coat around her, suddenly chilled. It's freezing out here on the street, and she hates to imagine how cold it must be wherever Meta sleeps, more than likely alone, no one to share even a semblance of bodily heat. Max's philosophy crowds into her head: 'You can't save them all, my love,' she hears his voice say from somewhere inside.

147

'Just be careful,' Georgie says to Meta. 'Be safe, eh?'

'*Ja, Fräulein. Sicher.*' And then she's gone, swallowed by the darkness, clutching the case and her fresh bag of treasure.

CHAPTER TWENTY-ONE:
THE HUNTER AT HOME

13th February 1946

Meta

She broods. All the way back to her place, criss-crossing the slush-filled streets, through the alleyway which stinks of more than piss and out into the open expanse leading to her abandoned warehouse, Meta chews over Georgie's words. Fräulein Young said it, didn't she? That Meta had done well, intimated it was her who discovered the dead girl's identity, where the Kripo had failed. So why is she being dismissed? Or what feels like it. 'Just to keep your ears open, that's all. Nothing more,' Georgie said. But that means almost nothing, since her ears and eyes are always open, for survival. There's no longer any special aim, or target. So, how is Meta to earn her extras, the merchandise that will ensure a good profit, and her ticket out of this hellhole?

She stops at the warehouse entrance. Not the huge double doors welded shut, but the one that's been neatly fashioned by a bomb into the side of the brickwork, where she looks both ways and peers into the darkness before entering, listening for silence in the confines of what she calls 'her plaza'. Satisfied she's alone, Meta pulls aside the heavy tarpaulin held in place by a charred lintel, just enough for her and the suitcase to slip through, and then replugs the gap. Inside, her breath is visible in the vast, lofty space that was once filled with industry and people. A thin drift of snow falls in one corner where the roof slats finally succumbed to rot and winter. Like a fox, Meta sniffs the air once more, clicks her tongue and waits for the echo, in checking there are no trespassers. That her inner haven is untainted. *Sicher.* See? She knows how to keep herself safe.

She heads to one corner, to the refuge built from wood and sheet metal, and a patchwork of oily tarpaulins; a room within a room, that has its own roof, to ward off the vacuous chill of the warehouse. Her bones ache tonight and she would rather slip under the mound of blankets she's accrued and sink into her own oblivion, but Meta is too curious about Georgie's treasure trove. It needs unpicking and unpacking, stowing away for safekeeping.

She lights the paraffin lamp with one flick to her flint and opens up the paper bag. Inside are two eggs wrapped in tissue, which, when she shakes them, are not hardboiled, plus a shiny tin of sardines, glinting like a real cache of jewels, and the end of a loaf of bread. Not the dense black variety, but white British bread from the hotel kitchen. She buries her nose into its fabric and the grainy texture gives a little, releasing a comforting smell of yeast. She'll have a feast in the morning, gather some wood and . . . her hand goes to the bottom of the bag, fishing out one more treat, and she pushes it towards the lamp – a tiny old jam jar by the looks of it, containing granules of gold and a tiny piece of paper taped to the side. 'Maxwell House', it says. *Oh*. It will be a banquet of the sort she used to read about in fairy tales as a child. Her belly may even poke out a little again, bloated with coffee and eggs.

The fuel will fill her boots, reaching into her toes. Energy enough for Meta to go hunting again.

CHAPTER TWENTY-TWO:
PLANNING AND PROMISES

14th February 1946

Harri

Harri spends the previous evening and a good deal of the next day either searching for food or thinking about it, then pondering on why the approaching evening seems so important. Before the war, he and Hella entertained a lot, in their big old apartment in St Georg. He'd often invite friends over on a whim, Hella rolling her eyes and yet, being a far better cook, still producing a magical spread from the kitchen. Then when baby Lily arrived, talking late into the night over the dinner table became less frequent, but it was still pleasurable when they had the energy. Then the war. Now nothing.

Harri goes first to Fritz in the bar and 'borrows' his oven to roast two small pieces of chicken he's bartered for, which he and Georgie will eat cold, alongside potato salad and beetroot, paying Fritz's son to cycle out to a

smallholding on the city outskirts, with a range of
currencies to secure the vegetables. On his one small gas
ring, Harri will cook up a pot of soup, the one recipe
his mother forced him to perfect, insisting it would either
save his life or fill his belly. Or both. As a young rookie
policeman, his mother's potato and herb broth could well
have kept him from starvation for nigh on a year. Now,
it may just save his blushes in front of Georgie.

'Are you all right?' Paula asks him in the office. Her eyes
are wide with concern through the lenses of her glasses.

Harri snaps from his reverie. 'Yes, why?'

'You seem distracted, that's all.'

'Thinking.' But why so much time pondering about
Kartoffelsuppe? he asks himself. Perhaps because it smacks
of normality. Because the old existence will never return,
but when a slip of it nudges into your world, teasing and
tantalising, you snatch and hold on for dear life.

'You want to come with me?' Paula's voice cuts in
again. 'I'll even let you have the good bike.'

'Sorry, what was that?' Again, Harri has to force himself
back into the moment.

'I'm off to speak to a friend of Rita Essig, the second
victim. Anna thinks there might be a lead to follow up.'

'Fine. Let me get my coat.'

In the basement café at the far end of the Reeperbahn,
Rita's friend is granted only five minutes' break from
waiting tables by the sour-faced owner guarding his till.
The place is small, but does good business serving Tommies
and Germans who drop by on their way to work in the
line of municipal buildings further along the road.

Wilma draws hard on the Lucky Strike that Harri offers

and then lights for her, closing her eyes with pleasure at the taste that's inevitably far smoother than her own bitter, self-rolled smokes.

'So, what made you contact us again?' Paula asks. 'We interviewed you when Rita first went missing.'

'I don't know exactly,' Wilma says. 'I overheard a group of women talking last night and it sort of poked at my memory.'

'Talking about what?' Harri asks.

'One was boasting how she was going to get away from here soon, that she'd been proposed to by a Tommy, and this time next year she would be in England.'

'And you think Rita might have had an English suitor?' Paula quizzes.

'No, not that. I'm certain I would have known about a boyfriend.' The girl stares hard into the glowing end of her cigarette. 'But Rita did say once that she would be going away at some point. I laughed it off – I mean, where is there to go in Germany that's any better? But she had such a determined look on her face, as if she really meant it.'

'Did she mention if anyone would be helping her to get away – a soldier, for instance?' Harri is wondering if the trip has been wasted on mere hearsay, and yet he's known crimes in the past to be solved on a snippet far smaller.

The sour-faced owner gestures rudely from across the room that time is up, and Wilma douses the lighted end of her cigarette, tucking the butt into her pocket. 'She didn't say anything specific, but I do know that Rita was never a fantasist, not after the war. She wouldn't have been swept away by love or false promises, especially by a Tommy. That's why I thought it might be important.'

★　★　★

'What do you think?' Paula asks, sidestepping rubble as they get back on the bicycles.

'I'm wondering if that's what lured the girls into those dark places,' Harri muses. 'That we were right early on and it wasn't money, cigarettes or perfume. Or even the company of a good-looking man.'

'Then what?' Paula probes.

'Promises,' Harri says. 'Right now, the prospect of a different life is like a pot of gold at the end of a rainbow. And what wouldn't we all do for that?'

CHAPTER TWENTY-THREE:
GUILT OF A NATION

14th February 1946

Georgie

It hasn't escaped Georgie's notice that she's clutching a bottle of wine and two large slices of torte, on her way to dinner with a man who isn't her husband — on Valentine's, of all days. Fortunately, she'd been able to send a telegram to Max earlier, in response to his brief but sweet message, received at the Baseler Hof just before she left: Love you more and more every day, Georgie girl. Missing you. Mx

In reply, she'd sent: Sorry not to be with you today. Celebrate when I'm back. Gx

It felt sparse in dictating it. Insufficient. And yet, when the hotel receptionist asked if it was complete, she struggled to think of anything to add. While she's never viewed her and Max as an overly sentimental couple, marking the day this year does seem important, given

156

what they've been through. Duly dispatched across the North Sea, her missive is not enough to banish the ripples of guilt surfacing when she arrives at Harri's apartment block.

Using Meta's map, he's pencilled in where they are to meet with an X, at the corner of Murken Strasse. The updated version is a godsend, since few of the original landmarks survive, and she's navigated her way following Meta's scratchy notations:'large rubble pile' and 'bombed-out church', 'bakery in house'. It's when the six-storey block looms out of the landscape that she understands Harri's instructions not to climb to the top floor, but to wait for him below. 'DANGER! KEEP OUT!' the sign cautions in big, black lettering. Only yesterday, Georgie warned Meta to keep safe — should she be heeding her own advice?

There's no chance to consider, because Harri appears through the double entrance doors at that moment. 'Ah, you found it,' he says. More importantly, he looks pleased at her arrival.

'It's all right,' he says, as if he senses her careful steps climbing the once ornate granite stairway. 'A lot of buildings are tagged as condemned, and they haven't crumbled yet. There's been no significant cracks here for a while now.'

'Well, that's reassuring.' Except it's not, other than that Harri is still alive, three years on, despite his heavy stomp upwards.

Finally, up on the sixth floor, he hesitates at a solid wooden door. 'I really hope you're not too shocked,' he says, without humour. 'Or too cold.'

'I'm made of stern stuff,' she jokes.

Beyond the entrance is what might be classed as a typical bedsit back in London. Georgie looks out on one

157

large room, with a small kitchen and bathroom off it, a double bed cordoned off by a dark brocade curtain. The sloping ceiling on one side would have lent a cosy garret-style feel, but for the hole in one corner, shored up with a heavy tarpaulin, moving back and forth rhythmically in the breeze like a set of bellows. The cooking odour masks a slightly lived-in smell of bedding and brick dust, but it's a hundred times more fragrant than some billets she's been in. Slept in, too. Harri's place is raised well above shanty status by the plant pots dotted around, some with stoic-looking leaves, others withered by the temperature and made into mini statues with a series of candles flickering alongside, pushing out a minuscule amount of heat. Harri wasn't joking – it is cold. Georgie watches her breath billow, pleased she added a third layer of clothing just before leaving the Baseler Hof.

'I would offer to take your coat, but that's probably not such a good idea yet,' he jumps into the pause with light humour. He leads her towards a small portable burner, 'away from my source of natural ventilation', and beside what looks like a card table set for two. 'Here, if we huddle by the fire, we may not freeze,' he adds. 'And if we do begin to ice up, there's a decent bar around the corner to warm up in.'

'Something smells good,' she says when he disappears into the small kitchen.

'Oh, that's a relief,' he calls back. 'I thought I might have burnt the soup, only I wouldn't know – can't smell a thing still.'

Georgie's brain quickens. How did he lose his sense of smell, and when? Was it an accident, or trauma? In time, she stows her curiosity. *Enough, Georgie*. Ditch the notebook for one night, enjoy the meal and the company. Be human.

Harri comes back carrying two steaming bowls and several plates of food in relays. He lays down the last, and opens the wine she offers, pouring two glasses of the crisp, clear Riesling. Cold, naturally.

'Nothing so grand as starters, I'm afraid,' he says, sitting opposite. 'It's a sort of German smorgasbord.' In place of a coat, he has on a bulky, hand-knitted blue jumper, patched at the elbows and darned in several places. Again, he sees her looking. 'Warmest thing I have,' he explains, dishing out potato salad.

'I like it,' she says. 'I once tried to knit Max a sweater, but I got into such a terrible mess. There was wool everywhere. I battled with one cuff before I gave up and handed it over to my mother. I tell you, some of those boys in the army can knit way better than I'll ever manage. They even knitted their own socks!'

'And I suppose you wrote an article about that?' He's clearly teasing as he passes over a fork. Under her fingers, Georgie feels warped nodules of metal on the shaft – another reminder of the city's searing past. Nothing, it seems, escaped those flames.

'I did as a matter of fact,' she replies with pride, spooning hot soup into her mouth. 'It went down a storm with the housewives back home, and sold worldwide.'

'Hella made this for me,' Harri adds, stroking at his sleeve. His face turns rapidly towards his own bowl, the expression shrouded by the steam. It's difficult to determine pride or sorrow in his voice.

'I am so sorry you lost them,' is all Georgie can think to say.

'Some days it feels like yesterday, and others, a very long time ago,' he says. 'I suppose in the context of the war – this world now – it is a long way in the past.'

'But it doesn't stop you missing them,' she says. 'And nor should you try.'

Harri's troubled face seems almost melted by the heat of the bowl as he looks up, smiling. 'Thank you for that.' He swallows another mouthful and sits back, thoughtful. 'You know, almost everyone in this city has lost plenty of family members, and in the most horrific circumstances. There's so much damage that your own distress either gets buried in the collective loss, or you don't feel worthy of wearing your pain openly.' He picks at a non-existent speck in the jumper's weave. 'So, it's nice to remember and talk about them. With love instead of guilt.'

This time, Georgie has to ask – her curiosity won't be quashed, but it also seems rude not to. 'How old would your daughter be now?'

'Lily? Oh . . . seven this year,' he calculates. 'And more than likely, she'd be ruling the entire house.' His broad grin falls away as he dishes out more food. 'And you . . . have you and Max thought about a family? Eventually?'

She blames hot soup on her impromptu coughing. 'Erm . . . yes . . . one day, I think. We've been travelling so much, and then the war – it didn't seem right then.'

Her pain is too raw, her own guilt too fresh to air it now. Besides, she's having too nice a time.

He nods, knowingly. 'Lily was born just before the war, and we'd been planning to move to England, ironically. I was all set to work with the London Met, but with a new baby, it took more time to arrange, and then . . . well, you know . . . events overtook us.'

Georgie does know: how the lead-up to Germany's declaration of war was viewed by some, her fellow journalists in particular, as inevitable. From their bird's-eye position in Berlin, the press pack watched it brewing, the full scope of Hitler's arrogance and ambition. The cruelty of it, too. And yet, so many across Europe refused to see the fatal storm descend, relying on human nature in trusting it would blow over. Politicians on both sides were equally to blame, so what hope did the average citizen have in predicting five long years of malice?

'However, we live for today.' Harri stirs himself and raises his glass, the chip in its rim catching against the low candlelight. 'Thank you for forcing me to confront my mess and cook something decent for a change.'

'And very tasty it is too.'

'You can thank my mother. I'm about as good at cooking as you are at knitting,' he says. 'Except for her *Kartoffelsuppe.*'

'Then I am truly honoured.'

'Though it's still cold in here,' he pitches in.

'Yes, still cold. I can't deny it.'

As Harri empties the last of the Riesling, and they scoop up a final mouthful of torte while sitting on the lumpy, patchy sofa, Georgie begins to feel the warmth in her belly trickling down through her limbs. It's the alcohol, inevitably, but the conversation, too. At first meeting, she read Harri Schroder as doleful and tetchy, his frown hiding a complex and wounded persona. He is injured, that's evident, but tonight he is also open and amusing, his whiskered face more and more animated as he talks. In so many ways, he reminds her of Max and their first

161

months in Berlin, that complicated dance of working each other out.

She drops her head back against the worn covers and closes her eyes, suddenly exhausted. 'I've only been here a matter of days, yet it feels like weeks,' she says wearily.

'And what's your impression so far?'

Georgie purses her lips. 'Do you know something? I'm not even sure. It was so much easier in the war. Max and I rarely stayed in one place for too long, and it meant my skills at first impressions were finely tuned. And oddly, the war theatre was chaos with a structure — he hates you, you hate him. Simple. Everyone knew where they stood.'

She opens her eyes to see Harri nod his understanding.

'Now, the walls of the theatre have crumbled,' she goes on, 'and we're left with . . . I don't know, some kind of boggy mess. Exposed. I thought there would be more forgiveness by now, more tolerance, and I can't pin down what it feels like.'

There's a sudden snort of laughter or derision from Harri's direction, which causes Georgie's head to spring up. 'What on earth does that mean?'

Harri's lips form into what looks like a smile, hiding the gravity behind it. Cynicism and scorn combined, if she's reading it right. 'Did you seriously think we Germans would see the Allies as liberating angels, come to save us from ourselves?' he says.

And because there's no malice in Harri's voice, it lends extra weight to his words. Georgie's drowsiness is wiped clean away. 'No! Not at all,' she cries. 'I only thought people might be sick of hurting each other, that we could see others as people, now we're not trying blow our fellow man into oblivion.'

'*We*? Who's we?' Harri prods. The smile is gone and his shoulders tense. 'Georgie, when you've been here a bit longer, and the fog has cleared, you will understand how the Germans and British view each other. More importantly, how the Allies see us.'

'So, tell me,' she challenges. It's not only Harri who's capable of squaring up for a fight.

'All right.' His pupils are glinting redness against the candlelight. 'All Germans are seen as morally bankrupt – both then and now. That includes those considered to be "good Germans" – of which there appear to be few. But there's no respect on either side, and I fear there won't be for a long time. If ever.'

'Do you think that respect is deserved?' she tosses at him. 'After everything, after the camps . . .'

'Ah! Here we have it,' Harri hurls back sarcastically. 'The real reason.'

'What reason?' Georgie can't tell if she's actually annoyed by his tone, or enjoying the argument.

'The guilt,' he says plainly. 'The heavy weight of a nation, that we – people like me – were to blame for Hitler's crimes, that we must have been complicit. Because how could we have *not* known about Auschwitz and Dachau, right here in our own country?' He shakes his head in frustration. 'I see the British looking at us, even those that are in some way tolerant, and I know the question they are really asking: are we more ashamed of losing the war than of the atrocities committed? They think we're not wearing our disgrace openly enough, or begging for forgiveness, again and again.'

Georgie's mouth opens to speak, and then closes again. He has a point. Only yesterday at the Baseler Hof, she came across an old issue of the *British Zone Review*, the magazine of the occupying forces. There, on the front page, was General Montgomery's forthright declaration: 'The defeated enemy must be made to put his house in order.' And some way through the war, hadn't Churchill raged in the House of Commons about Germans as 'savages', an entire race naturally aligned to war and conflict? Harri is right: how can there ever be respect when victorious nations are too busy wagging the finger at the losing side?

She breathes, heavily. Her chest feels dense with sadness. 'If it's worth anything, it's not what I believe,' she says quietly.

'But I'm guessing you have asked that question at some point, to yourself, if not openly?' He cocks his head quizzically. 'How could Germans let it happen?'

'Probably. Yes, I suppose I have.'

'Lord knows, Georgie, I'm ashamed of what Hitler did,' Harri goes on. 'But did you know that in a free election – until he banned them – the Nazis never achieved more than thirty-eight per cent of the vote? Thirty-eight per cent! Well over half the German nation voted against him.'

Georgie *is* aware of that fact, but it doesn't seem the time to admit it, since Harri's passion clearly needs an outlet right now. 'But you can understand the bitterness?' she says instead. 'Why those in Britain and America, the Russians too, think like they do. That someone needs to be held to account.'

'Of course,' he agrees. 'And I would be the first to string up those Nazi bastards at the camps, in the SS or the Gestapo. The generals, too. I *will* apologise for those crimes carried out in the name of my country, but I will *not* apologise for being German. In the same way you would never feel shame for being British, and nor should you.'

He stops. Finally, he breathes. There's no flare, blaze or brimstone coming from across the sofa, but she has witnessed his quiet rage. And perhaps that of many Germans. The question for her remains: how to drive home that sentiment to the public reading their newspapers over their acute rationing of bacon and eggs in suburban Britain, side by side with reports from the ongoing Nuremberg trials, the atrocities of the concentration camps laid painfully bare? More and more, this is shaping up to be an impossible task.

Harri heaves himself off the sofa, runs towards the kitchen and comes back with a small enamel pot and cups. 'Peace offering,' he says. 'Fritz and his lovely Maxwell House again.'

'I wasn't aware you and I were at war,' she replies in surprise.

He looks up from pouring the hot coffee, frowning. 'We weren't – aren't. Are we? I just enjoy a good, meaty exchange every so often. It's another thing I miss.' He pauses, mid-pour. 'And I don't know what it is, Georgie Young, but you have a very strange effect on me. I feel I need to say things, about myself.'

'Maybe I should take up your suggestion and become a police officer after all?'

'Oh no,' he says lightly. 'I've changed my mind on that. You'd be far better placed interrogating for the Allies, weeding out the Nazis, the ones who are slinking away like the average man in the street. The ones slipping through the net. Georgie Young – crack Nazi-hunter.' He laughs at the thought.

'I'll bear that in mind if I ever need another career. In the meantime, I have an article to write. Or perhaps several.'

The coffee, and Harri's 'exchange', wakes them up, and although it's not late, he offers to walk her back to the U-Bahn. Georgie quickens her step down the stairwell as a sprinkling of plaster dust drifts from above.

'Happens all the time,' Harri assures glibly. 'A bit like the people here, there's plenty more to hold it together yet.'

'But isn't it this way?' She points towards the U-Bahn as he strides in the opposite direction.

'I want to show you something first – one more slice of Hamburg life.' He reaches for her hand, more in a bid to help her negotiate the mounds of rubble, then hesitates. 'That is, if you want.'

'Yes, of course.'

With a lighter in his other hand, they stumble towards darkened ruins, where either someone has cleared a pathway through the debris, or the footfall has created one. Aside from the tiny flame, it's pitch dark and bitterly cold, prompting Georgie to think of the girls on Harri's chalkboard back at the station, what they sensed in following their killer into the ruins: dread, or lust, or hope? Surely only hope of something much better would entice anyone into this black abyss?

She's roused from morbid thoughts by faint strains of music in the distance, and with them, a glow emerging between the blackened bones of the ruins. Gradually, the notes of a stringed instrument become more distinct, and soon she and Harri arrive at the seat of the sound:

a circle of listeners gathered around a lone, shabby violinist, a small fire beside him. The acoustics from his bow are soaring skywards, echoing off the roofless ruin, a crystal-clear tune that Georgie recognises as the beautiful and haunting Adagio for Strings by Albinoni. She's no music scholar, but it's the one already chosen for her funeral, she and Max having had that frank discussion at the war's outset, 'just in case something happens'. It's the saddest, and yet the most satisfying piece of music she's ever heard.

Georgie scans the faces of the audience that stands silent and still – at least half have tears running down their cheeks, small rivulets picked out by the flicker of firelight. Harri stops in front, his back to her; instantly they join the twenty or so people transfixed by the sorrow and the clarity of this man's playing, his face contorting with each effort and note. Those collected are freezing, inevitably, and yet unable to tear themselves away from the sound that acts like a magnet, because for a small portion of time they seem able to forget or remember – whichever is most comforting – and feel certain there is some beauty remaining in this otherwise ugly world.

The piece finishes, and there's a ripple of applause, muffled by hands bound in wool or material to act like gloves. The musician lifts up his head and smiles at the compliments pushed his way, more so at the empty violin case by his side, slowly filling with a few pfennigs, the odd cigarette, half a slice of something – whatever people have in their pockets and feel they can spare. The man bathes in their appreciation, knowing gratitude alone won't keep him warm or fed into the early hours.

'Beautiful,' Georgie breathes, plumbing the depths of

her satchel for some Reichsmarks. 'I don't think I've heard anything so lovely in a long time.'

'He's here almost every evening,' Harri says. 'Apparently, he used to be a key player in one of the main orchestras.'

'And is there no chance of going back to that?' she wonders. 'I thought the British were feeding some money into the arts.'

'Hmm, when I say he's here most evenings, I think there's a reason why he's not present every day,' Harri says, tapping at his temple. The musician may have his precious fingers intact, but plenty of wounds go beyond skin deep.

'Come on, let's get you to that train,' Harri says as the crowd disperses. 'You and I have got work to do in the morning.'

'Thank you for a lovely evening,' Georgie says at the U-Bahn entrance. 'Dinner *and* a concert. I couldn't have asked for more, especially as I bulldozed my way into your home so blatantly.'

Harri laughs. 'Think nothing of it. I now have a tidier hovel to go back to. I'll send a note if anything happens on the case. Have a good day tomorrow. Have you got plans?'

'More touring on foot with Zofia,' she says, stifling a yawn, followed by a groan. 'Then I'm facing dinner with a Major Stephens and his wife. I have to say that public relations is *not* my forte.' She stops suddenly. 'I don't suppose you would wan—'

'Oh no, no!' Harri holds his hands up in defence. 'I'm definitely not the major's favourite policeman. And can you imagine the conversation with a German present?

One that's technically ex–SS. Thanks, but I'll stick to my soup leftovers.'

'Coward,' she teases.

'Better coward than cowed,' he shoots back, waves and turns. 'Good night, Miss Young.'

CHAPTER TWENTY-FOUR: BITTER REALITY

15th February 1946

Georgie

Georgie stares up into the corner of the room, transfixed for some unknown reason by a square of cardboard stuck to the ceiling by damp – once a beer carton by the looks of the printed letters on the side. Its edges have melded into the plaster, and if this room ever sees a pot of paint again, it will simply be brushed over, adopted forever into the fabric. Underneath, two children, anywhere between six and eight years old, sit at a ramshackle table, stuffing the bread that Georgie has brought into their mouths, lips greasy with the tiny amount of butter she's haggled for.

'Why aren't these ones at school?' she asks their mother.

'We've only two pairs of shoes between four children,' the woman shrugs. 'It's not their turn today.'

'They call it "shoe-absenteeism",' Zofia adds as she translates. 'It's common across the city nowadays.'

The stories are repeated from hut to hut as Georgie and Zofia make their way down Langenhorner Chaussee, the lines of emergency wooden housing with four walls, but as many as eighteen people and six families under one roof, the floorspace reduced to inches. Malnutrition is rife, children and adults covered in small, flat carbuncles of vitamin deficiency, eyes bulging and complexions sallow. Georgie winces at a pitiful, weak wail coming from within blankets and the woman's resigned expression as she attaches her newborn with little hope of satisfying. It's hard for Georgie to tell which aches more – her belly or her heart.

After life in the camps, Zofia seems more stoic in the face of such distress, but it leaves Georgie hollowed out by the cold and the sorrow, one tragedy after another, the sight of men home from the front sitting listlessly in the corner, broken bones and minds with flat, vacant expressions. She wonders if they mirror some of the British forces, returning to women and wives hardened by war in the men's absence. How it's changed everyone, for better or worse.

At lunchtime, Georgie suggests heading back to the hotel, via the Victory Club and the NAAFI shop. Zofia's nose is blue and her fingertips white, but she's undeterred in her own search and heads off to the unofficial refugee camp at Fuhlsbüttel. Georgie never needs to ask why – that endless quest for her sister again. 'How long will you keep going?' she asks.

Zofia shrugs, though her answer is fully automatic. 'Until I find her,' she replies, stepping away with her usual determination.

In a corner of the hotel lobby furnished with a desk

and typewriter, Georgie spends the afternoon typing up her notes and slotting them into some sort of order. For some time, she's entirely locked in her own world, reliving the pained recollections of the refugees, focused on conjuring a thread to her piece so that it doesn't sound like one large sob story, but a measured essay on suffering, devoid of bias or nationality. A piece about people, full stop. It swallows her focus for almost two hours, and it's not until Klaus, the young receptionist, approaches and tentatively asks: 'Is everything all right, Miss Young?' that she appreciates the heavy clattering coming from her corner of the parlour, quite how much emotion is being driven into the keys under her fingers and the resulting racket.

'Yes, I'm fine, thank you,' she says. The tears welling in her eyes tell her otherwise, but Klaus isn't close enough to notice, and she blinks them back before he does. What she wouldn't do for Max to be close right now, to understand how deep this goes.

Back in her room, Georgie reviews her limited wardrobe, irritated by even having to make a choice. Ordinarily, a formal dinner with Hamburg's privileged forces would be low on her list of scenarios, and yet what's *not* being said could prove to be quite revealing. Over time, she's learnt the benefit of keeping the military on your side, the army wives and their gossip being a vital source.

Generally, she loathes this sort of thing, with its starchy decorum and the need to dress up. In fact, the one and only day of the year when she separates her glad rags from their mothballs is the annual press dance, a raucous and liquor-filled night at the Ritz in London, when the length and breadth of Fleet Street suspends any fierce rivalry for the day's best scoop, drinking and cavorting into the early hours. It holds a special place in her heart, too, since that's where she first encountered Max, though the memory of their initial exchange seems farcical now – like two pieces of flint sparking off each other. Not exactly love at first sight. The adoration and respect came some way after the initial irritation.

In front of the wardrobe mirror, she holds up the long-sleeved woollen dress rooted out from among the racks at the NAAFI shop and marries it with a silken scarf found in one of the surviving department stores facing onto the Alster. With a touch of lipstick and the tiny gold earrings Max gave her for Christmas, it will do. It will have to, because she has nothing else. As much as she begrudges the airs and graces of such occasions, it is work. *Lump it or like it, George.*

A long soak in the bath definitely helps. Pleased to hear Zofia moving about her room next door and that she is safely 'home', Georgie washes her hair and makes some attempt at styling it, plumps her lips with colour and draws a black kohl line on the insides of both eyelids, her only concession to wearing make-up, either at home or out in the field. She sits back, satisfied at her own reflection; Max once remarked the eyeliner transformed her into a cat.

'Do you mean smug, like the one that got the cream?' she'd asked.

He shook his head. 'Sleek and alluring, more like a Siamese, or even a tigress,' he replied. 'A little bit scary, in fact.'

'Oh good. I must wear it more often.'

'Come on, George,' she says aloud into the mirror now. 'Shall we put this cat among those army pigeons?'

CHAPTER TWENTY-FIVE:
BREWING

15th February 1946

Meta

All day there's been a mood across the city, an indistinct thrum under the concrete that Meta feels through the thin soles of her boots. At intervals, she's stopped at a crossroads or beside a mound of stacked bricks and raised her nose to the sky. There's been nothing to see, and no sound to pinpoint, merely a tension that sits heavy on the icy wind, like the pressure of an incoming storm. Now, as darkness descends across Hamburg's centre, she senses that – far from dissipating with the daylight – it's brewing. Simmering.

She's felt that flip to her stomach many times before, of impending disaster. Back then, it was accompanied by a drone from the clouds above, a swarm of angry bees in Allied formation ready to unleash their wrath. Deadly bees with a fiery, explosive sting. With her pin-sharp

175

hearing, Meta had become the reliable look-out in their neighbourhood in those early war years. When she ran for cover into the basement of her family's apartment, so did everyone else. Only some couldn't run fast enough, caught in the swarm and the flames aimed so accurately.

Now, she sniffs the air again and catches the tang off the Alster – there's no fire, not yet anyway. But something isn't right. This time, she goes not underground, but towards it. This is Meta's city, and her intent these days is to find out what's going on.

CHAPTER TWENTY-SIX:
TORTE AND TANTRUMS

15th February 1946

Georgie

It's dark when the army staff car deposits her outside a large, double-front door in Hamburg's suburbs at seven p.m., having travelled through relatively clear streets for about twenty minutes and onto a long gravel driveway.

'Are we anywhere near the Elbe?' Georgie asks the driver.

'Yes, miss. It's at the bottom of the garden here.'

She's trying to tune into any movement of water when the door opens and casts a rectangle of light on the broad step. 'Miss Young? Please do come in before you catch your death.' The accent is pure Home Counties, more friendly and less off-hand than expected.

Major Stephens' wife reflects the glow of the house, in being warm and welcoming, scooping Georgie into a large, well-lit hallway. 'Please, do call me Olivia,' she insists.

She's likely in her fifties, with only a few wisps of grey left untouched by brown hair dye. It hasn't, however, left Olivia Stephens looking harsh, as sometimes can happen with slightly older women. Her light maternal manner chips away at the mould of an army wife. 'Come in, come in, oh it's so nice to have a new face.' She leans into Georgie with a conspiratorial whisper as they walk towards the parlour: 'And someone with a fresh voice.'

Georgie takes off her coat and is just about to apologise for her lack of evening wear when the hostess steps in with her practised etiquette. 'I do love that dress, dear! So stylish, and also very sensible in these temperatures.'

Put at ease, Georgie decides she likes the major's wife already. The question is: will her husband kick against the stereotype too?

He doesn't. Not at first glance, anyway. He sports no typical moustache favoured by so many senior officers, but the parting in his precisely cut hair is razor-sharp, and the gleam in his eye tells Georgie he didn't gain his epaulettes without guile or valour, and perhaps a propensity to be callous when the situation demands. Like war. But that's just first impressions, and Georgie is well aware that if she relied on those alone, she wouldn't have a husband in Max.

'So lovely to meet you, Miss Young.' The major steps forward and grasps at her hand. His is firm and warm, and he leaves it there, holding Georgie's gaze in unison, and for a second she has the measure of him. Because it's exactly what she used to do when she wanted to engage the military hierarchy on or near the front line. She sought to enchant, because she wanted something of them. So, what does Major Stephens want from her?

'I've been an avid reader of your reports during the conflict,' he goes on. 'You leave no stone unturned.' His black pupils cut away finally.

'I try, Major.'

She's introduced to the other guests: an army captain and his wife, plus a naval officer apparently on manoeuvres nearby, and Lieutenant Howarth, who arrives minutes after she does and apologises for being late, shooting Georgie a knowing look. There's seven in total and it's better than she envisaged, in being swamped by army talk.

The first two courses go well enough, and the food is the freshest she's eaten since arriving in Hamburg. Being Georgie, she studies the face of the house Frau serving up dishes of buttery potatoes and vegetables that are not grey, wondering if, secretly, she harbours resentment at having to work for British occupiers, resigned that it's a simple trade for a warm house and well-stocked kitchen. There's nothing to discern, though, and the woman dishing up looks merely blank.

It's when dessert arrives and yet another bottle of wine is opened that the conversation rises several notches. Major Stephens has been fairly reserved up until this point, boasting in a small way about the progress the British are making with repatriation and reeling off a list of successes. Georgie glances at Howarth, who only nods when called upon by the major to confirm the vast numbers of refugees resettled and homed. Opinions about Germans are reserved to say the least, Mrs Stephens working hard to keep a lid on a simmering pot: 'Freya, more wine, please', or 'Shall we have the cheese now?'

But with the level of alcohol consumed around the table, the pot lid was never going to stay put.

'So, Miss Young, tell me what you think of the Hamburg you've seen so far,' the major challenges.

Glancing up, Georgie sees Howarth cease chewing, and a second of utter silence appears to be noted by all. More wine is sipped to fill the space.

'Gordon, you can't put poor Georgie on the spot like that,' Mrs Stephens chides, perhaps sensing that steam is about to escape.

'Nonsense! She's a reporter, and doubtless been in far hotter spots than this,' Stephens bristles, his words tossed at Georgie with an implacable nod. 'Isn't that right?'

'I suppose I have,' she concedes. Opposite, Howarth visibly stiffens.

'Well then?' Stephens won't leave it alone. 'What of the British zone?'

Georgie lays down her spoon. 'If I'm entirely honest, Major, I am surprised at the level of chaos.'

Poor Howarth appears to choke on his apple torte.

'Chaos?' the major blusters, entirely in keeping with the rising colour of his cheeks. 'Of course there's a level of unease. I mean the Germans don't want us here, that's obvious. But it's equally evident that this country is incapable of policing itself, and needs help to do it.'

Georgie's thoughts swerve instantly to Harri and his frustration. To last night and a very different conversation.

'Don't you agree, Miss Young?' the major prods firmly, the bonhomie of the evening suddenly tipped towards confrontation.

'I agree there is plenty to do, in rebuilding and rehoming,' Georgie begins tentatively, if only for the sake of her hostess. 'But what I also see is a lot of excess, breeding resentment among the Germans.'

180

'Excess? What excess?' the captain pipes up, his ratio of wine to water so far has caused his words to slur a little, and he evidently can't see his own crimson flesh as a prime example of indulgence. Nor can he hold back. 'They are never satisfied,' he says, waving his cutlery with overegged gestures. 'We give them places to live, food on the table – leaving the British at home on rations, I might add – and they repay us with endless complaints. We're not doing enough, fast enough, always whining. Maybe they ought to have Hitler back and see how that works out? Bloody ingrates.'

His wife reaches out a hand and places it gingerly over his knuckles, her face pale with embarrassment. Stephens does nothing but fiddle with his glass and Howarth appears not to be breathing at all.

Georgie only just refrains from sweeping her hand across the table as a case in point. *Diplomacy, girl. Part of the job.* 'I think the forces here are doing a good job, but the captain is right – she's pleased to turn his argument on its head – 'because it isn't enough, not yet.'

'What the . . .' the captain attempts to counter.

'Clearly, it's *not* enough when people are dying from TB or the effects of malnutrition,' she cuts him off firmly, 'or women are unable to feed their babies, suffering miscarriages because their bodies are too weak to sustain a pregnancy.'

The table is silent, even from a scraping of spoons. *May as well*, Georgie thinks, *while I have a captive audience.* 'I also think the situation is clouded by an abundance of alcohol. From what I've heard, tempers are fuelled, and there has been violence . . .'

'Well, it's clear that the Germans do like a drink.' The

major makes a stab at lightening the mood, sweeping the table with his eyes for endorsement.

'From the British side,' Georgie qualifies swiftly. 'The servicemen in particular. Assaults and robberies, for which the culprits are not held to account, as I understand it.' She takes a breath of courage. 'Possibly much worse.'

This time, Major Stephens stiffens visibly and the temperature in the room plummets, despite a roaring fire in the grate. 'What do you mean by that?' he demands. If anyone could be said to sober up instantly, then this is one such time.

'Well, only that—'

'Major?' The voice of the German housekeeper projects from the doorway into the dining room.

'Yes, Freya?' he barks in response.

'A messenger, sir. He says it's very urgent.'

Gordon Stephens gestures for the captain to follow him out into the hallway, and the relief around the table is palpable, on Howarth's face especially. 'They're never off duty, are they?' the captain's wife offers with an insipid smile.

'No, dear.' Poor Olivia Stephens looks as if she wants to be swallowed by the vast recesses of her own home.

Georgie, however, is more curious at what's being discussed in the hallway. She hears the urgency of whispers barely kept under control beyond the door. 'Where's your bathroom?' she asks lightly.

The major lowers his voice when he sees Georgie emerge into the hallway, pushing further into the small huddle that he and the captain have made with the messenger. 'Tell them I'll be there immediately,' she hears him say. She makes out only one word in the next sentence, but it's enough.

When she returns to the dining room, having employed the battlefield skill of emptying her bladder in double-quick time, the major is already pulling on his overcoat.

'Can't someone else go?' Olivia is entreating her husband. 'Really, Gordon, I know duty calls and all that, but there are others who can manage.'

He ignores her, turning to a driver who has arrived in the doorway. 'Rotherbaum, please, Private. Fast as you can. Good night, everyone.' He flashes Georgie a look, and a knowing, hesitant smile.

'I had better go too,' Georgie says to Mrs Stephens as the major's jeep accelerates away. 'Early start tomorrow.'

'I'll share a car with you,' Howarth jumps in, grabbing the opportunity of escape.

The look of dejection and disappointment on their hostess's face almost convinces Georgie to stay. But not quite.

In the back of the car, she taps the driver on the shoulder. 'Can you take me to Rotherbaum, please?'

Howarth turns to face her, half reproachful, part smile. 'Really, Miss Young, what are you up to?'

'Well, you don't think I'm going back to my hotel, do you? Not when there's a full-scale riot going on.'

CHAPTER TWENTY-SEVEN:
FIRES OF HELL

15th February 1946

Harri

The call comes in as he's leaving for the day, scuppering another visit to Fritz and his under-the-counter remedies.

'Damn it!' Harri mutters under his breath, though it's soon apparent the order is not for his squad alone, but the whole of Davidwache to attend. It won't be another murder, at least. Instead, there are whispers of 'riot' rippling along the ranks as they squat in the back of army trucks. Harri's insides lurch, with or without the potholes under the wheels: has the news of the Puppet Master leaked out? The public railing against a murderer picking off women – German women, with hints of Allied involvement – and the resultant frustration? He feels nauseous with hunger and wretched anticipation.

The air is already glowing red as Polizei spill from the truck, and yet tinged with a certain relief for Harri:

the crowd's fury is white hot, swelling with tension, but he senses very quickly that the root cause is *not* a homicidal maniac. This mass of bodies – hundreds, if not a thousand or more – is up in arms about something equally vital, though in this day and age, you could take your pick as to which issue would light the tinderbox of unrest.

As a senior officer, Harri directs the ranks to the outer limits, to skirt around and corral any spill of violence rather than rush at an already incensed horde. He hoists himself onto the upright girder of a factory wall to gain a better view, seeing not the frenzied faces of out-and-out rebels, but the gaunt expressions of ordinary people whose only desire is to survive. *What in the hell am I doing here, obstructing their right to live?*

A rapid, red heat arrests Harri's doubt in its tracks, a fiery missile exploding directly under his feet and flashing upwards, flames licking mercilessly at his ankles. But rather than jump free, he's suddenly frozen, rendered catatonic and rigid with fear as he clings with both hands onto the iron lintel. He's both mesmerised and terrified by the sea of orange below, fed with oxygen and his own memories – of that time, of death, of a world devoid of hope. In the near distance, the eyes of the mass glow like demons. He tastes desperation as the acrid smoke chokes into his nostrils, the heat prickling through the soles of his shoes, and yet his fingers refuse to let go of the jagged metal.

'Harri? HARRI! SCHRODER!' A voice cuts through the terror, one of the uniformed inspektors at Davidwache. 'Move, man! *MOVE!*'

The vehemence of the order finally overtakes the dread of the flames below and sense wins out. Harri's fingers release and he plunges into the ring of fire, as the inspektor rushes to pull him free, dousing the singeing of his ankles with his heavy jacket.

'Get into the truck,' the policeman orders.

'But . . . the crowd,' Harri protests. 'I need to . . .'

The inspektor stares at him intently. Knowingly. 'Into the truck, Schroder. We've got reinforcements coming any minute, and you need to get that hand seen to.'

Harri looks down and feels the throb on his right palm for the first time, watching it pulse red. 'All right.' In the back of the troop carrier, he's infused with a guilt that's outbid by relief, burying his head in the seared, scored flesh of his hands. *Oh Hella, my darling. When will the good memories triumph over the bad?*

CHAPTER TWENTY-EIGHT:
BREAD AND FURY

15th February 1946

Meta

Sparks flying, a volley of blazing bottles are tossed high into the air above, leaving Meta to wonder how many unwelcome memories are being stoked by the very sight. It's three years since the firestorm – the blistering inferno that engulfed Hamburg for seven long nights – and any blaze, however small, is enough to conjure nightmares of Hades on earth. At the same time, this crowd is outraged, too determined and deprived to be beaten back by flames, by the police who are fearful of forcing control, or the army troops just arrived, brandishing their guns. This is the tincture of unrest that's been hovering all day, disquiet bubbling under the icy crust of a frozen city, in the bunkers and rat runs of the homeless and dispossessed. Hunger breeds lethargy, but every so often something happens to galvanise even the starving.

A smouldering rage has melted a small hole in the crust and this is the result.

Word on the street told of a flour consignment being delivered in the west of the city, and flour means bread, the staff of life to so many these days. People had gathered, hoping to buy some off the Tommies willing to make money on the side before the raw ingredients reached the bread factory. It turned out to be Hamburg's worst-kept secret of the day, and too many had congregated, Meta similarly drawn to the fray. She has no means of baking loaves, but knows plenty who could, affording her a slice of the profits.

At first it was just pushing and shoving among those squeezed around the back of one supply truck, then a small retaliation by an overzealous squaddie – a woman and child had fallen to the ground, some blood spilt. In the context of the city's daily hardships, it was nothing. In among this throng, however, it's everything, the spark to light a dry dust of rebellion.

And now the air is ablaze. Molotov cocktails are tossed liberally at the military line being formed, quickly reinforced by squaddies attempting to push back the increasingly angry mob. Meta wonders where the dissidents sourced the fuel, perhaps reckoning that resistance will bring a bigger return, rather than bartering the prized commodity of petrol; gambling on the authorities releasing more bread in a fair exchange for sending their precious fuel up in smoke. But that's just her mind, always calculating. By the looks of it, the crowd itself is powered by passion and anger.

A chant rises up and echoes suddenly into the night sky: 'Give us bread, give us bread' – mouths spitting fury alongside sparks from the missiles. Meta joins in at first, raising her fist to add to the physical wave of unrest, but she soon skirts around the edges to do what she does best. To spy. For a brief second, Popo catches her eye, sidling between bodies; she guesses he'll be looking for quarry even now, to pick the little they have in their pockets. She sags with disappointment, because she likes Popo and it's a side of him she'd rather not see. Even thieves like her have morals, only targeting the wealthy and the British. But not Popo, it seems.

Meta turns away, assessing there's little of worth in staying. The crowd will spiral, peak and then the fire will go out in their bellies, as hunger and cold take over. The British may well release more resources in days to come, but not tonight. They won't yield when confronted with insurgence, since saving face is all part of keeping the peace. And so she's better served by getting sleep and hitting the streets early tomorrow, for any fresh prospects created by this turbulence.

It's then that she spots her – the woman. Georgie. Ploughing into the crowd and pulling something from her bag as she does so, a brief glimpse of her face that's lit by the glow, but also by something Meta is glad to see. Determination, if she's not wrong.

Her mouth curls into a tiny smile, because she likes that. Someone is on their side.

CHAPTER TWENTY-NINE:
THE SPILL

15th February 1946

Georgie

She curses her lack of boots as she leaps onto the pavement, barely hearing Howarth's call of 'Be careful' as she slams the car door. Georgie is only thankful she didn't buy a pair of heels from the NAAFI and instead made do with her brogues for the dinner – they are mercifully flat, though the soles cause her to slip on the ice underfoot. The dress she hitches up over her knees for easy movement.

In minutes, her German – less and less rusty through necessity – has gauged the reason for this uprising. 'They are holding back the bread,' one woman shouts into the crowd. 'My children are starving,' another rails. As Georgie pushes further towards the front, it's populated by taller, more imposing bodies of men, voicing their anger, the rage of each one feeding another and soaring to greater heights. She has that ripple in her gut she's felt multiple times, of something about to tip over the edge, out of control. She tastes danger. But that innate sense of her place as an observer, as somehow removed from the core of peril, cancels out any nerves. She's here to do a job, and it's then that Max floods her vision, darting around with his camera, flashbulb popping, adrenalin coursing through him and high on the images he commits to film. Suddenly, she misses the comfort of his firefly presence.

She watches as a staff car screeches to a halt, close to the supply trucks lined up, still the focal point of the protest as the crowd attempts to press forwards. Georgie easily recognises Major Stephens by his build and demeanour, locking heads with several military and striding towards the crowd. He and another man climb onto the open platform of one truck, each with a rudimentary loudhailer in hand.

'*ACHTUNG, RUHE!*' he bellows into the metal cone. '*RUHE! RUHE!*'

The crowd noise does fall, levelling slightly, enough for Stephens to raise the hailer again. 'I understand your grievance,' he continues in English, pausing as an army man beside him repeats the same in German. 'But this . . . gathering will not resolve the issues, of the supply or how you feel.'

The crowd whistles and groans. Shouts of 'Fuck off, Tommy!' in concise English are lobbed in his direction, loud enough for Stephens to hear.

The major is undeterred. 'You need to disperse,' he goes on. 'I pledge that we will meet with your representatives to improve the supply lines, endeavour to open more factories for food production.'

He waits for the translator to catch up, and then is forced to pause some more at the verbal outrage which follows, words and fuel-primed bottles fired like arrows towards the flatbed of the truck.

'FUCKING LIAR,' one man nearby screams.

'PIGS!' lobs another.

'How long will we have to wait?' A woman's shout is lost in the scornful whistles filling the air as Stephens neatly sidesteps a missile landing close to him. Having been introduced to his character so very recently, Georgie pictures his features trying to mask a contemptuous look, plus his smugness at the projectile missing its target.

Only the next one doesn't. And that's when it gets more than heated. When the crowd are tipped over the precipice, spores of poison spraying forth.

The first shot comes from somewhere near the truck, possibly aimed into the air as a warning. Except it has the opposite effect – a red rag to a bull. The mass surges violently and Georgie's last sight before she is sucked beneath the undertow of bodies is the face of the translator up on the platform, the full horror of what he sees reflected in his features.

In among the turmoil of flesh and fabric, further shots are muffled and covered by the screams. If Hamburg runs daily on chaos, now there is out-and-out pandemonium, women couching their young ones within coats, people desperate not to lose their footing and be trampled under the sea of bodies. Georgie stumbles several times, feeling limbs under her shoes, but can't see or help having to stand on them. She's grateful for another skill gained out of necessity in wartime, on many a transport vessel carrying troops somewhere in the midst of very rough seas – the ability to roll with the ground underneath you, not to lose your footing and keep the horizon within sight.

Staggering but still upright, she doesn't see an elbow pull back at head height, only feeling the glancing blow to her cheekbone and eye socket, felling her into the crowd. This time, there are no bodies below to cushion her fall; panic floods Georgie's brain as her hands are swept and pinned underneath her, leaving her head at the mercy of the lurching crowd. Instinctively, she curls as much as she can, arms still trapped under a swell of humanity pressing down on her right, her left side ground into concrete devoid of cushioning snow. It's more terrifying than anything on the battlefield, gasping for breath, wondering if – instead of a stray bullet – a heavy boot will rain down and rob her of consciousness. And more.

There's no life flashing before her eyes, only muddy boots and street sludge, and no helping hand either. It's up to her. Driven by dread, Georgie squirms frantically in her confined space, frees up her hands and – with every muscle and sinew in her body – rights herself on the ground like a crouched animal. With one more almighty effort, she pushes with her legs to standing and, using the apex of the truck as her sightline, staggers her way out of the crowd, the vista blurred with fiery orange and the bright white of army spotlights. Breathless and blinking, she sees the horde gradually dispersing as people are hauled up, one by one. The shooting has stopped, but the screaming hasn't, its volume rising when two bodies stay down, unable to be pulled up. Ever.

'There's one dead!' a man's voice hollers.

'It's two!' another adds.

Her vision clearing, Georgie looks towards the platform, where Stephens has no doubt been scooted away to safety. The poor translator is running the gamut of abuse and missiles, though in the panic the attacks are piecemeal and much less co-ordinated, fear and bullets having pierced the solidarity. In wartime, people have been killed over less than a slice of bread, but in the peace? Georgie feels bruised inside and out, her heart taking the full brunt.

'Go home,' the translator shrieks through the megaphone, over and over. 'All those remaining will be arrested.'

German police begin to flood the area, proving less incendiary than the army in trying to reclaim control. The two felled bodies are ghosted away quickly into ambulances, their weeping relatives bundled into the back. The cloying smoke rises and begins to disperse, and for a single second, the scene reminds Georgie of the Victory Day aftermath. Except then the streets were smeared with ticker-tape debris and she was awash with hysteria and the joy of relief, her cheeks damp with kisses from strangers. Now, there's grime underfoot and she puts a hand to her pulsing flesh to feel a wetness under her eye, pulls it away and sees a slick, viscous red that's already begun to congeal. She runs both hands over her head, knowing from experience that serious wounds don't always register pain, having once witnessed an American soldier trying to stand on a leg that was no longer there, almost oblivious to the grenade detonated right under him. Thankfully, Georgie feels her skull is intact, despite a monstrous headache already beginning to cloud her thinking.

She stumbles to the side of the road and sits on the wet, slushy pavement to centre herself, watching legs moving away and squinting into the distance to test her vision. The cold seeps into her dress and a shiver ripples through her entire body, pained and numbed in tandem.

'Georgie! What are you doing here?' Zofia stands before her, face racked with shock and disbelief.

'Uh, I got caught up in the crowd.' Inside her head, there's a jackhammer doing its worst.

'We need to get you to the hospital. Come on, I'll find a taxi.'

'No, no, not the hospital,' Georgie protests, trying to stand up but managing only halfway. 'They have enough to do. It looks worse than it is, really.'

'Are you sure about that?' Zofia says. 'At the very least, let's get you back to the hotel. They'll have a first-aid kit.' The tables have turned, and Zofia quickly assumes control of the situation, something Georgie is only too grateful for. Her body is suddenly begging for sleep.

'Just wait here,' Zofia instructs, levering Georgie down to the pavement edge again. 'I won't be long.'

She's back within minutes and guides Georgie to a waiting taxi, which must have taken some persuading after news of the riot spread across the city. At the Baseler Hof, Zofia swings into action, running a bath and helping Georgie sink gingerly under the warm water, the bruises on both sides of her body already blooming into deep purple welts.

Mercifully, the jackhammer has slowed to a dull ache, allowing some clarity of thought. 'What were *you* doing there tonight, Zofia?'

'I heard the rumours, and went to take a look,' she replies, gently cleaning Georgie's head wound with iodine.

'But why?'

'To look for her.' Zofia stops for a minute, hands hovering, as if the answer is obvious. 'Where there's a crowd, there's always a chance, isn't there?'

'Yes, I suppose so.'

It's Zofia who begins to question then. Mercifully, for Georgie, it's not the grilling she herself sometimes exerts, more a way of keeping the conversation moving and ensuring the 'patient' stays awake.

'Where did you learn to do this?' Georgie sighs, eyes closed, sensing the form of her mother leaning over the side of the bath and not a woman at least eight years younger. 'This nursing, and caring.'

There's a second's hesitation. 'I used to help in the infirmary. At the camp.'

'Oh.'

Zofia's breath halts. Is she deliberating, perhaps? On letting go. 'It was a way of keeping myself whole,' she says at last.

'Despite what you saw?'

'Yes.' Zofia sniffs and her tone lightens. 'Huh, perhaps it runs in the family. My sister did the same at Ravensbrück, apparently. And yet, when we were younger, you would never have pictured us as nurses. I always hoped to work in engineering. It must be what war brings out in you.'

Georgie nods her head gingerly, but even that hurts. 'And now, are you tempted – to make a career of it? In medicine perhaps?'

'Maybe.' Georgie opens her eyes to see Zofia's expression cloud over. 'After. Plenty of other things to do first.' She blinks twice and it's clear their discourse is over.

Despite protestations, Zofia refuses to let her patient sleep alone, making up a bed for herself on the small sofa in

Georgie's room. 'I'll need to check on you,' she says, in a voice that will brook no opposition.

Some aspirin dulls the headache enough for Georgie to sink into sleep, surfacing at intervals, with a wave of pain each time she shifts. In her sleep fog, she wonders when and how she could have been run over by a London bus, and why the spectre of Max looms over her, muttering reassurances and then retreating from sight.

CHAPTER THIRTY:
BLOOD AND BLACKMAIL

16th February 1946

Harri

He's managed only three hours' sleep, and it is a Saturday, but a heavy sense of remorse drives Harri into Davidwache the next morning. Besides which, it's the best distraction from the nagging pain under his heavily bandaged hand.

Or it was, until he sees Paula's face.

'Don't bother taking your coat off,' she says as he enters the Kripo office. She looks him straight in the eye, no explanation needed.

'Where is she?'

'Ruins just north of the docks.'

'Oh Christ.'

On the journey over, Harri's guilt stacks ever higher; while he was out playing policeman at the riot (and not a very effective one, either), their killer was busy taking advantage, doing his worst. Outside of what once acted as a front door on Sachsen Strasse, he swallows a lungful of crisp, cold air while his heart muscle shrinks. The word 'escalation' rams at his brain, a term generals use in wartime for conflict increasing day by day. In this so-called peace, another body so soon is significant; a *need* for their culprit to feed his murderous urge. Up until now, the Kripo team have had the luxury – if you can call it that – of weeks until their predator singles out another victim. This is just a matter of days.

Resigned, Harri steps into a scene of carnage, the air odourless in his nostrils, but cloying all the same, a metallic taint of someone's inner core on his tongue. He swallows back anger, sadness and bile. There's nothing right from the second he sees her, lying at the centre of her own slaughter. It's utterly wrong because she's lying butchered, but there is something else – he glances over at Paula, whose face reflects his reservations. From three previous murder scenes, they know the Puppet Master stages and controls his showground, taking his time. By contrast, this display is a frenzied slash and run, blood splatters sinking into the beige rubble dust, some still fresh and glistening like rubies under the morning light. The woman is blonde, like Ursula, but Paula makes a point of looking closely at the roots of her hair and eyelashes, turning to Harri: 'Natural blonde.'

But murder is murder, and they comb the area meticulously for a good twenty minutes, Paula with her nose and eyes to the ground. Harri watches her nostrils, no doubt sniffing for a mere trace of patchouli. When he raises his eyebrows at her, she shakes her head. 'Nothing so far, boss.'

And that's when the uniformed constable comes running in breathless, as if he's sprinted halfway across Hamburg, calling from the doorway, 'Inspektor?'

Harri's head snaps up from analysing a lengthy blood trail, more evidence that this woman had fought for her waning life with every last breath. 'Yes?'

'They've arrested a man not far from the British barracks, covered in blood. Drunk and raving. Says he's killed a girl.'

'A Tommy?' Harri queries. Now it's his stomach that constricts. Worse, it might be an officer.

'Not sure, sir. He's in uniform, that's all I know.'

'Thank you, Constable.' Harri is relieved, and feels bad for it. A woman has lost her life to a violent monster, and he's pledged never to forget each and every loss. And yet, this news does feel like a minor reprieve, that the Puppet Master is still biding his time. It's replaced with a fresh problem, of course: if this woman has died at the hands of a British squaddie, there will be the individual monoliths of the law, the army and politics to contend with.

Not forgetting Major Stephens. Oh shit.

'Mist!' Harri curses the official army request already waiting for him back at Davidwache, along with the arrested soldier, who is no longer covered in blood, but wears the legacy of far too much alcohol on his breath, his prior ravings turned to a teary contrition.

'I didn't mean to,' the private sobs into a cup of tea. 'But she said she would if I gave her . . . and then when she wouldn't . . . I don't know what came over me.'

'What did you do?' Harri presses, handing the man a lighted cigarette. Having seen the body, he knows exactly what injuries were inflicted, but it's important not to lead the suspect's answers. Important for the conviction they will never likely achieve.

'I . . . I . . . stabbed her. I'm so sorry, I didn't mean to . . .' The Tommy breaks down again, sobriety causing his regret to overwhelm. He's remorseful, but it doesn't help the poor woman in the morgue. Or explain the fact he had a knife so handy.

'And where did you do this, Private Thomas?'

The squaddie gives a full enough confession that Harri is satisfied they are not looking for another culprit. It was a crime of lust, ugly and foul, the motivation as old as man himself. So, no long investigation, but Harri knows equally that nothing is ever that straightforward, not in this day and age. Looking at the scribbled message already waiting for him, there's a meeting with the major to look forward to, and no chance to catch his breath or even swig some weak ersatz coffee, because army transport is already waiting outside. As he bumbles across town in a military jeep, he realises a man like Stephens will not be kept waiting and wants this 'squared away', as the British are so fond of saying.

In a second-floor office at the Hotel Atlantic, Stephens gets up from behind his desk, though shies away from a handshake even before he sees Harri's bandaged palm. Years of military training means the major looks starched rather than weary after the previous night's late hour, and for a second, Harri wishes he possessed that skill of masking the bloodshot eyes that were so prominent in the mirror this morning. Stephens sits, though there's a slight deference to his movement, too, leaving Harri to suspect the British man requires something of the Kripo. Discretion probably.

Or more plainly: for the inspektor and his team to keep their mouths shut.

'Schroder, have a seat.' He gestures to a solid leather chair in front of his large walnut desk.

Far too polite. He really must want something.

'Unfortunate business this morning.' The major steeples his hands above the desk surface. 'Are you confident you have the right man in custody?'

'As near to a hundred per cent as I can be,' Harri replies. 'Private Thomas has confessed and the details match up to the scene.'

'Motivation?' Stephens asks.

'Alcohol and lust by the looks of it. Nothing new.'

Stephens' chin lifts up, shooting Harri a dark look, but he says nothing to counter the obvious audacity. Possibly because it's true. Any British soldier has access to rations the Germans can only dream of – fifty cigarettes per week, with opportunities to buy more, brandy, and copious amounts of NAAFI beer. Not only has it fuelled reckless driving among the troops and plenty of pedestrian deaths, such spoils also attract young women with hungry families, and the average Tommy wants something in return. If it's not forthcoming, well . . .

'I see.' The major lowers his lips to his entwined fingers, brow wrinkled. He pulls up sharply. 'You do know what this could mean, don't you? If it gets out, particularly after last night's fiasco.'

Harri takes his time in contemplating the grave expression, hating himself for enjoying the sight of a British officer squirming in his eyeline, albeit with his shaven stiff upper lip. He relishes it all the same. 'I wouldn't like to think, sir.'

'Well, we might *have* to think about it, Schroder,'

Stephens says firmly. 'A German woman murdered in cold blood, by a squaddie. If they're made angry by a bloody loaf of bread, this will rank as totally livid.'

'Yes sir.' *And so they should be.*

'Although . . .' The major stands up and paces behind his desk. 'I wonder if the charge might well be manslaughter? An impulsive act, in the heat of the moment.'

'He was carrying a knife, sir. And by the look of the victim, it was a frenzied attack.'

'Yes, well . . .' Stephens paces again, running a hand over sandy hair shorn neatly into the nape of his neck.

Harri wonders why he's being consulted at all, since they both know the outcome. Private Thomas will be ghosted away, back to England and military prison, because he's under army jurisdiction. He'll serve some time, but not enough, and the woman's family will have no closure. As for justice – is it even worth mentioning?

But if the Kripo are indiscreet and the full facts leak, who knows what the starving savages of Hamburg will do? That's what Stephens is busy calculating, clearly. Keeping the peace, rather than winning it.

'I don't need to impress upon you, Schroder, that this must be kept within your station, between the occupying forces and yourselves. We can't afford yet another riot.'

'No, sir.'

Stephens frowns. He needs more. 'So, can I count on the discretion of your entire team in this matter?'

'Yes, sir.' Harri is irritated with this exchange and craves to be dismissed, curtly if necessary.

But the major continues to ruminate. 'Any progress on the other women?' he says, picking up a pipe and filling it ritually.

Harri deflates again. It's been all of four days since his last grilling from Stephens. What kind of miracles does this man expect? 'We're following up a few leads, sir.'

Stephens grunts displeasure. 'And you suspect there'll be more?'

'Sadly, that's our prediction. There's certainly an element of revenge, that our killer feels betrayed.'

'So, you suspect he's German?' The major appears to rally at this prospect.

'Not necessarily, sir. The truth is, we don't know enough about him yet to make any firm guesses. Inevitably, we're lacking resources.'

For the second time in their exchange, Stephens ignores Inspektor Schroder's small but obvious dig. Patently, he knows all too well about the Kripo's dire needs. 'Once more, I'm sure I don't need to emphasise how delicate this matter might be, if you get near to isolating the culprit,' the major drives home.

'You mean if he is British?' With that, Harri thinks he might have stoked the military fire too hard and too briskly, bracing himself for a reprimand.

But while the army man is clearly taken aback, he appears to swallow it. He only puffs rapidly on his pipe, evidence of machinations behind his eyes. 'I'm told, Schroder, that you once had ambitions of working with the Met,' he says.

Here we go. He's done his homework. 'I did, sir. Before the war.'

'And now?'

Harri considers his answer, but since he has nothing left to lose, what's the harm in honesty? 'There's very little to keep me in Germany.'

'Family?' Stephens ventures.

'My wife and child died, in '43.'

'Sorry to hear that.'

'Thank you, sir.' Harri is far from grateful, but it's what he's expected to say, isn't it? To acknowledge out loud that it wasn't the major who personally dropped thousands of tons of bombs on Hamburg, destroying people and homes and loved ones. His loved ones.

The major's sentiment is fleeting, however. His face darkens. 'It would be a shame, Inspector, if you did want to pursue the same path abroad, and your application was held up for some reason. Or worse, rejected.'

'It would, sir,' Harri says. It's the curse of a *mitlaufer* come to haunt him again – one cleared by the authorities for their association with the Nazis, but yet never quite trusted not to have had some former sympathy with Hitler and his kind, to have actually believed in the Fatherland and the mighty Reich. Is he destined to always have the stink of fascism steeped into the fibres of his being, never to be scrubbed away? Heinrich Himmler must be bloody laughing in his grave.

Major Stephens, it seems, is very happy to take advantage of Harri's embedded stench. His military stiffness and paternal pipe can't quite mask his disdain for people like Harri – Germans who may just be innocent. Or at least not eternally tainted.

'I want to know instantly of any developments,' Stephens goes on. 'Especially those which point towards the identity of your killer.'

Say it, you coward. Say: 'nationality'. Because that's what you mean.

'I understand, sir,' Harri chimes, like the good Kripo man he is.

'Do you, Schroder?' the major growls. His steely edge flashes like a shiny dagger. 'Because if you think public knowledge of last night's debacle would cause trouble, then word of a British killer on German soil – one who is hunting down vulnerable women – would set this fucking country alight. Far, far worse than we've ever seen.' Sustained puffing on his pipe creates a plume of smoke, as if to illustrate the fires of hell.

'I do understand your meaning, sir. Perfectly.' That if the monster currently scoring German words into female flesh for revenge or lust, or some sick pleasure, happens to be British, then Harri and his team will have to take their foot off the pedal, to falter, to show themselves as inept detectives, while their prime suspect is scooted away before any trial, and the killings will miraculously cease.

Oh yes, Harri understands his own role in this debacle all too well. And he's sick at the thought of it.

'Good man,' Stephens says, before summarily dismissing Inspektor Schroder with a sycophantic smile and a knowing nod. Harri descends the ornate stairway of the Atlantic, certain of only one thing: the Nazis were not the only side to have chiselled and honed their blackmail tactics to an expert level.

CHAPTER THIRTY-ONE: REFLECTIONS

16th February 1946

Georgie

Zofia brings breakfast on a tray the next morning, although when Georgie checks her watch, it's already eleven a.m. She shakes herself awake, provoking a fresh wave of aches and injecting a rapid recall of the previous night.

'We need to get out there and gauge the reaction to the riot.' She braces the right side of her ribs with one hand and hauls herself to sitting with the other.

'*You* need to stay in bed and rest,' Zofia asserts, with a distinct matronly air. 'I can go out and check what's going on.'

'But . . .'

'And what happens when your body decides it won't do what you're asking, and you're dragging yourself around?' Zofia argues with fervour. 'Your entire time in Hamburg will be wasted. You need to rest.'

Much as Georgie hates to admit, Zofia has a point. And judging by the effort it takes just to hobble to the bathroom, the diagnosis is spot on. What she can see of her ribcage is already turning a deep plum shade, and her left eye is a classic shiner, courtesy of the elbow and hitting the concrete. The gash has closed up but it's a sorry sight. *She* is a sorry sight.

From experience, these injuries are obviously nothing new to Zofia. In any camp hospital, she might have tended to victims of severe beatings almost daily, alongside malnutrition and the side effects of profound cruelty. Georgie's injuries are mild in comparison, but Zofia will know how the body needs time to heal. Aside from one bout of food poisoning, Georgie miraculously managed to dodge anything serious in the war theatre. Only Max had sustained a shrapnel wound (in the same ill-fated broken leg, as it happens), and she remembers visiting him in the field hospital for weeks, several more for rehabilitation. It was a stark warning for both of them to slow down, to be a little less gung-ho.

'Look, you tell me what sort of things to look out for, and I will go back to the site and ask some questions, test out the people's reactions,' Zofia suggests. 'Surely that's better than nothing?'

It's also the only option that newly appointed Matron Dreyfus will tolerate. Georgie nods, slumping back into her pillows and grateful once again that fate has planted such a worthy comrade into her path.

She spends the morning scribbling her recollections from the previous evening, the atmosphere and the rage of the people, the terror as live bullets strafed through the crowd.

Was there an order to shoot from the top brass, Georgie wonders (and perhaps Major Stephens as the ranking officer), or a careless, split-second reaction from a frightened squaddie, in the face of a crowd ready to spill their wrath? There's certain to be an investigation, but who knows if the truth will ever emerge. Chaos can do that, muddying the origin of war crimes and those responsible.

Not for the first time, Georgie questions how the world ever got into this mess. Surely it can't have been down to just one man? And that prods her to think of Harri, and their nearly heated exchange just two nights before – that 'guilt of the nation' debate. She wonders if he and other Kripo were drafted in last night, and what his take on it will be – sympathy or censure for the rioters? Half of her wants to leap out of bed and towards Davidwache station for his reaction. To her surprise, she realises the other half would rather not know at all.

Zofia returns in the early afternoon, with news that two have been confirmed dead, both men in their twenties. 'That's bad enough, but no children were hurt, thankfully,' she says. 'People are angry, but they are also wary of protesting again. I think the sound of bullets is all too fresh in their minds. It's made the women especially retreat into their underground holes. It's quieter than normal on the streets.'

'Did you hear anything from the military side, the squaddies talking?'

'Not much,' Zofia reports. 'A few whisperings, though they are definitely less vocal out on the streets. Perhaps even sheepish. I detect a sense of shame.'

Is Major Stephens feeling the same level of regret? Using her newfound acquaintance, Georgie would dearly love to appear on his doorstep and fire a barrage of questions at him, except a nosy journalist is the last person he'll want to encounter right now. Besides, her body continues to signal a firm 'no'.

Zofia brings both news and a late lunch, and something unexpected on the tray – a letter from Max. Georgie fingers the envelope, thinking of her own missive left sitting in the drawer. Unsent. *You coward, George.*

It doesn't stop her sniffing at the paper inside, hoping to detect the tiniest whiff of Old Spice, a favourite aftershave he adopted from some of the US soldiers in the field, and the bottle she'd bought him for Christmas. Disappointingly, there's only a dampness coming off the single sheet. Max was always concise with words when he started out in journalism, far less flowery than her pieces. Both sides, however, bear his distinctive hand-writing.

Darling George,

I hope you're well, and not finding Hamburg (and the post-war landscape) too hard to swallow. I had drinks with Jerry Strand from the Times a few days ago – he's just back from several weeks in Berlin, painting quite a gloomy picture of a very slow climb into any kind of normality. I know that you of all people will cope with whatever Europe throws at you, but I hope your heart isn't too bruised, my love. We all need some light in our lives.

Once again, Georgie blames the resulting cough on her hot soup, plus the lump quickly forming in her throat. It's not like Max to be so reflective on paper, usually reserving his feelings for their private moments. Is he referring to what's currently between them – a future family as their light? Or is that Georgie being overly sensitive, bruised in so many ways?

I'm bored stiff, of course, enough that I have pulled out my old typewriter and started putting some thoughts about the war on paper. Ha! I can almost hear you laughing from across the North Sea, having told me enough times that's what I should be doing. But, Georgie, I need you desperately as an editor – come and save me from my ramblings and grammar that's definitely wanting!

Seriously, darling, I miss you. I knew I would, but the hole in my life is far more vacuous than I imagined. That last night was far from perfect, I know. And I'm truly sorry if I upset you. I was hurt, and if I'm honest, I still am, about our baby. But I had no right to make you feel guilty for reacting differently. George, we'll work it out – and if that means it's just me and you, then that's how it will be. I promise. It's you I married, and you I want to be with.

I know you have a job to do in Hamburg, but please don't stay away because of that night. Come home and we will work it out. Talk it out. Haven't we always?

My love, ever and always, Max

P.S. The leg says hello – plaster comes off in three days. Hurray!

Trust Max to end on a light note. It's the bit in between which is actively diluting her bowl of already watery soup.

'What's wrong?' Zofia asks, her face askew as she returns with more aspirin. 'Are you in a lot of pain?'

'No,' Georgie sniffs. 'I'm fine. Honestly.'

It's an out-and-out lie. But it's what's expected, and what the British always say. Why can't everyone just be more honest?

CHAPTER THIRTY-TWO:
TIME BOMB TICKING

18th February 1946

Harri

Time is ticking. Harri stands before what he's already heard one uniformed officer label the 'murder board', and while the days have moved on, the board hasn't. Information that trickled in is now static, mouths firmly shut since Friday's riot, the one since tagged a 'disturbance' by British High Command. Over past days, he's heard Hamburgers on the streets talk constantly of *Aufstand* – revolt or riot – but apparently, it's not quite so serious if you apply a different label.

The weekend had meant long hours writing reports over the Private Thomas case, though Harri was glad to be occupied; time to himself nowadays feels more of a penance than leisure, endless hours when he seeks mostly to avoid areas where children play, huddling under the bedcovers instead, and subsequently hating himself for wasting a life that fate has gifted him. Had he not been out there doing Montgomery's bidding in keeping the peace, he would have worked on the case, perhaps checked out the areas where men scour the streetside dancefloors, and possibly identified the one man hunting for his next victim. So, yes, the sands of time are falling quickly, and too smoothly for their killer.

'Have we anything from circulation of the updated image of Ursula, the one where her hair is dark?' Harri asks.

'Possibly, boss.' Erwin shifts and consults his notes. 'By chance, I spoke to a woman who's a regular at these dance meets, but who also works in the records office. She recognised Ursula as coming into her office three weeks ago and enquiring about a birth certificate.'

'Her own?' Paula queries.

'No,' Erwin says. 'That's what struck my witness as odd. It was of a woman about the same age, but who – again by chance – she remembered as dying in the firestorm of '43. Ursula explained it away as her cousin.'

Anna moves close to the board and Harri watches her pupils dart from side to side. As with Paula, he can almost see the lightbulb switch on inside her. 'What is it, Anna?'

'Well, it's just that you mentioned one other victim telling a friend she was going to get away. From Hamburg.'

'Yes?'

'It's just a guess, but I have an idea of why these women willingly follow him down a dark alleyway. We thought he might be offering them fake travel documents, a route to getting away from here. But what if it's more? A lot more. I think he's offering them an entirely new life, and that's perhaps why Ursula was looking for documents. The intelligence services have done it for years, using the

214

names of the dead to build completely new identities. In their desperation, they believed him – Liselle, Rita, Ursula. Ironically, he's luring them to their death with their own future as bait.'

Finally, pieces of the puzzle are beginning to slot together, though the evidence is sorely lacking. As members of the team trickle in, they discuss which new avenues to pursue when there's a tentative knock on the Kripo door and a head peers through.

All eyes go to the doorway, but it's Harri who registers most shock. '*Scheisse!* Christ, Georgie, what happened to you?'

Her fingers go immediately to her face, as if she's only just remembered the crusted gash on her cheek and the swollen eye that's already on a spectrum between plum and yellow. He sees that, while she's not exactly limping, her steps are tentative.

'Er, I got caught up in the riot,' she says, 'before the weekend.'

'Shouldn't you still be in bed?'

'Oh, please, Harri, don't you start. I've had enough of Zofia's protests this morning. What I need is to get back to work.' She catches sight of his still bandaged hand. 'Besides, I could say the same to you.'

'It's not so bad, and certainly nothing like your war wounds.' He shrugs it away and offers her a chair alongside Anna, resuming the briefing. 'Erwin will follow up on any other searches for identities but, in the meantime, I think we target some of these dance places. It's the only lead we have which points to his hunting grounds. Paula, are you still a willing stooge?'

'Possibly, one or two nights,' she says apologetically, 'but I can't find sitters for much more.'

'I'll help,' Georgie pushes in, reacting swiftly to Harri's sceptical glance. 'I *can* dance, you know.'

'I don't doubt it,' he comes back. 'But Hamburg swing is famous for its energy. It's whether you're fit enough right now.'

Her loaded look quashes any doubt. 'Okay. Jonni has also agreed to being another look-out,' he goes on, 'and being a darned sight younger than the rest of us, he'll blend in well. If you're free, Paula, we'll start this evening.'

She nods.

'I'd be happy for Zofia and me to hover in the crowd this evening, and keep our eyes out,' Georgie offers. 'That's if I'm fit enough, of course.' She qualifies her sarcasm with a smile.

'The more the merrier,' Harri says. 'Let's get to it. Those working tonight can take the afternoon off.'

As the team disperses, Harri plants himself on the chair beside Georgie. Up close, he sees the depth of injuries to her face, small cuts where he imagines gravel had been painfully been ground in, wondering if it's even worse under her clothes. 'I thought you had a dinner date on Friday?' he queries.

'I did.'

'And, was it that eventful?'

'Not really, but the major – Stephens – got called away, to an emergency. I sort of followed him.'

'You *sort of* followed him?' His eyebrows arch with disbelief.

'Yes.'

'Georgie, you could have been seriously hurt.' Under

the bandage, his flesh smarts and his pride digs painfully. He knows all too well how bad it was for some.

'But I'm fine,' she insists. 'Were you there?'

'Yes, the whole station was drafted in.'

'And did you see where the first shot came from?' she asks.

Harri cocks his head, disappointed. 'Are you interviewing me now? For your article.'

'No, actually,' she answers firmly. 'Sad to say, the whole event made three lines in the *Times* and *Telegraph* foreign pages. It will be part of my feature, eventually, but for Fleet Street, it's already old news.'

'Well, in answer to your question, I didn't see the first shot fired,' he goes on. 'Officially, it was a stray bullet. Some poor bastard of a squaddie will be taking the blame, I expect.'

'And your injury?' she pushes.

'My own stupid fault,' he says. 'No one else involved, I promise you.'

'Harri, you don't need to explain your—'

'And where's Zofia today?' he cuts her off.

'I left her at the hotel, thought she needed a break from nursing me. By now, I expect she's out combing the city again.'

'You know she was in Dachau, don't you?' Harri says. 'Zofia, I mean.'

'No, I didn't. She hasn't volunteered it, and I haven't asked. Though I guessed it must have been bad. It explains why she's reluctant to talk. Her only goal at the moment seems to be finding her sister.' Georgie snaps her face towards him. 'And how is it you know this, about Zofia?'

'Curious, but it is in my nature – and my power – to check people out.'

'Harri!'

'I told you – blame it on Himmler. It's an unfortunate legacy of the SS.'

And being Georgie, he's glad to see it actually brings a smile to her face.

For a Monday night, and despite a dusting of snow on the ground, there are plenty of people who want to dance on Hamburg's streets. From the girl in the records office, Erwin has gleaned where it will be, and the surveillance crew assembles at around eight p.m. There are a few people lingering, but nothing of note, and so they retire in pairs to cafés and bars for an hour to keep warm and regroup.

By nine p.m., further snow has held off and the allotted place is in full swing. Harri never tires of his city's creativity when it comes to entertainment, and what he sees reflects both the tenacity of its people and the love of music in Hamburg. It was the fast and furious band tunes that first brought college-age 'Swing Kids' together before the war, uniting in their love of all things British and American; music from across the Atlantic, and a dress style reminiscent of Edwardian dandies, complete with swagger and hooked umbrellas. The *Swingjugend* also hated the Nazis. In turn, the Nazis loathed them, for their rejection of things Reich, their abandonment, but mostly, Harri thinks, for just having a good time. The strait-laced Hitler Youth constantly raided the dance halls, with many a Swing Kid arrested and sent to the camps, the boys to Moringen and the girls to Ravensbrück.

But the movement refused to die, going underground and simmering throughout the war. Some of the swingers didn't return, but the music lives on right here. In place of a band and stage, there's a wind-up gramophone squatting on a table against the stone pillar of the bridge, with one man in charge of the tunes, seamlessly changing each record.

'He's a former band leader,' Paula mutters in Harri's ear.

'I think we can discount him,' Harri reasons. 'Too busy to stalk any women, and too obvious. Also, he looks too old.'

He watches Georgie and Zofia peel off together and skirt around the crowd that has shaped itself into a circle around the 'floor', Jonni and Paula a little to the left, eyes already roaming. The wall of bodies forms a good-size arena on the flagstones, like the tables once set around the floor of the Alster Pavilion. Where the pavings are pocked by war, someone has laid out a rough round of thick green baize to cushion any falls. Inside the circle is a frenzy of what Harri can only describe as pure joy.

Lamentations from the violin he and Georgie heard in the ruins less than a week ago have been replaced by the upbeat, furious sound of a brass section pushing out from the gramophone at full volume; several couples respond to the first bar of familiarity and leap instantly into the circle, egged on by the clapping and stomping of feet. Dressed in their dance finery, the women spin, their mouths wide with glee and bright with cherished lipstick, the men seeming to delight in their strength as they lift and twirl the women around the space. Harri remembers how Hella loved this type of music, though with his two left feet, they rarely went dancing. Another in his stock of regret.

He catches Georgie's eye, but she neither smiles nor swipes her gaze away, and he senses she's done this type of surveillance before. Zofia seems more of a fish out of water, her head bobbing with interest, but then he imagines it must be her first time at any dance since . . . well, since before.

The circle thickens with those passing by and drawn into the spectacle, a few squaddies too. Harri notes a distant police presence looking on from the top of the bridge, observing only, and he's relieved in more ways than one. This crowd look to be regulars, hurrying to the floor and moving with abandon, and it's difficult to equate this side of Hamburg with the squat squalor of so many families, only a stone's throw away. But then, doesn't everyone deserve something to break the cycle of survival?

Paula is the one who sparks a real surprise in him. To get a better view, she's broken through the audience and is in the centre of the circle, energetically jiving with a smart-suited man who looks German. She's undoubtedly enjoying herself, but he knows all her Kripo senses will be on full alert, eyes skimming faces in the crowd as she spins. The gramophone man switches between a mixture of British and American swing, most of which Harri recognises but can't put a name to. Still, his fingers tap rhythmically against his leg as he heads towards the bar area, a fairly sophisticated contraption made of pallets and hinges snuck just under the bridge awning. Inevitably, it's designed to be set up promptly, packed even more swiftly if the Polizei come prying. There are bottles of beer and soda, and beyond his gaze, likely to be several varieties of moonshine for those who ask.

'Is it always this busy on a Monday night?' Harri says casually to the man stacking bottles, slipping him pfennigs for a cheap and gassy beer. Part of him craves the liquefying confidence of a good brew, enough to throw caution to the wind and join Paula in letting go, but not tonight, and not in front of the team. Or Georgie.

'Suppose so,' the barman grunts. 'Since the war ended, it's busy wherever we go. It's as if people are making up for what they missed. That or trying to forget what life has become.'

'Get many tussles between the Tommies and the local boys, over women?' Harri asks. As more men in uniform join the attendant crowd, he's working his way round to enquiries about male barflies and men who make a habit of watching, but it might take some time to light a flame under this barman.

'Some. Though the look-outs know more about that. I just dish out the drinks and watch.'

'I imagine there's a few locals wanting to court the women, what with the Tommies flashing their cigarettes and black market goods around.'

Perhaps the barman is too bored to notice he's being pumped, counting his takings in the dim light. 'Yeah, but the ones back from the war haven't got a hope, even if they have all their limbs. One look and the women sense their desperation.' He stops and gestures to a tall man on the outer rim, watching the proceedings intently over the heads of others. 'See him? Here at almost everywhere we set up. Never dances. Just stands and watches. Sad bastard.'

'Does he ever talk to the women?'

'Occasionally. Some try to get him to dance, to make up the numbers, but he won't.'

'And does he ever leave with a woman?' Harri asks, perhaps a little too keenly.

Now the bartender wakes up. 'What are you, some sort of spy? I thought we'd had enough of that with the Gestapo.'

Harri swigs to hide his unease. 'Just interested, that's all.'

'But you're here, aren't you? Looking at the women. Like him.'

'I'm here with my sister,' Harri lies, gesturing towards Paula on the floor. 'She loves to dance, but she won't come on her own. Because of the men.'

'Oh well.' He seems satisfied and goes back to fiddling with his stock.

Harri takes his drink and wanders to the edge of the crowd, feeling exactly like a voyeur with each passing minute. He smokes too many cigarettes as a way of hiding his unease, and declines two requests to dance (though feels secretly pleased at being asked), watching the men enticing women onto the floor, only to fling themselves about energetically and innocently. Aside from the tall man, no one looks particularly sinister, or shady. More as if they are trying hard to have a good time. Have they got the wrong day, or got it wrong completely, and this isn't their killer's hunting arena at all? If it isn't, how on earth will they find another lead to follow, and in time to prevent another killing? His anxiety throbs in time with the beat.

After an hour, Harri manages a brief word with Paula, who's pushed into the crowd for a respite, gesturing her towards the shadows of the stonework. She's flushed and breathless, having partnered as many men as she possibly could, both German and British in uniforms. 'Any hopefuls?' he asks.

'Nothing that's tweaking my radar,' she says. 'Though I'm sure you've noticed the guy just standing to the side, staring.'

'Yes, the barman pointed him out too. What about him?'

'I noticed he's been giving a fair bit of attention to Georgie's friend. Zofia, is it? Without being unkind, it is pretty obvious she's not long out of the camps, but still, she's attractive. I asked some of the girls if they knew him. He's here all the time, apparently, but they seemed to think he's pretty harmless.'

'Well, it is sometimes the quiet ones,' Harri says. 'Let's call it a night. I'll stay until he leaves, see where he goes. You get some rest, it's well-earned.'

Paula turns to seek out Jonni, as the music rhythm slows and couples pair up for less energetic dancing.

'Oh, and Paula?'

'Yes?'

'I was enjoying all your slick moves out there, you dark horse.'

She sticks her tongue out in response. 'One day, Harri Schroder, I'm going to get you out there and put you through your paces.'

He nudges back into the crowd a metre or so from Georgie, near enough for her to notice the slightest motion of his head. Subtly, she blinks an acknowledgement.

'What's up?' she says when they meet against the stone parapet. Even in the shadows, her unmarred eye is keen and bright.

'We're calling it a night,' he says.

Her shoulders seem to slump a little, though whether it's disappointment or relief he can't tell.

223

'How about a proper drink?' she suggests. 'I'm sick to death of drinking soda.'

Harri shifts uncomfortably. 'Another time, perhaps. I have some work to catch up on, back at the station.'

He can't escape her glare. Professional. Accusing. 'You're going to follow someone, aren't you?' she says.

Christ, how does she know?

'It's a long shot, and probably nothing,' he protests. 'It would be a big coincidence if we found our man on the first night. But I can't take that chance.'

'Then I'm coming with you.'

'No. Georgie, it could be dangerous.'

'You said yourself it's probably nothing!' She huffs displeasure. 'And I wish you would stop trying to protect me, or save me. I've done perfectly well myself throughout an entire life and war.'

'Sorry,' he says, with true remorse. 'It's a bad habit of mine.' *If only I could have saved them when it mattered.*

'So, come on then,' she says triumphantly. 'It will be far more convincing if you're walking a girl back home, rather than skulking after one man.'

'As much as I hate to admit it, you're probably right.'

CHAPTER THIRTY-THREE: LOITERING WITH INTENT

18th February 1946

Meta

At first it's a surprise when she sees Georgie mingling among the circle of observers, her face emerging between the bodies and the lights on the bridge. But then Meta reasons it's the sort of place a journalist might go if they wanted to experience the Hamburg of now, the highs and lows of life. Still, she shrinks further into the dark recesses cast by a newspaper kiosk, keen not to be spotted. Not today, and especially when she recalls her recent pledge *not* to go hunting.

As the dancing slows and people begin to drift away, Meta watches Georgie link arms with a man – a little shabby, in her view, and clearly not dressed to impress as some of the dancers have taken pains to do, even if close up their outfits are worn and darned. This one has made little effort, maybe a policeman, the folds of his face obvious and his posture telling. And he's one who has lost, she judges. Easy enough for her to visualise the burden of grief and guilt. It takes one to know one.

Georgie and her man move away, casually putting on the pretence of a couple, even if Meta senses they are also working. She's the queen of deceit, and can spot it in others at a glance. They'd just better hope their target isn't quite so shrewd.

She moves her gaze back to her own objective. While Georgie and her partner are trailing one of the event's regulars, Meta's eyes fix on another, close to a small cluster of dancers who collect in the chill night air by the bridge, sparking up cigarettes and stamping their feet against the cold. They go from the frenzied heat of the floor to the freezing wind whipping off the water in a matter of minutes, jogging on the spot to infuse some heat, like the moves she saw Popo demonstrate once. What did he call it – the jitterbug? It's the last time she remembers laughing so hard that her belly hurt. Some months ago now.

Her man isn't hopping. He stands back, alone under his black homburg, feet planted firmly and not smoking, so that Meta has to keep her eyes trained on him, without a glowing cigarette tip to fix his location. Just like her, he's in the shadows for a reason. She first spotted him four nights ago, hovering at a similar meet to the west of the city where the pickings were good. Flushed with liquor and drunk on music, the dancers are often more amenable to her requests for money or cigarettes as they head home; despite the windfalls from Georgie, she has to keep a good supply coming in. Like the nice Tommy, Georgie will leave, and she'll be here still.

On that night, Meta sensed he was waiting, and not for anyone in particular, the type of loitering that she spends her days perfecting. A tiny light flickered inside her: what was he doing there? Waiting for someone he knew, a girl perhaps, to escort home? But he met no one, and eventually sauntered away, close into the shadows. *What if . . .?* Hadn't Georgie mentioned a man who is dangerous to women? Pretty women, she reasoned, and not a ghost like her.

In the three consecutive days since, including the night of the riot, Meta sought out every dance meet around the city, and he's been present each night, lurking on the periphery.

Now, as the dancing comes to a close, he simply waits. The couples head off first, then women who walk home in twos or threes, for safety. She senses that he's biding his time for a lone woman to fall in step with and strike up a friendly conversation. He's done this once so far – on the night before last, sidling up to one such woman and asking for a light, then chatting innocently as they walked in the same direction. Meta found it easy to follow, since most people choose to screen her out from their vision, and what silly individual would be shadowing with a suitcase in tow, bashing against their reedy legs? She has a battered copy of an Agatha Christie mystery under her pillow, another method of improving her English, and she knows it's termed 'hiding in plain sight'. She's good at that.

On the night before last, Meta felt this man might have found his prey, except that he and the woman rounded a corner just as the streets became darker, she chancing upon a group of friends, then muttering a casual goodbye to the man as she joined the crowd. Meta watched with interest as he threw down his cigarette butt with a distinct impression of annoyance, pulled down his hat and melted into the darkness before she could follow. While scavenging for his half-smoked butt, she pondered whether the innocent woman had escaped merely a fondling, or with her life.

Is she certain this is the man Georgie speaks of? The one who has made women disappear? No. Isn't now the perfect time to alert Miss Young, with her policeman in tow? Perhaps.

But right now, it's just a suspicion worming its way through Meta's mind, in a time when her days are filled with mistrust; of those on the black market who strive to fleece her, authorities tempting her into a life of ill-paid labour, or dirty thieves who would strip her home of everything she has. It may well be her mind playing tricks. And yet, she feels compelled to follow him, since the hasty pace ensures blood will pulse through her veins (with no firewood back at her camp), keeping her senses sharp. The image of her suitcase packed to the brim with cigarette packs also floods her vision, of it being so full of tobacco rewards that she struggles to close it and fasten the clasps.

What a dream to have.

To the side, the man finally lights a cigarette and strides off with purpose, in the wake of a young woman pushing her dark hair under a beret as she walks. Without hesitation, Meta picks up her case and forms part of the human caravan.

CHAPTER THIRTY-FOUR:
THRILL OF THE CHASE

18th February 1946

Georgie

It feels odd walking arm in arm with a man again; the last time was in London, the week before Max broke his leg, after which point he formed an intimate relationship with a pair of crutches. Now it's Georgie who feels slightly dependent on Harri's support, the ache in her right leg turned to stiffness after standing for so long in the cold. She's distracted by having to focus on the pretence of their conversation, concentrating on her casual German in seeming like an average couple walking home, having ensured Paula and Zofia were safely dispatched together.

Harri keeps it simple: 'Did you have a good time tonight?'

'Yes, I liked the music.'

As they keep step with the man in front, their objective (and the thrill of it) overrides her discomfort, especially when Harri pulls them to a halt in line with their target at a late-night *Kafee* kiosk. The man sinks a small cup of ersatz while standing at the counter as they make small talk nearby. In minutes, they're back on his trail.

With purpose, they walk for fifteen minutes to a residential area pocked by ruins, but with enough houses and functioning apartment blocks to constitute a neighbourhood. Their target stops briefly under the only working streetlight, and it looks to Georgie as if he's fumbling in his coat for keys.

Suddenly, Harri yanks her to a stop and swivels to face her, his features skewed with apology. 'Sorry,' he whispers, and moves close. Very close. Now is the time, she realises, to enact the embrace of a real couple. She smells the weak beer on him, but it's not unpleasant, and a soapy odour as her face goes into his neck, along with the musk of the city carried on his coat. In the darkness, they are a man and woman in love.

'Can you see him?' Harri whispers close into her ear.

'Yes.' Over his shoulder, Georgie watches their suspect pull at his pockets with exasperation, and then, seeming to give up, stride towards the front door of a run-down house and knock loudly three times. Within seconds, a weak light shines through glass above the door, and it's opened by what looks like an old woman. She appears to mumble a word or two, turns her hunched body and he follows inside.

Harri pulls away, coughs and fusses with the collar of his coat. 'What did you see?'

'I think he lives there,' Georgie says. 'The woman who answered was definitely older. His mother perhaps?'

Harri's features deflate. Despite his low expectations of

230

their surveillance, perhaps he secretly hoped they were onto something, that fortune had afforded them a break in the case. Caught in a fleeting shard of light from a passing car, he looks weary. Of disappointment maybe. Of death, certainly.

'What do *you* think?' she says.

Harri sighs and blows into his gloveless hands. 'I will have Erwin check this guy out, of course,' he says. 'But in all honesty, it appears he's simply a lonely man who lives with his mother.'

Shoulders touching, she feels his optimism drain away, sensing a need to hoist him up. 'Then we'll just have to keep going, won't we? More dancing and more searching.'

'*We?*' he swipes back. 'How long are you planning on staying, Georgie? Don't you have a life and husband to go back to?' Evidently, it's frustration making his voice both caustic and despondent.

And yet, she knows he's right. Max's latest telegram, received only the day before, sharply distilled her responsibilities. I read there's been a riot. Are you OK? Caught up in it? She could hear his concern leaping off the tissuey paper. Her dictated answer had been brief and deliberately vague. All fine. Slow research, lots to do. Home asap. Love G.

The questions lingers: is she ready to face what awaits at home? For now, Georgie shakes away the burden and smiles. 'You know what the British say – in for a penny, in for a pound.'

He manages a weak laugh. 'You British and your sayings. Come on, Miss Young. I'll walk you home – for real this time.'

CHAPTER THIRTY-FIVE:
TO BE SOMETHING

18th February 1946

Meta

From the rear, his manner is assured, one arm hovering around the back of the woman's coat. Meta's eye is intent on the language of the man's body and the way he sways confidently, gently persuading her to fall in with his step. But the ground underfoot is rocky, and Meta has to watch her own footfall as they leave the relatively clear pavements of the city centre and venture into the rubbled streets. When she glances up again, his hand has crawled upwards, stretched across and cupped around the woman's waist. Already, there's an air of possession, perhaps even restraint. Does that make him The One? Should she intervene and disturb this calculated dance of his, securing the trust of his prey? Or is he just one of the many men in Hamburg who assume they own women with the offer of a drink and a good cigarette?

With few people or cars about, she hears the woman's tinkle of laughter rise into a coal-black sky, punctuated by a bright slice of crescent moon. Clearly, she doesn't feel threatened, responding to his flirtatious gallantry like that. But it's all a pretence on his part, Meta is certain of that. From everything she's learnt, every survival skill that she's honed through necessity over the last months and years, Meta is adept at sensing the bad ones. It's almost as if she can sniff out the fetid soul that squats within. Take her Tommy – he was a good one, and she knew that at their first meeting, could smell his purity. Clear, too, that he was never attracted to women, and although it was left unsaid, they both understood. She felt safe with him. He was kind, that was the main thing: generous with his copious rations, never asking for anything in return. He had a little sister back home, he said, and Meta was a nice reminder. Grubbier for sure, but he never once said anything about that or wrinkled his nose, just slipped her a tablet of fragrant Palmolive every so often. Why can't more men be like that? Just nice.

But this one up ahead – he's nothing like her Tommy. And although her nose can't detect it yet, she's sure there is a putrid odour lurking somewhere within him. Should she wait for it to rise up? Would an approach by a filthy street kid do anything to disturb his purpose anyway?

As with her everyday dealings, Meta swiftly calculates what action is likely to give the best return. Not in terms of dollars or cigarettes, but what has value to Georgie Young and her policeman in catching this man. It's clear that she needs to look at him squarely in the face, to sketch his features in her memory, and then onto paper, in helping to drag this monster off the street. To do something of worth, rather than fashion cigarettes from filthy butts. To be something.

So far, this man has shied away from the light, face obscured by the heavy brim of his hat for a reason. If she plays the poor urchin and approaches, Meta can get a good, long look, especially if she cajoles convincingly, hopping and coaxing him towards the thin shaft of the moon. But their current route into blackness means those chances are waning. It must be soon. Already, he's steering the woman away from the cracked pavement and towards a set of ruins, one where a good friend had an apartment, before '43. It's not part of Meta's current trading patch; the friend both lived and died here, and while the city is full of memories, this one is particularly raw. Best friends are hard to replace.

Meta scrabbles to keep pace over the knobbly ground, far enough back that he can't hear her stumble. Up ahead is a hole, black as pitch and where the moon doesn't reach; why is this woman content to be led somewhere so bleak? Only then does Meta notice the sway to her gait. So far, she's been focused solely on the man's dominance, assuming that the slight wobble to the woman's calves is down to the rough ground and not the alcohol she must have consumed. But now, he is supporting her more and more, bearing her weight rather than clutching her waist. It must mean . . . Now, Meta. GO NOW!

She does, or at least she makes to speed up. Stopped in her tracks by what looks like another of her kind, sprinting towards the couple. Is it? No, it can't be. Meta squints into the distance, her eyes adjusting to the darkness. But yes, it is. It's Popo. Bloody Popo! What the hell is he doing here? It won't be trade at this time of night, but blatant begging. He will have been sent out by the gang leader, his turn to bring in a few pfennigs. Rarely coming here nowadays, she hadn't realised it's part of his patch.

Popo bowls up like a circus clown, the couple startling as he appears out of nowhere. Up close, even the man recoils at the young boy's maimed face, Popo typically pushing his disfigurement forward as the best method of eliciting guilty offerings. Meta notes the man pulling down his hat further before reaching into his pocket for change. The woman's low laugh mixes with her inebriated chatter, and then a satisfied Popo darts away into nothingness.

The intervention has either spooked this man or it's fired his determination, because he begins to half steer, half drag her towards the black skeleton of a building at a pace. The woman squeaks a little in surprise, but she's in no position to object, with his build towering over her. All thanks to Popo, the opportunity for Meta to leap ahead and get a good look has disappeared and she's reduced to following at a discreet distance.

The couple enter the ruins, their exchange audible through a hole in the remaining structure that was once a window, the low tone of his voice against her high-pitched giggling, he urging her to keep quiet. The scoring of a match and its subsequent glow are a surprise, but raising her head above the window frame means Meta can locate where they are. To her further surprise, the match has become a small fire, and her first thought is: *Where does the wood come from?* Has he planned this, the location, and set the fire in advance? Inside her layers, she itches uncomfortably. Should she go for help? But where? The space around the ruins is a black abyss, with a few scurrying rats as the only living company.

She bobs again above the parapet. He's pulled the woman close and, in shadow, Meta can make out her flirtatious rebuff, pushing him away half-heartedly. In a flash, his gallantry switches to control and then aggression, forcing her down, her cries muffled with one hand. In the other, a thick strip of something stands obvious against the glow. Whatever it might be, its purpose is not good. Meta's heart beats in her own ears, thrusts against her bird-like ribs.

Now is the time, Meta. Now is the time it will matter.

CHAPTER THIRTY-SIX:
THE MARAUDING CAT

18th February 1946

Georgie

They hear the first scream in unison. Its shrill pitch cuts through the air that's relatively still in among the ruins settling for the night. More than distress or a call for help, it pierces Georgie's brain like a white-hot poker. The language of a woman under threat. Or a death cry.

'What the . . .?'

Harri halts instantly, swivelling left and right in locating the direction. Running back towards the centre, they're in a dark crumbletown of ruins, between civilisation it seems, and although it's only eleven p.m., there's no one about. Except for a woman in dire need. His arm slips from Georgie's and she watches him race towards the shrieking, now coming in short bursts, as though its energy is waning. Along with her life?

Harri is more sure-footed over the rubble, but she

follows at a stealthy, faltering pace, the ache in her leg long forgotten. The beacon of noise is replaced with a small light as they race towards a ruin bordered on three sides and enter what was once an interior, catching the glow of a fire amid the stones, its flame flailing and fighting to keep alive. In its shadow, a woman does the same.

Georgie glimpses the silhouette of a struggle, playing out like an early silent film – the dastardly villain exerting his masculine strength on the slighter body under him, her cries reduced to little more than a whimper. In the shadow of the firelight, Georgie spies something significant. Familiar. Personal.

The suitcase.

More battered, for sure. But what was once hers, and is now . . .

Meta!

The villain senses the intruders within a split second. Instantly, he begins to untangle himself from the woman, whose limp, bare limbs seem entwined with his like the roots of a tree. It's only then Georgie spies the third body in the scene, a small, rounded bundle who comes out of the darkness, launching like an animal from behind and pulling at the man's coat; a cat hanging on for dear life with claws, spitting and scratching.

With his height and strength, it takes only one swipe of a fist to connect with the marauding cat, who is thrown like a limp rag against the nearby stone wall and slumps, motionless. Harri hurls himself forward, but his target has already turned and is scrabbling across the gravel floor and out into the night.

'*SCHEISSE!*' Harri curses loudly. Georgie watches him deliberate on his duties in a heartbeat – two victims needing help, against a potentially futile chase into the darkness. He chooses the path of life. The right path.

Harri scrabbles to kneel by the woman lying on the floor, whose weak moan signals she's still breathing, while Georgie heads for the other body against the wall. It is her. It's Meta's face above the layers of cloth, dazed and with blood oozing from above her ear, but conscious. Just.

'Meta . . . Meta . . .' Georgie stoops and pulls the sour-smelling bundle towards her with one hand, bleats the name repeatedly, to draw the waif's wavering, rolling eyes towards her, tempted to shake Meta into consciousness, but knowing she shouldn't. Her other hand presses the thin weave of Meta's woollen hat into the weeping head wound.

'Fräulein Georgie,' Meta mumbles. Her bloody lips work themselves into a weak smile. 'What are . . .' And then she's gone, her pupils flickering and her lids closing, a lingering breath wheezing from her mouth.

'NO! No!' Georgie tears frantically at the heavy coat and cloth underneath, to expose Meta's skin and the top of her collarbone. Her own breath is absent as she angles Meta's limp frame towards the dying light of the fire. Seconds tick by as she watches for movement, a sign Meta is unconscious rather than . . . No. She won't let it be true. This can't happen.

A twitch of the flesh stretches over the bare bone, grime-encrusted skin rising a millimetre. Georgie stills her own body and looks again. A laugh shoots from her mouth, a near hysterical reaction to noting Meta's skin is flushed, air moving, blood running through her tiny, thready veins. She's still and unconscious . . . but present.

'Georgie?' Harri's urgency cuts into her bubble. 'Is she ali——?'

'Yes. Yes. Thank God.'

'This one too,' he pants, 'but we need help, one of us needs to go.' His voice is capped by the arrival of a guardian angel in a man's form, his alarm evident as he squints in the gloom and takes in the scene.

'*Hilfe, Arzt, Polizei!*' Harri barks. Help, doctor, police! He's crouching and cradling the woman's head in his lap, a hand clasped under her neck, perhaps to stem a flow of red that's more copious than Meta's. 'Come on,' Harri urges the woman in German. 'Stay with me. Please.' Georgie can hear the anguish in his voice as he pleads, and she wonders then what happened to his wife and child and whether he is thrust back there, bleeding desperation and hope. At that moment, he is a husband and father, citizen and human, as well as a Kripo detective frantic not to lose this most valuable witness.

Time is static and yet, all of a sudden, there are bodies crowding into the space, with torches and a rudimentary flame on a staff – some civilians, others in police and army uniforms, and men who lift Harri's victim onto a stretcher. 'Take care of her,' she hears him say as they leave. And then it's Meta's turn, a man's hand having to peel Georgie's fingers away from the clothing, her digits clamped in a tight, clawed fist. 'Let go, Fräulein. We'll see to her,' he gently cajoles. 'I promise.'

'I want to come with her,' she insists.

'There's no room, Fräulein.'

They're alive . . . they're alive. She has to repeat it over and over as Meta disappears from view. And yet, Georgie doesn't recall the self-same thoughts pounding into her head throughout the war, during any bloody battle or endless bombardment, lives succumbing all around her.

240

The rules had been different, all expected in the theatre of war. Reasonable even, if combat could ever be dubbed as such. But this – now – should not be happening, to women anywhere. And not to Meta, this waif-cum-thief who has no one, and who has somehow burrowed deep beneath Georgie's skin.

She feels numb as the space gradually empties, Harri drifting to the ruin's edge and talking with a single Polizei left to guard. From the corner of her eye, Georgie sees one other officer bend towards the rubble floor and reach to pick up something.

'NO!' she cries, causing his hand to recoil, as if it's molten metal. 'That's mine,' she qualifies, moving to grab at the handle of the suitcase. 'I'll take it to Inspector Schroder.'

The officer looks sceptical, swings his gaze towards Harri, who turns and nods silently. 'It's fine, officer. Let her have it.'

Georgie's fingers ease into the worn handle like they've never been parted. Meta has been true to her promise – she's looked after and cherished it. It's no longer a piece of Georgie, but the ties remain. And if it can't be with Meta for now, she can be its guardian until they are reunited.

She senses rather than sees Harri approach from behind, the visceral tincture of blood moving with him. Turning as he holds out both bloodied hands in a gesture of something like relief, she raises her one free hand, not steeped in red but tainted enough that she could be on some sort of stage in the guise of Lady Macbeth.

He doesn't need to utter a word, because his expression says it all, this man who has doubtless seen more death than she will ever witness, before and after war. Harri Schroder folds his bloody arms around her body and, for the second time that night, Georgie Young is pulled into a comfort more welcome than any she can ever remember.

CHAPTER THIRTY-SEVEN: WITNESSES

18th February 1946

Harri

'I'm so sorry,' she sniffs. 'It's not like me at all, and it isn't the time or place.'

'I don't mind,' he says. On the contrary, Harri thinks it must have been the right time, as Georgie sobbed on his shoulder in the midst of the ruins, feeling her heart break as he pulled her in closer, an eruption of emotion that he senses is long overdue.

In the back of an army jeep – one to miraculously appear as word spread of an 'incident' – she tells him why. Everything comes tumbling out of Georgie Young, crack reporter. About the baby, her reaction, and Max's disappointment at her grief and relief. Harri listens and nods, because he understands all too well about grief. But also about the dirty secret of relief too; that once they are gone, those you love, there is a gaping hole of sorrow so wide it threatens to swallow the whole world, and you with it. Except the world is not engulfed, meaning you have to go on living each day. And maybe once or twice in twenty-four hours there is a point where relief nudges out the grief, because you no longer have to worry about the next warning siren, or wave of bombers, or hungry flames looking for victims. Or your loved ones. Because the worst has already happened.

He doesn't say any of this to Georgie, only nods and squeezes her forearm in reassurance. It's not the right time for him. Only once has he ever broken down in the same manner, at the discovery of a small child in the ruins as the winter of 1945 approached, suspected at first to be foul play, but then discovered to be a combination of malnutrition and hypothermia. The girl had looked around the same age as Lily, and the sight of her curled up in the rubble, as if she were merely sleeping, broke him in two. His reliable sergeant was on hand to catch as Harri plunged emotionally to the depths, then and there, and so he knows the value of a good, sturdy shoulder at the right moment.

Georgie blows long and hard into her handkerchief, takes in breath and instructs herself: 'Pull yourself together, George.' Aside from her red eyes, she's back to being the formidable English reporter. 'I'm all right now, Harri. But thanks.'

'Any time.'

'What about the man?' she starts afresh. 'Shouldn't we be out searching for him?'

'I've got uniforms patrolling the area, but if he has any brains — which we suspect he has — he'll be long gone.' Harri peers eagerly through the greasy window of the jeep.

'It's better we get to the hospital and see if either woman is conscious and get a description. At least one of them must have seen his face.'

When they arrive, Hamburg's main hospital is quiet, its corridors giving off a hushed calm at nearing midnight. 'What a difference,' Georgie says. 'It was bedlam in here when I came last week. Where is everyone?'

'Even the desperate need to sleep,' Harri mutters. Flashing his Kripo ID at the stern gatekeeper on reception, they are led onto a first-floor ward, and towards two side rooms, each with a uniformed officer standing guard outside. 'I'm not taking any chances that he might get to them,' Harri explains.

But disappointment awaits again. After patching their respective head wounds, both Meta and the other victim, whose identity card names her as Sigrid Heike, have been heavily sedated.

'Did either of them say anything – anything at all?' Harri presses the attending doctor.

He shakes his head. 'Noises and mumbling, both were only half conscious,' he reports. 'No words that I could understand.'

'We'll wait here then,' Harri states firmly.

'Your choice,' the doctor shrugs, 'but it will be at least mid-morning before they're awake. If it were me, I'd get some sleep.'

'Perhaps he's right, Harri,' Georgie says when the doctor leaves. 'Neither of us will be any good if we're exhausted. And if we come back in the morning, I could always bring Zofia with us.'

'Why would we need Zofia?'

'Well, I don't know Meta well, but I am certain she's suspicious of anyone in authority. And that means you. She's met Zofia briefly, and I think she's more likely to open up to someone who's been in a similar position. You can guide us on the questioning.'

Harri pulls his hands – washed but still a faded red in the deep grooves of his rough flesh – across his face. The skin on his cheeks feels rough and grimy, and what he wouldn't give right now for a long soak in the huge tub that he and Hella had in their very first apartment. Big enough for the both of them, bubbles and all. He lets out a sigh that signifies how long this day has been. The adrenalin of the last few hours has drained from his body, like a tap left open until only drips remain.

'Maybe you're right,' he says at last. 'I'm too tired to think right now. Let's sleep on it, and I'll pick you up in the morning.'

For once, he's thankful to see an army jeep waiting outside the hospital – the same one that transported them over – its engine exhaust billowing in the freezing night air. Stephens, no doubt. Somehow, the astute major must have got wind of the incident in the ruins and sent officers to cast an eye, checking the Kripo were not arresting a British squaddie as their suspected killer. Which means Harri will be summoned yet again, to account for his actions in letting a potential killer flee.

But for now, he honestly doesn't care. Fatigue has triumphed, and all he wants is his cold apartment and to hear the flip–flap of tarpaulin as a lullaby to sleep. Georgie, too, by the way her head is lolling on his shoulder as they bumble over ruinous Hamburg.

The driver drops Georgie at the Baseler Hof first. 'Sleep well,' Harri says as she hauls herself out.

'I don't know about well,' she mumbles drowsily. 'I think I could pretty much snooze on a washing line right now.'

CHAPTER THIRTY-EIGHT:
THE HAVEN

19th February 1946

Georgie

'What do you mean, she's gone?'

'Exactly that,' the doctor explains, a little sheepishly. 'Got up and left this morning, when the nurses weren't looking. I thought the sedative would take some time to wear off, but she's obviously stronger than she looks.'

'And the guard on the door?' Harri queries.

'I assume she waited for him to answer the call of nature,' the doctor speculates.

Harri is clearly furious, venting his anger on a nearby officer, and while Georgie is alarmed, she is not surprised either. Any other stray who lives among the city's filth might relish clean sheets, half-decent food and tender care for as long as they could eke it out. But this is Meta they are talking about, and independence takes on a new meaning where she's concerned.

She, Harri and Zofia were late arriving at the hospital, having been forced to take the tram; once it became known there was neither an arrest, or suspicion involving the military, the convenience of army transport immediately vanished. Hence it's nearly midday, and Georgie senses Harri is anxious to catch up, his patience clearly not improved by only a few hours' sleep.

'She did leave something on the bed.' A nurse holds out a piece of paper folded into a tight wad. 'It's addressed to someone called "Georgie"?'

'That's me.' She near snatches at the note, and unfolds it as Harri looks over her shoulder.

'Smart girl, Meta,' she breathes, turning to face him. 'She's not trying to run away from us, Harri. Only this place. She's left us a map, for how to find her.'

In Meta's meticulous hand, and in a style similar to the map she crafted for Georgie, is a clear pathway to what must be her home. Georgie shows it to Zofia. 'Do you recognise where this is?'

Zofia squints and peers at the marks on the page. 'I think so. I've walked around that area a little. It's mostly bombed-out buildings and warehouses. But this has detail – I'm sure we can find it.'

Harri's frustration is extended by news that the other victim, Sigrid Heike, is still unconscious, 'And likely to remain so for a while,' the doctor adds. 'She's stable, but there are marks around her throat, as if there was an attempt at strangulation, and she lost blood from the wound to the back of her head.'

'Was that made with a weapon?' Harri asks.

'Difficult to tell,' the doctor replies. 'If I were to

249

guess, it's more that she struggled and fell on the rough ground. But it's still a head wound that could cause problems.'

Harri paces the length of the hospital corridor, deep in thought, one hand rubbing at fresh bristles on his chin. 'Well, it's clear that our first priority is to find Meta and talk to her,' he says at last.

'And check she's all right,' Georgie reminds him.

'Yes, yes, of course.' He locks his brows together. 'But until Fräulein Heike is awake, Meta may be our best witness – our only witness. So, we'll go there. Right now.'

Georgie steps forward and gently herds him into a corner, away from the others. 'Harri, do you remember what I said last night? I don't want to step on your toes, but I think Zofia and I should to talk to Meta alone.'

'But she's a material witness, Georgie.'

'Yes, and she's wary of the police. Terrified of a good many men after last night, I shouldn't wonder, strangers particularly. If we don't tread carefully, we'll end up scaring her away for good. She'll run.'

He looks at Georgie with alarm, as if she's doubting his reasoning, or sanity. She's not – merely recognises his fervent desire to catch this man. She's seen it on the battlefield, as officers zealously search out snipers who are picking off their men, one by one. The single-minded pursuit can make them almost crazy.

'Surely you need to survey the scene and meet with your team?' Georgie suggests.

'It's just that he was so close, almost in my grasp.' Harri draws a hand through his hair, releasing a slightly maniacal laugh. 'But you're right. Annoyingly so. I need to step back a little, don't I?'

'Like I say, you're the boss, but . . .' she purses her lips and then works to lighten her expression '. . . maybe just a little.'

'Well, all right,' he accedes. 'But write down every detail. If you can get a description, or even a sketch, since this Meta can clearly draw, then that will be a great leap forward.'

His subsequent look says that he does trust her; any journalist knows the bones of a story are the who, what, why and when, but each of them is equally aware that it's the tiniest of details – the 'nuggets' as Georgie calls them – which make a written piece stand out. Or catch a killer.

It's as she and Zofia leave the hospital that something else shifts. Not a seismic change, but enough to cause Georgie to swing her attention towards Zofia, whose own face turns ashen as they walk the corridor towards the entrance. Staff are coming and going, with patients waiting in chairs and on trolleys, in a daily routine of confusion. She watches as Zofia's eyes are pulled in one direction, glued to a group of women in the distance clustered around someone who – from the resonating wail – is patently in labour. Midwives in white are having trouble persuading her onto a stretcher.

Georgie's instinct is to swipe her gaze away, the sight and sound pricking at her uncomfortably. Instead, Zofia's reaction draws her towards it.

'What's wrong?' Georgie quizzes. A thought looms large. 'Have you seen her – your sister?'

Zofia shakes her head, once, twice, three times in quick

succession, and swallows visibly. Then a fleeting hesitation. 'No. No. I thought for a second I might have, but no. It's not her. Come on, or we'll miss the tram.'

The journey takes them to what seems like the edge of an urban wilderness, and yet Georgie senses they aren't too far from the centre, whispers of the city clamour just audible. It's early afternoon, and a weak winter sun is playing peek-a-boo through a thick layer of cloud, much like her first day in Hamburg. The rubblescape is similar, but there are no landmarks Georgie recognises, and she thinks this area must have been bombed quite early in the war, a few weeds here and there pushing upwards through the devastation.

Zofia is studying Meta's map carefully, turning it full circle like a compass and matching the pencil marks to what's in front of them. 'I think it's this way,' she says at last, leading them further across the barren ground. They approach the only edifice left standing, a damaged, abandoned factory, and Zofia peers at the paper again.

'Are you sure?' Georgie says.

Zofia points to the paper. 'It's what she's drawn.'

The dotted line Meta has scrawled – exactly like a fictional pirate map, where X marks the spot – takes them to the side of the factory, and it's Zofia who spies the hidden entrance under wood slats and tarpaulin. Crawling inside, they stand for a second or two in the cavernous space, their breath adjusting to a new chill. Has Meta sent them on a wild goose chase? But then, why would she do that?

With the nose of a refugee, it's Zofia who spots the shelter tucked in the corner, a ramshackle lean-to that's near to collapse in anyone else's eyes. 'This must be it,' she says with certainty.

Georgie is still in doubt until they duck under more tarpaulin and she sees it's a home – of sorts. Empty tin cans stand in a neat line, goods taken from the Baseler Hof kitchen.

'Meta? Meta – are you there?' she projects into the gloom.

Silence. *Oh God*. Has she crawled back to the only home she knows, just to die, like an animal in the wild?

Then, the slightest breath to disturb the stagnant air, a weak moan from the corner, and Georgie squints towards a mound of blankets, and the outline of a small body emerges.

'Meta, are you all right?' The groan intensifies and Georgie peels back several coverings, one of which is clearly an old curtain, to find Meta's face, cleaner than she's ever seen it, but hair still matted with blood, poking out from a bandage around her tiny skull. Georgie guesses the nurses must have washed her, but skirted around the head wound. Most importantly, her eyes are open – a thin slit under swollen, purple lids.

'Thank God!' Georgie cries, then in German: 'I thought you were dead.' Again, she's shocked at her own depth of feeling to discover Meta alive, the knot in her stomach and flood of relief as it loosens slightly. *Is that how a mother feels?*

A brief, weak smile spreads across Meta's lips, twisted seconds later into a ripple of pain. Zofia is already rifling through the bag they filled at the pharmacy – with aspirin, clean water, iodine and more bandages – and together they prop Meta forwards, just enough for her to sip at water and take in the aspirin that Zofia crushes with a can. She scans the bandage and nods at Georgie – a positive sign that blood hasn't seeped through the layers of lint.

'I'm all right,' Meta croaks.

'You don't look it. Why did you leave? Why wouldn't you stay and get help?' Georgie tries not to badger, but she can't stop herself, struggling to understand the reasoning of a runaway.

Meta merely glances at Zofia, but, in that brief exchange, Georgie grasps their connection. Each knows precisely why, and it's something she and others may never fathom, those lucky souls with a roof over their head and food on the table. And with family left alive. That when the most precious commodity of all is stolen – when your safety is cruelly robbed – it takes years to root and regrow, like those weeds pushing up through the rubble outside. In the meantime, you trust no one. You simply daren't.

What can Georgie do but respect that loss?

'She'll need a fire,' Zofia says, scanning the floor, 'and there's nothing here.' Given Zofia's initial reaction to Meta, which had been suspicious to say the least, Georgie is pleased at her keen attention. 'I'll go out and collect some firewood.'

'And any food you can buy, too.' Georgie reaches into her satchel for Reichsmarks and the cigarette packs she keeps handy for trade.

Meta drifts in and out of sleep; the doctor has warned of head injuries causing drowsiness, and, as Georgie tidies the area, she prods once or twice at Meta's shoulder to ensure signs of life. Half an hour after Zofia returns with wood and food, they've stoked a fire and boiled up coffee and eggs, Meta managing to sit herself up. She does allow Zofia to look over her slight body, checking the stitches to a gash on her shoulder and soaking away the crimson crusts with boiled water.

'Are you sure you don't want to go back to the hospital, or to the hotel with us?' Georgie tries again.

Meta's horrified expression says it all. 'I can look after myself.'

A silence descends as Meta drains the last of her coffee. Georgie fidgets uneasily, knowing she needs to conduct something like an interrogation.

'How is the other woman?' Meta asks. For someone so young, she has the intuition of someone twice her age.

'Alive – thanks to you. But she can't talk, not yet anyway.'

'Then you'll want to know about him, won't you?'

Georgie nods. 'In your own time, though.' She's aware Harri is a cat on hot bricks for any information but, like a flame, this has to be tended carefully and slowly.

'I have something better,' Meta says. She shifts in what passes for her bed, rifles under a makeshift pillow, and pushes out a clenched fist towards Georgie, her knuckles raw and grazed, dotted with iodine. One by one, her fingers unfurl to reveal something that glints against the firelight.

'It's his,' she says. 'I ripped it off in the struggle.'

CHAPTER THIRTY-NINE: ORDERS

19th February 1946

Harri

He's barely back at the Kripo office when there's a knock at the door and the desk sergeant pokes his head through, wearing the poker-faced expression he reserves for bad news. 'Inspektor, you've been summoned again.'

An army jeep is idling once more on the kerb outside Davidwache. While Harri is sometimes glad of the transport to save his weary legs, increasingly he likens it to one of those wagons ferrying the condemned to the gallows, knowing full well passengers will not enjoy what's at the other end.

'Where are we going?' he asks the driver.

'Atlantic,' he chirps back. 'Lucky for some.'

'But only for some, Sergeant.'

⋆　⋆　⋆

Major Stephens is not a patient man. Harri gauged as much at their last meeting, and now, in his office at the Atlantic, there's no pretence at diplomacy.

'You had him in your sights, Schroder!' he rails. 'What the fuck were you thinking in not giving chase?'

'There were victims in need, sir. More than one. I felt it was my duty—'

'Your duty, *Inspector*, was catching this bastard terrorising Hamburg. Putting this case to bed.' Stephens looks to the floor as he paces, clearly exasperated, rallying for a second attack. 'Don't you know that it's a fucking war out there, Schroder?'

Actually it's not. And yet, despite Monty's avowal to 'win the peace', the rest of the military elite obviously think the battle is ongoing. Against the defeated. Oh hell.

'Both victims are alive, sir,' Harri offers, 'which means we have two witnesses who will hopefully be able to give us descriptions. It's a major breakthrough.' He doesn't mention – for obvious reasons – that one remains unconscious, and the other has absconded from the hospital and is, at this moment, being hunted down with a rudimentary hand-drawn map. That just might be the last straw for Major Gordon Stephens. 'Both women need to be handled gently, sir. It will have been a terrifying experience.'

Stephens grunts a modicum of empathy, but not for long. 'Still, they need to come good – understood?' he demands, his sooty, rigid pupils directly on Harri. 'I want daily reports on your progress. And who this man is likely to be.'

You mean, if he's a squaddie, and if, by virtue, your own career is on the line? 'Yes, sir.'

But the major isn't finished yet. 'One more thing, Schroder.'

'Sir?' Harri struggles to banish a level of tedium in his reply.

'I hear you have a journalist in your midst. A British woman.'

'She has visited us once or twice, as part of a wider report on Hamburg, I believe,' he lies.

'Get rid of her,' Stephens says tartly, going back to the papers on his desk. 'She's too good, by all accounts, and that makes her trouble. Leave her to my man at the CCG to sort out. He can distract her.'

'Sir.' Harri doesn't nod, or say yes; within his own personal morality, it means he's committed to nothing, something that might stand as a meagre defence when Stephens attempts to kick him out of a job. He turns to leave, then hesitates. If he's already in the major's bad books, what is there to lose?

'Well, Schroder? Shouldn't you be getting on with it?' Stephens grunts from behind a cloud of fresh pipe smoke.

'I could get on with it a lot faster, sir, if we had some transport to hand.'

Now Stephens is irritated as well as confused. 'Surely the Kripo has cars available?'

'Minimal, sir, and only at headquarters.'

The face behind the cloud falls. He's clearly shocked. And perhaps there is some realisation in there, after all. 'Very well,' he says grudgingly. 'Take the driver you were given today. Clear it with my secretary outside.'

'Thank you, sir.' Harri makes to go then, satisfied he's achieved some success out of this grilling.

'And Schroder?'

Harri swivels again. Now what?

'I want an end to this – and fast,' the major reiterates. 'You do recall our previous conversation?'

'Yes, sir.' *No, sir, three fucking bags full, sir. Isn't that how the English express their disdain in rhyme?*

Harri climbs into the front passenger seat of the jeep. 'Looks like you're with us for the foreseeable future. Sorry, Sergeant.'

'Not a problem, sir,' the driver says. 'I like a bit of variety, and it beats hanging about with nothing to do. I'm glad your English is good, though, because I don't speak much Kraut. Er, sorry – German.'

'Then we'll be fine,' Harri says, wholly relieved not to have bagged a surly, reluctant army man. 'Welcome to the Kripo team, Sergeant . . .?'

'Dawson, sir. Robbie Dawson.'

'Back to the station then, Dawson. You never know, there might even be a pot of decent coffee on.'

CHAPTER FORTY:
A NEW FOCUS

19th February 1946

Georgie

Zofia insists on staying with Meta as Georgie leaves to head back to Davidwache. All notions of observing Hamburg for the purposes of her article have vanished; as far as Georgie is concerned, this *is* real life in post-war Europe. At least for today, her task now is far more urgent than satisfying some features editor hundreds of miles away in Fleet Street.

'I'll talk to Inspector Schroder about some kind of police patrol,' she whispers to Zofia, out of Meta's earshot. While they had trouble finding the bolthole, their killer is clever and determined. And after last night, with the prospect of being identified, he's likely to be wary, furious or paranoid. And possibly all three.

As Georgie suspected, Meta's makeshift home isn't too far from the city centre – it only seems to be buried in a wasteland – and the walk to the Rathaus takes only fifteen minutes. She stops briefly at a wurst stall in the plaza, and is on the U-Bahn in minutes. Rattling under the city, she keeps a constant hand on Meta's golden nugget, its significance burning a hole in her pocket.

'Fräulein Young!' Paula greets her with more enthusiasm than ever before. Harri must have briefed the team that she and Zofia were on the hunt for their star witness. 'Did you find her?'

There's an audible gasp when Georgie reveals the St Christopher pendant and chain that Meta yanked from her attacker's neck.

Paula lays it across her palm, as if it's long-lost treasure. 'Finally!' she cries, her face heavenwards. 'We've got something tangible to pin down this monster.'

Seconds later, Georgie is forced to dampen their newfound hope. Harri walks in, Dawson grinning in his wake, in time for Georgie to reveal that they have little more than a vague description of height and build, with hair colour that's 'not dark'.

'Meta trailed him from behind, in darkness,' she explains. 'When she saw him guiding the woman into the ruins, she hung back, and even when he lit a small fire, it only made shadows of them both.'

'But we saw her, almost on top of him,' Harri says, with obvious frustration.

'On top, yes, but she attacked from behind,' Georgie qualifies. 'In the next second, she was thrown against the wall. Out cold.'

'So, are we even sure this is our killer?' Anna comes in. 'Undoubtedly, this man attacked Sigrid, and we don't

261

like to imagine what his intentions were, but do we suspect that he engaged her previously, or was intent on killing her? It doesn't fit the pattern so far.'

Georgie nods. 'It's a good point, but I am inclined to think it is him.' She walks towards the board and presses a finger to a word scrawled in chalk. 'Meta didn't see him, but she's got a very good nose. And I mean that literally. She's adamant that she smelt something distinctive.'

Her fingernail rests on the word 'patchouli'.

'So, come on, let's review what's new after last night,' Harri says to the room. True to his promise, they each have a cup of good coffee in hand, largely down to Dawson reaching into the supply tucked under the seat of his jeep, courtesy of the British armed forces. The briefing is in English, too, in deference to the sergeant. 'Anna is right – this behaviour doesn't fit his previous attacks. But so much else does. Police work led us to his hunting ground, and although Georgie and I weren't on the right trail last night, when we look back over the previous victims, we now know they each went to these impromptu dance meets on at least one occasion.'

'But don't we suspect that, previously, he's met each woman several times?' Erwin queries. 'That he engages with some type of promise?'

'So far.' Harri sips at his coffee. 'And that's what worries me most about last night.'

'Why?' Georgie says.

'Because from what Meta has told you, there appears to be no lead-up to last night's attack. From her statement, he looked to be engaging Sigrid for the first time. He selected someone who was clearly tipsy, if not drunk, and took advantage of that. In such a short walk, he couldn't possibly have sold her the dream of a new life.'

'Does that mean, as of last night, he's getting braver or more reckless?' Paula wonders.

'Perhaps a bit of both,' Harri says gravely. 'Either way, he's clearly escalating. Less time between each target. Less planning, and his motivation seems to have shifted. He seems bent either on satisfying his own desires, or thirst for revenge. Quickly.'

'It's like his killing isn't a passion any more,' Paula says. 'It's need.'

'But surely now he'll be scared off?' Erwin queries. 'Isn't he likely to disappear from Hamburg?'

'It's possible,' Harri agrees. 'But these days, it's not so easy to leave a place and set up elsewhere. His actions so far tell us he's an egotist, with plenty of confidence. He might want to stay and watch what we do, hoping we fail. And pick up where he left off. Personally, that's my guess.'

Harri holds up Meta's captured treasure. 'We have new evidence to work with – we'll begin tracking down the St Christopher chain right now, although with the black market like it is, that will be difficult. But we shouldn't assume he will melt away.'

They sip silently, as if absorbing the enormity of this newest challenge.

'Maybe he'll just switch his hunting ground?' All eyes go to the back of the room and the unfamiliar voice of Sergeant Dawson.

'What are you thinking?' Harri queries.

Dawson shuffles his feet. Despite his cheery demeanour,

suddenly he seems shy. 'I only mean that, well, he might shift to where there's plenty of prey, if you'll excuse my being so blunt.'

'Which is where?' Anna asks.

'There's regular dancing at the Victory Club, and on certain nights, big crowds to hide within,' Dawson suggests. 'And lots of German women who are actively looking for a new life. If he's as clever as you say he is, he'll invent another ploy to attract them.'

'But wouldn't he stand out there, as a German?' Erwin challenges.

Dawson hesitates, then looks to Harri, who gives an encouraging nod. 'Your board suggests he speaks German, but I know plenty of British who do, and vice versa. Inspektor Schroder here could easily pass as an Englishman with his accent, so why not this man?'

Harri smiles. 'Well, thanks for the compliment, Dawson. But it is worth looking at. Once we've processed the scene last night, I think we need to organise another stakeout. We can't – won't – sit back and wait for him to do it again. Paula, how are your dancing feet?'

She groans. 'You'll be the death of me and my weary body, Harri Schroder.'

'Don't worry, Paula,' Georgie says. 'I'll join you this time. With the two of us, we may even persuade the boss onto the dancefloor. By force if necessary.'

'Then you have been warned,' Harri comes back. 'The Kripo offers no compensation for broken toes.'

Georgie takes a short diversion to Meta's place on her way back to the Baseler Hof, via the NAAFI shop, where she buys the last tablet of soap on the shelf, and several blankets that are second-hand, but washed and with enough weave left to afford some warmth.

In the factory shelter, the sour smell of cramped living has been overlaid by something more homely and inviting. Zofia has just left apparently, and Meta is still bundled under her layers, her pale face peeking out.

'Have you eaten?' Georgie asks.

'Yes, Zofia made me soup. It was nice, like my mother's.' Her voice is small and mouse-like, and Georgie wonders how much of a battering her slight body has taken on the inside. This is not the Meta who sits for an age outside the Baseler Hof, or walks the city endlessly. She wonders, too, how on earth Zofia managed to cook with so little to work with, then chides herself for a poor memory; Zofia had been in Dachau, where – as with any concentration camp – weak soup proved to be the only daily sustenance and the lifeblood of so many, made from scratchings and peelings, whatever could be scavenged from the surrounding scrub or the floor. She's heard those stories time and again. That particular recipe for life may never leave Zofia.

'Are you feeling any better?'

'My head aches less,' Meta says. 'I'll be up by tomorrow.'

'No!' Georgie is both horrified and adamant. 'Meta, you have a serious wound to your head. You could have died. And if you won't see a doctor, then you have to rest. One more day, at the very least. Zofia and I will look after you.'

Meta stares, fabric resting just under her tiny nose. 'But why?'

'*Why?*' Georgie repeats, incredulous. She squats beside the makeshift bed and tempers her voice, conscious of sounding overly maternal. 'Because we want to, Meta. Because you're a good person, who needs help.'

265

'Meta doesn't need help!'

'Only for a short while,' Georgie stresses. 'Because what you did, it gave us something. The investigation. Inspector Schroder says you've helped a lot.'

Under the blanket, the narrow eyes widen. 'He did?'

'Yes. But he also says you have to stop now. No more hunting. You promise?'

Meta breathes into the musty fibres of the cloth, her expression resigned. '*Ja. Versprochen.*'

Georgie reaches the Baseler Hof around five. She wants a bath, but more urgent is a need to unscramble her thoughts; she came here to do a job, but events have overtaken that. People have overtaken. So, what is her priority now? To work out an answer, she needs the clatter of a typewriter far more than a good soak. Settling herself into a corner of the downstairs lounge and cocooning herself with two walls and her own thoughts, she feeds in a blank sheet. Within seconds, the confusion rattles through her fingers at a pace:

What is it about? The life in Hamburg, or the investigation? Are they one and the same, murder a symptom of the life here? Can I separate them?

The chaos. Black market. Fraud or vital for survival?

Refugees? How much does the British public want to know? Have they reached saturation point?

Light and dark in Germany/Hamburg. Where is the light?

Are we really winning the peace?

What drives this man to hate women?

She sits back, sighs, fidgets, gets up and orders some tea from reception. Frustration squats heavily on her shoulders. Georgie has never experienced this before, this drought of reason. The words still flow, but they are jumbled, reflecting the blurring inside her head. In the field of war, the urgency of reporting, writing and searching out ways to send their goods back home had acted as a focus for both her and Max. In tandem, they worked like a well-oiled machine, artillery thumping around them; whatever the scene, they distilled it in words and pictures and dispatched it swiftly. Gone, and on to the next hair-raising tableau. Here, she has almost too much freedom to think, and the space is oddly suffocating. Dare she say it? Can she admit to herself that she almost misses the war? The very admission feels inhuman, after witnessing the reality, being so close to Zofia and Meta and seeing what the conflict has burnt away inside them.

What am I trying to say? What do I want to say? What is the POINT?

She throws herself back heavily and ponders the questions punched onto the page. The point of what? Her story, or everything? If she had solutions to the latter, life in her world would be a breeze.

Right now, she'd settle for a single answer to her most pressing personal challenge: *Why in the hell can't I write to my own husband?*

Georgie is saved from more uneasy reflection by Zofia's head appearing in the lounge door.

'I thought it was you.' Zofia takes off her beret and

pushes back wisps of hair. When she wears it loose, it flanks her thin face and Georgie thinks it makes her look almost healthy, masking the damage in her sunken cheeks.

'What, just by my typing?' Georgie laughs.

'The speed,' Zofia nods, 'and the fer . . . ah, I don't know that word too well.'

'Ferocity?'

'Yes, ferocity. No one else types like that, with your passion.'

'In this case, I'm afraid it's good old-fashioned angst.'

Over dinner in the near empty dining room, Georgie sees a marked change in Zofia, as if she's ever more distracted. In the eight days they've been together, she's never been overly talkative, if always focused on the work at hand. Georgie puts this new unease down to the added effort in caring for Meta, alongside scouring the streets for her sister. Inevitably, both pull on her emotions in different ways – maybe it is too much for her?

Perhaps now is the time to probe a little, allowing space for her thoughts?

'What makes you so convinced your sister is here in Hamburg?' Georgie asks casually as they eat.

Zofia's eyes slice sideways, though the dim dining room light deadens any clues within. Has Georgie overstepped the mark?

Slowly, she chews a forkful of potato. 'I . . . I just feel certain that she would come home. We talked about it before . . . when things got bad. We made plans and promised each other we wouldn't stop searching. Not unless we were sure.'

There is no gentle way to phrase the next question. 'And are you certain she's . . .?'

'Yes,' Zofia jumps in. 'She's alive. I know it.'

'Has she been sighted, by others?'

'I met a woman from Ravensbrück who saw her in the last days. They were waiting for transport out, and then they got separated. From what she described, it was my sister.'

'Then that's good,' Georgie nods. 'Clearly, she survived until the liberation.' She won't tell Zofia of the stories she's heard from fellow reporters, or the scenes witnessed with her own eyes, of camp survivors succumbing to sickness or disease on the journey out, or hijacked by roaming bands of the angry dispossessed, spraying bullets and fury. If war stands as a waste of life, that surely is inhumanity sinking to the depths. But Zofia doesn't need to know that. She needs only to clutch at her hope and keep searching.

The scrape of her empty plate echoes under the high ceiling. 'Georgie, I don't like to ask . . .' Zofia stutters.

'Ask away,' Georgie insists. 'Don't be afraid.'

'When you go home . . . I mean, you won't be here forever, and then you won't need . . .'

Georgie sets her knife and fork down. 'I'll make sure you have somewhere to go, and a way for you to stay in Hamburg,' she says with a confidence she doesn't yet possess. 'You won't need to go back to any camp, I promise.'

For the first time that evening, Zofia's entire face lifts. 'Thank you. It means so much.'

Such a task has been at the back of Georgie's mind for days now, but what with Meta and the killer out there, pushing herself into the investigation and then being drawn further into it, she hasn't given it enough effort. Her first hope is Lieutenant Howarth. He's a good man, and Zofia's already competent English is improving daily. With her Russian, too, there's sure to be a place at the CCG for paid work, enough for her to afford a room or a small flat.

Georgie resolves to tackle it first thing in the morning. In the meantime, a hot bath is calling, where she'll surely soak until the water goes cold.

CHAPTER FORTY-ONE:
HARRY'S NEW STYLE

20th February 1946

Harri

His fingers are so chilled he can barely peel off his gloves and reapply them each time he steps in and out of the pawn shops to the west of the city. Harri has been going most of the morning and, with so many new trading posts sprouting in the past months, fed by the desperation that's grown to epidemic proportions, he's still only halfway through those in his designated patch.

With each tinkle of the shop door bell, he trudges in with a little hope, pulling the St Christopher from his pocket and laying it on his palm. 'Seen this?'

So far, it's meant only a brief stay in gloomy shopfronts that have few fires and even less hope. With each shake of the pawnbroker's head, Harri's optimism is chipped away. Either they've not seen it, or the design is too common to be of any use. That it's English in origin is the only valuable clue his morning has established. But then so is a good portion of Hamburg, and signals only that their killer may have bartered with the occupying forces. Like most of the city's population.

By midday, he's already weary, cold and thirsty. Which is just as well, since he's arranged to meet Paula and Anna at Fritz's basement café, a central point between the areas they've been covering. Erwin has been dispatched with Dawson to the refugee camp over in Fuhlsbüttel, where the shanty market is more like the souks of Marrakesh, only with shoddier goods and odours that are much less piquant.

'There you are, troops,' Harri says, lowering three steaming coffee cups onto the table. Fritz's daughter follows behind with bowls of soup. Hard to determine the ingredients, but it smells good and looks edible. Even better, there's bread that isn't black and has some substance.

'Fabulous,' Anna breathes into her cup, sending a steam fog up towards her face.

'Are you sure I can't put in a chit for footwear, Harri?' Paula groans. 'What with this morning and the dancing, I'm down several centimetres of shoe sole.'

'You can certainly try,' he replies. 'I'll be sure to add it to the towering pile of requests for typewriters, pens and paper.'

'So, any progress?' Harri looks to each woman, eyebrows rising with optimism. They lower with news that both have received similar responses, each armed with Jonni's detailed illustration of the chain and pendant.

'With so much on the black market, no one's trading in the cheaper trinkets,' Paula says. 'There are too many well-to-do old ladies swapping good family heirlooms for a loaf of bread.'

It's merely a sign of such desperate times. Harri remembers

the days before the war, when pawnbrokers were an asset to the Kripo, always a good source of illegal trends in the city's underbelly, what was being robbed and who was doing the thieving. Now, everyone and everything is up for grabs.

Silence falls into the gaps between spoonfuls of soup, until Harri sees Anna glance at Paula, gesticulating with her eyes. 'What?' he says.

Paula swallows. 'Well, we were only wondering . . .' she ventures. Anna urges her on with a nod. 'Is this witness of Georgie's entirely reliable? I mean, none of us have seen or interviewed her, and we only have her word that she snatched the chain from him.'

Harri chews and wipes the side of his mouth. 'You mean like every witness in every other case we've had? That it's their word we are relying on.' His voice is quiet yet testing. The lively chatter in Fritz's seems suddenly screened out by an invisible wall.

'That's true, but we do normally have access to witnesses first-hand,' Anna argues.

Harri sighs into his soup. He's not annoyed. If anything, he's pleased both officers have the wherewithal to question everything and take nothing for granted. That makes them effective. Something else is niggling deep inside, perhaps that their scepticism surrounding *trümmerkinder* isn't too far from his own not so many days ago.

'I trust Georgie's judgement on this,' he says plainly, then looks to each of them. 'Do you? Trust her?'

Both women shift. 'I like her,' Paula says at last. 'I do.'

'That's not what I asked.'

'She means that however nice Georgie might be, she is still press,' Anna cuts in. 'British press.'

'True,' he concedes.

'But?' Anna adds. 'Because I know there's a "but" coming any second, Harri.'

'Only that we wouldn't be in the position we're in today without Georgie, given her connection to Meta. She has brought something to the investigation. Don't you agree?'

'I suppose,' Anna says, unconvinced. 'The fact remains she will gain whatever she wants, and then leave. That's what happens to all these do-gooders.'

Harri twitches visibly at Anna's open reproach. Warily, Paula flicks her eyes from one colleague to another, like a referee sensing trouble ahead.

Harri reins in his disappointment. Deep down, he's aware of nudging Georgie onto the team – and given his initial reticence towards her, he's equally surprised at wanting her so closely involved. Despite Stephens' overt warning to cut her loose, something compels him to defend her as a person and a journalist. Or is it that having Georgie around makes him feel more alive? Something he won't readily admit to himself, let alone colleagues.

'I do think she is different from other reporters,' he justifies. 'And yes, she may write about us in the English papers. But what do we care? The chances are, we'll never set eyes on it and, let's face it, no one else is interested in how the Kripo is falling apart, least of all the CCG or the British military.' Here, he pushes the major's censure, and the potential loss of his job, to the back of his mind. 'You never know, it might actually do us some good. A bit of recognition perhaps.'

'I'd settle for a decent bicycle,' Paula says, clearly trying to dissolve any tension. 'At the very least, a box of pens.'

'Then, Paula Koch, I see it as my life's work to obtain the best two-wheeled transport in Hamburg for you, and you alone.'

'Promises, promises, Harri Schroder.'

'Lord, give me strength that I should have to work with these two children,' Anna mutters as they leave.

Harri pounds the streets for another hour before returning to Davidwache and giving thanks there's a lick of flame in the office stove. He stokes the embers, feeds in the last of the wood and sets a kettle on the top for when Paula and Anna return. Finally, he turns to the chalkboard, as if something may have miraculously changed in his absence. A connection or a lead scratched in white, the clue to bind it all together. It hasn't. While their killer's fervour is apparent, anything tangible remains a mystery – a face, name or occupation. True, they know from Meta that his hair is lighter rather than dark, but given it was hidden by the homburg and in near darkness, that's all she can be sure of. That and his German accent. Absent-mindedly, Harri looks at his watch, as if it will tell him the day on which their man will next strike, as well as the hour. When he notes the hands have stopped, it feels like some sort of omen. Instantly, he wishes Georgie was here, her presence helping him to think, in the way her eyes dart back and forth, absorbing it all. Stupid, but he pictures her mind like some sort of German Enigma machine, rolling through a myriad of combinations to come up with the best possibilities. It leads him then to picturing Max, and what type of man would be able to first engage her, and then maintain her interest. Rather than igniting

275

envy or jealousy, the prospect intrigues. And it stops him from thinking about his own sorry state of a love life. Too soon after Hella, and too much like hard work in today's messed-up world.

More pointless inner ramblings are interrupted by the arrival of Erwin and Dawson from the refugee camp. Poor Erwin is so chilled his limbs look seized up, and Harri is touched to see Dawson clucking around him like an attentive nurse, pulling Erwin's chair to the fire and pouring out hot tea.

'It's not as strong as a London brew, but it will have to do,' the sergeant rattles on.

Through chattering teeth, Erwin relays the news that Harri has come to think of as inevitable – nothing to report on the St Christopher. Being fairly well covered himself, and with the benefit of an army greatcoat, Dawson appears largely unaffected by the cold. In fact, he seems galvanised by having more to do than ferry around military officials.

Seizing on the opportunity, Harri decides to capitalise on this new enthusiasm. 'Dawson, do you fancy taking me for a drink?'

'Pardon, sir?'

'I mean, do you want to show me around the Victory Club, starting with the bar?'

'Oh, yes, sir. My pleasure.'

'So, let me get this straight. You want me to treat you like a cousin, over from England on business?' Dawson repeats as they park up outside the Victory Club.

'You said yourself I might pass as British with my accent,' Harri explains. 'I'm keen to test out a theory.'

'Which is?' Dawson is still beyond perplexed.

'That our man might be German, but is fluent enough to pass as English.'

'Or vice versa?'

'Absolutely, Dawson. If I can fake it here, then it's possible our killer could put on a convincing front, too.'

'Which means we could be looking for a German or an Englishman, posing as the other? Won't that make it more difficult to track him down?'

'Yes, Dawson.'

'Shit! Sir.'

'Precisely, Sergeant.'

'Said like a true Englishman.'

At just approaching three on a Wednesday afternoon, the NAAFI bar is less than half full, mostly men in uniform, perhaps between shifts or on a day off. Some are standing at the counter, with others scattered around the basic tables, one group of women in a huddle in the corner, their laughter rising upwards like a plume of smoke.

'Just follow my lead,' Dawson hisses out the side of his mouth. 'There's a couple of blokes I recognise. Good to practise on.'

Harri nods, with the distinct feeling that Dawson is relishing this little slice of espionage. He itches inside his suit, the one he bought off a Tommy several months ago, who'd had a bad night at the card table. Though it's not the best tailoring, it is English-made and much less threadbare than his workday clothes. He and Dawson made a brief stop at the apartment to change and flatten down his hair with oil, the sergeant giving a thumbs-up to Harri's more Anglicised look.

'All right, lads?' Dawson breezes up, gesturing at two Tommies propping up the bar.

'Just about,' one replies. 'You?'

'Oh, you know, surviving, mate.'

This very British discourse over, Harri watches them peer past Dawson and towards the new man in tow.

Dawson is quick off the mark. 'Lads, I'd like you to meet Harry, my cousin who's just landed in this fair city for a few days.'

The Tommies nod, raising their near-empty glasses halfway.

'Harry, these two reprobates go by the names of Joe and Terry,' Dawson adds.

'Pleased to meet you. What will you have, lads?' Harri steps in and pulls out a wad of Reichsmarks with a small flourish, as if it doesn't represent a week's wages and a large bag of decent groceries.

'Don't mind if I do,' Joe says. 'Mine's a pint.'

'Same here,' Terry echoes.

The drinks buy them kudos and conversation, loosening up squaddie tongues.

'So, you here on business?' Joe says, when in receipt of his fresh pint. 'Though I can't imagine what there is to trade in this godforsaken place, except fags.'

'You'd be surprised,' Harri says. 'There's plenty of opportunities, and Monty is keen to encourage anyone who wants to put money into factories. I hear there's no shortage of labour.'

Terry scoffs. 'You're right there. But rather you than me in trying to get a day's work out of the Krauts. Always complaining they don't have this or that. Lazy bastards.'

The insult rolls off Harri's back – he both expects it, and he's heard it all before, quick to laugh it off. 'Then

278

I've got my work cut out, haven't I?' He swigs at his beer, mimicking Dawson's long gulps of the bitter, weak liquor. 'So, any night-life here? What about the women?'

The Tommies are suddenly animated, a certain smile creeping across both faces. 'Well, that's where Hamburg does come into its own,' Terry boasts. 'The German girls are good looking and desperate for rations and a passport, whenever Monty sees fit to grant us squaddies leave to marry them.' His smile turns to a sickening leer. 'They'll do almost anything to get either, and on a promise, too.'

Harri is saddened rather than shocked; there is some truth to the gossip, though Terry's words and the beer swill uncomfortably inside him. If he had a younger sister, it could so easily be her. But he's here to play the game, a game that – if successful – can only help to save women from pawing, dangerous men. And if he's to return to the Victory Club as 'Harry', his cover must remain intact.

'Well, I'd better be on the look-out for a pretty girl,' he says. 'Do you have any dancing here?'

'Only the best,' Joe chips in. 'There's a band on Friday night if you like swing. And that's when the girls come out to play.' He laughs into the dregs of his beer and, suddenly, Harri hates both his job and a good half of humanity, being faced with the worst of men's desires. He thinks back to how he loved Hella, her body and her mind in one, the late-night murmurings in bed and their strident debates over politics, the giggles and the sex. And the lows, too. Witnessing her exhaustion in those early days with Lily, barely able to brush her hair, and yet he felt overcome with love at the sight of the baby – *their* baby – at Hella's breast. Surely, he can't be alone, surely other men have those feelings, too, and not merely bodies running with lust?

'Harry? Harry? You ready to go, mate?' Dawson's voice cuts in. 'Some of us less fortunate buggers have got work to do.'

'Yes. Yes, let's make a move,' he says, mimicking some of the sergeant's easy patter. They slip over to a table of women on their way to the exit, Dawson striking up a brief conversation with those in ATS uniform, drawing Harri into the conversation and making polite small talk with others at the table.

'What was all that about?' Harri asks as they head back out to the jeep. 'Just before we left.'

'Oh, that was the real test,' Dawson says with satisfaction. 'Any squaddie will talk to you with the offer of a drink, but it's the women who've got the nose for an imposter. If you can get past them, you've succeeded.'

'And did I?'

'Pass muster, you mean?' Dawson is enjoying this far too much.

'Yes, Dawson, pass muster.'

'I think so. I noticed one or two of them giving you the once-over, and then the eye. As far as they are concerned, you are Harry the British businessmen. And perhaps a bit of a catch.'

While flattered, Harri sees his success as a double-edged sword; very possibly, their killer is a man who moves through two worlds, a German posing as an Englishman, or an Englishman with a convincing German manner.

'Which proves our potential pool of suspects has just doubled. Time to go hunting again, Dawson. So, have we got a date?'

'You really must stop propositioning me, sir. People will talk.'

Harri frowns. 'I mean Friday night, Sergeant. You and me at the Victory Club, with Paula and Georgie on look-out, too. It's work, Dawson. If Major Stephens were here, he would say it's an order.'

'Well, in that case . . . am I allowed to drink on the job?'

Harri considers. 'If the beer is as weak as that, then yes. What do you Brits call it . . . *piss-water*?'

'Then, sir, we do have a date.'

CHAPTER FORTY-TWO: NEEDING RESPITE

20th February 1946

Georgie

Following her doubts and unease the previous evening, Georgie's frustration is further compounded the next morning. While Zofia leaves to check on Meta, she heads to the Atlantic with the sole purpose of finding Lieutenant Howarth and securing future employment for her translator.

With great success, too; Howarth needs very little persuasion in pledging a job for Zofia after Georgie returns home. 'We're always in need of good linguists,' he says. 'Especially when we have tricky dealings with the Russians, and that's increasingly common these days.'

The relief is enormous and, as a return gesture, Georgie agrees to visit to several CCG-backed initiatives, though stops short of promising what she will write, and he knows better than to press her. The frustration manifests as she descends the stairs and feels herself skulking past the entrance to the Palm Court, wary of meeting anyone – Major Stephens especially – who might waylay her. Too late.

'Georgie!' a voice rings out across the lobby.

'Oh, Mrs Stephens, how nice to see you.' At least it's not the husband.

'Olivia, please.' She has the same easy manner in her welcome, kissing Georgie on both cheeks, as with good friends rather than one-time acquaintances. 'What are you doing here?'

'Oh, just checking something with the CCG,' Georgie offers. 'A few facts.'

'You're working, of course, but have you time for coffee?' In her manner of the quintessential host, Olivia is already steering Georgie with one hand towards the ornate tearoom. 'We're having one of our little gatherings, and I'm sure the girls would love to meet you. Might be something for your article, too.'

The 'girls', when they approach the table, are a group of ten or so women, with ages, at a guess, ranging from thirty-something to the eldest at seventy-plus.

All are service wives excepting one, whose husband is a chief engineer working on the city's sewerage system. 'Yes, dear, he deals in shit,' she says unashamedly, in a flat London accent from south of the river. Georgie warms to her instantly, more so when she sees that several of the group look down their noses at this woman with open derision. Olivia Stephens, thankfully, is not one of them. Between sips of strong, fragrant coffee, they discuss the weather, refugees (with varying degrees of sympathy), an upcoming party and the price of everything, as if they're forced to worry about half a dozen eggs breaking the bank. Georgie itches with impatience and boredom.

'We're also deciding on where the money from our recent fundraiser should go,' Olivia tells her. 'I'm advocating we should help fund the resettlement centre based at the old zoo, though there are several votes for improvements to the Victory Club.'

There's no contest, from what Georgie has seen so far: the refugees have infinitely more need of improvements than the well-supplied British club.

'Our boys – and girls – are away from home comforts and they shouldn't be denied the best we can provide,' one of the women argues, tossing her long nose in Georgie's direction and aiming not so much disdain as a challenge: *Beat that, if you dare contest our patriotism.*

'Well, I think you both have a case,' Georgie begins diplomatically. 'But in all honesty, having not long left England, I do feel the forces here receive a good deal more than the people back home, where rationing is still harsh. I wonder if the troops might feel a little uncomfortable in receiving luxuries that outstrip their families. Plus, there's a very dedicated band of British Red Cross at the zoo camp whose lives would be made so much easier by your generosity, I'm sure.'

Olivia Stephens masks a satisfied smile, though her eyes sparkle in triumph.

'It's a good point,' says the engineer's wife. 'My sister at home wrote to me recently – she spends an hour or two each day just queueing for bread. And let's face it, there are no shortages at the NAAFI.'

The long-noses issue a combined moue of surprise and doubt.

'I agree with Miss Young,' says the eldest of the group. 'My vote goes to the resettlement centre.'

'A show of hands?' Olivia chimes in, leaping on the momentum. The group makes a reluctant display of democracy. 'Wonderful!' She claps her hands. 'The centre will be delighted, I'm sure.'

Georgie is quick to make her excuses before a second round of coffee is threatened. Getting up, she reaches into her satchel and pulls out Jonni's illustration of the chain and pendant. It's a long shot, but serendipity has guided so much of her life that she never dismisses any potential.

'Does anyone recognise this?'

As expected, they peer and shake their heads. Those with noses put out of joint don't bother to hide their scorn for something seemingly cheap and common.

'Never mind,' Georgie says. 'It was worth a try.'

Olivia escorts her towards the Atlantic's main door. 'Thank you for being the voice of reason,' she says. 'They're a generous bunch at heart, if a little . . . sheltered, shall we say. I think you helped tip the balance in the right direction.'

'Glad to be of service.'

'Anything you need, just ring me,' Olivia adds, and by the look on her face, she means it. Yet again, Georgie wonders how such a nice woman stomachs life with her stiff-neck of a husband.

Beyond the hotel's front door, she steps towards the edge of the Alster basin, inviting the coarse, bitter wind to roll off the water and slam against her, standing long enough that the healing wound on her cheek begins to sting. She welcomes it. To help Zofia, and a genuinely good woman like Olivia, has rescued what otherwise would have been a wasted morning amid finery that, here in Hamburg, makes her squirm with shame. At home, she rarely refuses a dance at the Café Royal, but she's not alone among working people who similarly want to screen out the building site of London for a few hours. On the capital's streets, there are no more beggars than were present before the war. In Hamburg, however, you would need permanent blinkers to ignore the deprivation on every corner. So much conflict still present. *And so much of it in my brain*, Georgie thinks, her body leaning into the physical buffer of wind against her body. For several minutes, she gives in to its strength and almost enjoys a pounding from the elements, stripping away the irritations running through her.

Feeling lighter, she steps eventually along the waterline towards the Rathaus and the city centre. Harri has warned he won't be back at the Kripo office until late afternoon, so she has a decent sandwich in Café Paris, earwigs on a few more conversations and scribbles them in her notebook, resigned that the pages will remain a muddle until she lands back in London.

The script she considers next is more tangible but no less tricky to face; another letter from Max arrived that morning and is so far unopened, digging hard at her conscience. Dated the 17th, it's taken only three days to travel from London, via military mail by the look of it. Tentatively, she unfolds the paper.

Darling George,
    I can only imagine your letter (or letters) is lost somewhere over the North Sea, or that you are simply run off your feet in gathering material.

286

Or that maybe what you're seeing is too labile to set down in black and white just yet.

Georgie shifts in her chair, flushed with guilt. Max's reading of her is so acute, from so far away. Can he imagine her other feelings too?

There was never any doubt some sights would be hard to see, and I suppose we both became a little numb to the atrocities of war. And then that swell of relief once it was over. But now this ugly aftermath, after everything that was fought for – that is difficult to witness. Knowing you, my love, I am confident you will – 'take it in your stride' seems too flippant – but you know what I mean. You'll do it, in your unique, brilliant way. Of that I am certain.

Leg news (and I'm sure you're on the edge of your seat for this): the plaster came off two days ago, a little bit early. I had something of a mishap in the bath (nothing damaged but my pride) and so it needed to come off, but the doctor and an X-ray say both bones are healing well. Still on the crutches, but so much easier to get around without my lumbering friend. I'm working on my hopping for when you come home. After that we'll limp to the Café Royal, promise, and you can dance around me while I endeavour to stay upright.

Stan at the Telegraph has earmarked me for some feature work in a month's time, so I have a date to work to. Don't we hacks just love a deadline!

287

Don't groan, but having to dust off my camera has saved me from putting more thoughts about the war on paper. You're so much better at it than I am.

Otherwise, it's pretty dull here: cold, foggy and grimy. Don't know if you have access to the British papers, but the government is threatening more cuts if we don't secure loans from America, and that's unlikely to go down well with your average Brit, or help your story.

Lastly, but most importantly, I miss you. I know we both said some things that stung, but we WILL work it out, George, I'm certain of that much. I love you, here, now, forever. The world is still spinning, but my love is a constant. You are my rock – never, ever doubt it.

Must go, promised to buy Henry a drink after his shift at the Chronicle. That's my deadline for today, ha ha.

Oodles and doodles of love, your hopalong husband XXX

P.S. PLEASE send word to your mother. She's been writing to me for news of you!

Folding the letter back into her satchel, Georgie feels the uncomfortable itch subside. From the tone, his bitterness has abated and the old Max humour shines through. There will be negotiation on her return, and compromise on both sides. But isn't that marriage? That push/pull of life again, and yet it doesn't seem so arduous, compared with the here and now.

So, what now? Fuelled by bread, coffee and Max-isms,

Georgie springs from her chair and brushes off her languor. She walks the short distance to the Baseler Hof, picks up her old suitcase, stuffs in a few supplies from the kitchen and strides out to Meta's place, noting the deserted scrub outside the abandoned factory looks much less threatening in the daytime, when the weak winter sun is trying so hard to break through and even the weeds are infused with a certain brightness.

Again, she's just missed Zofia leaving, but Meta is brighter and sitting up in her makeshift bed. The bandage is gone and the wound visible, sporting a neat line of stitches, like a zipper to her soul. For the first time, her hair is clean and combed, lying flat to her head. Zofia's efforts again. Meta is beaming, too, at the sight of the suitcase back in her possession, stroking at the leather.

'How are you feeling?' Georgie asks.

'Better,' Meta replies firmly in English, another positive sign that her brain is unaffected by the blow. 'I have been up and walked about. I feel stronger.'

'That's good, but don't do too much. We're still here to help, until you're strong enough.'

'Soon.'

Georgie frowns at the girl's stubbornness.

'And the man?' Meta asks. Georgie notes her fingers grasp at the blanket.

'No arrest, I'm afraid,' she tells her. 'The other woman is still sedated, but the police are using the pendant to track him down. And there are people looking out for you, I promise.'

'Here?' Suddenly, Meta seems more nervous of strangers near her hideaway.

'In the distance,' Georgie reassures her, though in truth, she has no idea what form Harri's promised 'protection' takes, only assumes there are officers watching the area from afar. It's what she hopes.

Georgie stays long enough to open up the tin of ham brought from the Baseler Hof and make a sandwich that looks halfway decent (given her patent lack of skill in the kitchen), with Meta joking and gesturing that soon her belly will turn to fat when, in reality, there's scant chance of that. Zofia has promised to return in the morning, and yet it's clear Meta is feeling hemmed in by the attention. The flyaway bird won't be caged much longer.

'Keep safe, Meta,' Georgie says, ducking under the tarpaulin.

Meta nods, but there's little conviction in it.

Common sense tells Georgie to head back to the hotel, putting time and real effort into planning her remaining days in Hamburg. Realistically, they are limited and she will probably leave with the killer still on the loose. As much as she wants to see it through, Harri is right when he says it takes time to build a case. While the subject has consumed her, murder is not the only side of this city she needs to chronicle for demanding editors back home. That push/pull yet again. Logic, however, isn't having any of it; she turns her head into the bitter wind, the U-Bahn and Davidwache.

'Ah, I was beginning to think we might not see you today,' Harri says when she arrives in the Kripo office, as he pores over and ticks off lists of pawn shops.

'I couldn't very well keep away from the master at work,' Georgie says with a wink. 'Any luck with the pendant?'

Harri shakes his head, filling in the details of their search, and of his trip to the Victory Club.

'Damn it. I felt certain the pendant would lead somewhere,' she sighs.

'So did I,' Harri says. 'And it may still. But in the meantime, we have to go forward, Friday night dancing at the Victory Club being our next target. Time is ticking and he's become unpredictable. Rash is what I fear most.'

The case is taking its toll on everyone, she thinks. Paula and Anna have left to spend precious hours with their children, and despite his smartened, suited appearance, Harri looks more weary than normal. 'When did you last have a day off?' she says. 'I mean a proper one, not just a few hours.'

'That I can't remember.' He fiddles with the pot on the stove. 'In all honesty, I rarely know what to do with myself, aside from tackling my laundry. So, it's just as well.'

'Perhaps I can help,' she offers.

'With my laundry? I don't think so.'

'I was actually thinking of a trip out of the city. I badly need some perspective.'

He doesn't say no, merely cocks his head. 'Anywhere in particular?'

'Oh, I don't know. Begging or borrowing a car, and a trip to the countryside, to see life away from the city, as a contrast. Editors like that sort of thing. More to the point, so would I.'

Harri leans against the stove, deep in thought. Georgie worries she's crossed a line and become too familiar. The fact remains, she is married, and he is not. While war

291

relaxed so many ridiculous social constructs surrounding the sexes, it hasn't swept away every etiquette entirely.

'It doesn't matter,' she fills in quickly. 'I'll check in with Lieutenant Howarth and see what he can conjure up.'

'No, I would like to.' Harri pushes himself off the stove with energy. 'The team here can manage the enquiries for one day. Like you, I could do with some space, away from this bloody man who's taken up residence inside my head.'

'If you're sure,' she says. 'Where can I hire a car at short notice?'

The loose folds on Harri's face lift, his expression unusually boyish. 'Let me worry about that. I'll pick you up from the hotel at nine thirty tomorrow morning.'

'Should I bring anything?'

'Just your notebook, and perhaps some food,' he says. 'I'll show you a little slice of Germany to make you smile.'

CHAPTER FORTY-THREE: BREAKING FREE

21st February 1946

Harri

There's a certain thrill as he waits outside the Baseler Hof the next morning, a feeling Harri recognises from childhood, of surprising his parents with something he'd created and watching their faces crease with pleasure as he presented it to them. The tingle he'd felt inside himself, too. Is this endeavour equally childish for a supposedly hard-headed Kripo man? No, he decides quickly. It's simply nice and what they both need. What he needs especially.

It's worth every effort when he spies Georgie emerging from the front entrance, scanning left and right with a confused expression, and perhaps ever-so-slightly irritated at his not being there on time. When he hoots the horn, her head whips towards the sound and she squints at the car, her eyes finally settling on him in recognition. The look that floods her face is priceless.

'Hey, where did you get *this*?' Her voice is full of wonder as she lowers herself into the passenger seat and places a picnic basket in the back seat.

'Hmm, just something I had squirrelled away for a rainy day. Isn't that the phrase?'

'It's not raining, Harri.'

'I had noticed. But you said we needed transport, and so here she is.'

'Seriously, Harri, where did you get this? It's wonderful.' She runs a hand over the leather seats and the metal dashboard, fingering at the bowed roof above their heads. 'Despite their provenance, I've always coveted one of these.'

Once a rarity on Hamburg's streets, the Volkswagen Beetle has become a familiar sight post-war, though few can claim the prestige of Harri's model. When the first cars rolled off the production line in 1938, his good friend and chief engineer Emil needed new 'customers' to test-drive Hitler's home-grown pet project. The Beetle stood as a key part of the Führer's vision of a wealthy, industrialised Germany, where every family would be able to afford 'the people's car', his drive towards the mighty Reich. With such a gift, Harri, Hella and then Lily took every opportunity to venture out on day trips, the shiny new motor attracting admiring looks wherever they went.

But when war loomed, production halted and petrol rations forced Harri to mothball 'Griselda' in a lock-up. 'It's her first outing since the peace,' he tells Georgie, 'so forgive the old girl if she's a bit rusty.'

'I think she's beautiful,' Georgie asserts. 'How on earth did you get her going after all this time?'

'Plenty of elbow grease, real grease . . .' he holds up a hand still tainted with black '. . . and a friend with a spanner.' He thinks of Emil's old eagerness for mechanics as they pulled off the dustsheet and tinkered with the engine into the early hours. 'You can thank Sergeant Dawson for the petrol.'

He runs an affectionate hand over the steering wheel before drawing away from the pavement with a comforting pop and thrust of the exhaust, joining the traffic of jeeps, Mercedes, army trucks and other Beetles moving up and down Hamburg's highways. Griselda's paintwork is scuffed and she's badly in need of proper TLC, but the distinct chug of her heart instantly lifts Harri's mood as he steers out of the city centre.

'So, where is your "other woman" taking us?' Georgie asks.

'Aha! That's for me and Griselda to know,' he says.

'A mystery tour then?' She issues a small laugh to herself.

'What's so funny?'

'It's only that the last time I got into a car with a German officer for a mystery tour, I ended up in a hot air balloon over Berlin.'

'And was that so unpleasant?' Harri asks.

'I'm not one for heights, so I suppose scary and pleasant . . .'

'And . . .?'

'And the same man ended up kidnapping and beating my husband-to-be, as well as hounding us both out of Berlin. He was SS.'

'Oh.' Harri shoots a look at her. 'I can see the similarities. But I promise you, Miss Young, there will be no hot air balloons, and I have left my keys to the Kripo cells back at the station. Which is where I suggest we leave all talk of the case, just for today. Agreed?'

'Agreed.'

Mercifully it isn't raining, or snowing, the day being typically February-like and overcast, but not enough to dampen their mood. They move through the grey-black sludge of ice remnants bound with grime, where the moving shoals of wanderers gradually stretch out to a few walkers here and there as the city streets become country lanes.

The sky remains uninspiring but the torque of muscles around Harri's neck and shoulders already feels looser; he will not let the Puppet Master become a dark shadow today. He notes Georgie's eyes switching from left to right in absorbing everything around her.

'Is any of this familiar?' he asks.

'I did a little bit of touring in Germany before the war,' she says. 'But it was summertime, extremely hot, and it looked very different. Mainly because there were swastikas everywhere.'

'And the country wasn't in pieces?'

'Yes, that too.'

He can't deny it feels good to be driving again, with a woman sitting beside him. When was the last time? It was the summer after war was declared, Hella alongside and Lily sleeping, snug in her arms. They weren't to know it was their last real trip out, or that life was about to get a lot harder, their time together a precious jewel. They'd packed a picnic on a whim, Harri nosing the car into the countryside looking for a spot to lay out their blanket, where they could breathe beyond the city limits, the Brownshirts and the oppression already taking its toll. Where they could feel free for a few hours.

Just like Georgie, Hella had stared in wonder at life speeding by the car window. 'When it's all over,' she murmured, 'if we can't go to London, then I think we should move out of the city. A place in the country, for us to really grow as a family. What do you think, Harri?'

'You mean me as a country policeman?' he'd joked, eyebrows raised.

'Why not? I can picture you propping up the local bar with all the farmers, arresting cow rustlers as your public duty.'

Harri couldn't see it, but he said nothing in response. The end of the war seemed a long way off, even then. The outcome, too, for Germany and for him, was something he dared not imagine.

He checks his dark nostalgia; he's already told Georgie that gloomy thoughts are not for today. It's about enjoying the here and now. Regrets he can easily mull over in the long hours of the night.

After an hour and a half he steers Griselda into a forest clearing, laying out a blanket and Georgie's picnic on a dry patch of grass.

'You must be popular in the Baseler Hof kitchen,' Harri remarks, at an array of food he hasn't seen in some time.

'I'll admit to swiping a few extras when the chef turned his back,' she says. 'Plus, I gave him my one and only pair of stockings for his wife. Happily, that means I can no longer dress up to attend insufferable military dinners.'

'Technically, I should arrest you for theft.'

'Or you could eat the evidence?'

'That is a much better prospect. And it means no paperwork, for which I have no paper anyway.'

Stomachs full (and Harri can't honestly remember a time when he did feel so sated), they both seem reluctant to move on. Despite the cold, the midday sun is edging its way through the grey, while he and Georgie lie on the blanket, wrapped in their outer layers, staring skywards, each end of it tucked around them like a human sandwich. Lying there, he feels different, as if from the moment Georgie climbed into Griselda, they had somehow altered – from acquaintances to friends, sharing their time through choice. He likes it, both the company and intimacy of friendship.

'What *are* you going to do, Harri?' Georgie breaks the lengthy silence, her eyes fixed on the sky above.

'When? Right now, I'm trapped by a mad woman under a blanket.'

'Idiot. No, I'm thinking, after all this?'

'You mean after I catch this killer, am hailed as a hero of the Kripo by the British forces, given a medal and my choice of command?' He's well aware the humour masks the stark truth, of Major Stephens' intolerance, plus his forthright orders. Not least the mandate to cut loose a certain journalist lying not a million miles away.

'Yes, after that,' she pushes. 'Seriously, why don't you come to England, as you planned? You'll know me, and Max, too. I mean, I know it will be strange at first . . .'

'We'll see,' he caps her off, partly because he doesn't want to think about either element: the life he and Hella had planned in London, or the fact that Stephens will move to scupper any chances if the Puppet Master is not arrested very soon.

'Come on,' he urges, throwing off the blanket. 'We've still a few kilometres to go, and if Griselda gets too jealous, she may not start again.'

'Where is it we're going?' she entreats. 'Tell me, please.'

'There is a saying in your own language, Georgie Young. Patience is a virtue. You'll just have to wait.'

CHAPTER FORTY-FOUR: STRIKING A DEAL

21st February 1946

Meta

Thanks to Zofia's diligence, Meta no longer itches with insect life nesting in her clothes or the roots of her hair. What she runs with now is impatience, and then guilt in waiting for Zofia to leave. It's true that all the nursing and good food has been a lifeline, plus friendship that she'd forgotten ever existed. But she's better now, mobile enough to do her own foraging. And something else. Georgie's policeman has said she needs to stop looking for the man, but he hasn't instructed her to stop everything, has he?

With a brisk wind in her face, Meta takes in the view of scrubland outside the factory, listening intently for signs of patrolling Polizei. As if she needs those clowns looking out for her! Satisfied of neither sight nor sound, she moves towards the hum of civilisation. Annoyingly, her pace is slowed by the stiffness of her limbs from lying down so long and the bruises still present, plus the suitcase that swings in line with her right leg. Reluctantly, she has almost emptied it, save for a few tools vital to her task and one pack of cigarettes. She passes the Rathaus, nodding in deference to the city's solid, symbolic edifice, as her marker that the world hasn't collapsed in her absence. Beyond it, she makes one trade from a street seller, and is back on her route that sees her hunting out a familiar face.

'Is he here?' Meta stands on the threshold of the *trümmerkinder* camp, as if respecting the imaginary walls to their home-hovel. The older boy loitering inside a makeshift doorway looks her up and down, no doubt assessing her newly clean hair and clothes that are not yet on their way to being rags. Her cheeks, while fuller, are still pinched enough to pass as one of them.

'Hey, Popo! Your girlfriend's here,' he sneers, peeling away towards the fire, where Popo is busy stoking the embers.

He barely turns a good eye towards her as she approaches, feigning disinterest. Meta isn't offended; he's done it before, only to be fully animated when they are left alone. That's what she doesn't like about the gangs – the façade of resilience that's demanded at all times, and the obvious hierarchy of the tough over the weak. Meta may suffer loneliness, but there's no pretence either. Well, not all the time.

Tentatively, she approaches the fire and squats, as Popo shows some scant attention. Then, when he brings his seeing eye onto her properly, it widens with alarm. 'What happened to you?' he grunts. There's a grudging concern in his voice, perhaps the only type he dare expose.

'I got attacked,' she says, her voice low enough that only he can hear.

'Where?' Popo sidles up to her, reading her need to keep things between them.

'Near where you were, the other night, over in St Pauli. You begged from a couple – a drunk woman and a man, remember? He gave you some coins.'

She watches Popo's memory grinding inside his maimed head, toiling behind the opaque blind eye. There's a flicker inside. 'You mean the one with the homburg hat, having to hold up that giggling woman?' he says at last.

'Yes!' Meta's dormant heart actually leaps inside her battered chest. But now the real test for Popo. 'Did you see his face?'

The milky eye rolls. 'It was dark, but yes, I did.'

'Enough to describe it, so that I can draw him?' Meta can barely control her excitement. A tangible help to the Kripo yet again. Better still, something solid for Georgie, and Zofia, in gratitude.

'Yes, I think so.' His seeing eye, the one that can look both mean and determined, narrows.

'What, Popo?'

'I'll need something in return.'

Meta sags. How many precious cigarettes will she have to relinquish for a slice of his memory?

'Not cigarettes,' he says. In the background, a raucous argument has struck up between two of the boys, but Popo ignores it and keeps his voice low. 'I need your help. On a raid.'

She slumps again. The thieving she can do in her sleep, but it'll mean more of a delay on getting her image to Georgie. Equally, she knows Popo and his stubborn

302

nature, doggedness that's a product of war. What choice does she have?

'Where?'

'There's an empty house on the Elbe. The family only moved out a few days ago, so I heard. In a hurry.'

If Meta were to have gathered the same information – and if it's reliable – she would be targeting the house, too. Popo's strengths are in begging, his charm in eliciting money from strangers. The face helps, of course. He's less skilled in night-time raids, largely because of his limited sight. The gang, however, is unforgiving and demands he takes a turn in the real money-spinner, raiding houses for valuable trinkets that the occupiers have left behind in their rush to pack.

'All right,' she concedes. 'When?'

'Tonight.'

'So, when do I get my description?'

He smiles with an artful slant. 'Afterwards, of course.'

Irritated, Meta takes a punt on her superior thieving skills as a bargaining chip. 'We make the picture before, Popo. I give you my word I'll come to the raid. But then I have to go. Is that a deal?'

He sighs, considering, and she sees the old Popo struggling to get out, the persona before his face was burnt to wax. 'Deal. It's a good thing I like you, Meta.'

CHAPTER FORTY-FIVE:
THE FACTORY

21st February 1946

Georgie

'Is this it? Is this where we're going?' Georgie squints through Griselda's windscreen as a flat terrain of ploughed winter fields gives way to rows upon rows of wooden huts. A particular type of hut, those that remind her of hidden horrors, of those she saw with her own eyes in Sachsenhausen after the liberation, alongside the grotesque images of Bergen-Belsen. In all honesty, she's seen enough degradation. Today is supposed to be a reprieve, so where on earth is Harri taking her?

By contrast, he can't contain a very wide smile, his enthusiasm evident. 'You know, if such a thing ever existed, this was one of Hitler's better ideas,' he says.

He's lost his mind, she thinks. 'Harri, where exactly are we?'

It has the sprawl of a small town, yet none of the elements

of a community that sprouts organically around a church, a river, small stores or a schoolhouse. And then she sees it. Griselda motors around a bend to reveal the view so far screened by trees on one side, a huge brick structure dominating the landscape and dwarfing the made-to-measure village. Its style is solid and stark, the clean lines of the Teutonic building mirrored by five concrete chimneys soaring into the air like soldiers on parade. Georgie shudders: it's Hitler all right, reminiscent of the towering columns stretching down Berlin's principal highway of Unter den Linden back in 1938. Except now, there are no swastikas evident and Harri seems more than happy to forge on through the main gate, announcing himself and being waved through without delay.

He stops the engine in a car park alongside scores of other Beetles, clearly noting the surprise – no, shock – on her face. 'You wanted to see something positive, didn't you?'

'And this is it?' So far, it's just a telling reminder of the Reich.

'Yes!' he cries. 'It's a perfect example of British-German co-operation, or if I'm being entirely accurate – and a little bit cynical – a British driver of German pioneering. More importantly, it's Griselda's home. It's where she came from.'

They get out to face a large *Volkswagen* sign, amid the manufactured 'town' of Wolfsburg, grandly named as the 'City of Strength Through Joy' in Hitler's day. Before the war, the Führer commissioned an entire city to house engineers, production line workers and their families, and even a grandiose hotel for potential buyers. All this is relayed with some element of pride by a foreman called Hans, who greets Harri at the door with a firm handshake and a familiarity that's a nod to their past.

'So, this is the journalist I told you about, Miss Georgina Young,' Harri introduces.

'Pleased to meet anyone who admires our beloved Beetle, Fräulein Young.'

Hans steers them through the lofty, busy industry of the factory floor, cars in varying stages of production, their parts gleaming and new, distinct bodywork shining. 'Just six hundred and thirty Beetles rolled off out of Wolfsburg before the war . . .' he shouts over the din.

'Griselda being one of those,' Harri whispers in Georgie's ear.

'. . . but then production was halted when war came, and the factory turned over to building jeeps and military vehicles.'

Hans doesn't elaborate on who manned the lines during the conflict, but it's not a great leap to imagine the forced labour of Russians, Poles and Italians. Hence the huts that look suspiciously like concentration camps, their residents churning out Kubelwagen - distinctive German jeeps – by the thousand. How must those workers have felt, manufacturing vehicles used in the fight against their own countrymen?

But Hans is keen not to dwell on the factory's inauspicious past. 'And now we're up to almost a thousand Beetles rolling out per month,' he says proudly.

'And who controls all of this?' Georgie asks.

'We have an English engineer in charge,' he tells her. 'An army major who worked on British tanks in the war, and he's taken on the Beetle as "his baby", he likes to say. He would speak to you personally, but he's not here today.'

Instead, Georgie is given free access to any of the men on the production line, with Hans hovering nearby, though well out of earshot. Harri busies himself peering under the bonnets at the gleaming engines, seeming relaxed as he talks with the workers. Once or twice, Georgie catches him staring into the high structured ceiling, and she wonders if he is somewhere in the past, with bitter-sweet memories, or else battling thoughts of Hamburg's killer, the man who squats firmly inside his head. He's pledged to leave it behind for today, but can he? There is, however, plenty to occupy her: she pulls out her notebook with relish, quizzing those on the vast factory floor about wages and working conditions, moving to the offices and the canteen to gauge the women's point of view. After almost two hours, she can detect no animosity from the German staff, only relief at having work and a pay packet at the end of the month. And as much love for their product as Harri bestows on Griselda.

'I told you,' Harri says as they climb back into the car. 'Incredible as it may seem, it's a success story to come out of this whole mess.'

She looks at him sideways, at his self-satisfied expression. 'But it's controlled by the British. Doesn't that bother you?'

'Ah, but it won't always be,' he says. 'I'm not certain of much, Georgie, yet that's one thing I have high hopes for. Germany will return as an industrial force. Just watch.'

Georgie wakes with a start as Harri draws up to the Baseler Hof, disorientated in the encroaching darkness and her neck at an awkward angle. 'Oh Lord, Harri, I'm so sorry. I must have dropped off. There's something about the sound of Griselda's engine, lulling me to sleep.'

He bats away her apology. 'She does tend to have that effect. My wife used to . . . Anyway, did you have a good trip, manage to throw off the city shackles for a few hours?'

She leans to peck at his stubbly cheek. 'I had the most wonderful day, thank you. Productive, too. I'll owe you a portion of the profits from my article, because once I get some pictures organised, it's sure to warrant a separate piece. If nothing else, Lieutenant Howarth will be delighted.'

'Forget the profits, I'll take a decent dinner in return,' he says. 'After that picnic, I think you've reactivated my stomach.'

'Then I'll pledge to stand you three courses at the London Ritz when you come to stay,' she teases. 'Meanwhile, what time at the Victory Club tomorrow?'

'Seven p.m. Dancing shoes essential,' he says.

'Ditto,' she says, hauling herself out of the car. 'And that's an order, Inspector Schroder.'

Wearily, Georgie climbs towards reception. Despite a blast of icy wind on the hotel steps, she's awash with a warmth she hasn't known in ages, of a day spent pleasantly, in good company. It was work and yet felt like anything but. Then the swift aftermath, a sharp twist to her heart, Max uppermost. When was the last time they'd spent a day lazily doing nothing, or roaming London's art galleries, taking tea and hurrying for nothing and no one? Guilt, too, at having shared that time with someone other than her husband. And enjoying it.

She resolves to write to Max after catching up with Zofia at dinner, her way of reconnecting with the man she does love, even if their bond won't be immediate. The very act of putting pen to paper will soothe her own conscience, and for that, she endures a second stab of remorse.

'Is Fräulein Dreyfus in?' Georgie asks the receptionist on the way to her room.

'Yes, I saw her return about thirty minutes ago,' he says. 'And there's a message for you, Fräulein Young. It came late this afternoon.'

When she flips open the paper, it's both brief and surprising:

Georgie – please ring me at home. I have some information about the picture you showed us at the Atlantic. Regards, Olivia Stephens

Picture? In her sleep fog, Georgie needs to wind her memory back. Oh yes, the St Christopher. What on earth would the major's wife know about that?

The telephone at the Stephens' residence is answered by the nonchalant maid, but Olivia is quick to the receiver. 'Georgie! How nice to hear from you.'

'Your note said you have some information,' she says, dispensing with any niceties.

'Oh yes. Well, it's not me as such. Do you remember Marion, the engineer's wife?'

'The one whose husband deals in shi—'

'Yes, that one,' Olivia cuts in. 'She didn't want to say anything at the time, not being entirely sure. But, on reflection, she's fairly certain she's seen that St Christopher.'

At the other end of the line, Georgie is wide awake. 'And does Marion remember exactly where?'

'Oh yes,' Mrs Stephens says. 'In fact, she knows who it belongs to.'

CHAPTER FORTY-SIX:
BANG TO RIGHTS

21st February 1946

Meta

She has the scroll of treasure tucked safely inside her coat, Popo's recollections of the man's face sketched in pencil. After a good hour with Meta scratching away by the weak firelight, he'd concluded it was a good likeness, and for once she believes he's not faking it. Now, it's her turn to come good on their deal.

Meta feels almost naked without the suitcase, left back at her place, knowing that she couldn't bear to dump it, even in a chase for her liberty. Against army patrols and hungry dogs, the bulk of it might be her undoing. She's also cold, having shed several layers in anticipating squeezing through tight gaps to gain access, plus a quick and nimble exit.

'Is this the one?' she whispers to Popo over the gentle slap of the black-water Elbe just feet away. She thinks how nice it would be to wake up each morning, in a sumptuous, warm bed, and hear that rhythmic sound, but it's a fantasy cut short by the reality of the moment.

'Yes, this is it,' he says, his voice hoarse with nerves.

Meta puts a foot on his shoulder and launches herself up against a brick wall, her face peering over the garden boundary.

'See anything?' Popo says, fully blinded by the flap of her coat in his face.

She drops down. 'No lights. No car on the driveway. It looks empty to me.'

This time, it's Popo who goes over the wall first, sitting atop and pulling Meta up by the hand, both landing like statues when they hit the ground on the other side. Popo's ears virtually twitch in the moonlight as he listens for the pounding of heavy canine footfall beating towards them. Nothing.

Like cats, they steal across the lawn and make for the back entrance, the doors always less solid than the grandiose front of these houses. This is where Popo's skill comes to the fore; Meta's never known a lock that he can't feel his way around, tuning into the faintest of clicks as the catch gives, and she's relieved not to have to squeeze through the tiniest of windows, not when her body is still smarting from the attack.

Once inside, it's silent running, using a sign language unique to *trümmerkinder* as they steal through the house on tiptoe. It's Meta's eyes that Popo needs most in assessing the treasure swiftly, what they can pocket and carry, but also what brings the best return on the street. She knows his status within the gang will rise in line with the value of tonight's spoils.

311

Upstairs, in the bedrooms, he holds up one or two items and she shakes her head. Surely, there's something better? Gingerly, Meta rolls her foot carefully over each floorboard – experience tells her the wealthy like to hide their valuables from roaming eyes, those rich German industrialists forced to leave items behind as they fled in the wake of the Reich's defeat. The British military aren't beyond the same ruse, either, especially when black market goods are way cheaper than 'back home', and the one-time German elite are trading tiaras for tins of food.

To Meta's acute senses, one board feels just a tad looser. She gestures silently to Popo and they prise up the wooden slat, Meta pushing in her skinny arm to ferret under the floor. She nods as her hand paws at something solid, pulling out a single package, layers of cloth tightly bound. Hastily unwrapped, the moonlight instantly catches what's inside, and it's a toss-up as to what glows the most – Popo's face or the jewellery nestled within the cloth.

With satisfaction, Meta sees his one eye widen with pleasure. Then alarm. His attention swivels to the door, at the noise from downstairs – footsteps, shuffling. Did they leave the back door open? A stray cat, or perhaps a brave rat, venturing this far from the river's edge.

'Hey, anyone there?' A muffled voice from below. Not a rat, then. More shuffling and footsteps.

Popo's whisper is barely audible in Meta's ear. 'Must be a watchman, but he sounds old. We can barge past and outrun him.'

Meta nods, while mentally testing her stiffened legs. It's better than the alternative of a sizable drop from the bedroom window. Popo pockets his treasure and together they creep towards the crest of the sweeping staircase, watching the man hobble underneath in his search and waiting for the patter of dog's claws in his wake. Both breathe with relief when there is none. Meta goes first as the look-out, descending with stealth down the carpeted stairway, Popo and his distinct odour not far behind. She signals that the watchman is towards the front parlour and they should pick up speed in their aim for the kitchen. His good eye almost bursting from its socket, Popo swallows and nods, fear exuding from his face.

They move. In the same moment as the watchman turns and heads in their direction. 'HEY, YOU!' he cries. 'Stop! Stop!'

As if they would, especially with the glint of metal close to his body. The old man isn't fast, but his shotgun has reach, the first blast contained inside the house and sending splinters flying in their wake.

'*SCHEISSE!*' Popo screams as he hurls himself past Meta and through the back door, streaking across the lawn and leaping as if with springs on his feet. She's running with every effort, but her legs are like lead; they buckle to a fall as another blast rings out into the night air. Meta picks herself up, her only goal being Popo hovering on top of the brick wall, his hand dangling and ready to haul her up.

Then the sound they both dread: the dogs' bark echoing in the night air, a vicious baying of killers in hot pursuit. Big dogs with teeth to match.

Meta makes it to the wall, Popo's face above. 'Jump! Jump!' he's screaming. But her once-lithe form is spent, and his hand might as well be several hundred metres in the air for all the energy she has left. The animals move in close enough that she smells their rancid dog-breath, flecks of spittle flying to the side of her vision. As Meta turns, they are almost on her.

And then the sound that she never thought to welcome. 'Halt! Down!'

The dogs freeze, stood down by the command as two men in uniform approach, a bright torch shining in her face. Instantly, they must see she's a waif in still too many clothes, a threat easily dealt with.

'*Polizei!*' one yells in unconvincing German, his voice sounding disheartened as the torch strobes over her, revealing their pathetic catch. 'You're under arrest, Fräulein.'

Fuck it. *Bang to rights*, as her Tommy used to say.

A night in the cells is never a welcome prospect for a thief, but this one is warmer than her own place, and that's something at least. A hot cup of tea, too, though it's bitter, in the way the English brew it, and it wakes her up. Swallowing the last drop, Meta lies down again on the thin mattress, wrapping herself in a decent blanket. Aside from the fact that she's in the custody of British military police, she thinks it's not such a bad predicament. Until she reaches inside her innermost blouson and feels the crinkle of paper against her skin, the drawing nestled close to her flesh for safekeeping. Damn! It's crucial she gets it to Georgie, and soon. And yet she knows the timing depends on military police, and probably the level of disdain a magistrate might have for the 'menace' of rubble kids. It will be just her luck to face one who thinks she deserves a lesson – behind bars.

At least Popo got away. He dropped over the wall when it became obvious she had no hope of escape, but Meta is neither bitter nor angry at his apparent abandonment. In their world, the accepted code says you do everything to help each other flee. Beyond that, you save yourself and the goods. Popo will earn fresh kudos in the gang after last night, and she may, in time, benefit a little from that. More pressing for her is that she gets his visual recollection to Fräulein Young.

There's a jangle of keys, the lock turns noisily and Meta stiffens, then relaxes when she sees it's a military guard with a benign expression and a tray, steam rising and the inviting smell jabbing at her empty stomach. Food. Hot food. At any other time, she might relish being a guest at this hotel for a few nights.

'Get this down yer,' he says, but it's without revulsion, unlike the German police, who generally treat her kind as a type of pestilence.

'I . . . I need to get information to someone,' she chances, in her best English, her face petitioning any goodwill he possesses. 'Do you know Fräulein Young?'

'Eh?'

'She's a reporter. British. She's at the hotel Baseler Hof. Please, it is . . .' she struggles to pick out the word '. . . vital.'

'Vital, you say?' There's no animosity but he's not hearing her desperation.

'Please, sir. She's working with the Kripo, with an Inspektor . . .' And here Meta digs deep to remember his name, through the fog of her head wound and convalescence. 'Schmidt . . . erm, no . . . Schroder. *Ja!* Inspektor Schroder. I need to see him.'

The soldier looks blank and bored, tired in what is now the end of his long night shift. 'Listen, Fräulein. I have orders to keep you here until the local police see fit to take you. Nothing more, nothing less. I'll get skinned alive by my sergeant if I disobey.'

Skinned? What does that mean? Meta only knows from

his dogged, army-speak tone that he won't shift or break ranks. The door clangs shut and she's alone again, but with food that's the best she's eaten since Zofia last cooked for her. It's when she's downed the last scrap that the walls begin to close in, a sense of panic rising at the world out there, without her in it. When will she get to see it again, to push towards something other than drudgery?

She brings out the drawing and smooths the paper flat, determined not to distort the carefully pencilled image with too many folds. She slips it under the limp pillow and lays her head down, bringing her knees up to her chest under the blanket, like she does at her own place.

There's no choice but to wait, to endure this world she's not used to, where fate – and not Meta Hertzig – will determine her next steps.

CHAPTER FORTY-SEVEN: A STEP FORWARD

22nd February 1946

Harri

He dreams of Hella into the early hours, though it's not the gut-churning nightmare that sours his sleep most nights. In these latest visions, he and Hella are happy and carefree, under a sky that is bright with sunshine and not burning like hell. Lily features, too, stomping around in her first baby shoes and making them laugh. Harri wakes with aching cheeks and wonders if people smile in their sleep, then feels the lines of salt crust running across his face. It's certainly possible to cry.

Overall, though, his mood is good, motivating him to wash and shave with vigour. He's halfway through one side of his face when there's a frantic knock on his door. It can only be his downstairs neighbour at this hour, with gossip she's desperate to pass on, or some frustration to vent.

'Georgie! What are you doing . . .?' Her mouth warps

slightly at the sight of him, perhaps at a face still half-lathered white, like a circus clown. 'Sorry, come in. I'm just getting ready.'

'I thought it best to come early, and save you a trip to the station,' she says, breathing heavily from the climb, and perhaps with the urgency that's etched into her brow.

'Why wouldn't I go to the station?' He leads her towards the kitchen and skates the razor hastily over the remaining cheek.

'Because we need to go out to Altona immediately. I think I have a sighting of the pendant. And possibly the owner, too.'

No wonder she looks less well-slept than him. No wonder she's unable to contain her excitement. 'Then let's go, Detective Young. Dawson should be here any minute.'

Predictably, the engineer and his wife live in a largely untouched suburb of Hamburg, the Elbe bordering their capacious back garden like an oversized stream. Harri notes a military jeep parked in the long, circular driveway.

'Oh, they're just checking the garden,' Marion Peabody explains when she shows them in. 'There was a break-in last night next door – a house just vacated. One of them got away, apparently, and the police just want to be sure the thief isn't hiding out in our grounds.'

Mrs Peabody – 'Marion, please' – leads them into a neat, cosy parlour that's typically English, right down to a reproduction of Constable's *Hay Wain* on one wall. Quickly, though, Harri sees that this British woman is neither starchy nor fluffy; she offers tea and gets straight to the point.

'I couldn't stop thinking about it after that day at the

Atlantic,' she tells them. 'It niggled at me for hours, and then it came to me in a flash.'

'What did?' Georgie asks.

'Where I'd seen it. And who I'd seen wearing it.'

'So, he works in your husband's office, the man who you think owns or owned this pendant?' Harri asks. So far, it feels too good to be true.

'I don't *think*, Inspector,' she says firmly. 'I know. He came to a party here late last summer. It was an informal occasion, and the men were largely in open-neck shirts. I remember being a touch surprised at him wearing something religious.'

'Why surprised?'

Marion considers. 'Hmm, nothing to base it on, other than he didn't seem the type.'

Georgie and Harri exchange looks. While Harri favours hard and fast evidence, he knows Georgie gives plenty of credence to gut feeling. Not surprising, since her survival in wartime may have depended on it.

'But I know for certain it's the same pendant, because of what's on the back,' Marion goes on. 'What's very clearly sketched in your drawing.'

'Yes?' Now she has Harri's attention.

'I remarked that it was very nice, and he put a hand to it, saying his mother had given it to him. As he fingered it, I noticed the metal was incised on the back, and said what a shame it had been damaged.'

There's little doubt in Harri's mind then both that Marion is a reliable witness, and their St Christopher did belong to this man at some juncture. Several questions remain: did he lose it, or have it robbed before the attack on Meta? Could he realistically be their killer?

'So, what sort of man is he, this Martin Sexton?'

Marion fusses with the teapot. 'Oh, I don't know him well. He's been here all of three times, but he seems nice enough. David, my husband, could tell you much more. He was the one who employed him.'

'Do you know how long he's been with your husband's company?' Georgie asks. Side by side on the sofa, Harri senses the quiver running through her.

'Only since late summer, I think. He'd just joined when we had the party, and that was the first of September.'

This time, it's Harri who can't sit still. Three murders in three months, starting in November '45. Is it just a coincidence? Or the break they so desperately need? 'Can we speak to your husband?'

'I'm afraid David is away until Saturday,' she adds, 'and I can't contact him — silly man likes to go hiking up in the hills in this freezing weather. But I'm sure the company secretary can give you details, or you can speak to Martin himself, if he's not away on a site visit. I'm certain he has a perfectly reasonable explanation, but once it came back to me where I'd seen it, I couldn't ignore the fact.'

'Thank you, Marion,' Georgie says as they leave. 'You've been a great help.'

'I hope to see you again, Georgie. Come to the Atlantic. Apart from Olivia, that gaggle of women do need shaking up a bit.'

'I promise that I'll try.'

'What do you think?' Georgie says, the instant they're in the rear of Dawson's jeep.

'I almost don't like to,' Harri replies. 'We know our killer could be English, posing as German. So, it depends on this Sexton man and his language skills. Let's go and find out.'

A portion of David Peabody's engineering firm has been afforded a temporary base by the CCG amid the bustling town hall grandeur of the Rathaus. On the first floor, they locate his efficient secretary, one Fräulein Geller, who dishes out both good and bad news. Yes, Martin Sexton has been in the office today and they do have a personnel file on him, but no, he's already left for the weekend.

'But it's only ten thirty,' Harri questions.

'I know,' Fräulein Geller says apologetically. 'He came in briefly to check some reports.'

'Do you know where he's going, or where he lives? Even better, do you have a photograph?'

Her suspicions clearly aroused, Miss Geller pulls out a buff file and opens it. 'All employees submit one when they join the firm,' she says, flicking through the pages. 'Oh.'

'What is it?' Harri sounds, and is, impatient.

'There doesn't seem to be a picture here,' she relays. 'Only a chit with a request for one. Herr Sexton must have forgotten to do it.'

Harri doesn't need to turn to see Georgie's eyes boring into him; he feels their heat.

She steps forward. 'What about any photographs on site, or some that might have been taken at a party, for instance?'

'Oh yes! I hadn't thought of that.' Fräulein Geller rifles in the filing cabinet again. 'Here. These were taken at Herr Peabody's house.'

All three peer at the black and white images of smiling people in the ornate garden, posing in a group. 'Which one is Herr Sexton?' Harri asks wearily. He has a nasty feeling that after the initial gains with Marion Peabody, their luck might be running out.

'Hmm, I can't see him,' Fräulein Geller says. 'Perhaps he's that one, behind Herr Trent. You can just see his shoulder.'

Harri is right. Good fortune has gone astray, with Herr Trent towering over most of the crowd. Has Martin Sexton purposely snuck behind him for the photograph, to stay out of sight?

Harri tries another tack with Fräulein Geller. 'Can you describe Martin Sexton for us?'

'Let's see. He's taller than most, average build, fairish hair, and well, quite ordinary looking,' she says.

'Any moles or birthmarks, scars or unusual features?' Georgie presses. 'A beard or moustache?'

'No. Like I say, he's not someone that stands out.'

In more ways than one, thinks Harri. Word for word, it's the same description Marion Peabody offered up – a blank canvas of a man, who melts easily into the background. Amid the chaos of Hamburg, he really is that English needle in a haystack.

'And how is his German?'

'Oh, perfect,' the secretary reports. 'In fact, sometimes you'd never guess he's English.'

'*Now* what do you think?' Georgie echoes, back in the jeep.

'He's certainly more than a person of interest,' Harri says. 'I've phoned through details of his personnel file to Anna, and she'll follow up on his references with the British authorities. We'll check out the address he has on record.'

By their third stop, Harri is unsurprised at another dead end.

'No, he hasn't lived here for the past two months or so,' the landlady says. 'Left all of a sudden. Paid his rent and was gone.'

'Description?' It's worth a go, he thinks.

'Never really looked at him much,' she remarks. 'Though he did have a peculiar smell, too sweet for me. I thought it must be some type of English cologne.'

Harri has almost forgotten about the patchouli that was so distinct to Paula's nose. Now, it's become a vital piece slotted into this infuriating puzzle, and yet they're still way off completing the picture.

'And you took him to be English?' he asks.

'Well, yes, with a name like that.' The woman frowns. 'But, you know, his German was so good he could easily be one of us.'

Harri clomps heavily down the stairs of the apartment block. 'If you're going to ask me again what I think,' he pre-empts Georgie's question, 'I'd say there's a high chance that Martin Sexton – if that's his real persona – is our man. Except we're not any nearer to knowing what he looks like, where he lives or what he's doing now.'

'Oh, one thing,' the old Frau shouts after them, leaning over the banister. 'He played that music they used to have in the clubs before the war. My son loved it. Lots of trumpets and such.'

'Swing music?' Harri calls up the stairs.

'That's it,' she says. 'Swing. Infernal noise to me, but he played it constantly.'

★ ★ ★

Returning to Davidwache, Harri chalks the name in large letters on the board, followed by several question marks. Anna has come up blank on a Martin Sexton registered at the British Embassy, and the CCG have even less to offer than Peabody & Co.

'I'll try immigration next,' Anna says from her corner of the office. 'But that will take some time persuading them to even look.'

'And time is what we don't have,' Harri mutters to himself, then with volume: 'Tell them it's urgent. Tell them it's bloody life and death!' He senses a thick, oily slick rise into his chest, knowing his anger is propelled by fear. Fear that time is running out. 'Any word from the hospital on Sigrid Heike?' he hectors irritably to anyone within earshot. 'Isn't she conscious yet?'

'Only just,' Anna says weakly. 'Paula went over to get a statement. Only . . .'

'Only *what*?'

'She's very confused, apparently, and can't remember much. Paula has nothing worthwhile.'

'*Mist!*' Harri slams down his coffee cup, seeing Anna flinch from the corner of his eye. His fury is helping no one. 'Sorry,' he says limply.

He wanders over to Georgie, who stands in front of the board, arms folded, with that distinct expression he's come to recognise. The cogs are churning.

'What is it?' Harri draws close to stand by her.

'What if he was already here?' she muses, thinking aloud. 'What if he didn't arrive to take up a post, but was in Germany all this time? It explains his perfect accent, knowing the way of life and how to blend in when it suits him.'

Harri's fingers go to the growth on his chin that he's missed with the morning's swift shave. 'You mean as a correspondent, like you, or an ex-army man?'

'Maybe,' she says, her eyes swinging towards him. 'Or perhaps one step further?'

'Any ideas?' Harri's brain is aching with all manner of combinations, most of which lead to another dead body – and soon.

Georgie sucks in a breath. 'A traitor perhaps? Like the British Free Corps – British fascists fighting on the German side – or a propagandist.'

'Like Lord Haw-Haw, spreading fear on the radio?'

Georgie shrugs. 'It's not impossible and, let's face it, with the chaos just after the surrender, it would have been easy to fake a death and be cleansed of your own past. And it would explain the motivation you've been working on, that he's harbouring some kind of deep betrayal. If you'd given over your allegiance to one country, only to be cast aside in defeat, how bitter would you feel? I've no idea why he would take it out on those women, but then what drives any man to assault?'

Harri's eyes crawl over the board. 'I think you might have something.' Still, his tone bleeds frustration. 'And yet, we still have no address, description or whereabouts. And possibly a chameleon with a dual nationality. Can it get any worse?'

'Oh, you're such a pessimist, Harri Schroder,' she rebukes.

'And tell me why I shouldn't be?'

'Because we have two advantages over him.' Her smile is wide and satisfied.

'Which are?'

'We know he won't – he can't – stop. And he's addicted to the spectacle of dancing.'

'So?'

'So, Inspector Schroder, you must don your dancing shoes like the rest of us, slip on your British persona, and take to the floor at the Victory Club tonight.'

'That sounds suspiciously like another order.'

'It is – suit up and stop moaning. I'll see you all later.'

CHAPTER FORTY-EIGHT:
DANCE, DANCE, DANCE

22nd February 1946

Georgie

Heading back to the Baseler Hof in the early afternoon, Georgie is acutely aware of abandoning Zofia yet again. Not that a German national needs a guide – far from it – but the case has robbed the focus from their joint exploration of the city. Had it not been for Marion Peabody's revelation stealing her attention yet again, they would be sailing down the Elbe, to witness the devastation in the docks and life along the riverbank. She feels so conflicted, between what stands as her work and what needs her attention most. Georgie had slipped a hasty note of apology under Zofia's bedroom door on the way to Harri's apartment that morning. Equally, she knows Zofia won't have spent the day idle, using the time to search for her sister, plus checking in on Meta.

When she arrives, Zofia is sitting in the small lobby, hands clasped and her face drawn.

'What's wrong?' Georgie asks.

'It's probably nothing,' Zofia says. 'But I looked in on Meta quite early this morning and she wasn't there. The place felt very empty, and there was no heat to any fire or hot water.'

Georgie sits down heavily next to her. 'You and I might not think she's fit enough, but we both know Meta has been itching to get back out on the street for days. She's probably out haggling, making up for lost time. But, Zofia, without the care you've given her, that would not have been possible.'

'I suppose. But I do want to look in on her tomorrow.' Her expression is strained. 'Georgie, she's just a child, only sixteen, younger than my smallest cousin would have been. And she's so alone. She has no one.'

'Aside from you, and me, for the time being. And she has grown up fast. Knowing Meta, she's getting the better of traders twice her age. Life hasn't given her many options, but she is making the choices she wants. And it's clear that she doesn't want a keeper.'

Zofia nods, resigned.

'In the meantime, we've a dance to dress for,' Georgie adds. 'I'm not sure I can bear the heat of my woollen dress tonight and I've no stockings. What say we both go to the NAAFI and look for something more suitable?'

Zofia's face moves from concern to pleasure. 'Yes, I'd like that.'

They've scraped out the kohl liner, sharing the lipstick bought in one of the department stores, and it's with some pride that Georgie and Zofia step out of the Baseler Hof towards Dawson's jeep and the Victory Club. On the way

328

back from the NAAFI that afternoon, they'd spotted a tiny hairdressing salon run from someone's living room, and on a whim dived in, so that Zofia's hair is now sleek and set in a beautiful French plait. Georgie's curls have been snipped for a sharper look; in the mirror, she liked the slightly androgynous look, coupled with a full-skirted feminine dress she discovered on the second-hand racks. Zofia is in a neat, fitted turquoise dress which accentuates her slim form in a good way, since her hips are slightly fuller after a little more than a week of decent food. There are no stockings to be had anywhere, so they both sprint towards Dawson and the relative warmth of the jeep, after Harri insisted that they be picked up.

'Ladies, you look very fetching, if you don't mind me saying.' The sergeant bows in mock deference as they climb in.

'You don't scrub up so badly yourself,' Georgie counters. Dawson is in uniform, as befits a night out at the Victory Club, but it's clean and pressed, his hair slicked with what looks like a month's supply of Brylcreem.

'The band on tonight is very good,' he says as they drive away. 'So, I'll be honoured if both of you will agree to a dance. All in the service of the operation, of course.'

'I'm not sure how we can possibly refuse, Sergeant.'

They'd been at the Victory Club only hours before in rifling through the NAAFI stocks, but now it has a different feel as Dawson parks up near the entrance. Groups of chattering women in ATS uniform are filing in, leaving Georgie to feel suddenly uncomfortable in her femininity and yearning for her own, unofficial livery of trousers, shirt and flat brogues. The pumps she's managed to squeeze into are flat but not particularly sturdy, and the only saving grace is that she's not teetering on heels.

The buzz exuding from inside the club, though, is engaging and hypnotic, pulling them through the doors and towards the music that's just starting up, the ballroom rapidly filling up with servicemen from the surrounding bases and women in uniform, a few more in their finery. She can't be sure, but the women dressed to the nines look German, those searching for their darling Tommy, perhaps, and a passport away from here. Or perhaps they just want to take advantage of good music?

Georgie scans the vast, high-ceilinged room for signs of Harri, at the bar or among the tables, but nothing so far. Dawson has entered separately, as tonight's agreed plan is for the watchers to operate singly or in pairs: Georgie and Zofia, Paula and Jonni, with Harri and Dawson mingling alone. It means they can circulate around the dancers, the surrounding tables and the bar area, meeting on the floor if they need to pass information, or pick out potential suspects. She and Zofia buy a drink and settle into one of the tables, just back from the floor. There's no gentle introduction; the band is in full swing and the dedicated dance fans are soon spinning on the floor, faces fixed with true abandon.

'I'm not sure I can go that fast,' Zofia says, staring at her feet.

'Me neither,' Georgie agrees. 'We'll wait for something a bit slower, shall we?'

She watches Dawson moving through the crowd opposite, jovially talking to men and women in uniform, but when he focuses, she notes his gaze switch to survey the other men in suits, the off-duty CCG, plus business entrepreneurs who see Hamburg as the goose laying a golden egg of the future. She thinks Harri would be impressed with Dawson's surveillance skills. Talking of which, where *is* Harri?

Just at that moment, there's a light touch to her shoulder and a body sidles by. Instinctively, she gets up and follows, knowing that the twist in her stomach should register as trepidation, when, in fact, it's exhilaration. *Spying for the Kripo!* What would Max say?

The suited man eases his way into a cluster of bodies looking onto the floor.

'Aren't you the Anglophile?' Georgie stands to his side and leans in, catching a whiff of pleasant cologne. Had he not tagged her, she would have struggled to recognise Harri Schroder in his latest guise of English suit, brogues surely from a good London shop, his hair newly cut and combed flat with a modicum of oil. With a neat shave, even his jowls look lifted.

'I try my best,' he says, chancing a look sideways. 'Ditto, *Miss* Young. I might even be tempted to a dance.'

'Very funny. Anyone that's caught your eye so far?'

'I'm looking at those out of uniform first, while Dawson is doing the rounds of his own tribe,' he says. 'So far, only a few with fairish hair.'

'Though we ignore the convenient use of hair dye at our peril,' Georgie reminds him.

'Spot on, as usual, Miss Young. There's three or so suited men by the bar.' Harri gestures subtly. 'One is quite fair. I wonder if you can engage them with your blistering wit and repartee, if only to ensure one isn't our Martin Sexton.'

She purses her lips, in a way that suddenly feels

familiar from years ago in Berlin, before she and Max agreed to like each other, let alone love; that static of disdain between them which both infuriated and fired her, and which slowly adapted into good-natured respect. Sarcasm to sardonic, and then something softer. Love was the last, and hopefully the most enduring, of their shared emotions. It means Harri's sharp repartee makes her feel comfortable.

'I'll try my utmost to be charming, Herr Schroder.'

From her sideview, she watches his cheek ripple with hidden amusement.

On her way to the bar, Georgie glances over at Zofia. There's a second of alarm when the seat is empty, until her eyes sweep towards the dancefloor and the turquoise dress being spun around by a man in a CCG uniform. Atop, Zofia looks animated, entranced. Enjoying herself. In the mix is Paula, already in the thick of it and being courted by an RAF man. Good – two in the middle and four on the periphery. Georgie barrels towards the bar with purpose, intent on using the premise that a woman who doesn't seem in the least bit bothered by male company tends to present a challenge to the masculine ego. It's worked before in trying to engage an unwitting contact. What's more, it's preferable to the role of Helpless Female.

'Allow me.' One of the suits breaks free from their cluster and pushes forward. 'What will you have?'

'I'm fine, thank you,' she says, with barely a sideways glance. Barely.

'Really, I'd like to buy you a drink,' he presses. 'This barman seems almost blind to the women in front of him.'

332

Conveniently, he has a point. Her head swivels quickly towards him. 'You're right, and thank you. A gin and tonic, please.'

Drinks acquired, the man draws her into the group to make introductions – one from the CCG (black hair and eyebrows to match), a building contractor (white-blond with eyelashes that can't possibly be faked), and the last, an admin clerk with fair hair. Not only is his name Benjamin, but Georgie wagers he couldn't easily unscrew a jam jar; it's not what Harri would rate as elimination by evidence, but she strikes him off the list. Having glimpsed the killer's build briefly during Meta's attack, her own knight in shining armour is far too short and broad to make a convincing suspect.

Satisfied this group represents no threat, Georgie excuses herself, circulates for a while and rejoins Zofia at the table. 'That last number looked energetic.'

'Yes,' Zofia says, still breathless. 'I hadn't realised how much I've missed it.'

It's good to see her so animated and, for a time, they watch as the activity on the floor spirals, the music gaining tempo and the dancers matching it step for step, twirling, whooping, releasing energy and angst as the band barely takes a breath between each number. It's a wild, smoky spectacle that Georgie hasn't seen in a while, or enjoyed quite so much. 'Come on, let's have a dance together.' She pulls Zofia by the hand towards the floor.

They join plenty of women pairing up for a moderately fast jive, and she's buoyed by the music, the hot and heady atmosphere, spinning and swirling. Not too distracted, however, to spot the man on the edge, the one who – each time she turns and catches his eye – is tracking their progress around the floor. When Georgie spins away for a second, she realises his focus is on the turquoise of one particular dress, his gaze on the woman in it. On Zofia. What's more, his hair is fair to dark.

As the music tails off, they return to their table. Oblivious to the man's attention, Zofia is grinning from ear to ear. 'Oh, I loved that number,' she pants.

'Stay here,' Georgie instructs firmly. 'Don't go anywhere. No dancing, just for a while, all right?'

'Yes, but anything wrong, Georgie?'

'I just need to talk to Harri for a moment.'

She finds him in a clutch of men, his best English apparent as she draws near. 'Harry darling!' She launches herself into the group. 'I thought it was you! What on earth are you doing in Hamburg? Let's catch up while we dance.'

'That's one way to get a man onto the floor,' he says, as they shuffle to the edge of the dancers. 'Your acting skills are noted, Miss Young. To what do I owe this pleasure?'

'There's a man to the right of the band, just behind the woman in the yellow dress.'

He turns her in time with the music. 'Spotted him,' he says into her ear.

'He's been looking very intently at Zofia. Fits the description and, so far, I've yet to see him dance.'

'Noted, so let's test him out, shall we? You go back to Zofia and sit tight.'

They part as the music dies, before the band strikes up again, and Georgie returns to her table. Through the bottom of her glass, she watches Harri make the briefest of contacts with Paula and then move towards their target. Clumsily, he barges the man's shoulder, spilling his drink and making a meal of apologising. Harri returns quickly to his side with a replacement drink and tries to engage the man in casual conversation, nudging at him and gesturing at women on the floor. More and more, Georgie thinks they may have isolated their man – his awkward body language, the clear irritation on his face at being bothered by Harri, who's playing at being slightly drunk. But it's not proof, is it? Far from it. So, what now? If he is their killer, how do they draw him out without scaring him away?

With one eye on Paula as she approaches what must be their suspect, Georgie is almost blind to the change in Zofia's demeanour next to her, with only the faintest sense of her slight body tensing: has Zofia finally detected the man's eyes on her? Then, as her attention is drawn towards the dance floor, Georgie barely notes a fresh influx of people into the hall, her focus fixed on the interplay with Paula. Despite a good deal of good-natured cajoling, their man won't be enticed onto the floor, even when Paula pulls him by the hand flirtatiously, her role as the good-time girl with a drink or two inside her. Still, he won't budge.

The band strikes up with the distinct, thundering drumbeat of 'Sing, Sing, Sing' and the crowd erupts, dancers swarming like bees onto the floor. Paula is swallowed by an eddy of bodies, the man's dark suit disappearing with her. Georgie stands, craning her neck to see, eyes combing the crowd, but it's near to impossible with the bobbing, hopping throng.

'Did you see where he went?' Harri's hectoring voice is suddenly next to her.

'No.'

'*Scheisse!* I think we've lost him.'

Paula threads through the crowd towards them, her normally calm face skewed with concern. 'Where is he, Harri?'

'I don't know. He was there one minute, then gone.'

'He's our man, I'm certain of it,' she pants.

'What makes you so sure?'

Paula stares at him in amazement. 'Didn't you smell it? Didn't you smell the patchouli on him? It's the same scent from the murder scenes.'

Georgie's gaze goes to Harri's stricken face, and then to Paula, who is looking past her and towards the table. And the empty chairs around it. One chair in particular. 'Where's Zofia?' she says.

Harri and Georgie weave through the crowd towards the Victory Club entrance, Georgie frantically checking the ladies' toilets on the way. But there's no sign. As they hit the street, Dawson and Paula are close behind.

'Sergeant, you search in the jeep, main roads and side streets,' Harri instructs. 'Paula, you go with him. No one is to go it alone, understood?'

'Yes, boss.'

Georgie follows Harri out into the city streets, the freezing air slamming at her face and causing a fresh panic. *Not Zofia, please. Not after what she's already been through.*

'Where? Which way?' she pleads.

Harri squints into the darkness of his own city, looking beyond the blackness and using the innate radar honed during wartime to pinpoint the ruins their killer favours so much.

'This way,' he says, though there's little certainty in his voice. He's clearly praying as much as she is.

336

They half-run, half-walk towards the enveloping nothingness that's in the shadow of the busy city streets, shards of stone looming to Georgie's left and right as her eyes are fixed at head height for the turquoise of Zofia. Even when a large rat scurries across her path just a foot in front she doesn't falter, just forges ahead.

'ZOFIA! Zofia!' Harri bellows into the freezing air. It's desperation on his part, surely, but also it's intended to put their man on his guard, to scare him away before the act. The question is: has their killer become so desperate in his desires that he will condense the chase and risk capture? He is a madman, after all.

Georgie's mind calculates while her feet move at a pace, and only a flash of turquoise in her eyeline forces her to stop. Was it real, or a trick of the mind? No, she saw it, the same shade, the wispy form of Zofia.

'Harri!' Her voice is a hoarse, urgent whisper. 'Over there.' He swivels to where she's pointing, the blue streak absorbed by a substantial ruin, surrounded by stacks of salvaged bricks. She and Harri slalom around the mounds, moving nearer to sounds of distress now echoing upwards. His face carries the same dread as hers: is this Meta and Sigrid Heike all over again?

They track a woman's shriek, punctuating the air like radar, until they reach the two forms up against a solid wall. 'Zofia!' Georgie cries.

Thank God! The neat plait of dark hair has been pulled loose, but she's moving still, and upright. The relief lasts half a second, until confusion crashes in, pushing away any sense of reality. Why is Zofia facing the wall, with someone crouching under her? Has she somehow managed to overpower him? As Harri lunges forward, they hear the source of distress – a female shriek of alarm. And she's not being tended by caring, gentle Zofia. Quite the opposite.

'NO! NO! I didn't do it, you have to believe me,' the woman under Zofia is pleading in German. Above her, Zofia grapples, ramming the woman's head against the wall with force, hands around her neck. Throttling. With real intent.

'You killed her, you bitch! You killed her!' Zofia screams. Her face as Georgie comes near is that of a rabid animal, spit and hatred spewing forth, like Jekyll and Hyde playing out in real time.

It takes all of Harri's strength and bulk to pull her off, prising away Zofia's clawed fingers from the woman's already bruised neck, pinning Zofia's arms back as she lunges and fights against his tethering, possessed by the strength of ten men.

'Let me go!' she hisses. 'Let me finish her off, like she did to my sister.'

The woman is choking and pawing at her own neck, coughing and drawing breath. 'Stupid cow. Who does she think I am?' Pulling herself upright, she's older and thickset, short hair, someone you might pass in the street and not look at twice.

Zofia is finally calming, though Harri still grasps her with both hands. Georgie rounds on her friend: 'Who *do* you think this woman is?' With the shock, her own displeasure and disappointment are obvious.

Zofia's mouth is set, thin and dogged. 'I don't *think*,' she says through gritted teeth. 'I *know* exactly who she is.'

'And?'

'She is – was – a guard at Ravensbrück. One of their

338

best, by all accounts. One they tasked with all sorts of special jobs.'

Georgie swivels towards Zofia's target. Before her face can flood with denial – a classic case of wrong identity, the woman might claim – Georgie catches a hair's breadth of realisation flash across the stern features. She's seen it before, in those caught red-handed: Nazi officers disguised in peasants' clothes when the Americans and British swarmed across Germany as the Reich crumbled in April '45. Hiding in plain sight. For God's sake, even Heinrich Himmler tried the same ruse before being captured.

Perhaps Harri caught that snapshot of guilt too, because he dares to let go of Zofia and steps towards the woman. 'Name? Identity card, please.'

'Her name is Greta Wollf,' Zofia says with certainty.

'She attacked me!' the woman spits, turning on Zofia and neatly sidestepping the question. She turns to Harri for sympathy. 'You saw for yourself – she tried to kill me. Why aren't you arresting *her*?'

Harri looks to Zofia and her face of granite, and then to the woman, whose feet are beginning to shift. Georgie takes one step closer to her.

'Because I would like to know if there's any truth in her claims,' Harri says firmly. 'If you're who you say you are, you won't have any trouble confirming it.'

'There's a tattoo on her right forearm,' Zofia offers. Her voice is steely, no trace of the kind and generous, damaged woman Georgie has come to know. 'It will say "88".'

Harri and Georgie exchange looks. The eighth letter of the alphabet is H. If it's present, it's damning, signifying 'Heil Hitler' and an enduring support for the dead Führer, a determination to continue in his name and resurrect the Reich.

'So?' Harri presses.

'It means nothing,' the woman stutters defiantly. 'People had tattoos all the time.'

'*People* did not,' Harri shoots back. 'Die-hard Nazis marked themselves, especially those who worked in the camps.'

'And others,' she counters, but her defiance is waning the longer she stands.

'Yes, others too. But it might warrant my checking a little further.' Kripo Inspektor Schroder is unwavering. 'Show me.'

She makes a meal of peeling off her coat, loudly muttering complaints about harassment and the audacity of Polizei to hound their own, doing the job of the 'bastard British'. Her hand is on the sleeve of her sweater when she goes, turning and leaping for what passes as an entrance. Having been half prepared, Georgie is nonetheless surprised at the speed for such a heavy-set woman. But she is faster – perhaps she has Meta to thank for such lightning reactions in the face of an absconder. Despite her feminine dancing skirt and flimsy pumps, Georgie is quickly on the woman, hurling her entire body down, as both land heavily onto the stone.

The target felled, Georgie whips up her head to look at Zofia. There's no satisfaction in her face, merely sadness, and what looks like the weight of a war lifting off her shoulders.

'I'm so sorry.' Zofia's head is shaking, quivering fingers clutched around a hot coffee mug at Davidwache. It's delayed shock at the events of the previous hour, so out of character. And that it's finally over.

'Sorry for what?' Georgie asks. She saw no remorse on Zofia's face as the woman was led away to face interrogation far more in-depth than the ridiculous *Fragebogen* form. Say what you like about the occupation, but British forces are determined in weeding out former Nazis, especially those accused of working in the camps. The subsequent grilling will be thorough and uncompromising.

'I didn't mean to put you in that position.' Zofia looks at her dolefully, awash with penitence. 'I betrayed your trust. And Harri's.'

Did she? Or has Zofia simply been consumed by the need for justice? When grief is not addressed, it can fester, with no body or burial to effect closure; it grinds away, leaving people blind to everything else. So, no, Georgie doesn't feel betrayed.

Her sister's life, Zofia explains, was over long before the war's end. She knew it, and has known it for months. Her quest was in finding the woman responsible for Rosa's murder, a camp guard who had mercilessly hounded her sister, merely for helping pregnant women give birth with dignity, even if their babies were taken soon after by starvation, disease or abject cruelty. Eventually, the constant beatings – at the behest of camp guard Greta Wollf – proved too much for Rosa.

'She might not have aimed the final kick, but it was her spite that killed my sister.'

'And how do you know this for sure, that it was the woman we saw tonight?' Georgie has every sympathy, but it's a question that needs posing.

Zofia's eyes are teary but intent. 'I have proof, people's own accounts,' she says firmly. 'From not one, but several women who made it out of Ravensbrück. I've been tracking them down and they all tell the same story, give the same description. I heard this guard came from Hamburg originally, and that's why I came back.' She sips at the coffee and swallows with difficulty. 'And then I met you, offering me a safe place – and I'm so grateful for that – but of course being out there every day, I was always searching. Still, I couldn't believe it when I found her, right in front of me.'

A tiny lightbulb illuminates Georgie's memory. 'Was that when we were leaving the hospital, the day after Meta was attacked?'

Zofia nods. 'She was in the group of nurses and midwives trying to help that woman in the corridor.' She scoffs with bitter contempt. 'I'm sure there's a word for it in English?'

'Irony?' Georgie suggests.

'Yes, irony. A nurse, pretending to be someone who cares. How dare she? But I know she's a *Wollf* by name and a wolf by nature. Except she disappeared again.'

'So, what happened tonight?'

'I saw her by chance at the Victory Club, arriving with a group of women. She didn't stay long, so I followed her out, and when I called her name across the street – her real name – she ran. I knew I had the right woman then. The rest you know.'

There's one more question Georgie has to ask, more for herself than the authorities. 'And what if we hadn't arrived when we did? What would you have done?'

A myriad of emotion ripples behind Zofia's eyes. 'I honestly don't know,' she says eventually. 'Until the war, I suppose none of us really knew what we were capable of, good or bad. It frightens me that I might have killed her, matched the monster she was. Is.'

Georgie reaches out a hand. 'Zofia, I really don't think there's any comparison.'

Harri's arrival back into the office breaks their silent contemplation. He stops short at the two women huddled together in the corner and raises his eyes at Georgie, as if wary of stomping on eggshells.

When she nods, he tells them what he knows. 'She's in custody, though still insisting her name is "Marta Pohl". Eventually, they'll find out who she really is, but until then, she's not going anywhere.'

'And me?' Zofia asks. The question of assault, or even attempted murder, hangs over her.

'I don't think you need to worry. Judging by Fräulein Pohl's silence and indignation so far, she won't be pressing any charges. She's got other priorities – namely saving her own skin.'

Georgie follows Harri over to his desk and plants herself on the rickety chair opposite. 'Does all this mean tonight was a complete washout?'

'No, not if we – or Zofia, to be precise – apprehended a former Nazi. Certainly not.'

'I mean our killer,' she urges. 'Do you think he might suspect, or noticed the surveillance, enough that we've frightened him off?'

Harri looks up and ponders. 'I hope not. Paula did a good job of flirting without being too obvious. My main worry is that we've missed our chance. We simply haven't got the numbers to target the street dances and those at the Victory Club night after night.'

'So . . .?' Georgie can almost hear the time bomb ticking inside Harri's head.

'We keep going,' he says defiantly. 'I'm not just going

343

to sit here and wait for him to decide when he's ready. First thing tomorrow, we go looking for this Martin Sexton again. He has to surface at some point. At least now we've managed a good look at him.'

CHAPTER FORTY-NINE: KRIPO MAN

23rd February 1946

Meta

Compared to fellow detainees who emerge from the cells at seven a.m. looking sleep–deprived and dishevelled, Meta feels both rested and wired. Once she realised there was next to no chance of gaining liberty until the morning, she'd slept well that first night on the thin but proper mattress. But when one night turned into two, her frustrations multiplied as she petitioned any or all squaddies who even peeked through the cell hatch. 'I have information, for the police. Important.' But they were in no hurry to move her.

Finally, after a second breakfast, she's led out of the cell. Only then does she realise it's Saturday, meaning the magistrate will consent to dealing with urgent cases and nothing more. The panic resurfaces.

'But I *have* to get to Inspektor Schroder,' she pleads

again to yet another guard. 'Just ring him. Davidwache station. He'll vouch for me. *Bitte.*'

She has no idea if he will, or even if Detective Schroder works weekends, but she has to get that picture to Georgie. Having felt the killer's rage first-hand (and still feeling her bruising through the paltry mattress filling), it drives Meta's urgency.

'*Please*, nice Tommy,' she beseeches. 'Tell the inspektor that Meta has the face of his killer.'

He's either a soft touch or bored from her constant requests, because the guard gives a cursory nod and leaves her alone in the bare room that she guesses is for interrogations. She only hopes it won't be for hers. Some time later, long enough that the nice Tommy brings her an extra cup of tea, the door lock clicks and a man enters. Her thin face snaps up: it is him, the one with the jowly face at the dance with Georgie. And yes, from the front, he looks like a Kripo inspektor. His expression is set hard, less than happy to be dragged out among the British on a Saturday morning to vouch for a thieving wretch.

'Meta,' he says flatly, sitting opposite. 'A proper meeting at last, while you're conscious.' His lips thin out. 'More than conscious – fairly active, so they tell me.'

She expects nothing less than his disdain, and certainly not the empathy of Georgie. No doubt, his desk is bowing under the weight of complaints or crime reports involving *trümmerkinder*. What can she say in defence? She merely sits opposite, holding the precious portrait close into her body like a talisman, allowing him to vent frustration before she speaks.

'And you're in here because?' he goes on.

'Attempted robbery,' she says. *Badly executed crime* is a

better description of the fiasco, but she reasons it's best to curb any impertinence in the face of his current mood.

'Are you guilty?' he says. His pupils centre on hers, fixed and unyielding.

No wonder he's Kripo, she thinks. He's good. Meta can only drop her eyes in response.

'Thought so,' he grunts. 'The British say you have something for me. Now I know Georgie rates you highly, and that you've helped us before and paid dearly for it. However, don't make me regret traipsing halfway across town for one of your games.'

'It's not a game!' she cries, shifting forwards. Meta reaches to the inner lining of her coat, retrieving the paper and smoothing it out on the table. 'Here.'

As he bends forward, she watches his face intently, from the lowest of expectations to genuine surprise as his eyebrows rise several notches. 'Where did you get this?' he asks.

'I drew it, but a friend described him.'

'Does this friend have a name?'

'Why? This is the man who attacked me and that other woman,' she says with exasperation. 'Isn't this what you need to catch him?'

Inspektor Schroder sits back heavily and scratches his head. '*Why*? Because I have be sure your friend is not sending me on a wild goose chase, possibly at the behest of this man here.' He flicks a finger at the portrait.

'He wouldn't do that,' Meta entreats. How can she persuade him that Popo is a lot of things, some of them bad, but he's not heartless, not in the way he's looked out for her in the past? Okay, Popo had demanded a trade for his information, but that's just second nature for their kind. On another day, she might do the same.

347

'So, who is your source?' Schroder presses with a shrug. 'I can't realistically get you out of here without a name, something to check on.'

She sighs. The four walls are beginning to close in, and the thought of another night in the cell makes her feel nauseous. 'Popo,' she says. 'But you won't find him. He'll have disappeared by now.'

'So, I assume he was the other half of your thieving duo?'

Again, she can't look him in the eye, either with a lie, or nothing. She cuts away.

'All right,' the inspektor says, picking up the portrait and signalling to the guard that he's done.

'All right what?' Meta's voice is unusually panicked. 'You're not leaving me here?'

'I damn well should,' he says. 'You've created more headaches for the Polizei than I care to count, but I'll never hear the end of it from Georgie if I leave you to stew, so you've got her to thank.'

He mutters something like: 'What the hell am I . . .' but Meta is too busy scrabbling upright to hear properly. With authority, the inspektor tells the guard: 'I'll take it from here.' The squaddie shrugs, no doubt delighted to be rid of another pilfering, smelly Kraut.

Being Popo, he hasn't gone to ground, as anyone with half a brain would. As she and Harri approach the *trümmerkinder* camp, Popo is poking at the fire in plain sight; Meta does wonder if some other part of his head melted in that firestorm, the bit where common sense is supposed to dwell.

Harri keeps to the rear, while Popo's eye swivels on

hearing footsteps. 'Meta!' The working side of his face runs with shock, and a modicum of remorse. 'I . . . I couldn't . . . I thought . . .'

'Don't worry, Popo.' She stands down his guilt. 'You couldn't have done anything.'

He's relieved, clearly, then alarm rises. 'I only got away with that one trinket, haven't had a chance to sell it on yet. But I will.'

'I'm not here for my share, Popo.'

'Then what?' he stutters. 'Though, of course, it's good to see you, Meta.'

In that second, Harri steps from the shadows; one side of Popo's face drops to mirror the other. He looks betrayed.

'It's fine,' Meta rushes to reassure. 'He's not here to arrest you.'

Popo's feet shuffle, as if he's debating whether to run. 'He's Kripo,' he says nervously.

'Yes, I am,' Harri says. 'But I don't want trouble – from you or for you. That robbery is out of my jurisdiction and I definitely don't want the paperwork, which means I can ignore it. If I choose to.'

'Then what do you want?'

'Confirmation,' Harri says, pulling out the sketch. 'I want everything you can remember about this man. And I mean everything.'

CHAPTER FIFTY:
PULLING STRINGS

23rd February 1946

Harri

'Fuck!' Harri lets his frustration fly as he climbs in the jeep's passenger seat beside Dawson. He bangs the metal dashboard to drive home the point.

'Trouble, sir?'

'You could say that, Sergeant.' His mind runs with irritation – of missed opportunities. But if he's really honest, he is furious with himself, for being duped all over again.

'Anything I can help with, sir?'

Harri unfurls the sketch rolled in his hand and turns it towards Dawson. 'I have it on good authority – or the best we're going to get – that this is our killer.'

The army man squints, and Harri watches realisation dawn across his features. 'Oh.'

'Yes, oh, Sergeant. Can you take me to the Rathaus please, and then to Davidwache. We have a plan to make.'

Being Saturday, the offices of Peabody & Co are closed, and the unhelpful woman on general reception at the Rathaus either doesn't know where the obliging secretary lives, or refuses to say. A swift call to the Peabody residence confirms that not only is David Peabody still away on his hiking trip, but his wife has now left for the weekend, leaving the secretary as their only reliable source of identification.

Harri bangs the receiver down, echoing loudly in the lofty opulence of Hamburg's symbolic heart. 'Christ, isn't there anybody who can confirm what Martin Sexton really looks like?' he mutters.

They drive by Paula's residence, where she seems almost glad to be plucked from an overcrowded, strained apartment and the attentions of her mother and children. 'What's up?' she queries from the back seat. 'And where's Georgie?'

'Uh, Georgie is . . . attending to some other business,' Harri says, skating over last night's escapade, and Georgie's insistence that she needs to spend at least a few hours with Zofia. 'Let's get to the office and we'll put our heads together.'

'But that's not the man we were watching last night,' Paula says plainly, when Harri unrolls Meta's image.

'Full marks,' he quips sarcastically, then mutters 'Sorry' at Paula's dark look. 'I'm just as flabbergasted as you. I felt sure we'd identified the right man at the Victory.'

'Me too,' she says, 'especially when I smelt that patchouli.' She points to the sketch. 'So, do we know for certain if this is Martin Sexton, or not?'

'Not yet. It's either poor fortune on our part that it's the weekend, or a huge stroke of luck for him. I don't think we can get a positive ID until Monday. But the witness who helped with this sketch swears blind he smelt something "weird" when he drew close.' Harri's eyes follow Paula across the room. 'What is it?'

She's circling the floor, the sketch in hand, nose pointed towards the ground like at a crime scene – the thinking stance – as her eyes flick to and from the image. 'Except I have seen this face,' she says, still pacing. 'I'm sure I have. In fact, I know I have. Give me a minute.'

Harri knows better than to interrupt; Paula's 'moments' are often productive if she's left to deliberate. He can only hope this is one of those times, wearing down the shabby floorboards as she paces. Her lips ripple with concentration and the thoughts spinning inside.

'Got it!' Paula's eyes pop open as the ripple irons out to a broad smile. 'Slippery bastard.'

'So?' Desperation means Harri can barely contain his curiosity.

'He *was* there, Harri. Last night. I saw him. What's more, I smelt him too.'

'Where? How?'

'He was standing right next to the man we *thought* was Sexton the whole time. Which is why I must have caught the patchouli as I went close. Shit – we had the wrong man all along. By a few inches.'

It's shit all right, Harri thinks. They were on the right track, but somehow took a dangerous detour. When he looks at the portrait, mining his own memory of the night before and the image of their suspect who refused Paula a dance, the two men look similar; same height and build, sandy hair under the club lights. Nothing really to make either stand out in a crowd. So, is that why the portrait man chose to stand close to his near-doppelganger? What's more, if his actions are that deliberate, it means he's spotted their surveillance. And he didn't run. Harri calculates a more worrying possibility: he's playing with them. He is the Puppet Master – pulling all the strings. Yanking at them now.

Harri goes one step further. If their man does suspect, and he hasn't fled, then will he be driven to kill? Or worse, take flight into the ether.

'What do we do now?' Paula cuts into Harri's negative reasoning.

'It's vital we know if our image really is Martin Sexton,' he says, 'and we're not waiting two days. Get down to the Rathaus right now and work your charms on the staff there – we need a home address for the Peabody secretary. If that desk Frau is unhelpful this time, arrest her.'

'Yes, boss. What will you do?'

'Think.' *Think like a killer. And pray.*

He can't do that alone, though, and while Harri does deliberate at his desk, head in hands, for a good twenty minutes, he's resigned to surrender, to seeking out what he needs most. Eventually, he steps heavily towards the Davidwache reception and finds Dawson practising his awkward German on the uniformed officers downstairs.

'The Baseler Hof, Sergeant. *Bitte.*'

CHAPTER FIFTY-ONE:
A FINAL SEARCH

23rd February 1946

Georgie

She descends the hotel steps and pulls her scarf tight, tipping her head towards a welcome slice of sun that's doing battle with heavy grey clouds buffering in the sky. Georgie sighs loudly, and with some relief.

She wanted to spend the entire day with Zofia – she truly did – but her heartstrings feel stretched and bruised, as the finality of Zofia's loss poured forth onto Georgie's shoulder. The emotional deluge was long overdue, as was Zofia's need to talk of what she had gleaned about Rosa, from letters and witness accounts; both her mother and sister together in Ravensbrück, the birth of her mother's baby (the result of rape by a factory foreman), and how – like many Jewish babies born in the camps – he was dispatched soon after with cold, calculating cruelty by a female guard. A guard like Greta Wollf. It was after the loss of her newborn brother that Rosa apparently began helping one of the camp midwives in the infirmary, and then in the huts. Even if they knew the babies were not long for this world, those birth-helpers strived to afford dignity and care, ensuring the women kept healthy to face the gruelling work schedules ahead. With that determination, Rosa somehow attracted the attentions of Wollf and her malevolence, singled out for spurious rule-breaking and rewarded with persistent beatings. For daring to care. Both Rosa and her mother succumbed eventually to the savagery, their malnourished bodies unable to sustain the fight any longer.

'She killed my family,' Zofia sobbed on Georgie. 'And there she was, in full view, living a good life. *Pretending*.' Zofia spat the last word through her tears. 'That animal needs to face justice.'

'And she will,' Georgie assured, crossing every finger that the testimonies would stand up if it came to a military court. For every suspect standing in the dock at Nuremberg right now, there must be ten Greta Wollfs living a false but ultimately free life.

She's left Zofia asleep, drained by the past twenty-four hours and the entirety of the war. On waking, Zofia will have lost everything still, but a closure of sorts might help her to build a good future. Georgie strides with purpose to the Café Paris, drinking strong coffee to revive her, and yet unable to spoon in the sweet cream of her torte, as if such luxury is still too dissolute, and should leave a bitter taste after what she's learnt in the last twelve hours. Her eyes go over the chattering crowd, and the men whose heads are buried in the day's newspaper, one or two faces she recognises from the Atlantic and the Rathaus.

Sipping, Georgie wonders what their stories are, and whether they are scarred, wounded or fixed.

She found herself wincing as Zofia recounted Rosa's life – of the countless new lives she helped bring into the world, before being forced to watch them be extinguished with total barbarism. Georgie's own loss has been nothing like that. *Nothing.* She was surrounded by care and sympathy in the hospital, and family. Love. But a hole is a hole. A vacuum where life should have been inhabits the same space in the world. Georgie's cavity is cushioned with a layer of guilt, but still she mourns. Despite the bustle of a busy café, the biggest void for her is Max. How, right now, he would say something uplifting, or funny, or just plain sensible that would animate her face, for her to push at him and exclaim: 'Oh you!'

God, she misses him. Harri is right: despite how close they came last night, she can't stay here forever, tagged onto this mystery that might still be some time in solving. She feels immersed, but can't put her own life on hold because of it. There is more than enough for several articles, and a future at home that is the right one. Georgie is certain of that. After what she's heard today, life really is too short to go wasting a single second. She will miss Harri acutely. Zofia and Meta, too, but their lives are here, and hers isn't. So, time to put a few things in order and she will be gone. Determined, and relieved to have made that decision, Georgie is ready. She tears a page from her notebook.

Max, darling,
So sorry this is only a brief note, but enough to say that I'm coming home in a day or so – I'm not sure exactly when but not long, I promise.

Hamburg has been enlightening in so many ways, but it's time to gather all my notes and thoughts, and sort them out. I can't do that here. I need you, to be fiddling with your camera lens, or even perhaps limping about the flat, as my soundtrack and my grounding. I wonder if only the great writers of the time can claim to have a muse, but hell, I'm going to claim it anyway. You are mine, Max. My comfort and my world.

You are right. We will work it out.

I love you, G. xx

Georgie doesn't question the tear running down her cheek; emotion has run amok all morning, and she barely contained it with Zofia in her arms. With her torte left untouched, she folds the paper, pays her bill and walks the short distance to the Rathaus, where she flashes her press credentials at the CCG staff, who allow her to slip Max's letter into the postbag destined for a military flight and home.

Much like that first day in Hamburg, Georgie has an urge to roam and, always the hungry hack, she can't help wondering if there isn't just one story out there waiting to be picked up, a little cherry on the cake before home. She's left a note at the Baseler Hof for Harri, just in case he comes calling. It's Saturday, and she's no idea if he will take a day's rest after last night's fracas. With her concern for Zofia front and foremost, she hadn't quizzed him about immediate plans for the investigation. Knowing Harri, though, he won't be dormant for long, so she might as well head in the direction of Davidwache, in search of stories and familiar faces. A weak sun is still jousting with the bulbous clouds, it's cold but not freezing, and her feet point towards the length of the Reeperbahn, bent on drinking in every last drop of this bitter-sweet cocktail that is Hamburg.

Georgie's good intentions are postponed by the ripples of the Alster basin as a brisk wind gusts off the surface, enticing her towards the water's edge. There's something else, too – a strangeness that she's struggling to pin down. A heaviness, something lurking, or someone. Or could it be the leaden mood of the last twelve hours?

She commits the view to memory, determined she will leave this city with something of beauty to remember, and not just the caved-in roof of the once-grand pavilion that perches alongside. The same Alster Pavilion where Harri has admitted dancing very badly with his now dead wife, in a sad legacy of war. But while the ornate structure lies in tatters, the basin endures, so too the mighty Elbe, the trade and life that will rise again one day, the towering cranes sure to grind with industry once more. That's what she will take back to England, and to British readers. Her own shutter-click recollections won't suffice for needy editors, however, and there's still a need to engage a photographer before she leaves, to illustrate each piece she intends to write. Distracted by details, Georgie barely notices a man sidle up to her and stand, gazing down on the shallow waves pushing against the basin wall.

'Penny for them?' Lieutenant Howarth begins, leaning in playfully.

She startles. 'Oh, hello! I didn't see you there.'

'You were miles away,' he says. 'Back home, in London, by any chance?'

'Hmm, perhaps. Just thinking about that time before. Before the world went mad.'

'Oh yes, that. I know exactly what you mean.' He casts around the busy street behind, at people variously leaning into the wind and glancing at the darkening clouds above, the sun having given up on the fight. 'It looks like snow. What say we take refuge inside? There's a nice café nearby that does very good soup.'

Georgie glances discreetly at her watch. Just gone two. Ideally, she wants to meander towards Davidwache before the weather closes in, finding the U-Bahn stuffy and a poor source of stories. But her stay has been made much easier by Howarth, so repaying the lieutenant's generosity is vital. She's suddenly hungry, too.

'I'd love to. Lead the way.'

The *Kartoffelsuppe* is good, especially with recognisable chunks of sausage to chew on, though secretly Georgie thinks Harri's own effort easily matches up. Opposite, Howarth seems at ease on his day off, away from the combined politics and tittle-tattle of the Atlantic.

'It can get a bit much at times,' he admits with his usual candour. 'There's far too much red tape, enough that I'd cheerily round up all the top brass and bang their heads together. They really can't see the woods for the trees sometimes.' He flashes her the same look of exasperation from that first day at the Atlantic Palm Court.

'It sounds to me as if you should be running this rebirth, rather than our illustrious Monty,' Georgie suggests.

'It's simply that they don't give the Germans any credit for intelligence, or remember that they were on the way to a thriving economy before the war. Even without

Hitler's arrogance and brutality, it was always going to be a hard-working, industrious nation. And yet we treat them like children.' He takes a sip of the broth like it's medicine. 'Sorry, I'm ranting. It's just that I don't get to mix much with any like-minded people.' He flicks up his eyes. 'Sensible people.'

'Perhaps it's time for a bit of a break,' she suggests. 'Have you any leave coming up, a chance to go home for a while? Is there anyone back in London, someone special?'

Then he does stare deep into his bowl. 'No. Well, I mean there was. She died, in the war.'

'I'm sorry.'

Howarth sits back, his sadness suddenly apparent. 'Ironic, really. She was killed by one of our own bombs, a stray. There I was, working all hours at the Ministry to combat Luftwaffe attacks, and all the time she was more in danger from the RAF.'

What can Georgie say to that? The injustice is too much to bear, from a man who has only ever exuded charm and a willingness to help. A sense of humour, too. 'Well, when you are back in London, be sure to give me a call,' she says. 'We'll meet up, and have a drink. My husband, Max, would love to meet you.'

'I'd like that,' he says. 'Most of my old crew have moved out, or are . . . you know. London has changed.'

It's gone three by the time they say goodbye, with Howarth offering to arrange her flight home for the day after tomorrow. The snow has held off, though dark clouds squat in the sky above, pregnant with promise. Georgie watches a homeless man push himself further into a shop doorway, his eyes reflecting the dread of nature's load to come. She drops several coins in his upturned hat and hates herself for such a feeble offering.

The walk westwards helps Georgie reacquaint herself with the thoroughfares leading out of the city centre. She stops and talks to some of the street sellers, hardy traders who will close up their battered suitcases only if the deluge is enough to drive their custom away.

'Yes, it's a hard life,' one of them agrees, without complaint. 'But we'll come through. In Hamburg, we always have.' Georgie looks over the sparse display, paying way over the odds for a tiny pocket knife that she thinks might be useful for Max in prising open his stubborn film canisters. She distributes the few remaining cigarettes from her bag and sets off again.

Trudging past several blocks of ruins, she's aware of a tingling under her heavy coat, hot and cold prickling at her flesh. That leaden feeling has returned, too, enough that once or twice she whips her head around to see what's behind her, to catch out any trail, slipping behind a wall or into a shop doorway at the last minute. But nothing obvious. By now, the few people about are hurriedly taking shelter as the sky begins to spill its load, fat but gentle flakes at first, then a steady curtain of white within seconds. Georgie considers ducking into a doorway, but imagines Fritz's bar isn't far away, and she'd rather sit out a snowstorm in the warmth. Ploughing on, head into the wind and her beret pulled down low, the cold flakes settle on her face and eyelashes, skewing her vision. Damn it! Yet again, she's quickly disorientated in these streets, this time by a world of white.

But Fritz's place isn't where she remembers it to be. Instead, every door is shut tight against what now counts as a blizzard, the wind spinning flakes into flurries, so that the curtain of snow billows like sheets on a washing line and even the few solid buildings disappear like ghosts. She swivels again, trying desperately to find her bearings. Any bearing. Blinded by snow, Georgie just makes out a single, solid element in the near distance, something tall, dark and mobile and moving towards her, crouched against the wind. If fate is kind, and fairy tales are reality, it will be Harri come to drag from her another misadventure of her own making. But twice in a lifetime, let alone the space of two weeks? That really is fantasy.

It is a man, though, that much she detects as he approaches, her own feet frozen to the spot, cold rapidly seeping through the leather of her boots.

'You look lost,' he shouts in German over the squall, clamping down his own hat with a gloved hand. 'Do you need some help?'

'Just to some shelter,' she cries. 'Until the worst is over.'

He scans left and right. 'Over here.' He points to what was once a building, and might still be, but Georgie can't see through the blanket of flakes. There's perhaps a doorway of sorts, but beyond that, who knows? She pivots full circle again: nothing and nobody, bar the white. What choice does she have?

He hooks his arm into hers, though it feels like a friendly gesture to help her navigate the jagged rubble now carpeted in white. Once or twice Georgie stumbles, though he seems sure-footed. If he's a native Hamburger, he'll have spent the last three years dodging debris.

As they duck under a lintel, it's obvious that it's a ruin they've come into, a partial ceiling clinging to the uneven

362

walls. But it's a shelter of some sort, and it means they are out of the wind.

'Whoo!' he pants, stamping his feet and clapping the snow from his gloves. 'That came on pretty fast. We haven't had a deluge like that in ages.'

'Sorry?' Georgie's German can't quite keep pace. She's busy shaking out her beret and her hair, brushing the worst of the snow off her coat.

'I mean, it's pretty bad,' he says. In English. Perfect diction. The King's English.

'Oh,' she says. Despite the cold, her skin pricks white hot. He looks somehow familiar. 'I imagined you were German, what with your accent, and the homburg.'

'Funny you should say that,' he replies, 'but so do a lot of people.'

CHAPTER FIFTY-TWO:
GUT INSTINCT

23rd February 1946

Harri

'I'm sorry, sir, but she left some time ago,' the Baseler Hof receptionist says. 'I saw her go myself.'

'Thank you.' Harri strokes his chin, trying not to feel too deflated at missing Georgie. Yes, he wanted to bounce ideas off her, as if she were standing in front of the chalkboard, rubbing her nose in thought. Why or how he doesn't know, but it settles him, allows his own mind to ruminate. He shakes his head, remonstrating with himself. *Idiot.*

'Inspektor?'

Harri turns to see Zofia, red-eyed and cried out, but undoubtedly lighter. 'Fräulein Dreyfus, how are you?'

'I'm all right, thank you. But I am worried about Georgie.' She gestures to beyond the hotel door and the flakes now falling heavily.

'Oh, that is coming down fast now.' It was a mere flutter as Dawson drove him over. 'Do you know where she was heading?'

'She mentioned something about going to the Rathaus to make arrangements,' Zofia says, 'and then heading over to the police station. She was keen to walk.'

'Well, she won't get far in this.' He hopes that, on noting the weighty sky, Georgie will have hunkered down in some café, as any veteran of Hamburg's weather would do. But she isn't of this city, and this is Georgie.

Harri makes two phone calls: one to the Rathaus, to confirm a 'blonde, British woman' has indeed been and gone, and to Davidwache, where Paula confirms Georgie hasn't turned up at the office. She has other news, too, from England: their sketched portrait *is* Martin Sexton.

'Strangely, it is his real name, but he lied about his references and his past,' Paula adds. 'He was in the British army in 1940, but was given dishonourable discharge.'

'What for?' Harri queries.

'Doesn't say. The records office hinted that it's heavily censored.'

'Which explains why Peabody & Co wouldn't have known,' Harri thinks aloud. 'Anything else?'

'Yes, Sexton's father was a businessman, meaning Martin was born in England but educated in Germany until the age of fifteen,' Paula reports. 'The school has closed down now, but it was in a small town, and I managed to locate the mayor. He remembers the incident well.'

'Incident?' Now Harri's attention is at full pitch.

'With a girl. After that, the whole family moved away.'

'Damn it!'

'One more thing, boss,' Paula says.

'Yes?' For a second, he wonders if he's ready to hear it.

'The Peabody secretary says she spoke to him this morning. Unusually, he rang her at home and said he wouldn't be into work on Monday, and needed to take some urgent leave.'

'Did he say what for or where?'

'No. But the secretary said he sounded odd. Anxious, and . . . I'm not sure how much we can read into this, but her actual word was "unhinged".'

'Oh Christ.'

'That's not all.' Paula's voice is unusually tentative. 'The secretary can't be a hundred per cent sure, but she thinks he was calling from somewhere in Hamburg, sounds of the Rathaus clock in the background apparently.'

Oh fuck.

Harri is out of the Baseler Hof in seconds. 'Dawson, head towards Davidwache. You'll have to drive slowly in this blizzard, but we need to keep our eyes sharp. We're on the hunt.'

'Who for, sir?'

'Miss Young. And if I'm right, a very nasty predator. One Mr Martin Sexton.'

The roads are near deserted, enabling Dawson to steer the jeep westwards at a snail's pace. Harri prays Georgie won't have strayed into the side streets, though he can't be sure where curiosity will lead her, and he doesn't want to imagine. He has absolutely no evidence that Sexton will target her, either now or in the future, except for the very uncomfortable torque in his gut. Tightening with every second. As a reporter, she's always relied on gut instinct, and something tells Harri Schroder he should heed that advice right now. He squints through the double smear of the scratched windscreen and curtain of heavy snowfall. At intervals, he orders Dawson to stop, leaping out of the jeep and disappearing through what now amounts to a hole in a white wall – some bar or café he knows – but emerges disappointed, more so when Fritz hasn't seen her. Neither has anyone else set eyes on a blonde woman with striking, short hair.

'Surely she won't stay out in this, sir?' Dawson queries.

'By choice, I hope not. It's whether she has that choice.'

A kilometre or so out, they hit the worst of the fallen buildings, where only snow on a solid roof distinguishes ruins from a residence.

'Shit! Sorry, sir.' Dawson is finding it hard to pick out road from battered pavement, the wheels bumping and rocking the inside of the jeep as if they're on some remote rural track.

'This is impossible,' Harri growls with frustration. 'I can't see a thing. Stop here, Dawson. We'll search a couple of blocks on foot. You take the right side, I'll go left. Stick to the ruins.' He fishes in his overcoat pocket and pulls out two whistles – nothing like the old methods when you have nothing else. 'Anything you see, blow hard on this. Meet back here in ten minutes, and then we'll move on.'

Stepping out of the jeep, he pulls on a thick woollen hat and looks up at the unrelenting deluge. It's that bloody needle in a haystack again. But if something were to happen to her . . .

Harri's boots are already beginning to let in molten snow when he reaches the first ruin. 'Georgie! GEORGIE!' he shouts, the volume swallowed by the snow blanket.

Where there's no remaining roof and the visibility is low, he skirts around the inner walls, ensuring she's not huddled in a corner, or within a tiny nook. Two structures on, there's still nothing. Dawson has had no luck either, and back in the jeep they crawl along for several minutes more.

'Stop, Sergeant,' Harri says, his faith waning. His real hope is that Georgie is sitting somewhere with her feet up and fingers wrapped around a warm mug. But that scenario feels overly optimistic. 'Let's try again.'

Trudging back out into the street, Harri pivots full circle amid a panorama of white. Where the hell can she have gone? His gut grinds painfully again, this instinct far sharper than his radar for danger during the war. Where has that bastard Sexton taken her? So far, nothing has stopped the deadly pursuit, and a snowstorm is the least of a killer's problems. An asset, in fact, masking his fresh tracks perfectly.

He looks at his watch. Five minutes until he and Dawson hook up again, much less until his feet turn to solid blocks of ice. He eyes the next building, pulls his overcoat tighter and heads towards it.

CHAPTER FIFTY-THREE:
A HEAVY SHADOW OF WHITE

23rd February 1946

Georgie

This man's perfect diction sends up a flare within Georgie's core, but it's not what sets her teeth fully on edge. Nor the temperature. Her nose is freezing, but still able to pick up the scent in his orbit: earthy and woody, a little like the sandalwood her mother uses, but far stronger and more masculine. Musky. It's the odour of patchouli which sets her heart reeling and her pulse into override. The tiniest spark in her memory, too. Of a face. But where? And when?

'I've a feeling we've met before,' she says with a smile, desperate to hide the tremor in her voice as that spark of recognition ignites. 'At the Atlantic perhaps, in the tearoom?' *Keep it steady, George. Show no fear. It may not be him.*

'Observant of you,' is all he says, unsmiling. 'I wondered how long it would take you. Though you seemed too engrossed to notice me at the Café Paris earlier.'

His tone is odd rather than threatening. It's when he looks furtively around, left and right, as if listening intently for something beyond the near-silent fall of flakes, that she becomes certain. Before, their killer used nightfall as a protective shroud. Now black has turned to white, and he's checking this veil is dense enough.

Georgie mimics his search, her eyes and ears probing instead for means of escape, a last resort if she can't talk her way out of this. 'Do you know, I think it might be easing up a bit,' she says, in what she thinks of as her 'pretty girl' English, a tone that has helped her out of plenty of scrapes by playing the oh-so-grateful damsel. Sometimes, in war and this world, needs must.

Predictably, he's not falling for it. He takes off the homburg as he moves a step closer, and it's no surprise that his hair is sandy. He scoffs a little, a mean, reluctant smile glancing over his lips.

'I don't think so. We'll just have to sit it out here a bit longer. It's no bad thing – I've been wanting to have a proper chat since we first met, about your *crime* reporting, and how you and the good detective are getting along.'

'So, it was you at the Atlantic, when I first arrived?' She smiles again, feeling the fake whimsy is rapidly wearing thin. 'I never did catch your name.'

'Martin,' he says. 'You can call me Martin.'

The chill turns solid inside her. He's no longer afraid to reveal himself, a sign of supreme confidence, or worse, that he's resigned to being uncovered. *I'm his last. This is his swansong.*

'Martin what? I once knew a Martin in London, a friend of my mother's. And so do you live in Hamburg?' The stream of drivel spills from her automatically, beyond which her mind is racing. *Who will hear me? How loud will I have to scream? How strong is he under that thick overcoat?*

'That's not important right now,' he says flatly. 'What's crucial is that we get to know each other a little better, don't you think?'

'I mean, I'm grateful,' Georgie says. Stutters, because now there's no hiding it. 'And a drink would be fine, but . . .'

'But you're married, I know that, Georgina Young. And what's more, I don't mind one little bit.' His eyes glint against the reflection of white, a different smile creeping across his lips, while his face sports anticipation and glee. A hand goes up to touch the blonde wisps poking from under her hat. Hunger and lust. 'I don't even mind that you're blonde. It's always good to try something different, don't you think? You're smart, and because you already know something about me, I don't have to promise anything, or make pathetic overtures, like those others.'

I have to get out.

His eyes are fixed on her as he reaches for the inside pocket of his coat, his hand just inches away, the taint of his cigarettes in her nose. She looks down to see a thick weave of rope.

Scream or run?

In the second before his hand reaches out to grab at her, she manages both. The air rings with what feels like a lungful of noise, capped off by the snow ceiling, while her feet turn and push, push, push. But this is not the gravelled airport pavement in her pursuit of Meta; the white carpet underfoot is thin but hides jagged bricks which stymie any effort to move forwards. Georgie

371

stumbles and lurches, stumbles again, voice waning as her face hurtles towards the snowy covering, her brow smacking against a rock with full force. She feels her skin give way and the intense pain pulsing through her skull, sparking the only human reflex she needs right now: flight or fight.

Now it will have to be the fight, because Sexton is on her already, a knee into her back as he grapples with the thrash of her arms and legs.

'Keep still, you bitch!' The veiled charm has gone and he punctuates the air with pure anger. 'It. Will. Be. Easier. If you don't fight.' He's panting and having to push his entire weight on Georgie, the breath almost squeezed from her body. In one deft move, he turns her over, falling flakes stinging her open wound. But it acts like a volt of electricity in keeping her sharp.

He looms over her, a stream of rhetoric spewing from his reddened face and saliva pooling around his mouth. 'This is what I mean,' he growls. 'You bitches. You won't do it, will you? You won't play the game. Fucking traitors. To me, to Germany. To the Führer. You know nothing about loyalty. You deserve to fucking *die*.'

From lucid to frantic in seconds. Georgie's mind flips instantly to the chalkboard back at Davidwache, and Jonni's accurate rendering of the dead women. Harri's assessment echoes in her brain: 'Calculated, and yet frenzied,' he'd said. Is that all she will be, after years of ugly, global, grotesque conflict – a drawing on a police station wall?

Well, she won't. She bloody well won't.

With every scrap of will and effort she possesses, Georgie swallows down sour bile and a swell of panic. Only once before has she stared death so acutely in the face, stumbling upon a lone German escapee hiding out behind American lines. He looked a mere child, starving and terrified. But he had a gun, his fear making him jittery – and deadly. For almost twenty minutes, though it felt like a lifetime, Georgie stared into the barrel of his Luger and his wide, wild eyes. And talked. By degrees, the wild shifted to weary and the frenzy in him was quelled, enough that she summoned courage to turn and walk away, expecting to hear the click of a trigger and feel the fatal rip of a bullet in her back. But the only noise behind was a soft, strangulated sobbing and the pad of his footsteps into the distance.

It's time to dampen that same frenzy again.

'We can go away,' she pants eagerly, her eyes fixed firmly on Sexton's. 'I'm due to leave Hamburg any day now. You and me. Away from here. No one will know. Think about it, where we could go and what we could do.' She's weaving words on the hoof, gambling on his turmoil leaving him suggestible. Anything to buy her time, for him to release his iron grip. And for several seconds his grasp does ebb. His pin-prick pupils search hers and she thinks, in his madness, that he may be considering it. Perhaps no other woman has suggested as much, only pleaded for their lives. Is there a slim chance her reaction has thrown him off kilter?

No. In a half second, she watches the insanity flick like a switch to lucidity. And then to evil. Worse, it spills over to rabidity, spittle flying as he hauls her up by the rope now looped around her hands. 'Bitch! Bitch, bitch, BITCH! You think . . . well you can't fool me. You're all liars. Weaklings.'

Sexton slams her against the wall of the ruin, the force of it buckling her legs and causing the rope to loosen.

From the board at Davidwache, Georgie knows what comes next, how this monster sets out his scene. How he will reposition the rope, sucking the breath from her neck, and then she will become just a diagram. A messy one.

Georgie is out of options. His violence has winded her, the icy chill and the fear sucking every ounce of energy from her. But this isn't the end, because she will not let Max be made to view her on a cold slab in a stinking, overcrowded morgue, far from home.

For him, she draws in every particle of freezing air, and she lets rip.

Georgie Young screams with all her might. For her life.

CHAPTER FIFTY-FOUR:
THE PUPPET MASTER PERFORMS

23rd February 1946

Harri

The shrill noise pushes like an arrow through the fug of white, piercing the near silence of drifting flakes. Harri's head whips towards it. Georgie? Whoever — whatever — it is, it's a noise of need, the same jarring distress of Meta's cry once before. Instantly, he pulls the whistle from his pocket, struggling to grip in hands that have stiffened with cold. He puts it to his lips and blows hard, a second, prolonged squeal pushing against the dense air. Will Dawson even hear it?

Knowing from bitter experience that hesitation can prove fatal, Harri doesn't wait for a reaction. He runs, feet sinking and slipping on the fresh, thickening snow, despite the tread of his boots, staggering towards the scream that has now stopped. Muzzled? By him? The innate radar points Harri to its origin, the cluster of ruins just metres ahead now. What will he find there?

The squall above has waned, replaced with thick, steady flakes that push at his face while he stumbles in earnest. *Faster, faster!* One icy sliver hits him squarely in the eye, and he's suddenly blinded, swiping furiously at his wet lashes, sprawling face first onto the ground. When he opens his eyes, it's no longer winter white in his vision, but the yellow and orange of three years ago, a fiery red tempest of flames rising up in front, the roar of a windstorm and searing heat creating a blast of death. So present and real. There are shouts and screams ringing in his ears, the echo of death. Where are they? How can he reach them both? It's too late, surely. It's always too late.

'NO, NO!' Harri croaks, his lungs choked by the icy air. 'Wait, Hella, Lily, WAIT! WAIT FOR ME!'

The chill in his ungloved fingers becomes a burn, agonising pain shooting through. Half aware of his mind playing cruel tricks, Harri plunges his face into the freezing snow a second time, jolting him back to reality. *Georgie.* It's Georgie he's searching for. Not Hella, not now. Only the same question looms: is he too late?

Reaching the wall of the ruin, years of police training force Harri to hang back, crouching and peering over the rim of an old window ledge. He sees a black spectre in an overcoat, looming over her. He recognises her coat and bag. Flaccid and lifeless? He can't tell. Pulling out the small truncheon deep in his pocket, Harri hurls himself forward into the space. Surprise causes the man's head to pull up, sudden reflexes yanking her close and in front, transforming Georgie's limp form into a human shield. It means she's facing outwards, her features contorted by the rope now around her neck, one of her hands grasping at its tension and keeping the thick hessian from pressing into her flesh. But it means she's moving. Harri watches her legs struggling to hold herself upright, her body not an inert sack. She's alive. There's a moan coming from her mouth, blooming with red and reflecting off the knife blade that Sexton pulls out and holds close.

'Georgie! Georgie, it's me,' Harri barks. 'Open your eyes. Look at me. You'll be all right.' It could so easily be a lie, but right now it's necessary – for her and him.

'Will she?' Sexton sneers in his King's English, through his own bloodied lips, and it's clear then that Georgie hasn't surrendered without a fight. 'You're very confident, Herr Policeman. Sir bloody Galahad. Is this your idea of saving her? Saving them all?' He tips the knife towards Harri, the fat blade catching what little light exists in the roofless but dull ruin.

'Let her go,' Harri says evenly, neither pleading not challenging. 'Just let her go.'

'And you'll do what, *Inspector*?' Sexton mocks. 'Let me go, too? Scot-free?'

'Maybe.' For a minute, Harri considers that he might. He would, if it means saving one more life. Hers. Except that when his gaze settles on Georgie's face and the eyes now fully open, fully alert, they say not. Categorically, they say: *Don't you dare, Harri Schroder.*

Sexton isn't buying it, anyway. 'I think the best way is for you to step back, and for me and the lovely Miss Young to leave. Together. That way she has half a chance. If not' – he seesaws the blade with threat – 'she has none. Zero.'

'Fuck you,' Harri growls under his breath, a cloud puffing into the icy air. It's inflammatory, and he knows it will rile Sexton. Equally, Harri is goading for a reason, because he can see what Sexton can't – that with her free hand, Georgie is fumbling in her coat pocket, her fingers struggling to find purchase on something she pulls out, then a near-silent flick of a second blade.

'You have absolutely no fucking bargaining power,' Sexton rails, one arm now locked around Georgie's neck. His eyes are demonic. Unhinged all right. But one glance tells Harri that Georgie's determination to survive matches that of any killer, her tongue reaching out to lick at her bottom lip. A signal. Her knees lock as she pulls her hand away from the rope and swipes blindly with her arm, up and behind, making heavy contact with Sexton's face, enough for him to reel with shock and pain. His grasp on her neck loosens instantly and she squirms away, stumbling to the side and hurling the penknife towards Harri, who leans and snatches at it with his fingertips, thanking fate that he was made to practise cricket endlessly during his English holidays.

But Sexton's fury and zeal make him resilient and still dangerous. As Harri rights himself, Sexton clutches at his nose, a flesh wound at most. Within seconds, he's recovered, his blade still in hand, a bigger, sharper and more fatal weapon than the tiny penknife Harri holds aloft.

They dance like boxers in a ring, a short lunge here and there to put the opponent on guard and off balance, the snow underfoot not helping. Sexton is grinning like the maniac he is, seeming to enjoy what he perhaps imagines is his victory dance, and yet knowing it's the end too; a rabid rat trapped in an alleyway with nowhere to go. Having nothing to lose gives him the sharper edge.

Harri has half an eye on Georgie, who is struggling to keep herself upright. 'Stay back!' he wants to warn her, but all his attention is on Sexton's hand and a single jab that might prove disastrous for him, and for Georgie, too.

Sexton's feverish grin wavers – Harri sees it too late, the drop of his arm and the lurch of his body sideways, adrenalin powering his body towards what was once a wall and is now a gaping hole into a white nothingness. There's no dilemma over the chase this time: he must be stopped. Harri is a second or more behind, scrabbling with every ounce of energy to catch up, the flapping tail of Sexton's black coat still in his sights.

And then, like a train hitting buffers at speed, it stops dead.

'No, you fucking don't!' Dawson's voice slams into the air as he comes out of nowhere and tackles Sexton with surprise and body weight, the knife twisted away and falling with a muffled thud on the soft blanket.

It takes both Dawson and Harri to wrestle with Sexton's zeal, his muscles coursing with the need to escape what he knows will be the hangman's noose. And God knows, he fights for what's left of his life. Dawson's heft, though, wins out, and Sexton is finally trussed and contained, seething but silent in his failure.

'Good timing, Sergeant,' Harri gasps. 'Can you hold him?'

'Yes, sir. He's not getting away again. Over my dead body.'

Harri picks himself up and hurries the few metres into the ruins, a sprained ankle thwarting his speed with a pronounced limp. The chase is less deadly, but no less urgent. He has to reach her, to know she's all right. He has to.

He rounds the side of the ruin as the flakes finally stop falling and the sky holds back on its grey threat. The floor of the ruin reflects some white but around is still dark, and he makes out her form against the wall, no longer sitting but lying on the icy ground. Unmoving. *Hella.* Harri blinks away the vision. It's gone, replaced only with the tinier form of Lily. A lifeless Lily. *Not again.*

He bounds forward, knees scraping on the jagged rubble, looming over her, clutching at her coat and shaking. Pleading. 'Wake up, wake up! *Please.*'

It's Georgie who stirs, disorientated, pawing at her own face. Harri sees it's red, but with blood both inside and out, life not running away. 'Suddenly, I just felt so weak,' she murmurs.

'Oh, Jesus.' The relief overwhelms. Harri Schroder can only lay his head into her lap and sob for the present, while weeping up the past.

CHAPTER FIFTY-FIVE:
CONFESSION

23rd February 1946

Georgie

Paula's face peers around the ruin walls, takes in the scene for all of a second and aims a knowing look at Georgie, then retreats again. It's another of Paula's intuitive moments, growling at the crowd of uniformed crew to 'Stay out of there.' Harri lies alongside, silent and still, seemingly empty.

Hours later, after the hospital and three stitches to her brow, he places a cup of Fritz's best coffee in front of Georgie. 'Real stuff, no Maxwell House this time.' Harri's smiling through his discomfort, of a badly bruised ankle, but of so much more, laying down two further shot glasses. 'I felt we needed whisky.'

They both contemplate the amber liquid, as bitter medicine and sweet panacea combined. Harri downs his in one and Georgie follows suit, she wincing at the soreness in her throat from a rope so recently applied.

'Are you sure you're all right?' he asks.

'Fine. And better for this.'

'I'm so sorry,' he begins after a brief pause. 'For afterwards. My timing was appalling, not to mention very unprofessional.'

She thinks of excusing it with a joke, his breakdown into tears, the way he clutched at her clothes, sobbing for an age into the cloth and grasping so tightly. But this is no time to make light or skate over grief.

'I seem to remember uttering those very words not so long ago,' she says. 'You wouldn't let me apologise for showing emotion, and so neither am I. Grief – *your* grief, Harri – doesn't go away, whether it's for one of millions who died or not. *You* still loved and lost. And you deserve to own that loss, for however long it takes.'

He sips and sighs. 'You're right, of course.' Smiles into his cup. 'Don't you ever get sick of being right?'

'Perhaps tell that to my husband. In fact, please come and tell that to Max!'

A gulp of his coffee and he's serious again. 'I think I need to tell you why – what happened back there, at the ruin, why I . . .'

'Why you were upset?'

'Upset. That's an understatement, but yes.'

Georgie smiles meekly. 'You don't have to.'

'But I want to. I need to,' he says. 'I've never told anyone, about Hella and Lily, and the truth of how they died.' Harri swallows, but he is dry of tears now, his tone bent on confessional. 'People – those I work with, who I know – think they perished in the fire, and I've been guilty of not putting them right. Of hiding the reality.'

Georgie says nothing, since she doesn't need to.

He pulls in courage of a different nature. 'Because I am ashamed. And guilty of much more.'

'Of what?'

'Failing them,' Harri says firmly. 'Those first few nights when the bombers came, in '43, I was working, couldn't – didn't – make it home through the chaos. I wasn't there to help them, protect them.'

'But how could anyone predict the level of devastation, what it would be like?' Georgie asks.

'I couldn't – no one could,' he says. 'Not on that first night. But when the raids came again and again, each worse than the last, I should have been there, with the people I loved.' His hands go from the coffee cup to his face, drag down on the loose folds. When his fingers peel away, he seems determined to go on. 'On the fourth night, it was worse than ever. I can't begin to tell you of the sights I saw on the streets, of people dying, being swept away by that ferocious red wind. Somehow, I made it back to our apartment block, to find it engulfed, the fires raging. I spent what seemed like hours searching in the flames, and then the debris, desperate to find them, then not to discover them, maimed or burnt.'

'And?' Georgie says softly. In truth, she prefers not to hear the grim details, but he clearly needs to reveal all.

'I did find them – alive. Huddled in the basement, delirious with smoke, but alive. We went to a neighbour's house that hadn't been hit.' Harri lays a hand over his eyes, either to screen out the guilt or to picture it with clarity. 'But, Georgie, I was blind to the effect on Hella. Everyone was frightened – the entire city petrified – but I, stupid man that I was, didn't see it in my own wife. How utterly terrified she was, of what might come next. Of the nights to come, and the chances of dying so horribly.'

Harri's breathing becomes shallow, and Georgie wonders for a minute if his heart, too, has slowed, stuttering with grief.

'She begged me to take them out of the city, but it was total chaos, and all Polizei were called into work,' he croaks. 'When I came home the next afternoon, I found them, in the neighbour's attic cupboard, untouched by fire. In her utter panic, Hella wouldn't have been thinking straight, about the smoke rising. She was wrapped around Lily, and they both looked so calm, at peace.' He looks up at Georgie, guilt exposed across his entire face. 'I didn't listen to her. I wasn't there for them.'

Georgie says nothing for a time, minutes perhaps. Shock at this dreadful scenario, the waste of life and cruelty of war still taking its toll, and the creasing hurt it will likely inflict for decades. But also because of what bubbles inside her: the realisation. That Hella's actions, though fatal, were fuelled only by the deepest love, a mother's instinct to protect, at all costs. Doing the best for her child. Right then, Georgie understands it fully. Her pregnancy amounted to a nuance of motherhood, which, at the time, she didn't grasp. But sitting opposite Harri, she knows – without a shadow of a doubt – that she would have laid down her life for the child inside her, in a heartbeat.

Harri is unmoving, looking intently into his coffee cup, as Georgie searches for solace to give him. What can she say? Who knows anything any more?

'I don't know how you mend from that, Harri,' she begins.

'Only that it was the most extraordinary time, when the rulebook on humanity was ripped to pieces. And that the *only* person to blame, the catalyst for all that death, was one man, sitting high in his bloody ivory tower, playing God, when he had no right to, either in the name of Germans and Germany, or people as a whole. Dead or not, *he* is the one to bear that guilt.'

Finally, he looks up. 'But I could have done more, *known* my own wife.'

'Did any of us really know what others might do, how we might react ourselves?'

What of that first dead soul Georgie encountered in wartime, in a tiny village in Poland, swamped by the mire of battle? She'd imagined herself so worldly-wise, having witnessed her own bureau boss on the mortuary slab in Berlin. And yet she froze at the sight of the staring, empty eyes of a young Polish soldier. Worse, his friend was writhing and dying beside him, wounded in the neck. It was Max who stoppered the blood pumping with a bare hand, talked to him in his last moment, as the boy cried out for his mother in the delirium of near-death. Would he have survived if Georgie had been quicker, administered aid? Or been comforted by a female voice in his ear? Had she just been *better*?

Probably not, but it doesn't stop the wondering. It's guilt of a different nature to Harri's, but with roots fixed firmly in shame and remorse. 'No one *knew* anything, Harri,' she asserts, 'only that we needed to take in the next breath. And the one after that.'

'You're right,' he says. 'Again. But I think the time has come when I need help to understand it. When I have to ask for that help.'

'Always the first step,' she says. 'And it will change, Harri, because the world changes. That's the only certainty, even now.'

'I'll settle for different. Better would be nice, but different will do.' He raises his coffee cup and clinks it against hers. 'Here's to a changed world, Georgie Young.'

CHAPTER FIFTY-SIX:
THE STRINGS ARE SNAPPED

24th February 1946

Harri

Major Stephens sidles up beside Harri as he peers into the tiny barred hatch of the cell door, where Martin Sexton lies on the sparse bunk, knees up to his chest. Somehow, their nemesis looks much less threatening now, stripped of his own clothes and bravado.

Stephens coughs his presence. 'Schroder,' he says.

'Oh, hello, sir.' The surprise is that the major has made a visit to the holding cells on a Sunday, in full uniform, so it must be important.

'I just wanted to say, er . . . good work yesterday,' he manages. The words are mined from somewhere deep inside, coated in reluctance.

'Thank you, sir.' Harri smiles, determined to wring every ounce of humility from the cynical army man. 'But we also had plenty of help from Miss Young, and

387

your own Sergeant Dawson. He deserves a medal as far as I'm concerned.'

'Yes, well . . .' he coughs again, nervously if Harri isn't mistaken. 'And how is Miss Young? I hear she sustained some injuries.'

'Nothing that will stop her,' Harri reports. 'But she'll be on her way home soon. Back to England.'

'And our man here.' Stephens gestures towards the cell window. 'What do we know so far?'

'We're just about to go digging,' Harri says.

He's been 'allowed' to lead on Sexton's interrogation, given that the multiple murder of civilians stands officially as a Kripo affair, though the military have insisted on overall control. As they can and often do where matters are considered 'delicate'.

Sexton is led shuffling into the interview room, hands and feet cuffed. Harri stands, and although Sexton is a few inches taller, he looks small. Cowed. His right eye is purple and swollen, and his left jaw grazed and bruised; Harri knows that's not from the encounter with Dawson or himself. He can only guess the squaddies have exacted their own revenge on a former comrade whose actions have brought shame on the military.

Harri gestures that they both sit, an army lieutenant joining them on Harri's side of the table.

'Cigarette?' Harri pushes a pack of Lucky Strikes towards Sexton, and the cuffs jangle as he takes one.

'At least they're the Yankee variety,' Sexton snorts. 'Neutral.'

He's resigned, Harri detects. Nothing to lose but his life, which has gone already. Nothing to gain but surety against another beating. 'So?' he begins.

'Why should I tell you anything?' Sexton's resignation has turned bitter. 'I've already got the rope around my neck.'

Harri fiddles with the pack of cigarettes. 'Because I want to know. To understand. And because if you say nothing, you will go to the gallows, your existence snuffed out. Nothing left but your bones in a pathetic grave.'

This uncompromising rhetoric seems to have an effect on the prisoner, as he draws hard on his lit cigarette.

'But if you do explain, it will be a matter of record,' Harri adds. 'Officially, it has to be. You won't gain any accolades, but your words will be etched in some kind of history. People will know *why*.'

He's appealing to Sexton's vanity for one reason only; Harri doesn't give a shit about this monster's legacy, hates him with every fibre in his body, but he does care about the victims and their families. They will never recover, but he of all people understands the need for explanation. That all-important closure. And God knows, he wants to fathom what makes a man able to do that to another human, when war is no longer an excuse for barbarity.

'We know from your records that your real name is Martin Sexton,' Harri coaxes. 'But I don't believe for a minute that's the full picture. So, tell me.'

Sexton stubs out his cigarette and reaches for another. Sensing the cogs churning across the table, Harri lights the end and sits back. Waiting.

Sexton draws slowly. 'You . . .' his hand sweeps beyond the room, 'you won't understand, because you're all traitors.'

'To whom?'

'To him. Our leader.'

'Our leader being?' Harri is goading again. It's not

professional but – now Sexton is off the streets – he is actually enjoying it.

Sexton's eyes fill with contempt. 'You of all people should know. Being German.'

'And yet you are not German?' Harri challenges.

A second flash of scorn across the table. 'You don't have to be born here to understand the Führer's vision. His genius.'

'And you do – understand it?' Harri needs Sexton to say it, plainly and for the record, that he was – is – a Nazi.

Suddenly, Sexton is animated. 'Yes! I grew up here, I saw it take shape, the promise of the Reich. And if the Allies and the rest of Europe had recognised that, we wouldn't be in this shit-hole, would we?'

He's utterly deluded, that's clear to Harri. But the progression from Nazi to a serial killer of women needs establishing. Too many in the post-war trials have escaped justice on a technicality, or pleaded insanity and fooled the legal system. Sexton's ideas are grotesque and immoral, but he is lucid in his thinking.

'So, tell me, Martin – how does a former British army man come to be in custody, in what I sense is your adopted country, for murdering women? Where is your logic?' Harri isn't blasé or smug as he says it. In contrast, he adopts a mawkish expression, as if he really doesn't know, calling on Sexton to educate him. With fervour, the man in chains obliges.

Frustration and rage discharge in a torrent of vitriol; how Sexton was discharged from the army following a complaint from a woman, a 'promising officer' (his words) who was never given a chance by the 'bastard hierarchy'.

Robbed of his future. Drifting to London, he found himself sharing opinions being spouted by Oswald Mosley and his British Union of Fascists. Such was Sexton's commitment, he offered his services to the Führer, 'in whatever needed doing'.

'And what did you do?' Harri asks.

The handcuffs clink against the wooden table as Sexton pulls himself up, infused with his own standing. 'I was the voice of the Führer,' he says. 'Right here in Hamburg. Over the airwaves, until the bastard British drove us out. And I've been here ever since, under your great, fat noses.' He grins with conceit.

So, Georgie's speculation was spot on, yet again. Harri had almost forgotten the nights he and Hella scrolled through the dial on their state-issued radio set, landing once on a frequency pointed towards British shores. With perfect diction, a self-appointed Englishman who called himself 'Ralph Pearson' spewed Nazi propaganda, threatening British listeners with a nightmarish scenario of Nazi occupation once the Reich had secured victory. Switching to exact German halfway through the broadcast, Pearson addressed those in the Fatherland, describing in detail how 'unbelievers' across the Channel would soon 'see the light'. So, this is the faceless Pearson they heard that night through the wireless, the voice of a traitor, to the English and humanity.

'You were something of a Lord Haw-Haw then?' Harri is inciting again, this time for his own pleasure. 'Though, I seem to remember he was better known?'

'Fuck Haw-Haw!' Sexton explodes. 'He was nowhere near as committed, or effective. I had it on good authority – from Berlin – that Hitler valued me more.'

Bored with Sexton's self-aggrandisement, Harri pushes it along. 'What happened then?'

Sexton shrugs. 'There were some who were too cowardly to stand by the Führer at the crucial point. They let the British and the Allies in. Traitors, all of them. They pledged to resist, to forsake their lives and futures, but when it came to giving either, they caved. They ran. Bloody liars and weaklings.'

Sensing a link beginning to emerge, Harri exploits a break in Sexton's rant. 'Does that include women, these liars you talk about?'

'Bitches – all of them,' Sexton growls under his breath. 'Especially that one who gave us up at the end, the last of us loyal to the Führer. I had no choice but to run back then, because of her. But, you know, they're all the same – weak. Loyalty is about standing firm. Nowadays, women promise you everything and lead you on, tell you they'll do anything because they want a passport, or cigarettes or coffee. In the end, they all bail. Every single one. You can't trust them.'

'So, you lured the women with what? The promise of a new life, away from Hamburg?'

Sexton's maniacal cackle echoes around the room, a true madman's laugh. 'So bloody naïve! Told them I was from the government – British or German, it didn't matter – and they would be doing important work overseas. In time, I would have had them believing in the Führer's vision, if only they'd just done as I asked.' He shakes his head, convinced of his own righteousness. 'It's all their own fault.'

Harri balls his fists under the table. Unlike some of his colleagues, he's never been prone to violence during

392

interrogations, but right now he's glad there are witnesses present, or else he might be risking an assault charge.

'How many women did you recruit?' he asks instead.

Sexton tips his head side to side, as if lazily totting up how many beers he might have had the night before. Harri's nails dig into his palms.

'Four, I think, if you count the one that got away, and five if you include the lovely Miss Young.' He directs a concerted leer at Harri.

'So, you killed Liselle Mauser, Rita Essig and Ursula Reinhart, and attacked Sigrid Heike and Meta Hertzig?'

'Yes, though I don't know the names of the last two. Just women who got in the way.' His eyelids blink slowly with contempt.

'And why did you target Miss Young? I mean, she's not your usual type – blonde and English.'

'Easy. I saw she was smart, and more of a challenge. And because of you, of course, getting a bit too close. Teaming up like bloody Bonnie and Clyde. It was irresistible. Is that enough of a reason for you?'

'She *is* smart,' Harri says with satisfaction. 'And the thing is, she got the better of you. Didn't she?'

His chair scrapes as he stands and heads for the door, nausea rising in his throat, in thinking that he might have been responsible for another woman's death, letting Georgie into the investigation. Using her, perhaps. But no, he can't reason like that. A man with Sexton's hunger would have targeted other women, found any excuse to kill. Sometimes there are no explanations for men like him, Hitler or Himmler, no matter how much you search or analyse. Harri is in a job because such individuals exist. What matters is that Georgie, Meta and Sigrid Heike are still out there – alive.

He's done. The military man alongside can take down the details of Sexton's grotesque confession, but Harri has heard his fill of this man's sickening morality. He leaves the room with a brief backward glance at the man who terrorised Hamburg's streets for no other reason than a slavish devotion to an egomaniac who went before him. For a brief second, Harri wonders when Sexton's bravado will desert him, if it will on his first sighting of that noose, the infamous last meal, or well before, as he's sitting alone in his cell, contemplating the dead Führer and his pathetic legacy.

Stephens is outside, having clearly listened to the exchange from a neighbouring room via a speaker. He stands and nods as Harri appears, but says nothing.

Should I stay equally quiet? Harri wonders. In the war, it was his nature and a survival technique to utter very little to his superiors, to 'keep his head down' as Dawson is apt to say. Now there's no SS, no Gestapo. And no reason to keep his mouth shut.

'He was a British army man,' he says, looking Stephens directly in the eye. 'An army man whose conduct raised suspicions even before he served in the war.' The bitterness in his voice threatens to spill over. 'But no one in authority cared, or said anything. The army just wanted rid of him, so he wasn't their problem.'

Stephens' feet shift. 'It was a failing, undoubtedly,' the major concedes. 'Some of that fault lies with us. I can only pledge, Schroder, that I will take it to the highest level. To make sure it doesn't happen again. That it can't.'

Harri only nods.

'Inspector, can I buy you a drink? As some small measure of my thanks.'

'I'd prefer a few more decent typewriters, or even some bicycles with functioning wheels.'

'Done,' Stephens says. 'And that drink?'

'Another time, thank you, Major. I have somewhere I need to be.'

The office isn't open on a Sunday, but Gunter's flat is just above the office of his practice, sharing the same door, newly inscribed: *Dr G. Vogel, Psychiatrist*.

'Hello, stranger!' he greets Harri at the door, dressed in his leisure attire, a sweater and trousers overlaid with a silken dressing gown. 'Come in, come in. You've caught me having a lazy day. I've just put some coffee on.'

'Perfect timing then.'

'Well, it's from under the counter. If you want to partake rather than arrest me, just close your eyes as you're swallowing.'

'So,' Gunter goes on, when they're sitting in front of a very good fire. 'Is this a social call?'

'Yes and no,' Harri says tentatively.

'Oh?'

'It's time, Gunter, that I faced up to it. To Hella and Lily, and what's left behind. I don't want to be a knotty mess any more. And if I want to unravel myself, I realise now that I will have to talk. And I would rather do that with you, a friend and a professional.'

'And as your friend, I can say it's not before time. As a doctor, it's way overdue.' He smiles. 'But I'm glad, Harri. It might not be easy, but I promise you won't regret it.'

CHAPTER FIFTY-SEVEN:
TOWARDS A FUTURE

26th February 1946

Meta

She barely recognises the woman, even when staring hard at her leather shoes, second-hand, but clean, then upwards to unpocked stockings and a neat woollen jacket. Finally, the face, also clean and with short, cropped hair, crowned with a felt beret. Meta peers hard into the smeared reflection of a shop window and adjusts her soft cap – another gift from Georgie – pushing wisps of hair under the rim. It is her. Meta Hertzig. Beyond the filth of the glass and the mask of good clothes, there is a shade of who she once was.

She imagined feeling underdone without her huge bivouac of a coat and her too-big boots. Almost naked. But she doesn't regret their loss, since the most essential comfort is still with her, tethered by need and the grip of her fingers on the leather handle of her suitcase.

'Come on, Meta,' Zofia urges, 'we should get to the platform. It'll be leaving soon.'

'Okay.' Yet she hesitates at the sight of a tiny form hovering to her side – a girl, she thinks – so thin and pale that her skin is near transparent above her rags. Meta turns and responds to the begging, outstretched hand, scrabbling in the case for what cigarettes she has left. She has money in her purse now, enough for several weeks, but old habits die hard when it comes to a pack of Lucky Strikes. Her entire stash of Chesterfields she bestowed on Popo as they said goodbye, and for a second she considered asking him to come too, but he seemed incredulous anyone would even want a different life.

'Why?' he asked her. 'Why, when the streets give us all we need?'

'Just look me up if you're ever in Berlin,' she said instead, which he won't, of course. He kissed her cheek and coughed away what looked to her like sadness, and went back to poking at his meagre fire.

The girl–beggar grabs at the proffered cigarettes, turns and runs like a savvy street kid, and Meta finds herself raising a hand, as if she's saying a final farewell to herself.

'Wait for me, I'm coming,' she calls to Zofia.

Georgie is already on the platform, ready to greet Zofia with tickets and directions, while Harri hangs back a little, his gaze towards the metal bones of the station roof, seeming to take in the echo of station announcements, joyous greetings and sad goodbyes. Meta has been wary of him before, given his visit to the prison, and her previous run-ins with the Polizei. Less so now, when she sees him alongside Georgie, as a true ally. And especially since he caught the bastard who put her in hospital. Thanks to Georgie, Meta is off those streets now, for good hopefully, while Harri has made them mildly safer for those who remain, forced by circumstance to make their home there. 'A team effort', as the squaddies are apt to say.

'So, the apartment is about half a mile from the station,' Georgie repeats to Zofia, 'and you're to report to the British headquarters the day after tomorrow, ask for Sam Blundon. He'll direct you to the translation department.'

'Don't worry, we'll be fine, won't we, Meta?' Zofia says with surety.

'Of course.' Were Meta planning to venture onto Berlin's thoroughfares as a vagrant, she might be more certain, but as a pretend adult, with a life to plan, she is a little less confident. She will, however, give this real life a go, and search for the aunt who may have survived the last bloody battle for the capital city in '45. If no relative exists, Meta is determined to forge a different future, with a roof over her head, to get a job – she was a decent student before the war – and not waste the luck that has been afforded in the most bizarre of fashions, in trying to steal the suitcase of a random woman at an airport.

Georgie approaches and wraps her arms around Meta's wiry body, still yet to fill out properly.

'You will write, won't you?' she breathes into her ear, and it's that sentiment, rather than Georgie's firm embrace, that squeezes a droplet out of Meta's eye, from the girl who has not spilt emotion openly since well before the war's end. Someone cares, enough to want to know. About her, and her future. Even if she had the words, she couldn't voice them in that precious second, her nose deep into the weave of Georgie's coat.

Steam rises and the train whistle lets loose with a long, resonant whine. Everyone looks relieved as it drives forward the lingering, unwelcome farewell.

'We'd better board,' Zofia says, with a last hug for Georgie, and one for Harri too.

The suitcase bashes against Meta's leg as she climbs on – no jewellery or contraband within, but a decent change of clothes, and a second-hand suit to wear for job interviews. Tucked into the lining are her bent and faded family photographs, the only remnants from before. Still, they are her own things, in her case.

Both women hang from the window as the train shunts out of the station, waving furiously until the platform is out of sight.

Finally, Zofia sits back into her seat, the salty track marks on her cheeks dried by the chill wind. She must glimpse Meta's worried look and the doubt it creates, and she's quick to reassure.

'It's a good thing, isn't it, Meta, that we have this new start?'

'Yes. If you're sure. I mean, we can do things separately, we don't have to . . .'

'Together, I mean,' Zofia affirms. 'A new life together. We didn't both lose everything only to push away what good fortune comes our way. Don't you think?'

'Yes, that's exactly what I think,' Meta says. She fingers the worn but soft leather of her case. 'A new life.'

CHAPTER FIFTY-EIGHT:
GOODBYE AND HELLO

26th February 1946

Georgie

'Two on the same day, and I bloody hate goodbyes.' Georgie pouts and sighs as she moves through the military airport towards the makeshift gate. She's undergone her quota of farewells over the last years, too many of which have proved permanent.

'Although it generally means there will be a pleasant greeting at the other end,' Harri offers.

Georgie stops abruptly and spins on her heel. 'Harri Schroder! Did I just hear a shining pearl of optimism come from your very lips?' She makes a play of fainting with shock.

'Would you believe me if I said it's a new me?' he says.

'Probably not. But it's definitely a start, and I look forward to seeing more.'

They both stare through the door, where aircraft

engines are pushing out warm thermals, distorting the cold, grey vista of the runway. A man in khaki signals for Georgie to move on to the hard stand. There's no delaying it any longer.

'You will come to visit, won't you?' Georgie presses him. 'We've plenty of room, and Max would love to meet you. I feel sure you and he will get on famously. Though you might gang up on me if I'm not careful.'

'I doubt it. You're more than a match for both of us,' he says. 'In the meantime, Dawson has pretty much adopted me – he's threatening to take me dancing at the Victory again, God help me. But it means I will be street-smart if I ever get to London.'

'*When* you get to London, Harri.'

'All right, when.'

Harri reaches for her hand, runs a finger over her knuckles and squeezes down. He looks straight into her, as she's done plenty of times with men in authority, those she aimed to win over. Only this time, she's certain Inspektor Schroder isn't trying to score, or triumph, or ask anything of her.

'Seriously, Georgie, thank you.'

'What for?'

'Well, there's the little matter of the investigation, and a very dangerous man in the cells,' he says. 'But you know what else. For letting me . . . allowing me to . . .'

She silences him with a kiss to his rough, stubbly cheek. 'Same here. I've been altered by a lot over the last few years, but I didn't imagine that two weeks in a post-war German city would be quite so life-changing. For a whole host of reasons.'

'Then that's good, isn't it?'

'I like to think it is. For both of us.'

The man in khaki hollers over the roar of the engine and beckons impatiently. 'Better go,' she says, and picks up her case, a battered cardboard version hastily acquired at the NAAFI.

'Send me a telegram when you reach home,' Harri calls behind her. 'And your articles, too. I'm almost sure Stephens will try to buy up all the copies so we don't read them.'

'Will do.' She turns and waves, as the door to the terminal shuts behind her and Inspektor Schroder disappears from sight.

She scans left and right as they emerge through little more than a corrugated shed – a military terminal British-style, with the ubiquitous tea stall stationed in the corner, a kettle puffing out steam. Welcome home. When Georgie doesn't see Max amid the small, waiting cluster, she looks instead for an office, somewhere she might phone for a taxi. She'd forwarded the flight details by telegram, though it's unlikely Max will have received them in time. In truth, she's a little disappointed, though she can't be angry. Just weary and resigned, and in desperate need of a long soak in her own bath.

'Can I help you, madam?'

Georgie turns at the voice. 'Oh you! Where did you come from?' She throws her arms around him, careful not to knock her husband off balance and send his walking stick flying.

'You didn't think I wouldn't come, did you?' His one free hand circles her waist, drawing her whole body in tightly.

Georgie clings onto it, and him. It's there. She feels it.

The thrill of seeing Max, what they once had. Still have. Now she's certain; of why she came home, why she felt butterflies in her stomach as the plane came in to land. Why she wants to reach home so badly. Their home. With only Max for company, to wake up with, to spend and end the day with. Every day.

Eventually, she peels away and he looks intently at her face, with love but also concern, at the stitches still prominent on her brow. 'Been in the wars?'

Georgie laughs at their age-old joke, something they'd said repeatedly, like a good luck charm, each time they emerged from close-up combat, or a risky situation. 'Something like that,' she says. 'But I'm fine, honestly.'

She catches a quizzical look as Max stoops to pick up her luggage. 'New case?' he says.

'Oh, that's another story. A long one, too. Let's get home and I'll tell you everything.'

News Review, Thursday 7th March 1946
The Circus Is in Town
Correspondent GEORGIE YOUNG reports from the streets of Hamburg, the first in a series of snapshot articles on post-war life in the German city

With the heft of his body and an agile, probing trunk, the elephant makes short work of nudging the mangled metal debris – in this case, righting a battered three-wheeled military jeep amid the aftermath of a hand grenade. There's no applause from the small cluster looking on, because this creature's work is essential, rather than a performance in a resplendent big top, even if those observers might argue that the Hamburg of today *is* a circus of sorts, with its wealth of eye-opening sights. Not to mention the ever-present frisson of impending danger around every corner.

Add 'chaos' into that mix and it's nearing a fair description of a post-war existence, as seen by this correspondent. Because while the ticker-tape of victory in Allied nations has blown away, and with Britons settling into a new peace, war continues to rage elsewhere. Hitler is dead, the Reich defeated, but daily struggles endure in German cities like Hamburg: for bread, soup, clothes to ward off the freezing winter and precious cigarettes to trade with, to buy the tiniest nugget of luxury that equates, at times, to little more than a sliver of soap or a fingernail of butter. Everyone here trades, in tobacco and trinkets. In life.

It was the illustrious 'Monty' who set out the challenge of 'winning the peace' in a defeated Germany, as British troops moved into the industrial heartlands of the Ruhr, occupiers alongside the Americans and French to the south and west of the country, Russians to the east. The British Army of the Rhine (BAOR) has a mission, principally to keep order and root out those Nazis who have gone to ground, in a long and complicated process of 'de-Nazification', overseeing a population of twenty million. Their colleagues in the Control Commission Germany, or CCG, aim to house, rebuild and employ a nation left confused and unseated after five long years of conflict.

Have the British triumphed this time? Perhaps not yet. Much like the elephant who stands as a surviving remnant of Hamburg's bombed-out zoo, the task ahead is a mammoth one. The Germany of 1946 is a movable beast, made up of Voelkerwanderung, or the 'wandering people' – the expelled, uprooted, evacuated and formerly imprisoned. Refugees, camp-dwellers, POWs and the stranded are now classified under one umbrella as Displaced Persons, or 'DPs' in military-speak.

From dawn till dark, Hamburg's streets ripple with this nomadic shoal, plodding on foot and in donkey-drawn carts, en route to resettlement centres, soup kitchens, unofficial refugee camps, and sometimes to nowhere at all. Just putting one foot in front of the other. Because moving is all they've come to know, having shuffled from one place to another, one meal to the next, for eternity.

'It's as if they are frightened of putting down new roots,' one British soldier remarked, shaking his head in bewilderment.

What this human traffic creates is need – for food, shelter and employment. It's estimated some seventy thousand residents still live in the city's concrete underbelly, the bunkers and cellars in which they sheltered during the RAF's bombing campaign of 1943. Above ground, whole neighbourhoods have been reduced to charred skeletons of buildings and apartment blocks, so that now, the windowless dwellings below can be twelve to a bunker, a single table accommodating three or four families. With little ventilation, the stench is beyond words, the walls streaming with damp, and in one I visited, fungi flourished nicely in a corner. 'At least we might get a meal from it eventually,' one mother said with a weary optimism.

Each morning, the underground dwellers emerge from their burrows, to partake in the city's newest and most buoyant industry: foraging. The once thriving shipyards on the mighty Elbe are now a mangled mesh of steel, and factories have all but ground to a halt, leaving many Hamburgers to scavenge – for food, coal, trinkets, ephemera, and the currency on which street-life exists: cigarettes. In the makeshift refugee camp which has mushroomed close to the military airport, a sparkling family heirloom might be exchanged for a loaf of bread, a functioning camera for a live goose, and a seatless bicycle swapped for a bag of potatoes. The marketplace knows no bounds.

The army and the CCG does its best to bring in grain for bread, struggling against a poor harvest in the winter of 1945, a legacy of damaged train tracks and the complex politics of negotiating supply 'corridors' with the Russians. On the streets, it leaves hungry mouths, the average daily ration now down to one thousand calories per day. Cats, dogs and rats do as meat, while frogs and snails make for a filling soup, I'm told. It is a daily battle, without guns or bombs.

And what of the people? Much like Britons in the endless days of the Blitz, they sometimes complain. There are brief flashes of rebellion, created in part by the gnawing hunger. The simple act of unloading flour for bread can spark an ugly riot, British troops as the target for the crowd's frustrations. Desperation feeds the anger and, during my brief visit, two Germans were shot dead by stray bullets, terror flashing in the protesters' eyes at the unwelcome memory of a very recent combat. They shrank from the horror, back into their freezing bunkers.

Mostly, the people soldier on, because they have no choice. Is there a sense of bitterness towards their British overseers? Yes, in certain circles. I wager Britons would feel the same, if the boot was on the other foot. Among others, there's a relief that the Nazi scourge is gone and order may be restored, enough that Germany will one day govern itself without the grey shadow of the Reich hovering above.

Mercifully, there is some light: the soaring

tower of the ornate, solid and beautiful Rathaus in the city centre, untouched by bombs and standing as a symbol of survival. The people's spirit shines through the dark, bitter months, with the tenacity of the British, the French, the Poles and all nations emerging from the recent storm. But make no mistake: Hamburg, and Germany, remains a battlefield, at war against nature, the elements and a legacy it struggles to shake off. Monty's trophy of peace will be hard-won.

For now, Hamburg tackles life one day – and one shuffling step – at a time.

News Review, Thursday 14th March 1946
Thick as Thieves
GEORGIE YOUNG reports from British-controlled Hamburg, in the second of her articles on life in post-war Germany

'They steal everything,' the man says with a sigh. 'They'd steal your shadow if they could sell or barter it.' Unconsciously, he looks at the ground adjacent to the tram stop where he's waiting, as if checking he's still in possession of his own soul.

This man is German, and he's talking with some regret of his own countryfolk, and of what life around him has sunk to in the city he calls home. Equally, he's not wrong. Within hours of arrival as a visitor to Hamburg, I had been mugged not once, but twice. I was unhurt, though shaken by a physical tug-of-war with desperate thieves half my size and weight. Each time, it was for something we Britons might consider a trifle, but to post-war survivors represents hard currency and the chance of fending off hunger for another day: a smattering of American dollars, and the 'prize' of my old, battered suitcase.

After a sprint outside the airport, I caught up with the first would-be thief – let's call her 'Inga'. She'd been quick to make her escape, but was hampered by the layers of clothes – some nearing rags – that she's forced to wear in warding off the cruel German winter. In her competent English gleaned from occupying British soldiers, Inga revealed how an ancient valise such as mine has become a coveted status symbol, and a receptacle for stowing life. Her entire life. Because sixteen-year-old Inga has nothing in this world beyond a stash of cigarettes that she barters for food, her resolve, and a good deal of guile. In the bombed-out factory she calls home, Inga proudly revealed the photograph she clutches close to her heart each night, curled up against the brutal temperatures. One by one, she introduced the faces smiling into the camera: her father killed in Russia, her mother and sisters, all victims of the firestorm which raged through Hamburg in 1943. The sadness she hides well. Her loneliness perhaps less so.

Lonely, but not entirely alone, because Inga is one of many – millions of children across Europe who live without the protection of parents, forced to grow up swiftly and fend for themselves on the streets of a post-war world that has sympathy and resources in short supply. What else can Inga and her cohorts do but steal? By necessity, she belongs to a network of street kids, or *trümmerkinder* – lone orphans who pick over the city's ruins for any morsel they can reuse or trade. Like urchins from the pages of Dickens, they pillage empty houses for trinkets left behind by the German elite who fled in defeat.

There are those who despair of this 'pestilence', including the British military and the overworked police departments, plus the man at the tram stop. Doubtless, he has a job and food on the table, a roof of slate (rather than Inga's filthy tarpaulin) to hold off the rain and snow, and a decent coat to keep from freezing. Perhaps a family to offer comfort.

Inga does not. She has cunning and pace (on the days when there are calories in her system), and a certain will. It's a spirit that just a year ago we would have applauded. Now, it's one that classifies her as an outlaw, along with her fellow waifs and strays.

Having seen beyond the rags and the ingrained dirt of her face, I would argue that what Inga possesses in today's Hamburg counts as priceless: the will to survive.

If I could track down that man at the tram stop again, I would tell him that she needs his sympathy and not his censure, a hand to hold as well as four solid walls within which to construct a new life in this war-weary world.

Swing, Swing, Swing
In her third and final article, correspondent
GEORGIE YOUNG reports from Hamburg
on life after Hitler's Germany

Like tiny fires in a grey wasteland, there are small
spots dotted across Hamburg that burn brightly
amid the daily struggle of survival. As darkness
descends, the young don their finest, press their
uniforms and put on their dancing shoes. When
the rain and snow hold off, they collect around
the bridges of Hamburg's mighty Elbe river and
the Alster basin, setting up an impromptu club
for the evening, complete with gramophone,
record spinner and portable bar. They are German,
mainly, though a small cluster of uniforms are
often enticed by the spectacle and welcomed into
the fold. Because when the music strikes up and
people spill into the makeshift circle of a 'floor',
they are no longer German or British, victor or
defeated, occupiers or not. They are dancers, in
total harmony.

Through the many divisions of this city, swing
music cuts a swathe AND forges a connection.
Quite plainly, people have fun.

This newfound unity is similarly apparent on
dance nights at the British Victory Club, a large,
imposing building close to Dammtor station, which
houses the NAAFI bar, shop, cinema and, most
crucially, a ballroom. Each Friday, the Tommies and
squaddies of the British occupying forces pull out

411

their Brylcreem and dust down the khaki. Women of the ATS and BAOR admin staff tease their hair, while the German contingent (women mostly) primp and preen to look their best. In the ballroom, the band strikes up with 'Boogie Woogie Bugle Boy' and the barriers between nations vanish, the dancefloor a twirling, swirling mass of smiling faces. The words may hail back to a time of war, but it matters not. The beat is everything, sparking a compulsion to jive, those on the sidelines unconsciously tapping their feet in time. You just can't help it.

Neither can you ignore the personal liaisons forged on such nights at the Victory Club: British men with women both far from home, and British with German. Plainly, Hamburg women are keen to escape the chaos of a country that no longer feels their own. Officially, the British forces frowns on 'fraternisation', but it happens.

'All week, I look forward to coming here,' Kristel tells me in the English that she's quickly mastering. 'The men are polite and courteous, and when we dance, we can forget everything on the outside. My mother doesn't like me coming here, but I don't care – I feel alive again.'

'The German women are beautiful, and they make a real effort,' says Billy, an army mechanic from south London, as he keeps one roving eye on the dancefloor. 'We're not fools. We know they want our rations too, but who can blame them?'

He takes a swig of NAAFI beer and surveys the crowd like a sage. 'When you stand here, it's hard to believe there was ever a war at all.'

The band strikes up the opening bar of all-time favourite 'Sing, Sing, Sing', and couples swarm onto the floor with a combined whoop of excitement. Setting aside his glass, Billy grabs instinctively at my hand. 'Come on, let's forget it all and just dance.'

And do you know, I did just that.

Swing, swing, swing.

ACKNOWLEDGEMENTS

Every one of my novels to date have been moulded by those around me, and – in the case of *The Hidden Storyteller* – by one in particular. As with the character of Georgie, I owe the contact to serendipity; I met Gordon Drane on a trip to the lovely city of Hamburg, as my designated city guide. Not only is he an Englishman who speaks fluent German, but he harbours a love of his adopted home and its history. Gordon went above and beyond for our tour, researching and translating throughout the writing and editing process. So, *danke* Gordon. Very, very much. Despite its sad wartime record, you made Hamburg a joy and embroidered this book.

I owe so much to my outgoing editor, Molly Walker-Sharp, whose love of Georgie inspired me to take her on another adventure, and then to my incoming editor, Sarah Bauer, who assumed the tricky job of birthing a 'baby' late into the gestation. Around them, there is the ever-present Team Avon, shaping, promoting, bartering and building on behalf of my books, alongside those in the wider world who shout loud about historical fiction. Much gratitude to you all.

To my fabulous agent, Broo Doherty at DHH Literary Agency, I say cheers, for her forbearance, enthusiasm and ability to make me chuckle with her quirky emails.

Friends. Well, where do I start? The 'ground crew' in my beloved home of Stroud are my link to sanity, with dog walks, coffee and laughs: Gez, Sarah, Jo, Annie, Isobel, Heidi, Marion, Kirsty, Ruth, Micki and Hayley, plus a whole host of others.

In the writing world, I am so lucky to be among a rich and varied seam of scribes that chivvy and support when needed: workmate Sarah Steele, who types like a demon opposite and shames me into keeping up, with the dark sisterhood of Mel Golding and Emma Flint pitching their irreverent humour. The Gloucestershire tribe are too many to mention, but thanks for allowing me to feel one of you. At the end of a WhatsApp or an email, there is Lorna (Elle) Cook, and long-term writing pal LP (Loraine) Fergusson, with wisdom and friendship.

Readers – whether you're new to Georgie or a veteran of the books, a huge thanks. I do it because of you, because I'm a reader, and because books are my world.

Germany, 1944. Anke Hoff is assigned
as midwife to one of Hitler's inner circle.
If she refuses, her family will die.

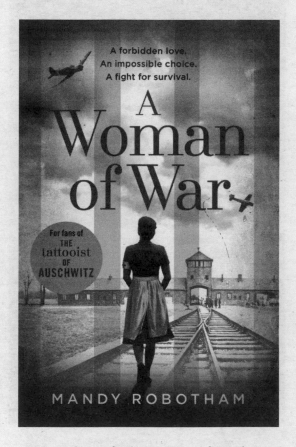

For readers of *The Tattooist of Auschwitz*
comes a gritty tale of courage, betrayal
and love in the most unlikely of places.

The world is at war, and Stella Jilani is leading a double life.

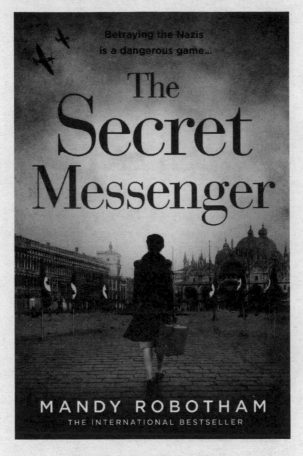

Set between German–occupied 1940s Venice
and modern-day London, this is a fascinating
tale of the bravery of everyday women
in the darkest corners of WWII.

Berlin, 1938. **It's the height of summer, and Germany is on the brink of war.**

A country on the brink of war.
A woman who will uncover its secrets.

The Berlin Girl

MANDY ROBOTHAM

THE INTERNATIONAL BESTSELLER

From the internationally bestselling author comes the heart-wrenching story of a world about to be forever changed.

A city divided.
Two sisters torn apart.
One impossible choice . . .

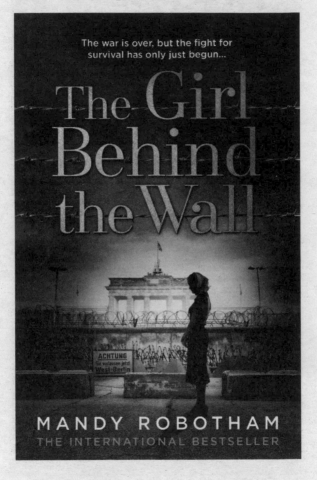

The war is over, but the fight for
survival has only just begun...

The Girl
Behind
the Wall

ACHTUNG
Sie verlassen jetzt
West-Berlin

MANDY ROBOTHAM
THE INTERNATIONAL BESTSELLER

Set against the dawn of the cold war,
this is a timely reminder that, even in the darkest
of places, love will guide you home.

Norway, 1942. **Rumi Orlstad is grieving the loss of her husband at the hands of Hitler. And now she will make them pay.**

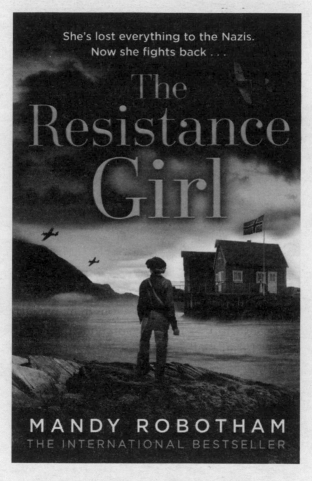

She's lost everything to the Nazis.
Now she fights back . . .

The Resistance Girl

MANDY ROBOTHAM
THE INTERNATIONAL BESTSELLER

A heartbreaking tale of the sacrifices ordinary people made to keep friends, family, strangers – and hope – alive.

Two cities.
Two spies.
Which woman survives?

Two cities. Two spies.
Which woman survives?

The War Pianist

MANDY ROBOTHAM
THE INTERNATIONAL BESTSELLER

From the internationally bestselling author
comes a gripping historical fiction novel about love,
loss and the worst kind of betrayal.

EXCLUSIVE ADDITIONAL CONTENT

Includes exclusive author content and details
of how to get involved in *Fern's Picks*

Dear lovely readers,

This month's read is Mandy Robotham's latest emotional historical fiction novel, *The Hidden Storyteller*.

It is 1946 and the war is over, but the effects can still be felt throughout Europe – and beyond. Germany is in ruins. We follow Georgie Young, an intrepid reporter, who is posted to an Allied-run Hamburg. Returning to a country she fled seven years prior at the start of the war, Georgie discovers it is almost unrecognisable.

It's soon evident there are many more stories to tell – and secrets to reveal – than Georgie first imagined. When she meets local detective, Harri, she finds herself entangled in an investigation into a killer who is targeting the women of Hamburg. Mandy provides her readers with exquisite writing, heart-breaking history and lots of intrigue – this beautifully researched novel is filled with rich detail, drawing back the curtain on a post-war Germany.

I do hope you enjoy it, I can't wait to hear what you think!

With love
Fern x

A Q&A with
Mandy Robotham

Warning: contains spoilers

**You've written about Georgie before; did you always know
you'd write about her again? How did you find it writing
a character you knew, but who will have changed a lot in
the intervening years?**

At the time, I felt I'd 'rounded up' Georgie at the end of
The Berlin Girl – she'd found love and was going onto a
different life. It was the readers who told me otherwise, asking
frequently if there would be a sequel featuring Georgie. In a
strange way, I felt her wartime adventures were not mine to
tell, but I did ponder on what she would do after the war, and
whether her spirit would be tamed eventually. Or not.

**Are there any other characters in *The Hidden Storyteller*
that you would like to revisit?**

Oh yes! Whilst writing *The Hidden Storyteller* I thought
Harri might be a secondary character, but he soon stamped
his mark on me and the book, and I fell in love very quickly
with his grumpy, slightly irascible nature. There will be
definitely be more of Harri, and I'm also quite curious about
Meta's future, too…

This is your first book that is set in this post-WWII era, was your research different?

The war is very well documented by historians, and although it doesn't stop at the surrender, there's definitely much less detail, or enthusiasm to write about it. I had to look harder for the 'nitty-gritty' of day-to-day life, but there were some writers, like the publisher Victor Gollancz, who were equally appalled at the fate of the wandering masses, enough to visit places like Hamburg and document what they saw. And, of course, there were Allied soldiers who fell in love with German women; luckily for me, some of them wrote about it.

Is there another period of history that you're fascinated by but are yet to write about?

Lots. I would love to write more about the Cold War in Europe, and the changing world for women in the 1960s, but I'm also a big fan of historical fiction set in Tudor times and the 1700s. I'd like to write about any period that provides an escape for readers like me.

There's a mystery element to *The Hidden Storyteller*, did you enjoy writing this? Did you plan who it was from the beginning, or did it come to you during the writing process?

With this book, I definitely set out to write a novel with a crime element, but the growth of Georgie, Harri and Meta as characters happened day by day. I usually have a set beginning, a slightly fuzzier ending in mind, and the bit in between is created, literally, as I open up the laptop and type. Working this way can sometimes cause headaches, and I have tried to be a better planner, but somehow it never works!

It is, however, much harder writing without the backdrop of war and conflict, and I needed to dig deep with my characters for this book.

What does a normal writing day look like for you? Do you have a routine?

Being a midwife for twenty years and getting up at all hours means that, nowadays, I'm quite a later starter. I'll walk my dog, Basil, and then gear up with a few emails. I also need to go out to a coffee shop and start writing with a good flat white beside me. Sometimes, I'll work opposite a friend and fellow writer, Sarah Steele – she types likes the wind, so I'm inspired and pressured to keep up!

I aim for a thousand words per day, and when I've done that, I'll spend the rest of the day checking up on research, or writing something totally different – I like to have a 'hobby' project on the go at the same time.

Georgie and Meta are very different characters and in very different circumstances, but they are both such strong women. Is having strong female leads in your novels something that is important to you?

Definitely. Again, being a midwife meant that I was surrounded by resilient colleagues for years. Plus, there's no one stronger than a woman in labour. Equally, I have to take account of the position of women in the 1940s, with fewer rights in the home and workplace than today. And yet in wartime they stepped up to the plate and became Britain's backbone. So, it's a balancing act between the real history and how I consistently view women – as true warriors of any era.

Whilst your books and characters are fictional, they are set against true historical events. Do you find it hard to balance the two? Particularly when you find something or someone very interesting during your research?

There's always a tendency to cram as much research in as possible, but I have to remember that my books are fiction – the story is the key driver of the book. So, I use the facts, or a real event in history, as a sort of hat stand on which to hang my characters and weave into the fabric. With *The Hidden Storyteller*, I read about suitcases being valuable items post-war, and I thought: Bingo! There was my pivot, and out popped the character of Meta soon after.

It is rare we see this perspective of Germany following the war, was it something you set out to do?

I do always try to think of places and people that don't feature consistently in fiction, so that I come to it with an unbiased approach and a real hunger to discover the detail. Reading so much about the war years, I began to wonder: What happened to all those people? In truth, some of the research – the rates of civilian death in Europe once the fighting ended – shocked me more than the conflict itself. In terms of Georgie, I felt we could probably imagine what she did in the war, but what about after, when all the adrenalin and adventure stopped? Could she slot into the role of so many other women, back into the home? Would she even want to?

What are you writing next?

I grew to love Harri so much that I felt I didn't want to leave him behind. So, he's going to be sharing the stage with a new and equally feisty partner – this time in England – and a new decade of the 1950s. Watch out for the adventures of Inspektor Schroder and WPC Dexter, AKA 'Dexie'.

Questions for your Book Club

Warning: contains spoilers

- What three words would you use to describe *The Hidden Storyteller*, and why?

- Which character's perspective – Georgie, Harri or Meta – did you relate to the most, and why?

- Before reading this book, had you thought much about post-war Germany? If so, how have your perceptions changed since finishing the novel?

- How important was the character of Meta in creating a true sense of Hamburg in 1946?

- Which scene struck you the most, and why?

- Georgie's work is important, but also dangerous. Would you have travelled alone like she did? Do you think she took any unnecessary risks throughout the novel?

- How important do you feel a woman's intuition is to the plot of *The Hidden Storyteller*?

- Which other books would you compare *The Hidden Storyteller* to, and why?

An exclusive extract from Fern's new novel

The Good Servant

March 1932

Marion Crawford was not able to sleep on the train, or to eat the carefully packed sandwiches her mother had insisted on giving her. Anxiety, and a sudden bout of homesickness, prohibited both.

What on earth was she doing? Leaving Scotland, leaving everything she knew? And all on the whim of the Duchess of York, who had decided that her two girls needed a governess exactly like Miss Crawford.

Marion couldn't quite remember how or when she had agreed to the sudden change. Before she knew it, it was all arranged. The Duchess of York was hardly a woman you said no to.

Once her mother came round to the idea, she was in a state of high excitement and condemnation. 'Why would they want *you*?' she had asked, 'A girl from a good, working class family? What do you know about how these people live?' She had stared at Marion, almost in reverence. 'Working for the royal family . . . They must have seen something in you. My daughter.'

On arrival at King's Cross, Marion took the underground to Paddington. She found the right platform for the Windsor train and, as she had a little time to wait, ordered a cup of tea, a scone and a magazine from the station café.

She tried to imagine what her mother and stepfather were doing right now. They'd have eaten their tea and have the wireless on, tuned to news most likely. Her mother would have her mending basket by her side, telling her husband all about Marion's send off. She imagined her mother rambling on as the fire in the grate hissed and burned.

The train was rather full, but Marion found a seat and settled down to flick through her magazine. Her mind couldn't settle. Through the dusk she watched the alien landscape and houses spool out beside her. Dear God, what was she doing here, so far away from family and home? What was she walking into?

When the conductor walked through the carriage announcing that Windsor would be the next stop, she began to breathe deeply and calmly, as she had been taught to do before her exams. She took from her bag, for the umpteenth time, the letter from her new employers. The instructions were clear: she was to leave the station and look for a uniformed driver with a dark car.

She gazed out of the window as the train began to slow. She took a deep breath, stood up and collected her case and coat. *Come on, Marion. It's only for a few months. You can do this.*

Available now!

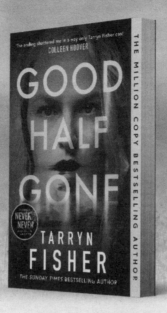

**Iris Walsh saw her twin sister, Piper,
get kidnapped – so why did no one believe her?**

Iris narrowly escaped her pretty, popular twin sister's fate
as a teen – vanished long before the cops agreed to investigate.
With no evidence to go on but a few fractured memories,
the case quickly went cold.

Now an adult, Iris wants one thing – proof. And if the police
still won't help, she'll just have to find it her own way;
by interning at the isolated Shoal Island Hospital for
the criminally insane, where secrets lurk in the
shadows and are kept under lock and key.

But Iris soon realizes that something even more sinister
is simmering beneath the surface of the Shoal, and that
the patients aren't the only ones being observed…